THE SHADOW PROJECT

Scott Mariani grew up in St Andrews, Scotland. He studied Modern Languages at Oxford and went on to work as a translator, a professional musician, a pistol shooting instructor and a freelance journalist before becoming a full-time writer. After spending several years in Italy and France, Scott discovered his secluded writer's haven in the wilds of west Wales, an 1830s country house complete with rambling woodland and a secret passage. When he isn't writing, Scott enjoys jazz, movies, classic motorcycles and astronomy. His books have sold worldwide and he is currently working on an exciting new vampire series, to be published by AVON in summer 2010.

To find out more about Scott Mariani go to www.scottmariani.com

By the same author:

The Alchemist's Secret
The Mozart Conspiracy
The Doomsday Prophecy
The Heretic's Treasure

SCOTT MARIANI

The Shadow Project

AVON

This novel is entirely a work of fiction.
The names, characters and incidents portrayed in it are
the work of the author's imagination. Any resemblance to
actual persons, living or dead, events or localities is
entirely coincidental.

AVON

A division of HarperCollins*Publishers*
77–85 Fulham Palace Road,
London W6 8JB

www.harpercollins.co.uk

A Paperback Original 2010
1

Copyright © Scott Mariani 2010

Scott Mariani asserts the moral right to
be identified as the author of this work

A catalogue record for this book is
available from the British Library

ISBN-13: 978-0-00-731190-3

Set in Minion by Palimpsest Book Production Limited,
Grangemouth, Stirlingshire

Printed and bound in Great Britain by
Clays Ltd, St Ives plc

Mixed Sources
Product group from well-managed
forests and other controlled sources
www.fsc.org Cert no. SW-COC-1806
© 1996 Forest Stewardship Council

FSC is a non-profit international organisation established
to promote the responsible management of the world's forests.
Products carrying the FSC label are independently certified
to assure consumers that they come from forests that are managed
to meet the social, economic and ecological needs
of present and future generations.

Find out more about HarperCollins and the environment at
www.harpercollins.co.uk/green

Once more, the author would like to thank the great team at Avon, Maxine Hitchcock, Keshini Naidoo and Sammia Rafique, for their enthusiasm and dedication.

Technological progress is like an axe in the hands of a pathological criminal.

Albert Einstein

The dogma of Christianity gets worn away before the advances of science.

Adolf Hitler

Chapter One

Rock and dust, scrub and cactus and the blinding white sun beating down. Nobody ever came out here.

The dust from two off-road vehicles drifted upwards into the still air as they bounced and lurched across the arid wilderness. The big silver Subaru 4x4 in front crunched to a halt on the stones, doors opened and three men got out.

One of them didn't want to be there. He stood out from the other two, and not just because he was the only Japanese guy and they were white Europeans. He was also the only one with a .45 auto to the back of his head and his wrists bound behind his back. Tape, not cord. Cord would leave a mark, and his captors didn't want that. A length of the same silver duct tape was pressed firmly to his face, muffling his protests. The T-shirt he was wearing was damp with sweat.

His captors knew his name – Michio Miyazaki – and that he was a scientist. Beyond that, it wasn't their concern why this was happening to him.

The bright red Jeep Cherokee following the Subaru pulled up alongside. Its driver killed the engine, stepped down, ran

1

her fingers through her blond hair and wiped the sweat on her jeans. There was no sound except the ticking of hot metal and the feeble protests of the prisoner as the two men started marching him away from the vehicles.

The Jeep was Miyazaki's, as was the technical equipment in the back. When this was over, it would look as though the scientist had been out here on a research trip, collecting samples. That fitted his profile. He was unmarried, single, no kids, tended to keep to himself, and he wasn't a well man. Nobody would question what was about to take place.

The woman walked around to the passenger side of the Jeep, opened the door and lifted out the small container she'd been riding uncomfortably beside through the desert. This was one item that didn't belong to Miyazaki. It was a pale blue plastic lunchbox, with tiny air holes pricked in the top. What was inside weighed almost nothing. The woman held it away from her at arm's length. With her other hand she grabbed a shoulder bag from the footwell, then shut the Jeep door and trotted to catch up with the others. As she joined them she could hear the prisoner pleading with them through his gag.

They all ignored him.

'This'll be fine,' the taller of the two white men said in their own language, glancing around him. The stocky guy with the muscles straining under his cotton shirt kept the .45 aimed at Miyazaki's head.

The woman set the container down on the ground and stepped back, happy to get some distance from it. She reached into the shoulder bag and pulled out a pair of thick leather gauntlets. Tossed the right glove to her colleague, then the left.

'You do it,' she said. 'I'm not touching that thing.'

The tall man pulled on the gloves. The one with the gun swept his foot out and Miyazaki crumpled on his back into

2

the dirt. He was crying now, tears streaking the dust on his face.

The tall man walked over to the container and squatted down beside it. The others watched as, very carefully, he unsnapped the lid, lifted a corner, peered inside, dipped his gloved hand into the container and stood up with the thing in his fist.

Miyazaki started struggling and protesting with renewed energy when he saw the glistening brown scorpion trapped between the man's fingers. He'd spent his life deeply involved in one small specialised corner of science, but he had enough knowledge of other disciplines to know that these people had done their research well. This was an Arizona bark scorpion, one of the most lethal arachnids on the planet.

Miyazaki couldn't take his eyes from the creature as the tall man walked towards him with a smile. He struggled against his bonds as the scorpion came closer and closer. He could see it wriggling, the long tail lashing out, the stinger turgid with venom. Now it was right over him, six inches above his heaving chest. He could feel his heart pounding dangerously fast.

The man dropped it on him.

The scorpion landed on its feet and froze, as if cautiously assessing its new surroundings. Miyazaki began to gibber, every muscle in his body racked tight as he strained to see the thing that was perched on his torso.

But the scorpion was more interested in flight. It scuttled away, slithered down his ribs and dropped down onto the sand.

'Shit.' The tall man stepped quickly over to where the creature was trying to dig itself in, and scooped it back up. Sand ran out from between his fingers as he clenched the scorpion tightly in his palm.

'Try again,' the woman said.

The tall man nodded. He admired the creature. These things were tough. They'd been around for millions of years, unchanged, perfect. And they'd still be around long after humankind had obliterated itself. He didn't want to harm it, just to stress it a little and activate its primal defence mechanisms. He squeezed hard and gave it a shake, feeling its hard carapace wriggle through the glove. Then he held it over Miyazaki's exposed neck, where sweat was pooling in the hollow at the base of his throat, and let it drop a second time.

This time the creature landed on Miyazaki's skin with its defences on full alert, poised to strike. The stinger lashed out, faster than a rattlesnake, and found its mark.

The scientist screamed behind the tape and thrashed on the sand as the creature scuttled away. His captors could see where the scorpion had stung him, a livid pin-prick already swelling on his neck three-quarters of an inch from the jugular artery.

'That should do it,' the woman said over the muffled cries of terror.

'Gonna kill the fucking thing now,' said the stocky guy, watching the scorpion as it ran towards the cover of the rocks. He pointed the pistol.

The woman slapped his arm down. 'No shooting.'

'Yeah, leave it be,' the tall one said.

The stocky guy gave a shrug and put the pistol away. They looked down at the prisoner. His movements were already slowing, eyes rolling back in his head as the toxic shock started shutting down his weak heart. After another minute he wasn't convulsing or kicking any more. His arched back sank down against the sand, his head lolled to one side and stayed there.

The tall man kneeled down next to the body and used a clasp knife to cut the tape from the dead man's wrists. Once that was done, he ripped away the gag.

'Now let's dress this thing up to look how it's meant to,' the woman said.

The Picos de Europa mountain range
Northern coast of Spain
Two days later

The killers set out early. Seven in the morning, the low sun was glinting over the mountain peaks.

They'd driven up until they ran out of track. It was a long way down to the tree line. The cold breeze buffeted the van and made it hard to open the door. The woman stepped down from the vehicle and shivered. Reaching for the Minolta binoculars that hung from her neck, she scanned the mountainside, up, down, left and right. Nothing but rocks and shrubs.

Her two colleagues got out and walked around the van to join her. 'OK?' the tall man asked her without a smile.

'Let's get it done.' She stepped over to the back of the van, opened up the back doors.

Julia Goodman blinked as the sunlight hit her eyes. Her heart was in her mouth and her hands wouldn't stop shaking. She knew what was coming. She'd known it for days. Just not how they'd do it.

'Let's go,' the woman said.

'Please.' Julia had repeated that word so often, it seemed to have lost all meaning. But all she could do was keep saying it and hope. Her eyes brimmed with tears. '*Please.*'

The woman looked at her impassively.

'I'm so sorry.' Julia had been saying that a lot, too. 'I'm sorry I couldn't make it work. I—'

'Save your breath.'

With a last glance around them, the two men dragged Julia from the van. She struggled and kicked, but they held her tight and her cries vanished in the wind.

The woman walked around to the side door, slid it open and yanked out the quilted jacket, the hiking boots, the rucksack. Everything inside it had been checked and double-checked, right down to the keys to the blue Renault Espace that had been leased in the university lecturer's name two months earlier. The Renault had already been transported to a hidden storage facility nearby. By the time the accident was reported, the car would be up here waiting for the police to find it.

Again, they'd thought of everything. They always did, every detail. It was what they were paid for.

The woman carried the gear over to Julia and dumped it at her feet. 'Put it on.'

Julia obeyed, weeping uncontrollably and shaking so badly she could barely tie the bootlaces.

'Please,' she kept saying. 'Please.'

'You want to die some other way?'

'I don't want to die,' she sobbed. She collapsed to her knees and sank down to the stony ground. 'I don't.'

The men yanked her up by the arms and held her steady as the woman grabbed the rucksack and looped the straps around Julia's arms, then walked round to her front and did up the fastenings. Julia was sagging at the knees, too weak to fight, making little whimpering sounds.

'See?' the woman told her. 'If you don't fight it, it'll be much easier.'

Twenty yards from where they were parked, the ground sloped sharply down to the edge of the precipice. The woman and the two men kept a tight hold of Julia as they walked her in that direction.

'Please don't do this,' Julia pleaded desperately. 'I'll keep trying. I'll work harder. I can make it work. I know I can. Give me another chance. Some more time. I—'

'Shut it,' the tall man commanded, and she did.

Then, with a sudden surge of energy, she ripped free of their grip. The stocky guy made a grab for her hair. She lashed out with a hiking boot, and he yelled in pain as the steel toecap caught his shin. Then she was dashing away from them, scrambling over the rocks.

She didn't get far before they caught up with her and dragged her back. Ten yards to the edge. Five. Three. A sheer, vertiginous, thousand-foot drop below. The wind was whipping her hair across her face, sticking to her tears. She let out a cry when she looked down.

'Nice view from up here,' said the stocky guy, still grimacing with the pain in his shin. Then three strong pairs of hands shoved her hard down the slope towards the edge. She lost her footing and stumbled and rolled, grasping for stones and rocks, anything that would halt her momentum as she slithered towards the drop. Her fingertips found a crack in the rock, and suddenly she stopped sliding and was dangling with her legs in space. Her eyes were crazed, teeth bared, her breathing rapid.

'Damn,' the woman breathed. 'Why do they always make things difficult?'

'Don't let me fall,' Julia implored them. 'Help me. Please. Don't let me die.'

'Could just leave her,' the tall man said. 'She won't hang on forever.'

The woman shook her head. 'I want to see her go over.' She thought about the options. Too risky to scramble down the slope towards the edge and kick her hands loose. A long stick would work, but there wasn't one around. She saw a jagged stone and picked it up. Hefted it in her hand. It was about the right size and weight.

'No,' Julia quavered.

The woman lobbed the stone. It caught Julia on the cheek-bone. She let go of the rock and went tumbling into empty space with a guttural shriek that died away as she spun and cartwheeled down to the rocks below.

Four long, drawn-out seconds later, the scream was cut short along with Julia Goodman's life.

Then the killers returned calmly, quietly, to the van, thinking about what to do with the rest of the day.

Chapter Two

Ben Hope was sitting at his desk facing a mountain of papers, letters, contracts, insurance policies and bank statements, feeling impatience mounting up inside him and wanting to dash the whole lot to the floor when his radio beeped and Raymond on the security gate informed him that the first of the new clients had arrived.

A few seconds later, a gleaming black Porsche Boxster roared into the yard. It circled between the buildings and let out two long blasts of its horn.

'Here comes Rollickin' Holligan,' said Jeff Dekker from his desk on the opposite side of the office and looking at his watch. 'Right on time.' Jeff was a former officer of the SBS, the Royal Navy's Special Forces regiment, and Ben's right-hand man at Le Val.

Ben threw a glance at his friend and felt like saying something about respecting clients, but kept his mouth shut. The truth was, he didn't like Rupert Shannon any more than Jeff did, and had been glad that almost two months had passed without the guy turning up. But business was business, and

9

the ex-Para and his new six-man bodyguard team had booked Le Val for an intensive two-day refresher course in VIP close protection after landing some new contract in Switzerland. That was what Ben did, pass on his special skills to men like Shannon, so that vulnerable people would be kept safe and protected. His opinion of the guy didn't matter.

Ben and Jeff both got up from their desks and walked over to the window.

'I was getting bored of paperwork anyway,' Jeff said, rubbing his hands together. 'Just think. This time next week I'll be in Nice, basking on a beach with a frosted glass in my hand. You should come along. Five days of doing nothing but sitting watching the girls go by.'

'And no paperwork,' Ben said with a smile.

Jeff rolled his eyes. 'Can't bloody wait.'

'It's been a busy time. You deserve a holiday.'

'So do you. The place is closing down for that week anyway.'

Ben laughed. 'Only so that I can catch up on all the other things that need doing around here.'

They watched through the window as the Porsche parked up across the yard, near the small bungalow that Ben had built for Jeff next to the trainee accommodation block. The early evening sunlight glittered off the car's sleek bodywork and tinted windows. The driver's door swung open and Rupert Shannon climbed out wearing aviator shades, a shiny black leather jacket and a wide grin. The breeze ruffled his sandy hair and he quickly patted it back into place as he glanced around him.

Jeff shook his head in disgust. 'Will you take a look at this guy? If the fucker was made of chocolate, he'd eat himself.'

Ben was about to head for the door to greet their new arrival, when the Porsche's passenger door opened.

'Shit,' Jeff muttered. 'I had a feeling she'd be with him.'

Ben followed Jeff's gaze and saw Brooke Marcel get out and walk around the side of the car. Her thick auburn hair was tied loosely back from her face, and she was wearing jeans and a plain white T-shirt that hugged her slim figure. She looked as good as she always did, but today Ben thought he could see a frown on her face, a certain self-consciousness in her body language. She looked down at her feet a couple of times as she followed Shannon across the yard towards the office building. Seemed to be trailing behind, holding back. It wasn't like her.

'Why is Brooke here?' Ben murmured. 'She's not needed for this course. This is purely practical. Shannon doesn't need lectures in hostage psychology.'

Jeff didn't say anything.

'And what's she doing with him?' Ben added.

Jeff gave a derisory snort. 'Can't you tell?'

'They're—'

'Yup. Looks like it. They're an item.'

'Since when?'

'Not sure. Since the last course, I think. I'd noticed they were spending a lot of time together. I was going to tell you. Must have slipped my mind. Or maybe I just didn't want it to happen. Denial, or something.'

Ben watched her approach. Dr Brooke Marcel. Expert in hostage psychology, with an alphabet of letters after her name. Based in London, she'd spent years as a consultant to specialised police and military units, but was recently spending more and more time lecturing at Le Val. She was thirty-five, maybe thirty-six. He suddenly realised that maybe he didn't know her as well as he'd thought.

'No reaction?' Jeff asked, watching him closely.

'Not my business,' Ben said.

'Come on. There's always been something between you

11

two. All those nights sitting together in the kitchen, drinking wine, listening to music. Going for walks. Don't act like you don't care.'

'There's never been anything going on between me and Brooke. Only in your head.'

'I don't know what she sees in that pumped-up twit, anyway. You're more her type.'

Ben ignored that. 'He is what he is, but he's paying a lot of money for this course.'

'I get it. You want me to be nice to the bastard.'

'Too much to ask?'

Jeff kept his eyes on Shannon as he chewed it over. 'It just might be, yeah.'

'Remember what we agreed, Jeff,' Ben said. 'At Le Val we always respect our clients, no matter what. OK?' But he didn't like the lecturing way it came out.

'Even the arseholes.'

'*Especially* the arseholes.' Ben walked over to the door, opened it and stepped out just as Shannon reached the building. Jeff followed him outside, muttering something that Ben didn't catch.

Shannon's grin broadened as he greeted them. He was a big guy. At six-three he was four inches taller than Ben, probably fifty pounds heavier, about five years younger. He raised his hand to his face and whipped off the shades.

'Ciao, Jeff, ciao, Benjamin,' he brayed at them. 'How's it going, boys?'

'It's Benedict, not Benjamin. And you can call me Ben.' Not a great start, he thought.

Shannon grunted with a dismissive gesture. 'Whatever. Benedict, Benjamin, Ben, it's all the same to me.'

Ben could feel Jeff bristling beside him. He threw him a quick warning glance. *Respect the client, no matter what.*

12

Brooke came up behind Shannon. 'Hello, Ben,' she said softly, and smiled.

'Hi, Brooke.' Ben patted her arm affectionately, like he always did. Shannon noticed it, and cleared his throat.

'The rest of the guys should be arriving soon,' he said.

'Fine. The accommodation's ready for you all.' Ben pointed over at the trainees' block, across the yard from the main farmhouse.

'I won't be kipping here,' Shannon said. He put a big arm around Brooke's shoulders and pulled her tightly against his side. 'Us two are booked into the Cour du Château. This little lady deserves a bit more luxury than this old place has to offer.'

'That's miles away,' Ben said.

Shannon grinned. 'Don't worry, I'll be here bright and early in the morning. Always punctual.'

'Nice wheels, Rupert,' Jeff said dryly, motioning towards the Porsche.

Shannon's eyes twinkled. 'Oh yes. I've hit the fucking jackpot this time.'

'So this would be the contract you were telling me about,' Ben said.

Shannon nodded. 'You don't know the half of it, Benjamin. Steiner Industries. Protecting the head honcho himself, Maximilian Steiner.'

'Kidnap threat?'

'One attempt so far,' Shannon said. 'Failed, but only just. What d'you expect? The guy's a billionaire, for Christ's sakes. Have I hit paydirt, or what? He's paying one point two million for this gig. And there's a shitload more to come. You should see the place we're going.'

'Congratulations, Rupert,' Ben said. 'Looks like this new business venture of yours is really taking off.'

'You bet your arse it is. And this is just the beginning, pal. I've been looking at new offices. Docklands, right on the river, three floors. PA, receptionists, you name it, the works.'

'Here's my advice, though,' Ben said. 'I know you're flush from getting this Steiner contract. That's great. I'm pleased for you. But take it easy. Don't go mad with it. This is a tough business, and you never know what's round the corner.'

Shannon reddened. 'Listen to this guy. Are you for real, Hope?'

'I just meant, be careful, that's all. Don't go spending it all at once, before you've even earned it.'

Shannon laughed and slapped him on the arm. 'You sound like my fucking nanny. You know what your problem is? You're getting old and slow.'

'Forty next birthday,' Ben said. 'Be dead soon.'

'Fucking forty,' Shannon guffawed. 'Five years from now you'll be just another flabby-arsed, ulcer-ridden businessman sitting behind a desk.'

'You might be right,' Ben said. Now he could sense indignation radiating from Jeff in waves. Couldn't say he blamed him.

Shannon grinned down at Brooke and squeezed her to his side. 'Now why don't we see about heading back to the hotel and grab some nosh?'

'Any plans for tomorrow?' Ben asked her.

She shrugged. 'Not really.'

'We'll be doing kidnap simulation exercises in the morning. How d'you feel about coming along and playing the principal?'

'Sounds fun,' she smiled. 'Looking forward to it.'

Chapter Three

The audience broke into enthusiastic applause as the speaker brought his presentation to an end. Up on the low stage, Dr Adam O'Connor smiled from the podium, thanked them all for listening and started gathering up his notes. People rose from their seats and started filtering out towards the exit. Adam folded up his laptop, walked over to the projector and turned it off.

He was pleased with himself. The last fifteen minutes of the talk had been a Q and A session and, judging by the level of interest, he was pretty sure he'd get back home to find some new orders coming in. 'The smart house is the home of the future' had been his closing line. It looked as though his audience felt that way too.

As he wound up the cable from the laptop to the projector, Adam cast his mind back, thinking about the last eighteen months and how well things were going. His academic colleagues at City University NY had all thought he was crazy, giving up a plum academic position to go off and start up a new business from the ground up. Back to the old country, they'd joked. But Adam was serious about his Irish

15

roots – virtually the first thing he'd done on hitting these shores was to change his surname from Connor and reinstate the missing 'O' that the English had forcibly removed from the names of his ancestors. *Adam O'Connor*. He liked the way it sounded. New name, new life.

As for the business side, what he didn't like to boast about to his former colleagues was that selling smart house technology installations was able to bring him in ten times his old academic salary, and rising fast every month. Not bad for a physics geek. He should have done this ages ago. Everything was better here – the air was cleaner, the countryside was lush and beautiful, the people were open and friendly. He felt he'd come home at last. The new environment in the Wicklow Hills was wonderful for his thirteen-year-old son, Rory, and the house itself was fantastic. Seven months of sweating over architect's plans, but it had been worth it. Stunning lakeside view, a dozen large open-plan rooms, beautiful wood and acres of glass, incorporating many of his own patented designs. *Teach na Loch* was the Gaelic name he'd chosen. He could pronounce it pretty well now, getting his tongue round the guttural consonants. *Tee-ach na Loch*: the Lake House.

For a fleeting moment he thought about Amy and wondered where she was now. Last seen heading off towards southern California on the pillion of a chopped Harley with her arms around some large, hairy guy in denim and leather. Never a thought for her kid, let alone her husband.

That's what you get for being a nerd, Adam thought to himself.

The last time they'd spoken was over a year ago. Seemed like a different life now. And Rory seldom asked about his mom any more.

The last of the delegates were filtering out of the entrance as Adam zipped up his bags, looked at his watch, picked up the copy of the *Irish Times* he'd bought that morning and thought about heading for home.

Just then, he heard a little cough behind him, and turned to see who was there. Stepping furtively out from behind one of the curtains that flanked the entrance was a figure he recognised. Someone he hadn't heard from in quite a while.

'Lenny,' he said, surprised.

'Hi, Adam,' Lenny Salt muttered in a low voice. He walked up between the empty rows of seats, glancing nervously about him.

So nothing had changed, then, Adam thought. Still the same old Lenny, always acting as though the Men in Black were just one step behind him. Physically, he hadn't changed much either. A little more stooped, maybe. A little greyer and, as he came closer, it seemed to Adam as though his teeth were fewer and blacker.

Adam put out his hand. The limp handshake was still the same, too.

'What brings you here, Lenny?' he said, smiling pleasantly, while wondering what the hell this was about.

'Good presentation, man.'

'You're in the market for a smart house?' Adam knew he wasn't.

Salt shook his head. 'No, man. We need to talk.'

Ten minutes later they were sitting over coffees in the hotel bar downstairs. Adam wanted to make this quick. Salt was a rambler, especially when he got started on his pet subjects – and if it was radical and wacky enough, he was up for it. UFOs one year, the fake moon landings the next. He'd hold you with his glittering eye, and, three hours later, you'd still be sitting there none the wiser and your smile

17

beginning to freeze on your lips, wishing you were somewhere else or just had the courage to ask the silly old bastard to shut up.

Today, Lenny Salt looked especially spooked. Maybe he was just getting crazier with age, Adam thought.

'What did you want to talk about, Lenny? I don't have a lot of time.' He slipped a hand in his pocket and restlessly fingered the key to his Saab. 'My sister's coming to stay for a few days, I have a new housekeeper arriving after lunch, and Rory's on his own. Need to get back.' He reached for his cup.

But Lenny Salt didn't seem interested in Adam's home life. He leaned forward.

'Julia's dead.'

Adam's cup abruptly stopped halfway to his mouth. '*What?*'

'You heard me.'

'*Our* Julia? Julia Goodman?'

Salt nodded.

'What the hell happened?'

'She fell off a mountain in Spain. They found the body last week. She'd been down there a while. Very nasty.'

Adam put the cup down on its saucer with a rattle. Sank his head in his hands, his mind suddenly filled with images and memories. 'This is awful. Poor Julia.'

'It wasn't an accident, man.'

Adam looked up sharply.

'Nah. It was just made to look like one. Nobody had heard from her in three months. She apparently just went off on her own. Doesn't that sound a bit strange to you?'

'She was into hiking in a big way.'

Salt raised an eyebrow.

'Come on, Lenny. This is nuts. Isn't it awful enough that she's dead, without making up crazy—'

18

'I know what you think about me. But this isn't crazy.'

Adam felt a flush of anger in his cheeks. 'Then tell me how you know there's something strange about it. What makes you so sure?'

'Because there's more to it that I haven't told you,' Salt said. 'If you'd let me finish.'

'Then what?'

'Michio's gone too.'

'Michio often goes off places without warning,' O'Connor said testily. 'His research takes him to every desolate corner of the planet. He's probably wandering about on a glacier somewhere as we speak, collecting ice samples.'

Salt shook his head. 'You don't understand. He's dead as well.'

Adam stared at him.

'Died of a scorpion sting out in Arizona. Forgot to pack his anti-venom, apparently. Oh, and his heart pills too. Very convenient.'

Adam took a few seconds to digest all this, staring into his coffee. He couldn't drink any more.

'How come you know so much, Lenny? How come I haven't heard anything?'

'I'm not the one who cut himself away,' Salt replied. 'I didn't turn my back on my friends, man. I stayed in touch with the rest of the Krew.'

'Never mind the damn Kammler Krew. That was never a serious thing, and you know it.'

'It was for Julia, Michio and me.'

Adam didn't want to get into old arguments. 'How did you find out about Michio?'

'His brother emailed me a couple of weeks ago.'

'And you didn't call me about this? Two old friends die, and you don't think to tell me about it?'

'I didn't have your number.'

'I gave it to you.'

Salt shrugged. 'I didn't write it down. I don't like to use the phone. You never know who might be listening in.' He leaned across the table with a conspiratorial look. 'Listen to me, man. Something's up. Something bad.'

'You're not suggesting that Julia's and Michio's deaths are connected?'

'Of course that's what I'm suggesting. It's obvious. Someone murdered them, and now they're coming after us. We're all that's left of the old Kammler Krew. Now it's just you and me.'

Chapter Four

At that moment, deep within the acres of dense forest that surrounded the training facility at Le Val, Brooke was sitting reading a paperback in the specially adapted cottage that Ben Hope referred to as his killing house.

It was the place where the bulk of the tactical raid and assault exercises were carried out, the many bullet holes and ragged splinters in the plywood walls silent witnesses to the amount of live-fire practice that went on there. The two-seater sofa Brooke was reclining on, deep in her novel, had looked better in the days before it had become riddled with 9mm rounds; one end was resting on bricks, and the stuffing was hanging out all over the place.

Today, though, there was to be no live shooting. Brooke was playing the role of a VIP, albeit the kind of VIP that would be hanging out in a semi-derelict cottage wearing faded jeans and an old rugby top. Shannon's guys – Neville, Woodcock, Morgan, Burton, Powell and Jackson – were stationed at strategic points inside and outside the building, assigned to protect their charge from Ben's squad of 'kidnappers'. The imminent raid was a test designed to expose any weaknesses in Shannon's team and form the basis of the training sessions to come. They'd been waiting for what seemed like an eternity, and so far no sign.

As team leader, Shannon had insisted on remaining closest to his principal. He was padding up and down the room in his black tactical clothes, glancing at her occasionally, trying not to look edgy, the empty 9mm Glock slapping on his thigh in its holster. The only sounds outside were the singing of the birds and the whisper of the breeze in the trees.

'I don't like this place,' he muttered. 'Too quiet.'

Brooke flipped a page and went on reading.

'You've always got your face in a book,' he said irritably. 'You read too much. I don't know how anyone can read all the time.'

'Shut up,' she said. 'You're the bodyguard, remember? You're supposed to be protecting me, not chatting to me.'

He snorted and walked over to the window, stared out at the rustling greenery. 'What's keeping the bastard?'

Brooke glanced up at him. 'You mean the guy you came here to learn from?'

He ignored her. 'Come on, Hope,' he murmured to himself. 'He'll come.'

'He'll never get to you, you know. No way he and his guys are going to get past my boys. There's a reason why Steiner picked us, out of all the thousands of close protection outfits out there. It's simple. We're the best there is. Yeah.' Shannon made a fist.

'Nothing to do with your uncle the brigadier's connections, then,' Brooke said quietly, without looking up from her novel.

But Shannon didn't hear. He gazed out of the window for a while longer, breathing noisily.

'Maybe we didn't even need to come here. Maybe I'm wasting time and money here. I mean, we're ready. We're fucking ready. You can't improve on perfection.' He turned away from the window, grinning to himself.

Then his grin froze.

And so did he.

'Morning, Rupert,' Ben said. He was sitting on the sofa beside Brooke, a pistol dangling lazily in his hand. The worn cushions were sagging in the middle, pressing them together so that their thighs were touching.

The door swung open, and Jeff Dekker walked in with Paul Bonnard and Raoul de la Vega, the two ex-military fitness trainers Ben employed as assistants. The shapes of Shannon's men were visible through the doorway, face down on the bare floorboards, tape across their mouths, struggling against the plastic ties that bound their wrists and ankles. Trussed up like turkeys.

Shannon stared for a long moment. Next to Ben on the sofa, Brooke was trying to suppress a smile.

Ben stood up, slipping his pistol in its holster. 'You need to pay more attention, Rupert. A gang of clog dancers could have come hopping and skipping in here, and you wouldn't have noticed them. Maybe you should spend less time chatting to your principal, and more time focused on your job.'

'You set me up,' Shannon protested. 'It was your idea to make her the principal.'

'Good training,' Ben said. 'Teaches you to remain objective. That's something we can work on a bit more over the next couple of days.' He reached out a hand to Brooke and pulled her gently to her feet. 'Break for coffee?' he said to her.

She smiled. 'Love to.'

'Like fuck we will.' Shannon ripped his Glock from its holster and pointed it at Ben. 'Stand down. This isn't over. Give her back.'

Ben wasn't worried about having an empty pistol waved at him. But he was annoyed at the pointless gesture, and he didn't like the way Shannon was shoving it in his face.

'Drop it, Rupert. You're out of the game. Your principal

is taken. We're having a break, and then we're going to do this again, and keep doing it until your team's providing effective protection. You do want to be worth that million, don't you? You don't want to be sent home from Switzerland in disgrace.'

But Shannon wasn't listening. 'Stand down,' he yelled again. 'Get on your knees. Hand over the principal.'

'Rupert—' Brooke began. Shannon ignored her and took another step towards Ben.

'Put the weapon down,' Ben said quietly. 'You're wasting everybody's time. I'm not going to say it again, OK?'

Shannon kept the gun levelled. His face was burning red. 'On your fucking *knees*,' he bellowed. 'Throw down your guns and let her go.'

Ben stared at him for a second, then moved. He carried out the disarming technique gently and at half speed. Because doing it properly at full speed, he would have trapped Shannon's finger in the trigger guard and broken it like a twig when he twisted the weapon round out of his grip, disarming and crippling him at the same time. He didn't want to do that.

But Ben was quick enough that Shannon's hand was empty before he even knew what was happening. He tossed the weapon to Jeff, who was looking at Shannon in disgust.

'You think you're pretty fucking smart with your SAS tricks, don't you?' Shannon sneered. 'None of that stuff's worth shit in the real world.'

'Change of plan,' Ben said. 'No coffee break. We're going to work straight through the morning. Maybe through lunch, and through dinner if we have to. Nobody leaves this house until we get it right. Understood, Shannon?'

Shannon said nothing. Instead he came on another step and took a swing at Ben.

'Oh, for Christ's sake,' Jeff groaned.

The punch was long and curved, and Ben had plenty of time to anticipate it. He stepped easily back out of the arc of the blow. He didn't try to block it. He didn't want anyone getting hurt.

'What's wrong with you, Major Hope? Forgotten how to fight?' Shannon took another swing, and again Ben moved out of the way.

'You're being ridiculous, Rupert,' Brooke shouted. 'This is supposed to be an exercise, not a bar-room brawl. What's got into you?'

But Shannon had completely forgotten the exercise. 'Just like I said, Hope. You're getting too old and too slow for this, you fucker.'

Ben ignored him and calmly turned away. 'Enough. Everyone back into position.' He clapped his hands, twice. Pointed through the open door at Shannon's trussed-up team. 'Paul, Raoul, untie them. Let's go again.'

It was partly the look on Jeff's face, but mostly Ben's natural instinct that made him sense the movement behind him.

It happened fast. He half-turned. This time Shannon was flying at him with all his weight and power.

If Ben had done nothing and stayed where he was, the incoming punch was on course to take him on the side of the head. Shannon was a muscular guy, with a broad back and thick shoulders. A blow like that could do considerable damage. Loss of hearing in one ear. Damage to an eye. Or worse.

Naturally, the blow couldn't be allowed to land.

Instead, Ben moved again. And this time he moved at full speed.

Shannon hit the floor with a crash that almost broke

through the planks and sent him tumbling down into the foundations. He writhed and rolled and howled in agony, clutching his arm.

'You bastard!'

Brooke ran over to Shannon and kneeled down beside him. 'Let me see.'

'He's broken my fucking arm!'

She looked angrily up at Ben. 'What did you do to him?'

Ben didn't reply. Apart from Shannon's groans, there was absolute silence in the room. Shannon's men were lying there staring in horror through the open door at their prostrated leader.

Jeff had his arms folded and one eyebrow raised. Ben caught his look. Jeff didn't have to say it. *Respect the client, no matter what?*

Shannon was still whimpering on the floor.

Ben turned to his assistants. 'Raoul, call an ambulance, will you?'

Twenty minutes later, there were flashing blue lights in the yard at Le Val as paramedics took Shannon away on a stretcher. Ben watched from a distance, saying nothing, trying not to contemplate what had just happened. He looked on numbly as Brooke climbed into the back of the ambulance. The paramedics closed up the back doors and Ben lost sight of her.

'Ben?' said Jeff's voice behind him, and Ben turned.

'I'll go along too. Best you stay here, OK?'

Ben nodded. 'Fine.'

Jeff held his eye for a moment. It was hard to tell whether he was about to laugh or start yelling at him. Maybe both. Then he ran over to the ambulance and clambered in the front, leaving Ben standing there on his own. A blast of the siren, and the ambulance took off. He watched as it drove out of the yard and started making its way down the long drive towards the gates. He guessed they'd take Shannon to the hospital at Valognes, a few miles away.

There was nothing left to do except wait. Ben slumped on a low wall and lit up a cigarette. Storm, his favourite of the German Shepherds, and more of a pet than a guard dog, came running over and licked his face. Ben ran his fingers through the dog's fur, genuinely grateful for the company.

He sat on the wall and smoked as Shannon's team came filing past about thirty yards away, firing hostile looks across the yard at him and muttering among themselves in low voices. They disappeared one by one into the trainee block. Neville was the last to go in, shooting a long stare at Ben before slamming the olive-green door shut with a bang that echoed around the buildings. Paul and Raoul had repaired to the office, maybe awaiting his instructions.

He couldn't think of any to give them. They might as well go home now.

He blew out a cloud of smoke and ruffled the dog's ears. 'Well, Storm, that surely was a fine morning's work.'

Chapter Five

The outskirts of Dublin shrank away in the Saab's rearview mirror as Adam O'Connor drove southwards into the green countryside. A choral air by the medieval composer Thomas Tallis filled the car from the six-speaker CD player, but Adam hardly heard the music. He was thinking about the deaths of his old friends, and feeling sad. And just a little guilty, too, that he'd allowed himself to lose contact with them.

Michio and Julia and him. Part of Adam missed those days. The three of them might have seemed an unlikely bunch of friends – the sober American professor quietly going crazy with his marital problems, the ebullient, fun-loving Japanese planetary scientist and the brilliant, hard-driving young head of the Applied Physics Department at Manchester University – but it had been great for a while, a refreshing antidote to the daily drag of teaching and research, lectures and seminars and department politics. There'd been a kind of innocent camaraderie between them, almost like schoolkids. From the outside, it might have seemed even stranger that what had drawn the trio together from across the world was their shared interest in an obscure, all-but-forgotten, wartime Nazi engineer and SS general. Hans Kammler had been personally appointed by Adolf Hitler in 1943 to work on some very, very strange things indeed.

Their first meeting had been a chance encounter at a physics conference in Cambridge, just about the driest and most uninspiring series of lectures Adam had ever listened to. He'd actually fallen asleep in the middle of the morning session, until he'd been prodded awake by the grinning little Japanese guy sitting next to him and he'd realised with a flush of embarrassment that he'd been snoring.

When the lecture ended, Michio had laughed about it all the way to the delegates' lunch. Adam liked him right away, and sat with him. Across from them had been a bright-eyed, attentive and switched-on young British physics PhD who introduced herself as Julia Goodman.

Instant friends. Just one of those moments in life when people seemed to chime with one another. They'd endured the rest of the afternoon's lectures as a threesome, then got together again for the evening in the bar at the hotel where many of the delegates were staying.

That had been when the ever-smiling Michio had first mentioned the name Kammler to them. He'd kept them up until after midnight in the bar, babbling on about his discoveries. The little guy's almost hyperactive enthusiasm had been infectious, and it hadn't taken him long to persuade them that this obscure piece of science history was more than just bizarrely compelling. Adam could still remember the rush of amazement he'd felt, and the look on Julia's face, when Michio had told them what he reckoned the Nazis had really been into. If you were even half-alive, if academia hadn't yet dried out your soul, it was the kind of physics that could turn your blood to wine just thinking about it.

'Are you sure about this?' Adam had asked Michio. Sometimes the most exciting theories were nothing more than a cool idea waiting to be destroyed by an ugly, inconvenient truth. But even as he'd asked the question, the sparkle in Michio's eyes told him this was no fanciful notion.

'I'm more than sure. I know they could make it work.'

'But the implications of what you're saying—' Julia cut in.

'Blows your mind, doesn't it?' Michio had grinned. 'Get used to it. There's more.'

And there was. The more Adam and Julia listened to what Michio had to say, the more incredible it seemed. This was pure, beautiful, intoxicating science. Nothing to do with politics or ideology. Science the way it was meant to be. It was easy to forget that the man behind it all was an SS general, one of the minds behind the building of Hitler's death camps and, in the closing days of World War II, one of the top five figures in the dying Third Reich. Adam had found himself almost obsessively consumed with the Kammler theories, as the months went on. The three of them had started meeting up whenever they could – London, Tokyo, New York – and staying in touch via email in between, mulling over ideas, postulating what-if scenarios. It had become a little gang of three, and they'd even made up a fun name for it. The Kammler Krew. Almost as much as his relationship with his boy Rory, it had been what had sustained Adam through the dark times of his break-up with Amy.

About a year into their friendship, the trio had become a foursome with the arrival of Lenny Salt. Lenny liked to tell people that he was a physicist, but in fact he'd just been Julia's lab assistant at Manchester, doing basic routine jobs that any decent first-year student could do. Adam hadn't been too sure about his coming on board, and had thought that Julia was too soft in letting him join. She'd said that Lenny was deeply interested in the subject and that he'd be happy to do some research for them to help out. By the time they'd discovered he was unable to contribute much to their discussions except his own brand of conspiracy paranoia, it had been too late to say anything for fear of offending Julia.

Lenny Salt's arrival had cooled Adam's enthusiasm for the Kammler Krew. After another year and a couple more meetings, he could feel himself drifting away from the group. By that time the whole smart house thing had begun to take over Adam's life in any case; he'd been winding up his teaching career, heavily involved in buying the plot of land in Ireland and designing, and subsequently building, *Teach na Loch*. With all that going on, he'd had less and less time to keep in touch with his fellow Krew members.

What nobody knew was that, though he'd slackened his involvement with the gang, Adam hadn't lost his interest in the Kammler research. He'd still often sit up late into the night, day after day, working feverishly on his ideas, even after setting up in business and moving to Ireland. He had a bunch of notes on four CD-ROMS that he kept locked away in his safe at the house. Sometimes he'd think about it, when he was supposed to be working on his smart house business, and the possibilities would start to flood his mind all over again, coming so thick and fast he was almost choking.

The worst thing had been having to keep quiet. This stuff was just too hot, and not just because it derived from the work of a Nazi. It was hot because of its incredible, almost limitless implications. Never mind making millions from smart homes. If anyone could make the Kammler theories work, they'd be talking billions. Money on tap.

And maybe, Adam thought now as he drove, that was also the problem. With Julia and Michio dead and Lenny's warnings still echoing in his ears, he could feel his heart beating and an icy chill run down his spine.

He glanced in the rearview mirror. Had that black Mercedes been following him all the way from Dublin? He started to worry as he watched it, taking his eyes off the road so long that he had to hit the brakes hard to avoid crashing into the back of a slowing truck. He overtook the truck, glanced nervously in the mirror and saw the Mercedes indicate and move out to follow him.

Shit. They are tailing me.

Don't be ridiculous.

He drove faster nonetheless, and the Mercedes kept pace with him. Then, just as he was getting really edgy, a straight opened up ahead and the black car flashed by him, doing at least ninety. Adam laughed shakily to himself.

A couple of miles further on, he spotted the Mercedes in a fuel station forecourt and saw that the driver was a young woman with a small child.

He cursed Lenny Salt for putting daft ideas in his head. What a weirdo the guy was. What an insult to their poor friends to come out with such a cockamamie story and cheapen the tragedy of their deaths like that. It was typical of the conspiracy theory mindset. Pure ego. Like anyone would even think to come after a pathetic old fart who thought he was a real scientist.

Adam's thoughts wandered back to Julia and Michio. The coincidence was terrible; but surely a coincidence all the same.

Just then, his mobile ringtone chimed through the car's sound system.

It was the housekeeping agency. Adam frowned as he listened to the woman informing him that the new housekeeper wouldn't be able to come until tomorrow, due to a minor road accident.

'Nothing serious, I hope?'

'She just had a bit of a shock,' said the woman. 'She'll be right as rain in no time, and with you tomorrow afternoon.'

Adam said he was pleased to hear that. Tomorrow afternoon was no problem. He ended the call and huffed with irritation. Wonderful. Now he'd have to start clearing up the house himself for Sabrina's visit.

Don't be such a jerk, Adam. You'll survive. He stabbed at the CD player and switched from the Tallis to a lively Vivaldi violin concerto. Michio and Julia floated up in his thoughts again, and he tried to focus on driving.

A couple of minutes later, the phone rang again.

'Dad?'

'Hey, Rory.'

'Where are you?'

'Sorry I was held up. Be with you in about five minutes, all right?'

'Don't worry. Everything's under control. She just got here.'

'Sabrina's there already?'

'No, not Sabrina.'

'Then who?' Adam asked. Rory was like that. A separate question and answer for everything. You had to tease stuff out of him. He was at that age.

'The housekeeper, stoopid,' Rory said in an affected moronic voice. 'Remember?'

'I hate when you talk in that damn voice. And what are you going on about? The agency just called me to say she won't be arriving until tomorrow.'

'I don't know,' Rory said in a deadpan tone. 'Maybe they changed their mind.'

'How do you know it's the housekeeper?'

'Because I spoke to her just now on the security monitor. She said her name was Sue. I just buzzed her in the gate and she's parking her van up outside. I'm watching her right now, from the window.' A pause. 'Where's she from? Kinda weird accent.'

'I'll be there in exactly two minutes, all right?'

'Hey, there's a couple of guys with her,' Rory said.

'A couple of guys?'

'Yeah, they're walking towards the house.'

'Rory, hold on till I get there. *Don't* open the door.'

But the kid had already hung up.

The Saab was coming into the bends a mile and a half from the house as Adam dialled the number for the agency. 'This is Adam O'Connor. We spoke a couple of minutes ago.'

'Yes, Mr O'Connor?' the same woman replied pleasantly.

'Did I misunderstand you before? I thought you said nobody was coming out until tomorrow.'

'That's right.'

'Then where did this Sue come from?' he asked, letting his irritation flood out. 'And who are these two guys with her? You know, this kind of disorganisation doesn't make you people look very good.'

'We don't have anyone called Sue working for us,' the woman said archly. 'There must be some confusion. And I must say I don't like your tone, sir.'

'Fine. Shove it up your ass. I'll find someone else.'

Two seconds after the call was over, Adam started to feel the first trembles in his hands. He put his foot down and the needle soared as he rounded the side of the big hill and the solitary lake house came into view. Everything looked peaceful enough. Acres of glass and the surface of the lake glittered the sunlight back at him from between the rolling green hills. A perfect picture.

But he just knew something was terribly wrong.

The gates sensed his car approaching and opened

automatically to let him through. He roared into the gateway and up the long drive.

There was no van parked anywhere. The shakes got worse, and his step was wobbly as he got out of the cool Saab and into the hot sun. He strode to the front door and said 'Constantinople' to the sensor. The lock clicked open and he ran through into the wide, airy entrance hall.

'Rory?' It was a big house, and you sometimes had to yell to communicate from one part to another. But from the instant he stepped inside, something told him the place was empty. 'Rory?'

No reply. No Rory, no housekeeper. He checked the living room. Empty. Strode across the hall and thundered up the stairs and threw open his son's bedroom door.

'Dad, I wish you wouldn't burst in like that.' That was what Rory would have said to him, turning towards the door with a scowl. But Rory wasn't there. His chess computer and TV and Blu-ray player and drawing pad and the model spyplane he was building were all exactly where they should be. But no Rory.

Adam was sweating cold now. Back downstairs, he called and called. Nothing. Checked the garden, the pool. Still nothing.

Then the phone rang. He rushed over to it.

'Professor O'Connor?' said a voice. A man's voice, calm and soft. The accent was English, educated.

'Yes.'

'Professor Adam O'Connor?'

'Who is this?'

'We have your son.'

Adam almost collapsed at the words. His hands were shaking so violently that he needed both of them to keep the phone clasped tightly to his ear.

'You will follow my instructions to the letter,' the voice continued. 'Any attempt to contact the police, any calls or communication with anyone from this moment on, we will know and Rory will die. Any failure or hesitation to do exactly what I tell you, when I tell you to do it, he will die. There will be no second warning. Do you understand?'

Adam managed a tiny 'Yes'.

'Good. Now listen to me very carefully.'

Chapter Six

In the casualty department waiting room in Valognes, Jeff Dekker got two foam cups of coffee from a machine down the corridor and carried them over to the row of plastic chairs where Brooke was sitting staring into space. He handed her a cup, then slumped down next to her.

He tried to sound upbeat. 'Don't look so miserable. I'm sure he's going to be OK. We'll know soon. They should have finished the X-ray by now.' He took a loud slurp of coffee. 'Jesus, this is revolting.'

Brooke sipped hers expressionlessly, as though the finest Blue Mountain roast or liquid shit would have been all the same to her.

'He'll be fine,' Jeff said again cheerfully. His plastic chair creaked as he leaned back in it, stretching his legs out in front of him.

'I hope so,' Brooke murmured, taking another sip of the coffee.

'Though I have to say, he had it coming.'

She said nothing.

'And Ben hardly touched him, really.'

Brooke snorted. 'That's reassuring.'

'Don't be too pissed off with Ben. He was provoked.'

She paused, biting her lip. 'You know I'm not pissed off with him. I just wish this whole thing hadn't happened.'

'You can be sure that Ben feels that way too,' Jeff said. He shook his head in disbelief. 'What the hell was eating Shannon anyway? Acting like that—'

'I think this was all my fault,' she said miserably.

'Your fault?'

She nodded. 'Something I said.'

'I didn't hear you say a thing.'

'Not then. Yesterday, in the car, on the way down.'

'What did you say?'

She sucked air through her teeth. 'It was about Ben.'

'So?'

'I think I just mentioned his name once too often, that's all.'

'You're saying that Shannon's jealous. He can tell how you feel about Ben.'

She turned to look at him. There was a flush of red in her cheeks. 'It's that obvious?'

'To me, and everyone else,' Jeff said. 'Except Ben, that is.'

'Everyone except Ben,' she echoed sadly.

'And when he got you to act out the role of the principal, that was too much for matey boy. He saw it as some kind of competition.'

She nodded. 'Fighting over the female. Locking antlers like a couple of rutting stags.'

'Except one of the stags didn't even know what was going on.'

'And it's all because of me. Damn. I shouldn't have agreed to it. I'm supposed to be a psychologist, for God's sake! I'm supposed to know people's minds.'

'Why don't you just tell Ben the way you feel about him?'

She shook her head.

'We're all grown ups. What's the worst that can happen?'

'That I'd lose his friendship, scare him away,' she said. 'I'd

40

rather have him as a friend than not have him at all. You can't force someone to love you.'

Jeff raised his eyebrows. 'Whoa. Did you just use the L-word?'

Brooke closed her eyes and sank her head into her hands.

'You're actually in *love* with him?'

'For a long time,' she muttered, not looking up.

'Shit.'

'Don't I know it.'

'I didn't think it was that serious. I thought it was just – you know.'

'It wasn't always. But after a while I realised I wasn't just flirting with him.'

Jeff looked confused. 'So wait a minute. You're in love with Ben . . . but you're going out with Shannon?'

'Don't go there, Jeff, all right?'

He shrugged. 'I think it's great, though. You and Ben. I can see it. Really.'

'Apart from the fact that he doesn't seem to know I even exist.'

'You've got that all wrong. He loves spending time with you. I can always see he's looking forward to your visits. He really likes you.'

'But not in *that* way.'

Jeff didn't reply.

She ran her fingers through her hair. 'What a situation. Here we are in the hospital because my boyfriend's been injured and I'm more concerned about the guy who put him there. I shouldn't even have come with Rupert. I just wanted to see Ben.' She sighed.

Jeff paused a moment. 'I think Ben cares for you a lot more than you think. He just doesn't know it yet, because that's the kind of guy he is. But one day he's going to wake up and see it.'

41

'You're not going to say anything, are you?'

'Would I?'

'You'd better swear to that, Jeff Dekker. One word and—'

Brooke was interrupted by the sound of footsteps on the vinyl floor of the corridor. She and Jeff turned to see the doctor walking towards them. Brooke stood up, looking at him with a mixture of expectation and worry.

The doctor smiled. 'No need for alarm,' he said. 'There's no serious damage.'

'But he must be in a lot of pain, yeah?' Jeff asked hopefully, smiling back.

The doctor rubbed his chin pensively, glanced down at his clipboard and spent the next minute or so gravely reeling off a long list of medical terminology.

'Ben did all *that* to him?' Jeff said, eyes wide.

'Monsieur Shannon is also complaining about severe back pain, and although there's nothing showing up in the X-ray, it would be prudent to keep him under observation for a few days.'

'Are you saying he can start work again soon?' Brooke asked.

The doctor shook his head. 'Certainly not. Complete rest will be essential for at least three weeks.'

'Shit,' Jeff said to Brooke as the doctor walked away.

'There goes Switzerland,' she muttered. 'I was afraid of that.'

'Guess we'd better go and break the news to Ben.'

'You go. I ought to stay here with Rupert. It's probably for the best.'

Chapter Seven

Adam sat on the edge of an armchair in the living room at *Teach na Loch*, head in hands. He reached out for the tumbler in front of him and knocked back the inch of Bushmills malt that was still in it, then grabbed the bottle and swilled some more into it. His head was spinning with shock, the taste of vomit still on his lips from when he'd thrown up earlier on. He'd thought he was never going to stop.

Now he just felt numb. It was unreal. Lenny Salt had been right. The old weirdo hadn't imagined it after all.

The kidnappers' instructions had been simple. He was to get all his Kammler material together and get on a flight to Graz. He checked the atlas: it was in Austria, near the Hungarian border. They'd given him the name of a hotel in the city, where a reservation had been made for him, and he was to check in there no later than 10 p.m., local time, the following evening. The orders were to sit in his room, speak to no one, and wait to be contacted.

Adam suddenly felt hot tears welling up out of his eyes. He thought of Rory. What were they doing to him? Where was he? Would he ever see him again? He could imagine the look of terror on the boy's face when they took him, could hear his screams of protest.

43

If only Salt hadn't turned up at the presentation. I'd have been here. I could have done something.

A thought suddenly crossed his mind. Had Salt had something to do with it? Had he been deliberately planted there to delay him?

He stood up from the armchair, unsteady on his feet. Walked over to the bookcase across the room and picked up the framed black and white photo of Rory. Sabrina had taken that one, just after he'd turned twelve. They'd gone to London for a weekend and visited her photography studio there. It was such a beautiful shot of the kid. He was smiling and looked so happy in it. Sabrina had a giant blow-up of the same picture on her studio wall. Adam knew his younger sister doted on her nephew – he was the only real reason they stayed in touch.

Sabrina. What was he going to tell her when she got here? Adam glanced at his watch and winced. Any time now. His hand was trembling as he replaced the picture frame on the bookcase. Another acid lurch in his throat, and he turned and stumbled towards the downstairs bathroom.

He was bent over the toilet bowl, retching vomit and whiskey, when a smooth female electronic voice announced through the hidden speakers: 'You have a visitor.'

Sabrina Connor paid the taxi driver, got her bags from the back and watched as the car turned and disappeared out of the gates. She looked up at the house, shielded her eyes from the bright afternoon sunshine, and smiled. She was looking forward to this break. Seven whole days away from London, the hustle and humidity and bad air, her capricious celebrity clients. Perfect. And it was great to be able to spend some time with Rory – she hadn't seen him since Christmas. This time she might actually beat the little smartass at chess.

44

The door opened. Adam stepped out to greet her. When he came up and hugged her, it was more tightly than usual. She could smell the sharp tang of mouthwash on him, and when she broke the embrace and looked up at her elder brother, she could see his eyes were a little pink.

'You changed your hair again,' he said.

She ran her fingers through the spiky red highlights. 'I like it like this. You OK? You look a little wired.'

'I'm fine. Just working hard.' He smiled weakly. 'Come inside. It's good to see you. Want a drink?' He picked up her bags and ushered her inside.

'Coffee would be great. Oh, here. I got you something.' She unzipped one of her bags and took out a little package. 'Happy birthday. Forty-five.'

He took it. 'Forty-six. And it was nearly two months ago.'

'What a close-knit little family we are. Well, aren't you going to open it?'

He tore the wrapper. 'Handkerchiefs.'

'Irish linen,' she said. 'Had to scour London for them. I got them embroidered, too, see? Adam O'Connor.' She exaggerated the 'O'.

'I know you think it's stupid, me changing my name. But it's important to me. It's heritage.'

She shrugged. 'Do what you want. Fine by me.'

'Nice hankies.'

'Kind of a lame present, huh?'

'No, really. I like them.'

Sabrina glanced around. 'Where's Rory?'

'Tennis camp,' he replied instantly.

'Tennis camp? You're kidding me, right?'

Adam shook his head. 'Nope. Tennis camp.'

'When?'

'I drove him up there yesterday.'

45

'Where?'

He made a vague gesture with his hand. 'Up in Donegal.'

'They even *have* things like tennis camp in this place?'

'Whatever they call it. Activity holiday, something like that. Why, you think we're all bog paddies living in mud huts out here?'

'Oh, give it a rest with the whole Irish thing, Adam.'

'Anyway, so he's at tennis camp.'

She shrugged. 'Fine. It's just I thought he hated sports.'

Adam headed for the kitchen to put some coffee on. 'You know what kids are like. One of his friends plays and so he wanted to have a go. It'll do him good. Get him away from that damn chess computer of his.'

'When will he be back?'

'Couple of weeks.'

Sabrina made a face. 'Jesus, Adam. You didn't think to tell me about any of this before? I was really looking forward to seeing him, you know.'

He sighed. 'Look, the truth is that I totally forgot. I was meaning to call you about it ages ago. It just slipped my mind. I'm sorry.'

'I spoke to him on the phone not long ago, and he never said a word about going to any tennis camp.'

'Well, you know Rory. He moves in mysterious ways sometimes. Like I said, I'm really sorry.'

'I'm sorry too.' She sighed. 'Just disappointed, that's all.'

The coffee was beginning to bubble up in the percolator. Adam took two mugs from the shelf and poured it out for them. Sabrina settled on a stool at the mahogany breakfast bar and sipped her coffee. She felt soft fur brush her leg, and a Siamese cat jumped up on her lap. 'Hey, Cassini.' She stroked the cat and it rubbed its head against her.

'You're the one visitor he doesn't bite,' Adam said, pulling up another stool. 'He likes you.'

She forced a smile. 'Anyway, here I am. Rory or no Rory.'

'It's really good to see you, sis. Really good.'

She watched him. 'Is something wrong?'

'Like what?'

'I don't know. You just seem a little tense. Things going all right here?'

'Things are fine.'

'Thought maybe you'd heard from Amy or something.'

He snorted. 'Who? No, I don't think so.'

'How's business?'

'Business is great.'

She touched his arm. 'Look, I know that you and I aren't that close. But you'd tell me if something was wrong, wouldn't you?'

Adam forced a laugh. 'Don't be silly. You know I would. I'm just a little tired. I've been working late a lot the last couple of weeks. New project.' He paused. 'Speaking of which—'

She glanced up. 'What?'

He hesitated. 'I have to go away too.'

'What? When?'

'Tomorrow morning. Something really important just came up. There's this conference in Edinburgh, and someone dropped out, and I've got to speak in their place, and, well . . .'

'I just love your sense of timing.'

'I know. But you're more than welcome to stay here. As long as you like.'

'All alone?'

'You've got Cassini for company. And you don't even have to worry about feeding him or letting him out. All automated. The house takes care of everything.'

'Wonderful.'

'You should have everything you need. But if you need to go out for anything, the password to open the front door is "Constantinople".'

She raised an eyebrow. 'Constantinople?'

'Just say it into the sensor. It'll recognise any voice. And if you want to lock the guest bedroom door, just tell the house "lock" and it'll hear you. OK?'

'Yeah, like I'd need to, out here.'

'And if you lock it, I've set it up so you just say "Cassini" and it'll unlock again. It's the same password for all the bedrooms. Popular security feature. We never use it ourselves, though.'

She glared at him. 'Fantastic, bro.'

'Look, I'm really sorry. There's nothing I can do about it. Just bad timing, like you said. Why don't you call Nick? Maybe he could come over and join you.'

'Nick and I aren't together any more. Not since he started screwing the model I used in his last shoot.'

'That's a real shame,' Adam said absently. He bit his lip. 'Listen, I've got to go and get my things sorted out for this conference. Help yourself to more coffee. See you in a little while, OK?'

Sabrina watched him leave the room. He definitely seemed odd. She poured herself another cup and sat stroking Cassini.

'Tennis camp,' she muttered.

Chapter Eight

When Jeff walked into the office at Le Val, Ben was slamming down the phone. He sat down heavily in his desk chair, clapped his hands to his head and swore loudly.

'Listen, Ben, I've got to tell you something. The doctor said—'

'I already know what the doctor said,' Ben replied without looking up.

'You've spoken to him?'

'I didn't need to. Shannon's lawyer's just told me. Multiple contusions, possible lower back injury, out of action for at least three weeks.'

Jeff looked perplexed. 'The bastard's been talking to his lawyer? Already? From his hospital bed?'

Ben got up from the chair and went over to the window. 'Not one to waste time. He's threatening to press charges. Grievous bodily harm.'

'Nothing that grievous about a bit of a twisted elbow and a couple of bruises. Shannon can take it.'

'Tell that to the lawyer,' Ben said. 'But that's not all.'

Jeff was quiet for a second as the meaning sank in. He swallowed. 'He's suing us, isn't he?'

'For loss of earnings,' Ben said, still gazing out of the window. Over the roofs of the facility buildings he could see the trees beyond. He so much wanted to be there. Hidden deep within Le Val's sprawl of woodland was the tumble-down ivy-covered ruin of an old church that for the last seven hundred and fifty or so years had been home to the wild creatures of the forest. It was a place Ben loved to go and spend time away from everything, just him and the stillness of the sun-dappled woods, the whisper of the trees and the sound of the doves nesting in the remains of the steeple. At this moment, all that seemed infinitely beyond his reach.

'As in one point two million kind of earnings?' Jeff asked quietly.

Ben nodded. He tore himself away from the window, went back to his desk and reclined in his chair. 'The Swiss gig will have to be cancelled. Which basically leaves Shannon and the rest of the team out of a job. And I'm responsible for that.'

'Can't they manage without him?'

'Apparently not. He insists they need a leader. It's his contract, and he can do what he wants.'

'Then we're fucked,' Jeff said.

They sat in silence for a long time. Three minutes passed, then four. Both men sat staring into space.

'Why? Why?' Ben muttered under his breath. '*Why* did I have to hit him?'

'You didn't exactly hit him, Ben. If you'd really hit him, you'd be up for manslaughter now.'

'That's a comforting thought, Jeff. Thanks for that.' Ben took out his cigarettes and Zippo, and lit one up. Offered one to Jeff, and they sat smoking together.

'There's got to be a way out of this,' Jeff said. 'Is there no way we can just deny responsibility? Pretend it never happened?'

'Nice idea, if you can forget the six witnesses who saw him go down. Seven, if you include Brooke.'

'Brooke wouldn't say anything.'

'That's not the point, Jeff. If it comes down to it, I won't ask her to perjure herself for nothing.'

'It was self-defence. He made the first move.'

'But I overreacted. I didn't have to cripple the guy.'

'What about public liability insurance?'

'I don't think the policy underwriters would be happy about forking out a seven-figure sum because I beat up my client.'

'It wasn't your fault. The bastard had it coming.'

'It is my fault. No excuses. I've put the customer in hospital, and that's it. He has every right to sue for loss of earnings.'

Silence again for a few moments.

'How about this?' Jeff suggested suddenly. 'We go back to the hospital, you and me, right now. We hang around and wait until Brooke and the doctor are out of the way. And then we slip into Shannon's room and tell him that if he goes ahead with this, we'll—'

'Forget it. That's not going to work either.'

'Then we're fucked,' Jeff said again. 'Completely screwed. Dead in the water.'

'Maybe not,' Ben said. 'I've got another idea.'

Chapter Nine

The next morning

The rust-streaked prow of the ship cleaved through the waves at a steady ten knots, throwing up a bow wave of white spray. The tweendecker cargo vessel was more than forty years old, and every inch of her hundred-and-sixty-foot hull was crusted with salt and oily grime, but she was a fast and reliable ship. Her speed was one reason she'd been chosen for this assignment; the other was that her Icelandic captain and his crew of six were savvy enough to take the cash and ask no questions of the two men and the woman they were being hired to ferry eastwards across the northern tip of Scotland into Scandinavian waters. They wanted to know even less about the 'cargo' that their three passengers had stored down below.

The ship had sailed in the night from Clifden on the Irish west coast. A few hours into the voyage, the sun was shining but the salty sea wind was cool as they left the Outer Hebrides behind them, the Orkney Islands a few hours ahead. The diesels kept up their steady grind, the clouds drifted overhead and the sea foamed white in their wake as the vessel ploughed onwards towards Stavanger, Norway, where the plane would be waiting to deliver the package to its final destination.

The stocky guy was not feeling good. He hated this fucking pile of rust, the stink of oil and ocean, the nauseous pitch and yaw of the floor under his feet. He was ill all the time, and he'd have loved to shoot down one or two of those incessantly screeching fucking seabirds. Not the most rewarding job he'd been on. He couldn't wait for it to be over.

The things you have to do for money, he was thinking as he clanged open the hatch and carried the tray down into the part of the hold that was off-limits to the crew. He hated having to act as waiter to the damn kid, too, and carried the tray carelessly. Some water sloshed out of the tin cup and spilled onto the thin cheese sandwiches. If the kid complained, then fuck him. Let him starve.

Down in the murky shadows, the stink of oil was even stronger. The guy could make out the pale shape of the mattress on the floor and the dull glint of the handcuffs that secured the kid's left wrist to the pipe.

Hold on. He shone the torch. The white circle of light danced on the rusty wall.

The handcuff was dangling empty from the pipe.

He dropped the tray with a clatter and stood there, mouth hanging open as his rising fury quickly gave way to fear. He dropped into a squat and rubbed his chin. If he'd lost the kid, he was a dead man.

Spotting a twisted length of wire lying among the filth on the floor, he picked it up and examined it, and his rage started flooding back. *Little bastard.*

He couldn't be far away. The guy muttered and cursed and shone the torch this way and that in the shadows.

A soft sound came from behind him. He started to turn towards it, but then something came whooshing out of the darkness and caught him a glancing blow to the side of the head. His vision flashed white with pain. He dropped the torch and fell to the floor. The hard object hit him again and he felt unconsciousness washing over him.

Then he was dimly aware of someone bending over him, feeling through his pockets. Light footsteps running away.

He gritted his teeth and forced himself to clamber to his knees, just in time to see the kid momentarily framed in the sunlight that streamed through the open hatch. Then he was gone.

'Come back here, you little fucker,' the guy yelled out. His head felt ready to explode as he staggered to his feet and over towards the hatch, stumbling over the length of iron pipe that the prisoner had hit him with. He tore the .45 auto from his belt and went for the phone in his pocket to alert the others.

It was gone.

Rory's heart was pounding in his throat as he half-ran, half-clambered up a clanking metal stair and sprinted along a railed walkway. He glanced frantically up and down the length of the ship and over the side at the heaving grey-green ocean and shivered in the cold, wondering where on earth he was. Gulls and cormorants were swooping and circling overhead; he could see dark islands on the horizon. His mind was working so fast that he was tripping over his thoughts, but he knew he'd already made two mistakes.

First mistake: when he'd taken the kidnapper's phone he'd seen the black butt of a pistol sticking out of his belt. He should have taken it, even if he didn't know how to work a gun.

Second mistake: in his haste to get away, he hadn't shut the hatch behind him. They'd soon be searching the ship for him. He ran on, his footsteps ringing on the walkway.

A riveted door swung open a few yards ahead, and Rory

ducked behind a girder. The two men who came out of the doorway were wearing oil-stained overalls and talking in some language he didn't understand. They were rough-looking, dirt on their hands and faces unshaven. It sounded like they were sharing a joke. One of them was lighting up a cigarette, and Rory caught a whiff of the smoke as they came past. For a moment he thought he was going to cough, but he clamped it in tight and held his breath. His heart was thudding so hard that he was convinced they would hear it over the rumble of the ship. He shrank behind the girder, trying to make himself as small as possible.

They walked on by. Rory let his breath out very slowly, waited until they were around a corner and out of sight. Then he darted out from behind the girder and made for the lifeboats up ahead. He dropped down on his hands and knees and crawled under their rusty mountings, where a tattered piece of tarpaulin dangled down to offer some cover. Crammed as deep into the space as he could get, he reached into his jeans and took out the phone he'd stolen from the man. It was switched on, and there was a tiny flicker of reception.

Rory hesitated. Police or home? Home first. He suddenly wanted to hear his father's voice so badly. He quickly punched out the number.

Sabrina was sitting outside on the patio finishing a break-fast of coffee and croissants and gazing out across the lake with Cassini on her lap when she heard the phone ring from inside the house. She twisted her head towards the open sliding glass door. Two rings, three. Adam didn't come to pick up.

Of course not, she thought. Her dear brother was too busy bustling about in a panic getting ready for his stupid last-minute conference to think of such things as attending to his visitor or answering his phone. What the hell was wrong with him? He was definitely acting jumpy. He hadn't wanted breakfast, either, and looked like he hadn't slept a wink all night.

She shooed the cat away irritably, jumped up from the deck chair and trotted over to the house. Maybe her big bro wasn't cut out to be a businessman after all.

She picked up the phone on the seventh ring. 'Hello, Slaves 'R' Us. How may I help you?'

'Sabrina?'

'Rory?' She brightened momentarily. But then the tone of her nephew's voice made her frown. He sounded scared. No, he didn't. He sounded utterly terrorised. 'What's wrong, honey?'

'Is Dad there?'

'He's not around. You sound upset. What is it?'

'I'm in trouble. I mean really bad trouble. I've been kidnapped.'

Sabrina froze. '*What?*'

'I said—'

'Where are you?'

'I don't know. I'm on a boat. No, a ship, in the sea. There are islands.'

'Rory—'

'I'm scared. I'm scared.' He started sobbing. 'Where's my dad?'

Sabrina gripped the phone in horror. 'Tell me where you are.'

'Oh, shit. They're coming. I—'

There were scraping and scuffling sounds, and then the phone went dead.

'Rory? Rory?'

He was gone. Sabrina wanted to scream for Adam, but her throat was so dry and constricted no sound came out. Still clutching the phone, she went running through the house to find her brother. He was in the hallway, carrying a travel bag and a briefcase out to the car.

'There you are. Oh my God, Adam.'

He stopped and stared at her. His face was pale, dark rings around his eyes.

'Something's happened to Rory,' she blurted. 'He's been kidnapped.'

'*What*? Say that again.'

'I've just had a call from him. He's been *taken*, Adam. Said he was on board a ship or something.' Tears prickled her eyes. 'What's happening?'

He stared at her a second longer, then broke into a twisted grin. 'Sabrina, that's not possible. I talked to him just a few minutes ago.'

Sabrina looked at him incredulously.

'This is something he's been doing lately. Playing practical jokes. You're not the first person he's tricked this way. Last time it was he'd been taken up into an alien spacecraft.'

'But . . . it sounded real. He was terrified.'

Adam's grin widened an inch. 'He could be an actor one day, that one. Anyway, he called on his mobile to say hi to you and that he's sorry he missed you. He's having a great time at tennis camp.'

She scanned his face carefully, trying to read his expression. The smile was steady, but there was something in his eyes that made her wonder. 'What the hell's going on, Adam?'

He shrugged. 'Like I said. Consider yourself Rory's latest victim.'

'I don't know. It doesn't sound right.'

'Anyway, listen, I'm all ready to go.'

'You're leaving? Now?'

'I did say I had to go.'

'But the call—'

'Don't worry about it. Trust me.'

She sighed loudly. 'I still can't believe you're leaving me here alone like this.'

'I'll make it up to you next time, I promise.' He put down his bags and hugged her tightly the way he'd done when she'd arrived, and she could feel the tension in his body. It was almost as if he thought he was never going to see her again.

Chapter Ten

Within twenty-four hours of Rupert Shannon's admission to hospital, Ben's idea had become a detailed plan, and the plan had quickly developed into a reality. The two-day training course had been cancelled, and Shannon's close protection team had returned to London to gather their equipment and be picked up at Heathrow by a private jet belonging to Maximilian Steiner. Meanwhile, Ben was making his own way to Switzerland. He didn't know when he'd be back.

He hated the idea, but it was the only way to resolve the situation. After his conversation with Jeff, he'd called Shannon's lawyer in London to suggest the only course of action he could see: to take the injured man's place as team leader, unpaid, until the damaged arm was healed and Shannon was able to resume his role.

After letting Ben stew a little, the lawyer had called back to say that his client had agreed to the deal, and that the new arrangement had been squared with Steiner's people. In practice, it meant that the team would arrive in Switzerland a day earlier than planned, giving them time to settle in before meeting their billionaire employer.

So it was done. Ben was on his way to a new job. Jeff had been ready to drive him to the airport at Cherbourg, but he'd wanted to take the Mini Cooper. Sitting on a plane with nothing to do except stare out of the window and brood over his situation wasn't his idea of a good time. Driving to Switzerland to do a job he didn't want to do wasn't much better, but at least it would give him something to occupy his mind.

It was a long drive across France. He left early and stuck to the fast roads, cutting eastwards as directly as he could. By the time he bypassed Paris the traffic was building up, and it stayed busy until he hit the countryside beyond the city. He let the CD player loop the same Stefano Bollani jazz piano album round and round at high volume and kept his foot down at a steady eighty, stopping only for fuel and tolls. The concentration of driving helped, but it didn't completely silence the voices in his head that asked him over and over again: *Why? Why?*

When the voices reached a fever pitch he just gritted his teeth, gripped the wheel tightly in his fists and stared fixedly ahead as the white lines in the road zipped towards him and waited for his mind to go numb. It never really did.

Sometime in the afternoon he started seeing the first signs for Switzerland, and a little while after that he passed over the border. Most of the traffic was bound for Bern and Lausanne, and thinned out as he followed the winding route upwards into alpine country. The road carved through rolling valleys and pine forests, green fields criss-crossed with country lanes and dotted with farms and villages. He passed through golden acres of sunflowers under a vivid azure sky. Watched the sunlight glitter off the blue-white mountains that hovered over the landscape like distant mirages. The shimmering reflection of the trees was mirrored in the surface of a vast lake. A wooded island rose up out of the water, the grey stone towers of an old monastery peeping through the foliage.

It was the kind of scenery that could take a person's breath away. But Ben could leave it until another time to appreciate things like the majestic splendour of nature. He kept moving on hard, following the directions he'd been given, and, as the sun turned from gold to red and sank down to kiss the mountaintops, he found himself approaching the secluded Steiner residence.

The estate wall seemed to go on forever. Then, arriving at a set of high iron gates, Ben was stopped by uniformed guards who questioned him and scrutinised the photo on his ID very carefully before waving him inside.

The gates whirred open to let him pass. Cameras mounted on the gateposts and the pretty stone gatehouse swivelled to watch him as he drove on through. Then there was another mile or so of private road, winding through a wood so neat that it looked as if every tree had been placed there by a designer. Ben came to a second set of gates and more guards with radios who waved him on without a word. He drove through a high stone archway and down a broad gravel path, and the trees parted and he caught his first view of the great Maximilian Steiner's home.

Even with all the troubles on his mind, he whistled to himself at the sight of it. He'd been in some moneyed environments in his time, but this was the kind of property that mere millionaires could only dream of.

You couldn't call this a house, nor even a mansion. The alpine château was a thing of fantasy. The sun's dying rays glimmered off towers and turrets, columns and arches. It could have been the home of a Bavarian monarch from three centuries ago, but the gleaming white stonework looked as though it had been built yesterday. Around it, acre after endless acre of sweeping lawns and gardens that looked like they'd need an army of groundskeepers to maintain them.

Ben wondered at the size of the staff that Steiner must keep on site.

Now he was one of them. *Great. Just great.*

He ran back through what he knew about his new employer. He'd dug up plenty of information online to explain how the Steiner billions were generated: pharmaceutical companies, oil refineries, heavy industry and aviation, with one of Europe's largest fleets of corporate jets. By contrast, virtually nothing was revealed about the man himself that could have shed more light on the kidnap threat against him.

But even without knowing the full details, Ben could imagine the scenario pretty well. The kidnap business was just like any other. Ninety-nine per cent of the time, barring the occasional revenge job or sex abductions, it came down to money, pure and simple. And he'd seen enough of that world to know the kind of people who would be drawn to the idea of grabbing a guy of Steiner's extreme wealth, whisking him away to some dingy basement somewhere nobody could ever find him, keeping him chained and starving with a pair of bolt-croppers on standby in case the family needed persuasion of their serious intentions. A finger in the mail was a highly effective means of getting the ransom paid. Ben had seen it all before. And had kind of hoped he wasn't going to see it again.

The château loomed like a sculpted quartz mountain as he approached, and he felt ridiculously dwarfed by it. He pulled the Mini up on the gravel at the bottom of a flight of polished white stone steps that were maybe not quite wide enough to accommodate the wingspan of a Boeing 747 and climbed out, stretching his legs after the long drive.

Someone was coming down the steps to meet him. A man in a beige suit, around fifty, a little shorter than Ben and lightly built with the delicate frame of a lifelong desk guy. As the man walked closer, Ben could see his eyes were sharp and his face lean, the thin hair neatly parted and combed. He put out his hand and greeted Ben in English, which he spoke with only a trace of an accent. The warmth of his smile seemed genuine.

'Mr Hope? So pleased to meet you. My name is Heinrich Dorenkamp. I am Herr Steiner's PA. I trust you had a pleasant journey?'

Ben wasn't in the mood for niceties, but he returned the smile as Dorenkamp seemed to warrant it. 'Very pleasant, thank you.'

'Herr Steiner is very much looking forward to making your acquaintance. Regrettably it will not be today. He is tied up in meetings for the rest of the evening.'

'A busy man,' Ben commented.

Dorenkamp flashed a grin and chuckled. 'You have no idea.'

A guy in his early twenties who looked like a valet emerged from a side entrance and walked over to them.

'Dieter will take your car and have your luggage sent on to your quarters,' Dorenkamp told Ben. 'The garage blocks are situated to the rear of the east wing. All fully secure, naturally.'

Ben handed the Mini's key to Dieter, and watched as his little car was driven off across the gravel and round the side of the château. He wondered how anyone was ever going to find it again among the Rolls-Royces, Aston Martins and Bugattis that he imagined filled the garages of a man like Maximilian Steiner.

Dorenkamp smiled again. 'Now, please allow me to escort you to the guest accommodation, where the rest of your team are waiting for you. They arrived here late this afternoon.'

My team, Ben thought, and cursed himself one more time for good measure. From the opposite direction another member of staff came rolling up in a white golf buggy. Dorenkamp motioned to the back seats. 'We generally use these for getting around. It is a big place.'

Ben didn't reply as he climbed into the open buggy. Dorenkamp settled in beside him and the electric vehicle darted off through the grounds with surprising speed. As the sunlight faded, concealed floodlamps were beginning to burn brighter, lighting up the house and grounds. Around the side of the château, the view opened up to show more panoramic acres of perfectly clipped lawns, so green that they looked unreal. Ben said nothing, taking in his surroundings as they cut across the estate. In the distance he could see the little flags of a golf course waving in the light breeze.

'You play, Mr Hope?' Dorenkamp asked.

Ben shook his head and was about to reply when the buggy rounded another gigantic column and the PA said, 'And here are your quarters.'

The accommodation was no château, but it was still spectacular enough to make Le Val look like a rustic hovel. The ultra-modern building was built into the side of a hill, its roof grassed over and dotted with wildflowers. Its white facade was smooth and undulating, a post-modern complex of caves with huge oval windows. Stylistically it was completely at odds with the château itself, but Ben had never seen a building so organically blended into its natural environment.

Dorenkamp noted his reaction with approval. 'Designed by the architect Peter Vetsch. The inside is extremely well appointed. I don't think you will be unhappy here.'

The inside was as white as the outside, the lines clean and elegant. The floors were granite tile that had been polished to a mirrored sheen, and the furniture was gleaming oak and white leather. Kandinsky and Paul Klee adorned the walls, and Ben would have bet they weren't copies. A giant TV and sound system nestled discreetly in an oval wall alcove.

The worst thing about the place was the other occupants. Shannon's guys had already got comfortable, slouching on the leather armchairs with their feet up on tables and bags, cases, clothing, shoes and magazines scattered about the main sitting area. Their laughter and conversation died down abruptly as Ben and Dorenkamp walked in. Ben met the six pairs of hostile eyes and his first thought was to ask himself why he wanted to cringe with embarrassment on behalf of someone else's team. Shannon really could pick them.

If Dorenkamp noticed the change in the atmosphere or was shocked by the mess, he didn't show it. Peeling back the sleeve of his jacket, he looked at his watch.

'I'm pleased to see you are making yourselves at home, gentlemen. I must return to Herr Steiner's meeting. Dinner will be brought to you at seven thirty.'

He was about to leave, then seemed to remember something. 'One other point I should make clear to you all,' he said with an apologetic smile. 'I am unaware whether there are any smokers among you, but I should make it clear that smoking is strictly disallowed anywhere within the estate.' He pointed up at the ceiling, and Ben saw there was an alarm discreetly blended into the plasterwork. 'It is very sensitive, and it makes *quite* a noise, believe me.' Dorenkamp smiled again. 'Now, gentlemen, I shall leave you to settle in.'

With Dorenkamp gone, the atmosphere settled quickly into frosty silence as the rest of the team watched Ben resentfully. He ignored them and went about exploring the accommodation. Each team member had his own bedroom with en-suite shower room. There was a communal sauna room, Jacuzzi, and a well-equipped gym with stationary bikes, running and rowing machines, weight bench and racks of dumbbells. The separate dining area had a long table and seven chairs. Everything was neat, precise and laid out with the utmost thoughtfulness.

'Never had a gig like this before,' Ben heard Jackson say as he walked back into the living area. 'Awesome.'

'Shame Rupert couldn't be here, though,' Neville said in a pointed stage whisper that was plainly intended for Ben to hear. Ben said nothing.

Dinner was served promptly at seven thirty by three waiting staff in white jackets. The chicken casserole was simple but smelled great, and with it came five bottles of good wine. Ben filled up a plate, grabbed one of the bottles and went off to eat alone in his room. It might not be helping his popularity with the group any, but there wasn't much he could do about that. He wasn't here to make friends. No matter what, he knew they'd keep resenting his presence there until Shannon took over. Which couldn't happen soon enough.

Let's just get the damn job done, he thought to himself.

Chapter Eleven

At the same moment, Adam O'Connor was walking into a hotel room on the edge of the city of Graz, Austria. He dumped his travel bag and briefcase on the narrow bed, stared out of the window at the flickering neon sign of the bar across the road, then slumped in an armchair and closed his eyes.

Everything had gone exactly as the kidnappers had said it would. The room had been reserved for him, his key ready and waiting. The fat, greasy-looking guy behind the reception desk had taken only the most cursory look at his passport. No paperwork, no register to sign. Just a key and a grunt and a nod towards the lift. He wondered if the whole hotel staff were in on this too. The bastards probably were. He wanted to grab the television and shove it through the window, set the whole damn building on fire, run screaming through the streets.

But he had to do as they said. Now all he could do was wait. Wait and think about his thirteen-year-old son, imprisoned Christ knew where.

The whole journey, he'd been unable to stop thinking that Sabrina was bound to call the cops. What if she did? What if they found out what was happening? Rory would die.

And Adam wasn't fool enough to imagine that Rory wasn't

going to die anyway, if he just blindly went along with the kidnappers' demands. He knew enough about the way these things worked to know that things didn't just go back to normal afterwards.

Which was why, right from the first moment he'd stood there listening to their demands on the phone, he'd made his plans.

Fuck them. They didn't know who they were dealing with. He was going to get his son out of there unharmed, and he knew exactly how he was going to do it.

Downstairs in the hotel lobby, the fat receptionist picked up the phone and stabbed out the number he'd been given. Two rings, and someone answered. The same voice he'd heard before.

'The American is here,' the receptionist said. Then he put the phone down and went back to his internet poker.

Chapter Twelve

It had been a gloriously sunny day in the Wicklow Hills, and Sabrina had spent most of it by the pool listening to music in her earphones and reading photography magazines. Every so often she'd slip into the water and swim a couple of lengths. All the while, she'd been trying hard to forget about her brother's odd behaviour and the phone call from Rory.

A practical joke? She knew Rory well, better than most aunts knew their nephews, probably even better than Adam knew his son. He was a serious kind of boy, maybe even a little too serious sometimes. A thoughtless prank like pretending to be kidnapped just seemed beneath him somehow.

Then again, she'd thought, he was at the age where you could expect to start seeing behavioural and attitudinal changes. And maybe, in fact, as she'd turned it over in her mind, discovering the humorous side of his personality could be good for him. As for the tennis camp, it occurred to her that there might be more to that than met the eye. Maybe there was a girl involved, a teen romance going on there. Perhaps something that Adam didn't even know about. It was possible. Kind of sweet, too.

In any case, the alternative was unthinkable. Her nephew kidnapped, her brother acting cool about it? Completely absurd. Now she'd started to feel bad about the way she'd overreacted with Adam earlier. He was clearly under a lot of stress.

By the time her thoughts had worked their way round that far, the sun had started to dip behind the clouds and it was getting too chilly to stay out in her swimsuit. She'd wrapped a towel round herself, taken her iPod and magazines inside, showered and dried her hair and pulled on jeans and a blouse.

After a light dinner she'd settled in front of the TV and flipped through channels for a while, then got bored with the rubbish that was on and started combing idly through the ads in the back of one of the photography magazines. By chance, she came across a juicy special offer on a tele-photo lens, a top-notch piece of kit that she'd been toying with the idea of buying for a while. 'For more information, view our website' the ad proclaimed.

It was an attractive enough prospect to make her start thinking about logging on to Adam's computer and checking out the site. She got up from the sofa and padded upstairs in her bare feet.

But his study door on the top floor was locked. Damned if she knew what the password was for that one.

Then it occurred to her that she could use the PC across the hall in Rory's room. He'd often allowed her to go on it, and she was sure it wouldn't be intruding on his privacy if she used it in his absence. She gingerly tried the handle on his door and found it open.

She went inside. The room hadn't changed much since the last time she'd seen it. Going over to the desk, she was about to turn on his computer when she accidentally nudged the mouse with her hand and to her surprise the screen flashed awake. Why had he left it on standby if he wasn't going to be around for two whole weeks?

The screen had opened up in Rory's Outlook Express email program. She was about to close that box and go to Internet Explorer when she saw that there was a new message incoming. When the mail appeared on the screen, she saw that it was from someone called Declan. It was just a one-liner in reply to an email Rory had sent.

'Cool. Just watched it. Best one yet!'

Sabrina's eye flashed down the screen, and it was with a jolt that she saw the date on Rory's original message.

Yesterday.

She frowned. And the time the message had been sent was only about two hours before she'd arrived at the house.

But that was impossible. Adam had said he'd driven Rory to Donegal the day before.

She read it again, and the shivers down her back got colder. Could Rory have sent the message from another source, maybe at the tennis camp? She was no expert, but she was pretty sure that if the reply had come here, Rory's message must have come from here too.

Calm down, Sabby. There had to be a logical explanation. Maybe there was a glitch with the PC. *Unlikely.* Or else Rory had somehow managed to sneak home and then away again without anybody noticing. *Nuts.* Or Adam had written the message to Declan himself, pretending to be Rory. *Oh, come on.*

She turned away from the desk. Saw Rory's mobile phone lying among the rumpled sheets on his bed. The phone he took everywhere with him. The one he'd supposedly spoken to Adam on from the tennis camp.

'Oh my God,' she said out loud. 'What the hell's going on here?'

73

Chapter Thirteen

Next morning at eight o'clock sharp, Dorenkamp came for Ben and the team and escorted them to the main residence to meet Steiner. Ben was aware of Neville and the others gaping around them as the PA led the way inside the palatial house, into a hallway about a square mile in size. In its centre was a life-size cast of a medieval warhorse in full dress, rearing up dramatically on its hind legs and carrying a knight with plumed helmet, spiked mace and a shield with a red lion rampant herald. Maybe a ton of glittering armour plate in total between animal and rider, and Ben was fairly sure it wasn't reproduction antique. He paused a moment to admire it, then walked with Dorenkamp across the hall and through another doorway. The rest of the team followed a few yards behind, talking in low voices.

'Tell me, Mr Hope,' Dorenkamp said. 'How much do you know about Maximilian Steiner?'

'Very little,' Ben admitted.

'Try to avoid asking him too many direct questions,' Dorenkamp said. 'If there's anything you need to know, I would request that you address your queries to me. Herr Steiner is a very private man, and doesn't tolerate intrusion into his family life. He is notoriously hard to interview, and relatively few people even get to have an audience with him.'

'Sounds like I'm going to meet royalty,' Ben said.

'In some circles that's exactly what Maximilian Steiner is,' Dorenkamp replied. 'One thing. You may find him cold. Many people do. But that is just his manner, and you shouldn't be put off by it. I have known him for many years and I can tell you that he's a good man. Behind the scenes he is a tireless campaigner against violence in all its forms, a staunch opponent of the international arms trade. He donates a vast amount of money each year to support many worthy causes. The fact that he does so anonymously only reflects his desire for privacy.'

'If I'm going to protect him, I need to know everything,' Ben said. 'I need total access to every part of his life. I respect his desire for privacy, but there can't be any secrets.'

Dorenkamp nodded thoughtfully. 'Very well. We'll see what can be done.'

'Tell me about the kidnap attempt,' Ben said as they walked.

'It happened three weeks ago. Herr Steiner and his wife were on their way to a family wedding in one of the limousines. As they drove, they came across what at first appeared to be an accident. There was a car in the middle of the road, which seemed to have skidded to a halt, blocking the way. Next to the car was a man lying on the ground, apparently injured. A woman was with him, shouting for help as Herr Steiner's car arrived on the scene.'

'It's an old ploy,' Ben said. 'Exploiting people's humanity to trap them.'

'Naturally, the Steiners had their driver stop at the scene, in order to help. But in the very next instant, a van suddenly appeared with more men who tried to grab Herr Steiner and drag him inside it.'

'Armed?'

Dorenkamp nodded gravely. 'Heavily.'

'Masked?'

Dorenkamp nodded again.

'How did they get out of it?'

'Purely by good fortune and sheer coincidence,' Dorenkamp said. 'There had been a real accident further along the same road, a few kilometres away. It later transpired that the ambulance was already there, attending to the injured. But the police were late arriving on the scene, and happened to appear at the right moment to frighten off the kidnappers.'

'But they didn't catch any of them.'

'No, they escaped.'

'Did the Steiners and their driver get a good look at the injured man, or the woman who was with him?'

Dorenkamp shook his head. 'Sadly not. The injured man was lying face down, and the woman was wearing dark glasses and a headscarf. She had long black hair.'

'Which you can assume to be a wig,' Ben said. 'Now, you said they were on their way to a wedding when it happened. How many people knew about their travel plans that day?'

'You are thinking about sources on the inside?'

Ben nodded.

'It was a high society wedding,' Dorenkamp said. 'Well publicised, and the hotel additionally had a guest list.'

'So the information was openly accessible.'

'In any case, the police have already pursued these avenues of inquiry,' Dorenkamp said.

'Though they haven't come up with anything, apparently.'

'Not yet.'

'So does anyone have any idea who might have attempted the kidnap?' Ben asked.

'Herr Steiner has his own theories.'

'Which are?'

Dorenkamp smiled. 'To be revealed. He will tell you himself in just a moment.'

They came to a tall doorway, and Dorenkamp led the way through it and past a broad gilt-framed painting depicting a classical scene with semi-naked nymphs frolicking around Greek ruins. Ben heard one of the men behind him muttering something about nice tits. Again, if Dorenkamp noticed, he made a good show of hiding it.

'Do the Steiners have children?' Ben asked the PA. 'I ask because kidnappers will often target other family members, even if it's only to get to the main person they want.'

'No children,' Dorenkamp said. 'There is just him, his wife Silvia and their nephew, Otto Steiner, who is in line to take over the business when Herr Steiner retires.' He chuckled. 'Though I find it difficult to imagine that he ever would. Perhaps at the age of ninety-nine, when Otto is nearly seventy himself.'

'Where does Otto live?' Ben asked.

'Here, on the estate. He has his own villa within the compound.'

'What about Otto's parents?'

'Sadly deceased,' Dorenkamp answered. 'It was a long time ago. A car accident. Please don't mention it to Herr Steiner. He was extremely attached to his brother Karl.'

'I won't say a thing. Now tell me about Mrs Steiner.'

As he said it, Ben could hear the sound of someone playing the piano from a room somewhere nearby. Someone very good. The piece they were playing was fast and intricate, the kind of thing only a real virtuoso would attempt. It might have been Rachmaninov or Chopin – Ben wasn't sure.

'You are listening to her,' Dorenkamp said with a smile. 'She was once a concert pianist, before Herr Steiner and she were married.'

'What does she do now?'

Dorenkamp shrugged. 'She has her music, and he has his work. They spend each day largely in their separate worlds, and they dine together in the evenings when he is not working late or away on business. It is a simple and unobtrusive life they lead, despite their wealth. There isn't much to say. Frau Steiner tends to remain here on the estate. She has everything she needs.'

It seemed like a lonely life, Ben thought as they walked on and left the sound of the piano behind them. He followed Dorenkamp up two sweeping flights of stairs to the second floor. The PA stopped outside a grand double doorway. 'Here we are,' he said and twisted the ornate bronze knob to push open one of the huge doors.

Ben followed him inside, and found himself gazing around him at the enormous conference room. Sunlight streamed in through French windows overlooking the estate and the mountainscape in the distance. A massive oak table was surrounded by some thirty buttoned leather chairs. The ceiling was high and ornate, and the walls were lined with arrangements of shields and old swords, from cavalry sabres to fifteenth-century claymores. In between the weaponry displays hung more gilt-framed paintings. Around the edges of the room were display cabinets. Ben wandered over to one of them and bent down to peer through the glass at the old letter inside. The paper was yellowed, the quill-penned handwriting flamboyant. Ben read the signature at the bottom and turned to Dorenkamp. 'Is this an original Napoleon Bonaparte letter?'

'One of several in Herr Steiner's possession,' Dorenkamp said.

'I gather he's something of a collector.'

'It's quite a passion of his, in fact.' Dorenkamp motioned

towards the table. 'Please take a seat, gentlemen. Herr Steiner will be joining us shortly.'

Ben and the team pulled up chairs and settled around the table. Nobody spoke to Ben, and he in turn ignored everyone. Dorenkamp pulled up a chair near the top of the table, to Ben's left. The PA checked his watch again, and turned expectantly towards the door.

Ben heard footsteps outside in the corridor and, a moment later, the door swung open and Maximilian Steiner walked into the room.

Chapter Fourteen

Ben and Dorenkamp got up from their seats as Steiner entered, and the rest of the team followed their example.

Steiner might have been approaching his mid-sixties, but he looked several years younger. He was about Ben's height, a shade under six feet tall, though heavier in build. He exuded an air of seriousness and absolute self-confidence as he scanned each face in the room in turn intently, as though he could read their thoughts. His reddish-brown hair was still thick, turning just a little grey above the ears. He was wearing an elegant light grey suit and a formal navy tie.

His cool gaze settled on Ben, and his eyes narrowed. 'You must be Captain Shannon's replacement.' He spoke with even less accent than his PA. 'Mr Benjamin Hope.'

Ben groaned inwardly. Benjamin again. This was Shannon's doing. 'Please call me Ben,' he said, avoiding the issue.

Steiner raised an eyebrow. 'I prefer a more formal address, Mr Hope.'

Ben smiled. *Fine, have it your way.* 'Then you can call me Major Hope,' he said. Pulling rank wasn't something he normally liked to do, but he was damned if he was going to stand in Shannon's shadow.

Steiner shot a glance at Dorenkamp. 'We were not informed of this.'

'Must be a glitch in your communications,' Ben said. 'I served with the British Army, Special Air Service. Rank of Major, retired.' He felt like adding 'and it's *Benedict* Hope, not Benjamin' – but he didn't want to make Shannon look *too* foolish. Just a little bit.

Steiner gave a curt little nod. 'Now to business,' he said, moving on briskly. Clearly not a man to dally over small talk, Ben thought.

'You know why you are here,' Steiner continued. 'I have no doubt that the recent attempt to kidnap me will not be the last. While the perimeter of the estate offers full protection from intruders, I cannot remain a hermit. I have businesses to run, places to go and people to meet. Your team's assignment is to protect me whenever I leave home.'

'Have you left the estate since the attack?' Ben asked.

Steiner shook his head. 'I have not. An intolerable situation that cannot be allowed to continue.'

'Is there anything you can tell us about the kidnappers?' Ben said, thinking of what Dorenkamp had told him. 'The more we know, the more we can anticipate their moves. It might be worth liaising with the police, as the investigation is ongoing.'

'The police are useless,' Steiner answered harshly. 'There will be no need for that. But I do have an idea who is behind this, and am happy to share the information with you.' He cleared his throat.

Happy to share. Ben felt like saying something about that, but instead he kept his mouth shut and waited for more. Across the table, Dorenkamp looked uneasy.

'It is my belief that the kidnappers have a political motive,' Steiner went on. 'Of a very particular sort. You may have noticed my interest in collecting objects of historical value.' He waved a hand at the mounted swords and the display cabinets. 'One of the items in my collection, which I do not keep on display but securely under lock and key, for reasons that will become apparent, is a certain set of documents – design notes to be exact – dating back to 1944. Not especially old, then, but of enormous historical interest. The author of these extremely rare papers is one Hans Kammler, a wartime design engineer as well as an Obergruppenführer of Adolf Hitler's Schutzstaffel.'

In plain language, an SS general, Ben thought.

'It is my belief,' Steiner went on, 'that the kidnappers are interested in obtaining the Kammler papers from me, by force or coercion.'

'Why?' Ben's question cut through the silence. It was perhaps a little more direct than Steiner liked, judging by the glint of disapproval in the man's eye.

'Because, Major Hope, Hans Kammler was the engineer in charge of Hitler's SS Buildings and Works Division in the closing years of World War Two, and the mastermind and designer of the death camps. And because I further believe the kidnappers to be neo-Nazi activists who have falsely persuaded themselves that within these documents is proof that the historical records of the Nazi Final Solution have been grossly exaggerated, possibly even made up.'

'Holocaust deniers,' Ben said.

Steiner nodded. 'Correct, Major. As you obviously know, ever since the war, a growing number of twisted neo-fascists have been intent on demonstrating that the Allied forces simply fabricated much of the evidence of the Holocaust as a means of vilifying Hitler and justifying their own atrocities. Kammler's papers are quite certainly the most detailed plans in existence of what the Nazis *really* did at Auschwitz and the other death camps.'

'One question. How do you know that the kidnappers are neo-Nazis? Were they chanting "Sieg Heil", wearing armbands and leather boots?'

Steiner clearly didn't appreciate the humour. He stared icily at Ben. 'Because one of them had a swastika tattoo on his hand.'

'So do a lot of British football hooligans,' Ben replied. 'It doesn't necessarily prove anything.'

'Though I don't believe that the typical football hooligan would be interested in the Kammler papers. Herr Dorenkamp has described the kidnap incident to you?'

'He has.'

'When the police car arrived on the scene and inadvertently foiled the attempt, the thug who was holding my arm—'

'The one with the tattoo.'

'On the hand that was clutching the pistol pointed at my head,' Steiner said coolly. 'This thug began to scream "Where are the Kammler documents?" At that point, one of his fellow kidnappers urged him to keep quiet and let me go, and they retreated to their vehicle.'

'Sounds fair enough to me,' Neville said from across the table.

Ben hesitated for a moment. 'Another question, Herr Steiner. This all has to do with these Kammler documents, correct?'

Steiner replied with a slow nod and a narrowing of the eyes.

'And these people believe the documents contain certain proof, but you're saying that's a fallacy. That there's no such proof in them at all.'

Steiner looked uncomfortable. 'Correct.'

'Then why don't you just go public with them? Put them

on display in one of the many museums that would be delighted to have them, and show the world what they really say? If your theory is right, you'd be destroying the kidnappers' whole incentive to get hold of them.'

Steiner stared at him with a look that said: 'Aren't you asking questions above your pay grade?'

Dorenkamp interjected. 'An interesting point, Major. But not directly pertinent to the issue at hand.'

Ben shrugged. 'You're wrong,' he wanted to say. But he stayed quiet, and wished he'd said nothing at all. It struck him as ironic that, if he pressed the point, he risked ruining Shannon's contract altogether by solving the problem too quickly.

'Now,' Steiner said. 'To other matters.' He turned to Dorenkamp with a barely perceptible gesture of his hand, and the PA quickly got up and left the room. There was silence around the table as Steiner's gaze swept slowly around from man to man. Ben watched him. Across the table, he saw Neville looking down at his hands as Steiner's eyes fixed on him.

After a moment Dorenkamp returned. With him were two men in dark suits, each carrying a shiny aluminium flight-case about two feet long. Dorenkamp directed the men over to the table. They carefully laid the cases on its shiny surface, then turned without a word and left the room. The PA flipped open the metal catches on each case, then lifted each lid in turn and stepped back.

Steiner's gaze settled on Ben. 'Please,' he said, motioning to him. Ben got up from his seat and walked over to the open cases and looked down at what was inside them. He looked, blinked, looked again.

'What are these?' he asked Steiner. His consternation must have showed in his voice, because he caught an edgy look from Dorenkamp, as if to say 'Don't question him like that.'

'These are the items I have provided for you to use in your protective role,' Steiner said.

Chapter Fifteen

Ben looked back at the contents of the cases. Each box had a cavity cut out of its foam lining, and inset into each recess was a weapon, brand new and shining under the lights.

'Naturally, what you see is only a sample,' Steiner said with an air of indifference. 'Each team member will be issued his own.'

Ben didn't reply. He reached down and picked one up.

'You are not familiar with this type of weapon?' Steiner asked.

Ben turned the gun over in his hands. It was a double-barrelled device, with bores large enough to accommodate a wine bottle. It was bulky and clumsy in his hands. He knew what it was, and what it was for. A Flash-Ball rubber bullet gun, what riot and raid teams called a 'non-lethal option'. At close to medium range its hard rubber projectile could deliver a blow roughly equivalent to a punch from a champion boxer. Enough kinetic force to knock a large human being to the floor and incapacitate them without doing any serious damage. Ben could think of a lot of situations where such a weapon would be extremely useful. Home defence in those countries that allowed it, to take down an intruder without having to kill them. Bounty hunters, who needed to soften a tough target and bring them in alive. In those situations, fine. Ideal.

But for the purposes of close protection they were worse than useless.

He put the weapon back in the box and turned to Steiner. 'No chance,' he said.

Steiner stared at him again. 'I beg your pardon?'

'I said no chance,' Ben repeated. 'These—' He was going to say 'Mickey Mouse pieces of shit', but then thought better of it. 'These weapons are completely unsuitable for our purposes. They're heavy and clumsy and impossible to conceal, and they're going to compromise our ability to protect you. They put us at a serious disadvantage in the event of a further kidnap attempt.'

Steiner just stared at him coldly. Dorenkamp was pale and wide-eyed. Across the table, Pete Neville was sitting back in his chair with his arms folded, glaring at him angrily.

'In short, Ben said, 'they're useless. I recommend you ditch them and get something more appropriate.'

'And what exactly is it that you would recommend, Major?' Steiner asked curtly.

'In my experience, the Heckler & Koch MP5 machine carbine is a good companion to compact, concealable semi-automatic pistols such as the 9mm Glock, Browning or SIG,' Ben said. 'Whatever works.' He pointed at the Flash-Balls in the cases. 'These won't.'

Steiner's lips tightened. 'No firearms. That is a contractual condition of your employment. I want you to protect me, but there must be no loss of life. I will neither tolerate bloodshed nor authorise the use of lethal force.'

Ben could see he was resolute. 'Herr Steiner, these people who are after you aren't playing. They're evidently armed and serious.' He paused, remembering what Dorenkamp had told him about Steiner's anti-gun stance. 'I understand your principles, and I admire them. It's laudable that you want

88

to avoid any kind of violence. Believe me, so do I. That's what I'm here for. And the best way to avoid conflict is to ensure that we're as well equipped as, or better equipped than, your enemies.'

Steiner shook his head.

'Then I'd urge you to think about your family. Putting yourself at risk is one thing, but you also have the emotional interests of your wife and nephew to consider. I've seen too many families torn apart by kidnapping.'

Steiner's face became even harder. 'We are getting nowhere. Your proposal is out of the question.' He threw a look at Dorenkamp.

'The, ah, equipment requirements had already been discussed with Captain Shannon,' Dorenkamp said weakly. 'I'm surprised you weren't notified of that.'

No, Ben thought. *I damn well wasn't.* He sighed, knowing that he had no choice but to back down. In normal circumstances, in sane circumstances, if this had been his contract, being forced to use such inappropriate equipment would have been a deal-breaker. He would have found it unacceptable to risk the safety not only of his principal, but of the whole team. And any team leader who agreed to this kind of a deal was a cowboy. Shannon was clearly just agreeing to anything to get his hands on the money.

But Ben wasn't here to make Shannon look incompetent in front of his employers. He was here to make reparations, not trouble. It was intolerable, but that was the way it was.

He took a deep breath before replying, 'I apologise. You're quite right. I was notified. It must have slipped my mind. We'll make do with the items you've supplied.'

Steiner eyed him coolly. 'Good. Let us move on to the subject of your first assignment. I am due to attend an extremely important meeting at a conference centre outside

Lausanne early this afternoon. My presence there is vital, and I have no intention of letting a gang of Nazis prevent me from carrying on my business.'

Ben listened and nodded. It wasn't a long drive to Lausanne. But far enough to be cautious. 'I should have a look at the vehicles.'

Steiner shook his head. 'We are not travelling by road. As team leader, you may travel with myself and Herr Dorenkamp in my personal helicopter. The rest of the team will follow in the second craft as arranged.'

This was just getting worse. Ben knew it was the wrong thing to do, but he had to say something. 'I'm sorry, but that doesn't seem entirely secure.'

Dorenkamp was staring at the tabletop with a weary look of resignation.

'Why not?' Steiner demanded.

'Because in my experience it's bad practice to separate the principal, in this case, you, from most of the team. If anything kicks off—'

But Steiner silenced him with a gesture. 'I don't have time to waste on a long road trip. The aircraft will reach the destination within half an hour.'

'Fine,' Ben said. 'Then perhaps you'll agree to let at least one of my team ride with me in the lead chopper?'

'Regrettably, that is not possible,' Dorenkamp cut in. 'There are only five seats. Pilot, co-pilot, and three passengers.'

'Then perhaps one of the men could take your place?' Ben said.

Steiner shook his head impatiently. 'I cannot allow that. I need my Personal Assistant with me at all times. We will have important matters to discuss in the air, prior to the meeting.' He paused. 'We are wasting time here. I had already discussed my schedule with Captain Shannon, who seemed perfectly content with the plans. I am surprised you did not know this either. Or perhaps you did, and this *also* slipped your mind?'

Shannon again. Ben was silent.

'You are being paid to protect me, not to organise my business arrangements,' Steiner added.

'Then I apologise again,' Ben replied. He could feel the looks that the other team members were firing at him.

'Then all is settled,' Steiner said. He laid his hands on the table, palms down, fingers splayed. Put his weight on them and stood up with a nod. 'Gentlemen.' He turned and walked out of the room.

Dorenkamp got up. He looked tense, and there was a sheen of perspiration on his high forehead. 'Morning coffee will be served in the refectory downstairs,' he said. 'If you will follow me. Then at one fifteen we will reassemble at the helipad. My assistant Rolf will provide you with everything you need.'

Including the useless weaponry, Ben thought as he followed Dorenkamp out of the conference room and the rest of the team filed out after him. 'I'd like to take a look around the grounds,' he said to the PA. 'Just to assess security and familiarise myself with the layout.'

Dorenkamp nodded. 'If you wish. However, I should point out that the grounds are completely secure. We have seen to that.'

They made their way back down the stairs, and Dorenkamp led them along the corridor they'd come through earlier. The music had stopped. Dorenkamp pointed at a door. 'The refectory is through there. Gentlemen, if you would like to help yourselves to refreshments.'

As the men went into the room, he turned to Ben. 'May I have a word?'

Ben already knew what he was going to say. Dorenkamp waited until all the others were through the door, then closed it.

'Privately, I completely agree with the points you made,' he said quietly, just above a whisper. 'But Herr Steiner can be a stubborn man, and once he has made up his mind, he will not change it.'

'So I'd noticed,' Ben said. 'I can be like that too.'

Dorenkamp smiled. 'So *I* had noticed. But I would beg you: for the love of God, do not antagonise him.'

Ben returned the smile. 'I'll try to keep that in mind.'

Dorenkamp was about to reply, when the sound of approaching footsteps behind them made them turn.

A woman was walking up the corridor to meet them, her heels clicking on the polished floor. She was handsome, mid-fifties. Classic looks, slim and elegant, wearing a black dress and a string of pearls. The glossy, shoulder-length, red-gold hair didn't look dyed. She greeted Dorenkamp with a warm smile. 'Good morning, Heinrich.'

'Good morning, Frau Steiner. May I introduce you to Major Hope?'

So *this* was Silvia Steiner, Ben thought as he shook hands with her. She seemed altogether more approachable than her husband. But then he noticed something a little odd. It was the way she was looking at him, more quizzical than disapproving. It was over in a second, and he wondered what it meant.

'Have we met before, Major Hope?' she asked him.

'Please, call me Ben. And I'm afraid I don't believe I've had the pleasure.'

'The major is standing in for Captain Shannon,' Dorenkamp explained, 'who regrettably is unable to join us for a while. An unfortunate incident.'

Silvia Steiner raised her eyebrows in consternation. 'Oh, dear. Nothing serious, I hope?'

'He'll be fine,' Ben said uncomfortably. 'Let's just say he had an inconvenience.'

'What happened?'

'It's a long story.'

Her gaze lingered on him for a few seconds. Ben tried to read her thoughts. Had Shannon told the Steiners what had really happened? He didn't think so. Not even Shannon could be that unprofessional.

But then the awkward moment passed and Silvia Steiner smiled warmly again. 'It was a pleasure to meet you.'

'Likewise,' Ben said.

'I'm sure we'll meet again soon.' She turned to Dorenkamp. 'Have you seen Otto around, Heinrich? There was something I wanted to ask him.'

'I believe he is on the golf course,' the PA said.

'Again?' But her look of exasperation faded quickly. She smiled a last time at Ben, turned and headed back up the corridor, rounded a corner and disappeared from sight.

'Enjoy your coffee,' Dorenkamp said, pointing to the refectory door. 'I will see you later.'

Ben watched him go, thinking he didn't seem like a bad guy. He had a lot to put up with from Steiner. Then he pushed through the door. The refectory was a large dining hall, the walls panelled with ornate oak. On a side table were stacked plates and cups and a stand with a selection of cakes and pastries. Beside it was a large coffee machine that hissed steam and burbled and spat. The coffee smelled good. Ben grabbed a cup and filled it.

The others were milling around the table and talking in low voices while helping themselves to food. Ben carried his coffee over to the window and stood with his back to them, gazing out at the view.

'What the fuck?' said a voice behind him, hostile and challenging.

Ben turned slowly. He'd known who it was, and he'd been right. Pete Neville was standing glaring at him, a coffee in one hand and a Danish pastry in the other. 'What's the fucking idea of stirring things up, mate?' he went on.

Ben gave him a look and said nothing.

'Watch it, Pete,' Woodcock called out from across the room. 'He might try and break your arm.'

'Like to see him fucking try,' grunted Morgan.

'So tell us, mate,' Neville said. 'What the fuck you trying to do, get us all the boot?'

Ben looked at him. 'A tip. If you're going to come on the tough guy, try not to do it when you've got custard all over your chin.'

Neville quickly wiped his chin with the back of his hand.

Ben turned to address them all. 'Let's get one thing straight, people. I'm CO here, and you're going to answer to me and follow my lead.'

The team watched him sullenly.

'And from now on, Neville,' Ben said, 'you keep your mouth shut. If you speak to me, it's in reply to a direct question. Otherwise I'll shut it for you. Understood?' He finished his coffee and put down the empty cup. 'Now, Neville, you've just earned yourself a job. Go and collect the popguns from Rolf. Take them over to our quarters. Check everything's working and get them ready for this afternoon. You're responsible for them from now on. Any complaints, *mate*?'

Neville didn't say a word.

'Better,' Ben said. Then he walked past them all and left the refectory.

Chapter Sixteen

Ben spent a little while before lunch wandering about the estate, checking things over and familiarising himself with the layout. Peacocks strutted over the immaculate green lawns. Attached to the château's west wing was a large glass-domed conservatory filled with exotic plants, with an ornate fountain in its centre and a bronze statue of the Roman sea god Neptune standing amid the waves, his trident pointing upwards. Ben stopped to look at it, then walked on. Bees hummed around the flowers in the formal gardens. Gardeners in white uniforms were mowing the velvety turf of the tennis courts. Through a gated archway Ben could see the neatly-trimmed entrance to a maze. The sky was blue, and even with the mountain breeze the sun was beating down hard.

A little further on, he heard angry shouts in the distance, and followed the sound to see a man he instantly knew was Otto, heir to the Steiner fortune, storming angrily across the golf course. In a business suit, he might have passed for a younger version of his uncle, but the check trousers, the brightly coloured golf shirt and the jaunty white cap on his head made him appear faintly clownish. A miserable-looking caddie stumbled along after him. Otto turned and started raging at him, then grabbed a club from the golf bag, threw it clumsily at him and screamed at him in German to fuck off.

Any other time, Ben might have smiled to himself at the spectacle. Not today. The whole situation was a mess. He didn't want to be here, sandwiched between a prickly despot and a team of idiots. All he wanted was to be back home at Le Val. Even the idea of sitting at the desk doing paperwork seemed deeply attractive at this moment. And he'd brought the whole thing on himself.

Ben watched Otto stamp off towards his private villa, then turned and carried on, thinking about what a difference there was between the two Steiner men. He wondered how they got on.

As he walked, he spotted a building that made him stop and look. Nestling in among the trees, its stained glass windows caught the sunlight.

It was a little grey stone chapel. If the Steiners had had it built specially for them, it was the best reproduction of an eighteenth-century church that Ben had ever seen. He felt himself drawn towards it. Pushed open the studded oak door and walked in.

It was cool inside, and his footsteps echoed off the tiled floor. He wandered up the aisle, between the rows of glistening pews, and stopped in front of the altar. The light from the stained glass windows shone down on him. He looked up at the statue of the crucified Jesus on the back wall behind the altar. Sighed and closed his eyes.

He hadn't prayed for a long time.

Lord, I know you and I have had our differences. I know I've been inconstant and done a lot of bad things.

He paused.

But please give me the strength to see this through. Give me the patience not to tell them all to go to hell, drive straight

back to Le Val and make sure Rupert Shannon spends the next
year sucking his meals out of a tube.

He opened his eyes. It hadn't quite come out the way he'd intended. A little dark, perhaps. But it would have to do, and he hoped God understood. He turned away from the altar and walked back up the aisle feeling just a little lighter. Maybe prayer was good for you after all.

As he headed back towards the house, he heard the piano again. This time he recognised the piece. Bartók. Harmonically dissonant and jarring on the ear, it was the kind of music he liked. And Silvia Steiner played it beautifully, as though she really understood it.

The music was drifting from a pair of open French windows. He walked towards them, paused to listen and peered inside.

She was sitting at her concert grand in a large white room. A little way from the piano stool a gilt harp, and nearby a cello case was lying on the floor. There was a sofa piled with cushions, that looked as though people actually sat on it. In one corner was a messy stack of music books and manuscripts, and tatty rugs were arranged ad hoc on the floor. Flowers and plants spilled out of vases everywhere. Ben sensed that this was Silvia Steiner's personal haven, cosy and inviting, untainted by her husband's cold, rigid formality.

She noticed Ben standing there in the window, lifted her hands from the keys and smiled. 'Hello again.'

'Please don't stop,' he said. 'I didn't mean to interrupt you. I was just listening to the Bartók.'

Her smile broadened. She got up from the piano stool and walked round the side of the instrument towards him. 'In this house, most people keep their distance when I'm playing Bartók. Especially Max. He says it makes him feel tense and uncomfortable.'

'Not me,' he said. 'I find it relaxing.'

She laughed, and considered him for a moment with the same curious look she'd given him before. 'You're an unusual man,' she said.

'Not so unusual,' he replied.

'I'm sorry my husband spoke sharply to you earlier on.' Catching Ben's expression of surprise, she added, 'Heinrich told me. You know, Max has been under a lot of stress lately with all that's been happening. These awful terrorists. Pressure of the business. Family problems.' She looked out of the window, across the golf course to where Otto had been a few minutes earlier, and Ben thought he could see a look of sadness pass over her face. 'Max isn't normally difficult to deal with,' she went on. 'He's really a wonderful man.'

Ben found that hard to believe. 'I understand that Herr Steiner is under a lot of stress. It's perfectly normal, in these circumstances.'

'Thank you for being so understanding,' she said. 'You seem like a very kind, decent person.'

Ben didn't quite know how to respond to that. He glanced down at his feet.

'I believe you live in France?' she asked.

'Normandy.'

'But you're English.'

'Not quite,' he said. 'Half English, half Irish. Before I moved to France I had a place in Galway, by the sea.'

'How beautiful. You must miss it.'

'I do, sometimes. But life moves on.'

'It certainly does.' She sighed. For an instant she seemed far away, then caught herself. 'Are you sure we've never met?' she asked suddenly. 'Quite sure?'

'Pretty sure. Why?'

She shook her head slowly, as if trying to place him. Her eyes seemed to search his. 'It's strange. Somehow I feel that I know you. You seem terribly familiar to me.'

'I have a good memory for faces,' he said. 'If we'd ever met, I would remember.' He smiled. 'Now I'd better leave you to your music. I have to get back to my work.'

After he'd finished his rounds of the estate and made all the mental notes he needed, Ben went back to the security team's quarters. He got there just as lunch was being served. Once he'd checked that Neville had sorted out the Flash-Balls as instructed, he grabbed a ham salad baguette and a bottle of mineral water and went back to his room to eat alone once again.

As he ate, he could hear the laughter of the others over the blare of the TV. He shut the noise out of his thoughts, still angry with himself. When he'd finished eating, he picked up his phone and dialled the number for Le Val. Jeff answered.

'How are things going?'

'Not much to report,' Jeff said. 'Brooke's still here, getting ready for her lecture. She thought she might as well hang around.'

'I ought to be there,' Ben said glumly. 'I should be taking care of things.'

'It's just a bunch of insurance brokers wanting to be taught about hostage psychology and ransom negotiation techniques,' Jeff said. 'Nothing we can't cope with ourselves. You sit tight and we'll see you when we see you.'

'Any word on His Nibs?'

'Still in hospital. I reckon the bastard's malingering there. Getting paid for doing fuck all. Private room at our expense, probably ordering champagne round the clock. I tell you, he's having a whale of a time with this.'

It wasn't what Ben wanted to hear.

Just after one, the team filed back outside, carrying their clumsy weapons. There was no conversation between them as they made the ten-minute walk to the circular concrete helipad at the west side of the estate.

Chapter Seventeen

Ben and the team didn't have long to wait before the beat of rotor blades crept up in the distance and the two choppers appeared over the tree line. The helicopters drew quickly nearer, until they were hovering right overhead and settling down to land, their downdraught flattening out a wide circle in the lawn surrounding the helipad. Both craft were immaculate, the bright sun gleaming off identical red paintwork and the crisp white graphics of the Steiner company logo on their flanks. With his clothes and hair fluttering in the windstorm, Ben could see the men inside – a pilot and co-pilot for each chopper, all wearing matching red uniforms.

The helicopters touched down, skids flexing gently as they took the weight. The screech of the turbines dropped down to a roar and the rotors gradually slowed to an idle. The co-pilots jumped down and opened the rear hatches. Ben could see how much plusher Steiner's personal helicopter was inside. Max Steiner was clearly a man who liked to make a statement.

Only when the noise and the wind had diminished a minute later did their employer make his appearance. The golf buggy zipped across the lawns towards them, the billionaire in the front passenger seat and Dorenkamp riding shotgun, clutching a black leather attaché case on his lap. Ben checked his watch. It was exactly quarter past one.

Steiner climbed down from the buggy, straightened his suit and, with Dorenkamp following behind him, walked purposefully towards the lead chopper. Climbing into the rear, he turned and shot Ben a look that said, 'What are you waiting for?'

Ben waved the team towards the second craft, paused while Dorenkamp climbed on board, then hauled himself up through the hatch carrying his Flash-Ball. The seats were deep and comfortable. Ben slipped the rubber bullet gun into a space beneath his. Then the co-pilots closed the hatches of the two aircraft, like chauffeurs shutting limo doors. They ran round to take their places and put on their headsets as the shriek of the turbines started up again and the rotors began to spin faster.

In less than a minute, the ground was dropping away from them and Ben watched the château and surrounding estate shrink to the size of a model. The chopper climbed straight up to four hundred feet, then dipped its nose and accelerated hard towards the horizon. The cabin was well insulated against the noise. Ben barely had to raise his voice to ask Dorenkamp where the aircraft were usually kept. The PA turned and replied that they were stored at a private hangar a few miles from the estate.

Ben nodded and said no more. Out of the window, hills and forests rolled by far below.

Steiner nudged Dorenkamp and pointed at the back of the co-pilot's head. Ben wondered what he was doing, then saw that he was pointing at the ring the man was wearing in his left ear. Steiner leaned towards Dorenkamp and Ben heard him say in German, 'If that young man wants to continue working for me, he'll have to dispense with the decorations.'

'Must be new on the staff,' Dorenkamp replied. 'I'll have a word with Rolf.'

The two men went on to discussing the agenda for the upcoming conference, while Ben watched the alpine scenery. Twisting round in his seat, he could see the second chopper keeping pace behind them, the shapes of his team just visible through the side window.

Just as he was about to turn and face forward again, he saw the other aircraft suddenly give a violent judder, bank and peel off to starboard. Over the noise he heard the unmistakable crack of a rifle shot, and from somewhere down in the rolling fields below the yellow-white flame of a muzzle flash caught his eye as more shots were fired. Then another. Two shooters, using high-velocity semi-auto rifles.

It was happening already.

The rear helicopter veered away sharply, rapidly shrinking into the distance. Steiner's pilot banked the lead craft hard in the opposite direction, dropping altitude and heading for a thick patch of woodland on the port side.

'*Gott in Himmel*,' Steiner yelled as the floor tilted dramatically and his attaché case went tumbling away from him. Dorenkamp's hands gripped the arms of his seat, fingers white against the red fabric.

Ben knew immediately what was happening. The shooters on the ground weren't trying to bring the choppers down, but to divert their course and isolate Steiner's helicopter from its escort. It was a crude form of hijack. The question was, how did their attackers plan on forcing the chopper to the ground without shooting it down?

The question was answered a second later when the co-pilot swung round to face them, holding a gun. Not a big clumsy riot stun gun, but a purposeful 9mm Beretta semi-auto pistol. And it was pointed straight at them.

'This is outrageous,' Steiner thundered in German.

There wasn't much Ben could do without risking his life

and those of everyone on board. He sat calmly in his seat as Steiner continued to yell. The pilot worked the controls, bringing the chopper down lower towards the pine forest. Ben could see the green canopy skimming past under them, and the second chopper now far away, just a little dark red dot against the sky.

The crude hijack was turning out to be quite neatly orchestrated. When Ben saw the wide circular clearing in the trees opening up ahead, he knew the pilot had found his prearranged landing zone.

The instant the chopper touched down, the co-pilot was out of the cockpit and tearing open the rear door, still pointing the pistol at them, shouting '*Raus! Raus!*' The pilot quickly shut everything down, kicked open his hatch and hit the ground running.

In seconds, Steiner, Dorenkamp and Ben were herded out of the aircraft and marched impatiently at gunpoint across the leafy ground. The muzzle of the pistol swept from side to side, covering them all. The pilot grabbed Steiner's jacket collar, shoving him across the clearing towards the trees about thirty yards away. The billionaire was protesting violently, scarlet with fury. Dorenkamp was pale and subdued, glancing at his employer as if he wished he could say, 'Shut up, you'll only make this worse for us.'

Ben glanced up at the sky to see the second chopper still a long way off but banking round towards them and coming in fast. It looked to him as though the kidnappers had only managed to infiltrate part of Steiner's crew. He estimated that they had ninety seconds at best to get Steiner out of there before the rest of the team landed. Tight timing, but the kidnappers seemed right on schedule and things were going smoothly.

'Keep moving,' the co-pilot muttered, waving his gun at

Ben. They were just twenty yards from the trees now. Ben peered through the dense greenery and could just about make out the shape of a commercial van parked on the other side on a lane. It was white, rusty and battered, long wheelbase, maybe an old-model Fiat Ducato. The perfect disposable and inconspicuous kidnap getaway vehicle.

Fifteen yards to the trees. There was a movement in the foliage, and then branches parted and five figures stepped out of the forest to meet them. All were armed with pistols, all dressed from head to foot in black military gear: combat trousers, assault vests, ski masks. To his amazement, he realised that all five had little red, white and black metal swastika badges pinned to their jackets, like military insignia. The audacity of it stunned him.

'Move, *Scheisskopf*,' the co-pilot said in German behind him. Ben could feel the gun at his back. Ten yards from the trees and the approaching ground team. The second chopper was getting closer, its rapid drumbeat filling the air. But not close enough. A few more steps, and the men in black would take charge of Steiner and march him to the waiting van. Then it would be over.

Ben slowed his pace, feeling the co-pilot's hand shove him hard in the back. The guy barked in German to keep moving. Ben sensed the pistol muzzle come closer, just a few inches from the back of his head.

Which was precisely what he'd been waiting for. He needed the gun to be as close as possible for what he was about to do next.

It was a combination of the two moves he'd used at Le Val to disarm Rupert Shannon and take him down, except this time it was for real. He whirled round faster than the guy could react, took control of the gun wrist and threw a stamping kick to the knee. The co-pilot cried out in pain.

Ben twisted the Beretta out of his grip. He sensed the pilot making a lunge at him, and caught him across the face with the butt of the pistol. The man screamed and went down, letting go of Steiner.

Then it was mayhem. The two pilots were rolling on the ground, clutching their injuries. The ground team were suddenly all yelling and screaming, waving their pistols. Steiner was like a drunk, staggering and swaying wildly on his feet and roaring 'No shooting! No shooting!' at Ben. Complete chaos. But the ability to remain calm and lucid when everyone around him was losing their heads had been what had earned Ben his SAS badge all those years ago, and it was as natural to him as breathing. Inside his mind, time had slowed down to a crawl, the shouting a distant muffled roar as he contemplated the scenario and sped through the options facing him.

He'd been in enough volatile stand-off confrontations to know that the few seconds the element of surprise had bought him were going to run out fast. He was outgunned five to one. He could only get two, maybe three of them before they took him down. Then they were going to kill Dorenkamp too, stuff Steiner in the van and take him away. Mission failed, disastrously.

Out of all the overwhelming odds against him, there were only two things in his favour. The first was that he had a gun in his hand. The second was that it gave him control over the enemy's primary resource: Steiner himself. These people were kidnappers, not assassins. Which meant the businessman was worth something to them. Money, information, wartime documents, evidence, whatever it was, if anything happened to Steiner it was beyond their reach forever.

And that gave Ben an edge. A big one. It was crazy, but

the logic was perfect – and anyway, he'd been doing crazy things all his life.

Fuck it. He grabbed a fistful of Steiner's jacket and yanked him brutally towards him. Shoved the gun hard against the base of his skull.

'Back off and drop your weapons,' he yelled in German. 'Nobody does anything. Or I'll kill him.'

Chapter Eighteen

The kidnappers were stopped in their tracks. Suddenly the tables had turned, and now they were the ones running out of options and squandering precious seconds in indecision.

The second chopper was almost overhead now, hovering and circling, battering the trees with its downdraught as the pilot zeroed in on a safe landing point.

Then the kidnappers scattered in panic. The black-clad ground team went running wildly towards the trees. The pilots staggered up on their feet, hobbling away after them. Ben lowered the pistol and let go of Steiner's collar, ignoring the man's fury. He turned and saw the second chopper landing on the far side of Steiner's personal craft, the doors flying open, Neville and Woodcock and the others spilling out, clutching their weapons, sprinting across the clearing towards them.

Ben pushed Steiner towards Dorenkamp, who was staring at him wide-eyed, as if in a trance. 'Get him into the helicopter.' Then, as the PA gripped hold of his employer's arm and started tugging him away to safety, Ben took off towards the forest.

On the other side of the trees, he could hear the Fiat's engine revving up hard as the fleeing kidnappers darted through the thicket towards it. The sound of its side door sliding open. A voice inside screaming 'Come on! Move!'

The woods were dark after the sunlit clearing. He crashed through the bushes and whipping branches. If he could just catch one of them, he might be able to neutralise the threat against Steiner, end this whole thing. That would probably mean the end of Shannon's protection contract – but Ben didn't have time to worry too much about that right now.

Up ahead, he saw two of the men in black burst out of the trees and reach the van and leap inside. Then a third, followed by the bloody-nosed co-pilot. The van was rolling now. More screams and yells. The second pilot managed to scramble on board, another man in black right behind him.

They're going to get away.

There was just one kidnapper still in the woods, fifteen yards from the road and moving fast. Ben ran harder, forcing every ounce of power out of his legs. Suddenly the kidnapper tripped and went sprawling onto the ground. By the time he'd picked himself up again, Ben had gained precious yards on him. The guy threw a glance back over his shoulder, spotting his pursuer, the eyes in the mask opening wide in alarm.

Someone in the van had seen Ben, too. The flat report of a 9mm, and a bullet cracked off a tree near his head. He crouched low and let off a string of return shots from the captured Beretta, taking out the back window and blowing a rear light into fragments of red plastic. He didn't want to kill anyone, and he certainly didn't want to get into a firefight. But he might be able to convince the van driver to abandon the last of the gang, who was now dashing along almost parallel with the road to keep up with the accelerating vehicle.

The van surged ahead, braked hard, accelerated again, the driver unsure what to do.

Ben fired a couple more shots, driving the running man further off course, and now the terrain was sloping downwards away from road level, with a steep earth bank snarled with brambles. Nature's barbed wire, cutting off the kidnapper's access to the road.

The guy was lightly built, and a fast runner. Ben had to sprint hard to keep up with the flitting black figure. As he ran he levelled the gun out in front of him and considered trying to take him down with a shot to the lower leg. Tactically dangerous. You couldn't run and shoot accurately at the same time, and if the shot went high he might hit a vital organ, open up an artery. He wanted this one alive.

The van was now a fleeting white shape behind the trees. More shots cracked out from its open side door, but went wide as though the shooters were nervous. Nobody wanted to hit their own man by mistake.

The kidnapper vaulted a fallen trunk and crashed right into the heart of a thorn bush that slowed him down as he stumbled and wrenched his way through it. Ben was close now. Still clutching the pistol in his right hand, he threw out his left arm to grab a fistful of the running man's combat jacket, but the guy dodged and Ben's fingers closed on empty air. He could hear the man's rasping breath as he darted left and right through the undergrowth, zigzagging like a rabbit trying to shake off a fox. Then the ground became more uneven and they were running into what looked like an old river bed. The kidnapper took the lower path through the middle and Ben found himself running alongside him on higher ground. He timed it, estimated distances, then went for it and launched himself into the air.

A moment's weightlessness, and then a jarring impact as he slammed into the kidnapper and brought him rolling down in the dirt in a tumble of flailing limbs. Ben's arm whacked painfully against a root and his pistol spun out of his grip. The kidnapper might have been slender, but he was strong and determined, fighting like a wild animal. A knee slammed up and caught Ben's cheekbone, snapping his head sideways long enough for his opponent to scramble to his feet. Ben jumped up after him, ducked a punch aimed at his face, grabbed the fist and twisted it hard. The kidnapper let out a sharp yell of pain.

It was at that moment that Ben realised he was fighting a woman.

She twisted like a snake out of his grip as he dragged her to her feet, and threw another well-aimed punch that would have smashed his nose if it had landed. He made a grab for her right arm, misjudged it and got a fistful of her sleeve, ripping the black material from wrist to elbow. She danced away like a boxer, then came back in and fired a kick at his groin, and he ducked back out of the reach of her combat boot. The arm with the ripped sleeve came slicing towards his throat, the hand stiff like a blade. Fast, but not quite fast enough. His fingers closed on bare flesh, and now he had her. He could see the tight muscles in her forearm as she struggled against his grip. The fight was just about over. Then they'd find out who was trying to kidnap Steiner. Ben prepared to deliver an incapacitating blow to the neck.

And he saw something that made him stop.

He let go of the woman and took a step back, stunned, disorientated.

The eyes in the combat mask were narrowed, watching him fiercely like a panther's. His gaze locked on hers – maybe three-quarters of a second, but it felt like minutes. He was lost, unable to move.

Then she whirled towards him and her boot lashed out in a straight kick that caught him in the pit of the stomach. His breath burst out of his mouth and he staggered back and fell.

There was a report like a shotgun, and a heavy projectile flew through the air with a low thrumming sound and smacked off a tree trunk next to where the woman was standing. Ben heard Woodcock's voice yelling 'Take him down!' and twisted round in the dirt to see the rest of the bodyguard team approaching through the trees. A ragged series of blasts as the team let off their Flash-Balls. The humming whoosh of rubber bullets flying through the air. One snapped a branch, the rest ploughed harmlessly into the undergrowth.

The woman's gaze lingered just a fraction of a second on Ben, and then she took off like a deer. Grabbing a fistful of ivy, she scrabbled up the earth bank and made a dash for the road.

The van was just twenty yards ahead, waiting, revving. The driver threw it into reverse and floored the pedal. Yells of 'Come on! Move your arse!' Hands reached out of the sliding door and hauled her in, then the diesel roared, the exhaust kicked out a black cloud of smoke, and the van sped away, weaving down the road.

Ben slowly clambered to his feet as the men gathered round him. Spotting the fallen pistol in the leaves, he picked it up and slipped it absently into his belt, under his jacket. Nobody spoke. Burton and Powell appeared, and Ben suddenly wondered who the hell was looking after the principal.

His question was answered just a moment later when he turned to see Steiner walking towards them through the trees, his chest heaving with exertion. He didn't look happy. Dorenkamp was a few feet behind, pale and sheepish.

The billionaire stormed over. His face was a mottled purple-red, eyes almost popping, hair in disarray.

'We all saw what happened,' Neville said.

113

Steiner came right up close, toe to toe, so that Ben could virtually smell his rage.

'That was a very fine display, *Major* Hope.' His voice rose to a shout as he went on. 'Not only did you completely fail to protect me and then point a gun and threaten to *kill* me – *me*, your employer, your *client* – you then allowed that kidnapper to escape.'

Ben didn't speak, but Steiner ranted on as if he'd tried to protest.

'If I had not insisted on following, I would never have believed it. But I saw you. You did *nothing*. You just stood there, staring at him. Have you gone completely out of your *mind*?' Steiner virtually screamed the last word. There were flecks of spittle on his lips. He stared in disgusted, trembling fury.

Ben still didn't speak. There was nothing he could say, except maybe 'Don't spit in my face like that' – but he didn't have the energy.

'Don't even *try* to answer,' Steiner yelled. 'I don't wish to hear excuses. I have been almost kidnapped, threatened with a gun by my own bodyguard, and I have missed my meeting. What utter, unbelievable incompetence is this?' He paused, as if searching for more accusations but running out of things to shout in Ben's face. 'You're fired,' he added simply. Turned to the rest of the team. 'All of you. Dismissed. You hear? You are all going straight back home where you came from and I will hire a *proper* team to protect me.'

Then Maximilian Steiner turned and stormed away, back towards the choppers, his assistant following behind him.

Chapter Nineteen

The battered white Fiat Ducato van sped down the country lanes, skidding and weaving on the bends. There was chaos inside, bodies crammed together in the back and falling over each other, discarded weapons sliding around on the metal floor. The van was filled with shouting as frayed nerves spilled over into adrenaline-fuelled hysteria.

Of the van's eight occupants, just one was silent. The woman with the ripped sleeve sat quietly on the hard rear wheel arch, combat boots braced apart to steady herself against the wild rocking and bouncing of the vehicle. She peeled off her ski mask, let it drop to the floor. Ruffled her cropped blond hair and closed her eyes and leaned her head back against the side wall of the van.

The shrill arguing and jabbering went on all around her.

'And once again it's all fucked up,' the chopper co-pilot was complaining loudly from the passenger seat.

'Yeah, and who let the guy have the gun, Ernst, you stupid bastard?'

'I'm a pilot. I'm not trained to go up against some maniac. Look at my hand. I think he broke my fucking fingers, man.'

'Who the fuck *was* that guy?'

The driver glanced at Ernst. 'What guy are they talking about?' he yelled.

115

'The fucking bodyguard guy, Dominik,' said Thomas in the back. 'He was threatening to shoot Steiner.'

'He was *what*?' Dominik exploded. He took his eyes off the road for a second as he twisted round in his seat, and the van veered a little off course.

'Drive properly, cretin,' screamed Helmut, the chopper pilot. He was wiping blood off his face from where the pistol butt had slammed into him.

'He had a gun at Steiner's fucking head and he was going to shoot him,' Jürgen said. 'We all saw it, right? The guy was crazy. What were we supposed to do?'

The woman in the back spoke for the first time. 'He wasn't going to shoot anybody. It was a bluff, and you idiots fell for it.'

'Yeah? And how do you figure that?' Rudi fired from the opposite wheel arch. He ripped off his ski mask in disgust, then almost lost his balance as the van hammered violently over a pothole and the suspension grounded out with a crash.

'*Arschloch!*' he shouted at Dominik. 'You trying to get us killed?'

'Oh, *I'm* sorry,' Dominik yelled back at him. 'Maybe the cops would give you a smoother ride to jail. I hear Swiss prisons are really nice these days.'

'Shut your hole!'

'I just know, that's all,' the woman said quietly.

Rudi said, 'What's that, female intuition?'

She didn't reply.

'Shut up, Rudi,' said Franz from where he was kneeling by the back doors.

'Oh, sure, stand up for your girlfriend. This whole thing was her fucked-up idea.'

Franz raised his arms. 'Guys. Why don't we all just calm the fuck down, OK? We're all in this together. And we just have to accept that it isn't working.'

'So now what?' demanded Rudi.

'We need to find a better way,' Franz said.

'What're we going to do if Steiner's got a bodyguard team now?'

'It was only a question of time. Just be thankful none of us got killed back there.' He turned to the woman and held her hand, laced his fingers through hers and looked in her eyes with concern. 'You OK, Luna?'

She nodded. 'I will be. I got a fright, that's all.'

'How the hell did you manage to get away from him?'

'I don't know,' she said softly, barely audible over the roar of the van.

'Did he say anything to you?'

She shook her head. 'Don't ask me questions.'

Franz looked at her, puzzled. 'Why?'

'Just don't.'

By then they had reached the end of the rough lane. The van leaned heavily as Dominik took a hard right onto a tarmac road and accelerated away. The arguing subsided into a brooding silence as they all sat with their private thoughts. Rudi was muttering angrily to himself and shaking his head. Up front, Ernst was twiddling with the radio, looking for any breaking news that might concern them.

Less than ten minutes later, the van pulled off the road, followed another bumpy track for a couple of hundred yards, then came to a halt in a grassy layby next to a field gate.

The brown Volvo carrying Andreas and Victor was already there waiting for them. Ernst climbed out of the cab, opened the gate and Dominik drove the van over sun-hardened tractor ruts into the field. The Volvo followed, and the two vehicles parked up side by side as Ernst shut the gate behind them.

Dominik killed the engine, jumped down from the van,

opened up the side door with a screech of rusty metal, and everyone piled out. There wasn't a face that didn't look weary and miserable after the failed kidnap plan. Luna took a deep breath and scanned the forested horizon. The place was so tranquil. She just wished she was feeling that way inside.

Andreas had the rear hatch of the Volvo open and was lifting out the roll of sackcloth that contained the rifles the two-man diversion team had used to split up the choppers. Those rifles had taken up the biggest chunk of their limited budget, Luna thought as she watched. What a waste of money. Just like all the training and rehearsals had been a waste, and all the meticulous effort spent to get Helmut and Ernst inside Steiner's helicopter hangar.

Failed. Again. She clenched her teeth.

'We need to hurry,' Franz told the others. 'In a few minutes this whole area's going to be crawling with cops.'

They moved fast and spoke little. Helmut and Ernst unzipped the red jumpsuits they'd stolen from Steiner's chopper pilots after tying them up in a toilet at the hangar. Velcro fasteners made little tearing sounds as the others stripped off their combat gear. Everyone had T-shirts and jeans under their outer clothing, except Luna. The light cotton jodhpurs she was wearing had been part of the plan.

The jumpsuits were tossed into the open Fiat, while Thomas and Andreas stuffed the black combat clothes and boots into two big rubble sacks. Victor gathered up the rest of the weapons from the van and shoved them into a zip-up sports bag. Meanwhile, Rudi stepped over to the Volvo and took out the two motorcycle jackets and helmets, the cans of petrol and the riding boots that had been piled in the back. He tossed the boots over to Luna, and she started pulling them on while he donned the bike leathers and helmet.

Meanwhile, Franz was opening up the plastic jerrycans and, once everyone had what they needed, he started sloshing petrol over the two vehicles and all over the grass around them.

Luna reached into the pocket of her riding trousers and took out a soft pack of Camels. She lit one up, took a long drag and felt the nicotine rush hit her bloodstream. Then she flicked the cigarette through the Fiat's open passenger door and stepped back.

A couple of seconds' delay, and then there was a roaring, flat *whumph* as the petrol ignited and a big rolling mushroom of flame engulfed both vehicles. Luna felt the heat on her face, smelled the stink of burning plastic and rubber, and watched the blaze for a second until she felt Franz's hand on her shoulder.

'Let's move,' he said. They picked up their stuff and started walking away from the burning vehicles.

Fifty yards across the next field, beyond another gate, were an old VW Golf, a Honda 750 motorcycle and a double horse trailer hooked up to a silver Range Rover. The 4x4 wasn't brand new, but it looked respectable enough to get past the Swiss border officials. A few yards from the open trailer, a plump, ginger-haired woman was standing with a large chestnut gelding. The horse had been grazing contentedly on the lush alpine grass until the fire had started; now it was prancing about nervously, tossing its head and snorting, and the woman was having trouble keeping hold of the lead rope.

'This is all we need,' Rudi muttered as they walked up to the gate. 'By the time the cops get here, we'll still be running around trying to catch your fucking horse.'

Luna shot him a look. 'He'll be fine. He's calm with me.' She jumped the gate and ran across, took the rope from the ginger-haired woman and patted the horse gently, talking to him in a low voice. He nuzzled against her, already calming down. She pressed her brow to his big flat bony forehead, felt the warmth of his skin and closed her eyes.

'How did it go?' the woman asked her.

'Do you see any captive billionaires around here anywhere?'

'I guess not.'

'Well, that's because we didn't get him, Steffi.' Luna handed her back the rope. 'He'll be fine now,' she said, giving the horse a last pat. Then she went over to the Range Rover, opened up the back door. On the seat were a collection of riding trophies and rosettes. She grabbed the bag that was sitting next to them. Inside was a long blond wig and a neatly-pressed silk dressage shirt. She quickly stripped down to her bra, pulled on the shirt and put on the wig. Checked herself in the wing mirror. The transformation from black-clad warrior to middle-class horsewoman was complete. Meanwhile, Franz was putting on a clean blue polo shirt with an equestrian logo on the breast pocket.

The perfect front. Nobody would ever have guessed who or what they were. More importantly, the guards at the Swiss–German border wouldn't be likely to stop and search respectable-looking equestrian folks on their way home from a horse show bearing their prizes.

Which meant nobody would have had any idea of what they were really carrying. Under the straw in the trailer was a false floor, sturdy enough to take the weight of the horse. It had two concealed compartments. One was for their weapons and combat gear and, as Luna and Franz were changing their clothes, the others were stuffing the bags and rolled-up rifles inside and re-covering the floor with a deep layer of straw.

The second compartment was twice the size, big enough to accommodate a large man. It had been intended for Steiner, to smuggle him back into Germany. He'd have been able to breathe through some holes discreetly punched in the steel panelling. The dope they'd have used to tranquillise him was in the Range Rover's glove compartment, labelled to look like a veterinary product.

'It was a good plan,' Luna said wistfully to Franz as she led the horse up the ramp into the trailer with a clatter of hooves.

He smiled. 'It was. But don't worry. We'll get him.'

'Will we?' She patted the horse, then skipped back down the ramp, raised it up and made sure everything was secure before she bolted the trailer doors. Her face was grim as she worked.

'Don't beat yourself up over it,' Franz told her. 'We'll come up with another plan.'

'Let's not talk about it now,' she said.

They were ready to go their separate ways. 'Everyone remember the routes we talked about?' Luna said as they headed for their vehicles.

Nods and murmurs from the others.

'OK. See you back in Germany. Be careful.' She and Franz got into the front of the Range Rover with Steffi in the back. Andreas, Victor, Dominik and Thomas climbed into the VW Golf. Rudi threw a leg over the Honda, fired it up and blipped the throttle as Jürgen got on the pillion and snapped his visor shut.

The little convoy left the field by an open gate at the far side. Fifty yards up the lane they rejoined the main road, and a little way after that they came to a crossroads. The Range

Rover carried on straight ahead, the Golf went left and the Honda went right.

Behind them, the column of smoke from the burning vehicles was still rising into the clear blue sky.

Chapter Twenty

Steiner and Dorenkamp took off back for the château in the lead chopper with the second craft's pilot at the controls while his co-pilot took his place and flew the bodyguard team behind them.

Ben sat with the others and felt the hot stares on him like a poultice. He didn't make eye contact, didn't speak. A couple of times he thought he heard angry mutters over the blast of the turbine, but he didn't react.

They say the return journey is always quicker, but this one seemed to take forty times longer. Ben had the hatch open and was on the ground before the chopper had even settled down on the helipad. Steiner's personal helicopter was powering back up for take-off. The billionaire and his PA were already gone.

Ben strode towards the house. Behind him, the rest of the team slouched moodily off in the direction of their quarters, carrying their stun weapons.

The interior of the château was cool after the baking sun. Ben walked across the main entrance hall, past the mounted knight. A maid carrying a pile of linen stared at the muddied, torn state of him as he went by, but he barely registered her.

He found Dorenkamp in the corridor not far away.

'I want to speak to Steiner. Where is he?'

Dorenkamp's brows were knitted with worry and embarrassment.

'He won't see you. I'm sorry.'

'I'm not asking him to change his mind about firing me,' Ben said.

Dorenkamp's look of discomfort deepened even more, and he shifted from foot to foot, as though he couldn't wait to be out of there. 'That's good, because I think there's little chance he would agree.'

'I want to ask him to keep the rest of the team on,' Ben said. 'I'll go, but let them stay. As soon as Shannon's healed up, he can fly out and join them. Then things are back to the way they would have been, and I'll be out of the picture for good.'

Dorenkamp shook his head. 'I meant what I told you before. Once Herr Steiner has decided on something, he will not go back on it.'

'I personally don't think much of them as a team,' Ben said. 'I would never have hired them, and I think this whole set-up stinks. But what happened back there wasn't their fault. It was mine.'

Dorenkamp looked as if he was about to dash off. Then he seemed to change his mind, like someone struggling over whether or not to pass on a burdensome secret. He glanced up and down the empty corridor and spoke in a low voice.

'Listen. I personally believe that what you did was the right course of action. I think that if you hadn't acted as you did, Herr Steiner would have been taken captive by those people, and you and I would most certainly still be there in the woods with bullets in our heads. And I think that Herr Steiner knows it, too.'

'Then why is he acting like such a stubborn old goat?'

'Because he can't tolerate the way you humiliated him

back there. You held a *gun* to his head. Nobody does that to him.'

'Maybe he should try getting over himself a little bit. He'd have lost a lot more dignity than that if he'd ended up a kidnap victim.'

Dorenkamp shrugged.

Ben turned away. *I tried*, he thought. *And that's that.*

But now he had more important things on his mind. Things that he could hardly believe. He couldn't shut the image of the woman in the woods out of his head. As he walked back out of the house and headed for the team's quarters, he was playing the events over again and again.

It's impossible.

But maybe some things that were impossible were real.

He walked into the communal living space and met a dead silence from the others. He went to his room and locked the door behind him. In the en-suite bathroom he stripped off his dirty clothes and left them strewn on the tiles as he showered. He turned the water up hot, on full blast so that the force of it stung his skin. His neck and shoulders were aching with pent-up tension, and he rotated them under the pounding water to relax the muscles. It didn't work.

It's just not possible, he kept thinking.

He stepped out of the shower, grabbed a towel and dried himself off, then wrapped it around his waist and started making his way into the bedroom. Then he stopped. Looked down. The kidnappers' pistol was lying among the dirty clothes on the floor. He snatched it up, stared at it for a moment, wondering what to do with it, then carried it through to the bedroom and tossed it on the bed, deciding to drop it into Dorenkamp's office on his way out. Let them deal with the damn thing.

He changed into his black jeans and black T-shirt, pulled on his shoes and his battered old leather jacket, found his cigarettes and the familiar shape of his Zippo in the jacket pocket and started to feel a bit more like himself again – though not much. Then he stuffed the dirty clothes into a plastic bag, packed up the few things he'd brought with him and headed for the door.

A lot had happened in the last couple of hours. It was just after three in the afternoon. If he hurried, he could be home at Le Val before midnight.

As he came out of his room, there was a reception committee waiting for him. Neville seemed to have assumed control of the group. He was standing there with his arms crossed, feet planted apart, a scowl on his face.

'Oi, you,' he said as Ben went by.

Ben kept going, eyes front, aiming for the front door.

'*Oi*. Talking to you, you fucking piece of shit.'

Ben stopped with his hand on the door handle. Hung his head. Breathed out through his nose. Turned round to face them.

'We want words with you,' Neville said.

Woodcock was standing behind him, staring at Ben over his leader's shoulder. On the other side of Neville, there was a sneer on Morgan's face that said, 'You're in deep shit now, buddy boy.'

'You and us, outside,' Neville said. 'Now.'

Ben slowly set down his case. Reached into his pocket and took out the cigarettes and lighter. Picked out a cigarette, put it to his lips, thumbed the Zippo and lit up. He took his time blowing out the smoke. Then asked, 'Me and you lot outside? What for?'

'So that we can express our thanks to you for losing our fucking jobs for us,' Neville said. Woodcock laughed. Morgan just kept up the sneer. Burton, Powell and Jackson were nodding in agreement.

Ben took another drag on his cigarette and watched the smoke drift up to the ceiling. 'I don't think that would be a very wise idea,' he said. 'There's already one of you in the hospital.'

'Fucking smartarse,' Neville spat.

'You can't smoke in here, shithead,' Powell said, pointing at the cigarette.

Ben gave him a long, calm look and held it until the guy broke eye contact. He took another pull on the cigarette and savoured the taste of it. Then let out another cloud of smoke.

The alarm went off with a piercing electronic blast.

Ben looked up at it. It was right over the heads of the men. Just a little white plastic disc screwed to the ceiling, no bigger in diameter than an espresso saucer, but the volume of the furious, eardrum-rattling shriek it emitted was wildly, ridiculously disproportionate to its size. It sounded like a squadron of Tornado jet fighters taking off inside the room.

Ben frowned up at the alarm for about half a second, then reached his hand behind his hip. Drew out the kidnappers' Beretta and brought it up to aim, thumbing off the safety and squeezing the trigger almost simultaneously.

9mm Parabellum is not the biggest, fastest or most potent handgun calibre in the world, but the sound of an unsilenced round going off in an enclosed space is massive and stunning. The harsh bark of the gunshot swallowed the scream of the alarm, and – an indetectably tiny fraction of a second later – the copper-jacketed bullet blew the white disc, the circuit-board and miniature speaker into a million pieces of plastic and silicone and solder. Ben kept firing as fast as his finger could move – BLAM-BLAM-BLAM – so that the blasting shots almost blended into one continuous detonation, like a length of high-explosive demolition cord going off.

By the time he'd stopped firing, Ben had pumped out half the magazine. Plaster dust and pieces of ceiling and the shattered remains of the alarm rained down onto the heads of the team. Morgan was cowering with his hands over his ears. Neville blinked and spluttered, his hair and face white with dust.

Suddenly there was silence in the room, just the ringing in Ben's ears that made the coughs and yells of the men sound muffled and distant.

'Cathartic,' he said. He flung the half-empty pistol on the floor at their feet, snatched up his case and walked out of the building.

Outside, the sun was still warm.

He turned his face up to the sky. 'Yeah, I know. I'm sorry.'

It didn't take long to hunt down Dieter and get the key to the Mini from him. Ben walked over to the château's garage block and found his car squeezed up next to the boxy hulk of a brand new Rolls. He hit a button on the wall to open up the steel shutter, got in the Mini and left a long, deep pair of tyre ruts across the gravel. He didn't glance back once in the rearview mirror as he left the Steiner place behind.

Then it was the long journey home. And he'd thought he was preoccupied on the way out to Switzerland. As he pushed the car on hard and fast, the thoughts swirled furiously round inside his head.

What was wrong with him? Was this some kind of midlife crisis hitting? Was he losing his edge at last?

Maybe Rupert Shannon had been right. Maybe the best place for him was behind a desk, marking time until he became just another double-chinned, bloodshot-eyed, cigar-chewing businessman with his gut hanging out over his lap, arteries more furred up than a chinchilla coat and a resting heart-rate of a hundred and fifty beats a minute. The well-trodden road to an early death. Perhaps that was all he was good for.

But the thought that was lodged in his head more than any other – spinning round and round like a pinball as the miles flew by, long after he'd passed back over the Swiss border and was heading westwards across France – was of the woman.

Thinking the same thing over and over again. Round and round, getting louder and more bewildering with every passing mile.

It couldn't be true. And yet . . .

He gripped the wheel tightly as he drove, as though somehow by holding on he wouldn't lose his grip on reality. But he was scared that he was.

So scared that he was shaking. So scared, that he could hardly bring himself to dredge up out of the dark corners of his memory the things that had happened all those years ago. The events that had changed his life and shaped his whole destiny.

Chapter Twenty-One

Sometime after Paris, the first raindrop spattered out of the darkness onto his windscreen. By the time he reached Normandy, around eleven, his headlights were cutting a twin swathe through the hammering rain and the road was slick and shiny.

Rainwater was cascading off the roofs of the buildings at Le Val and streaming across the cobbled yard as Ben pulled up outside the farmhouse. On a normal night, in a normal mood, he might have run to the door to avoid getting soaked by the deluge. Tonight wasn't a normal night. He didn't care enough to hurry, and his hair and jacket were dripping wet as he walked inside the door and dumped his case in the hall.

He was about to head for the stairs and the sanctuary of his private apartment when he heard what sounded like a movie playing and noticed the flickering strip of light under the door of the living room down the hall. He walked down the hall, opened the door and stepped inside.

Two faces turned as he walked in. Brooke and Jeff, sitting among heaps of cushions at opposite ends of the three-seater sofa. The lights were off, and the big TV screen threw shadows across the room. Looked like some kind of vampire movie, loud and colourful and bloody. The table in front of Jeff was littered with beer cans. Brooke had a steaming mug of something. Cocoa was her favourite, and she had that homely way of clutching it with both hands.

It was good to see them again.

'What are you guys watching?'

'What the hell are *you* doing here?' Jeff said, shocked.

Brooke was staring at him. 'You're drenched.'

'It's raining,' Ben said.

Jeff snatched up the remote and paused the DVD. A big open red-fanged mouth was frozen on the screen.

'Why aren't you in Switzerland?'

'Job's over,' Ben said.

Jeff made a face. 'What are you going on about?'

Ben walked over to the sofa and sat down heavily between them. 'You haven't heard?'

'Heard what?' Brooke said.

'I'm surprised Shannon's gunslinger of a lawyer hasn't called yet. First thing in the morning, I expect we'll be hearing from him.'

Jeff and Brooke both looked baffled.

'Remember what I said to Shannon about being sent home in disgrace?' Ben said. 'Well, that's pretty much what's happened to me.'

He spent the next few minutes explaining the events of that afternoon, with just a few minor omissions. He didn't tell them about the woman in the woods. He felt guilty about lying to his friends – but there was no way he could admit the whole truth.

As he talked them through it, he could see the deepening frown on Brooke's face and the darkening flush of anger on Jeff's.

'Let me get this right,' Jeff said. 'You save the old bugger's arse, and then he gives you the boot just because you,

132

completely on your own, can't stop a whole team of armed kidnappers from legging it back to their van? Maybe if he'd taken your fucking advice about the choppers—'

'Anyway, what happened, happened,' Ben interrupted quickly. 'There's nothing I can do about it now. Just one thing I need to do, and this whole nightmare will be over.'

'What do you need to do, Ben?' Brooke asked quietly.

'The only thing I can. Pay Shannon off.'

Even in the dim light of the screen, Jeff's face went distinctly pale. 'Pay Shannon off?' he echoed.

Ben nodded. 'Every penny.'

'That's one point two million,' Jeff exploded.

'I know how much it is.'

Jeff gaped. 'Are you out of your mind?'

'I messed up,' Ben said. 'Now I have to pay the price.'

'We'll take this to court,' Jeff protested. 'Unfair dismissal. Steiner's put us in this position.'

'It can't get to court,' Ben said. 'Even if we won, we'd never survive the bad publicity. And if we lost, we'd end up paying legal costs on top of everything else. There's no other choice.'

'This is nuts,' Jeff muttered. 'Absolutely nuts.'

Brooke was watching Ben anxiously. Her drink sat cooling on the table in front of her.

'You're talking about an awful lot of money, Ben.'

'More than the business can afford,' he admitted. 'I'll have to take out a mortgage on Le Val, or go to the bank and beg for a loan. Scrape it together, somehow. Then we hand it over to Shannon, and we move on.' He tried to smile and look optimistic. He knew it wasn't a convincing act.

'What if you can't raise that much?' Brooke asked.

Ben shrugged. The answer was obvious, and the look on Brooke's face told him that she'd known it even before she'd finished asking the question.

133

'Then we'll have to sell up,' he said quietly. Hearing the words out loud was almost more than he could bear.

The three of them sat there in silence. Jeff looked thunderstruck, and Ben knew what he was thinking. Le Val was just as much home to Jeff now as it was to him. If it had to go on the market, all the work they'd both put into it would be lost. And all just to pay off shit like Rupert Shannon.

Jeff stood up. His face was tight.

'I'm sorry, Jeff.'

'It's not your doing, mate,' Jeff said. There was emotion in his voice. He turned to leave the room. 'See you in the morning,' he muttered.

Then he was gone, and Ben and Brooke were left alone.

'I think I'll turn in too,' she said, getting up. 'Though I doubt if I'll get any sleep tonight. Not now.'

'I know what I'm going to do. I'm going to get pissed out of my mind.'

She smiled. 'Come to think of it, that sounds like a very good idea. Mind if I join you?'

'Be my guest. There's enough wine on the rack to kill both of us.'

It was cold up in Ben's quarters, and he arranged kindling sticks and a couple of dry logs in the fireplace while Brooke filled a couple of glasses of wine. She sat cross-legged on the big soft rug next to the hearth, watching him. 'You're a pretty good firelighter,' she commented.

'I ought to be.' In a minute or so the blaze was crackling up the chimney, and he settled next to her on the rug. She handed him a glass.

'What can you drink to on a night like this?' she said.

'Here's to good old Saint Geneviève,' Ben said, raising his glass.

'Who's Saint Geneviève?'

'The patron saint of complete and utter disasters and fuck-ups. An old friend of mine.' He downed his wine. Reached for the bottle and refilled the glass.

They drank in silence as the rain lashed against the windows, and watched the flames curl and lick around the logs in the fireplace. Ben knocked the wine back hard and fast.

'We need another bottle,' he said. 'Or two.'

'So soon?'

'I mean business.' He started clambering to his feet.

'I'll go down for it,' she said, putting her hand on his shoulder and standing up. 'I've just had an idea.'

'What idea?'

'A brilliant one.'

He tossed a couple more logs on the fire while she was gone, poked them around so that orange sparks flew up the chimney, and felt the heat on his face. After a few minutes Brooke returned, balancing two more bottles on a tray along with a plate and a covered platter.

'So this is your brilliant idea,' he said.

She took the lid from the platter. 'Marie-Claire's famous chocolate gâteau.' She sat down beside him, laid the tray on the rug in front of them. He quickly opened the second bottle. As he poured their glasses, she dipped a fork into the cake and ate some. Her eyes sparkled in the firelight.

'God, this is good.' She loaded up another forkful and carried it towards his mouth.

He clamped his lips shut, shook his head. 'I don't like sweets much. You eat it.'

'Help you soak up all this booze.'

'I don't want to soak it up. Defeats the object. What I want is for it to get into my bloodstream and circulate round to my brain, as quickly and efficiently as possible. What's the point otherwise?'

'Come on, Ben. You really must eat some of this. It's a secret family recipe. People round here have gone to war for it. To have it offered to you and not eat it is a sacrilege. An insult to the gods.'

He smiled and put down his glass. 'OK, you persuaded me. It wouldn't do to offend the gods.'

'Definitely not.' She held the fork up to his mouth. He opened it, and she fed the cake to him. He drew away, sliding the piece off the fork with his teeth. Chewed once, paused, chewed again and swallowed. It tasted rich and creamy. Cognac and almonds and home-churned butter. A hint of coffee in there somewhere, and traces of flavours he could only guess at.

'You're right. It is pretty damn good.'

'Have another bit,' she said. 'It's the ultimate in comfort eating.'

'In that case, maybe just another bit.'

'Let's just chocolate ourselves to death,' she said. 'Right here, right now.'

He threw up his hands in a gesture of resignation. 'Fuck it. Why not?'

She fed him another forkful, and then had another herself.

'You were right,' he said. 'This was a brilliant idea.'

They sat in silence for a moment, watching the flames. Then Brooke turned towards him to say something.

'Hold on,' he said, interrupting her. Raised his finger and moved it towards her face. 'You've got a bit of cream right there.' He gently wiped it from the corner of her mouth, then carried it back towards his own mouth and licked his finger. 'You were about to say something,' he said.

She looked blank. 'I don't remember.'

'You're drunk.'

'Getting there.'

But it didn't matter that they didn't say much. Ben was thankful for the companionship. Brooke was someone he felt relaxed around and could comfortably share a silence with. Her presence made him feel better. He could smell her subtle perfume, and the fresh apple scent of shampoo when her hair brushed near his face. It made him think of sunshine, summer meadows, nice things that seemed to belong in some inaccessible parallel world.

'I don't get it,' he said eventually. The chocolate cake was finished now, the empty plate and the fork between them on the rug.

'What don't you get?'

'You and Rupert Shannon.'

Brooke sighed.

'What do you see in the guy?'

'You mean, what *did* I see in the guy?'

'Past tense?'

'Very past tense. It's over.'

'Since when?'

'Since when do you think? Since all this happened. I don't like the way he's behaved. I think it's disgusting, and I told him so at the hospital.'

Ben paused for a moment. 'OK, what *did* you see in him?'

'Why d'you want to know?'

'Fine. It's none of my business. Forget I ever mentioned it.'

She shrugged. 'He seemed fun, and exciting to be with. He made me laugh. And he's never been this obnoxious before.'

'He's a gobshite.'

She laughed. 'Definitely a gobshite. That's something I've come to realise.'

'I could have told you before.'

'Some psychologist, eh?' She paused, and her smile fell away. 'It's not that easy sometimes, you know. Being me, I mean.'

'Being you is hard? I can't imagine why.'

'I'm a professional woman living on her own. I work strange hours, I'm often not around. It's difficult to meet guys. Especially the right guy. You don't come across very many of those.'

'You're saying you're lonely.'

She thought about it, then nodded. 'I do get lonely, sometimes. London can be a very lonely place.'

'I don't understand why. You could get any guy you wanted.'

She snorted. 'Somehow I don't think so.'

'I mean it. You're fun to be with.'

She looked at him. 'Really? You think?'

'Absolutely. And you're smart.'

Her lips curled into a bitter smile. 'And opinionated.'

'Maybe. But I like that about you.'

'It drives most guys away.'

'Only the arseholes. Think of it as a kind of filter. Quality control.'

There was another silence, just the crackle of the fire and the rain against the window panes. The wind was up, gusting down the chimney.

'You know, Rupert wasn't my first choice,' she murmured.

Ben didn't say anything. Took another deep sip of wine, then reached in his pocket for his cigarettes.

'Of course, I couldn't *have* my first choice,' she added in an undertone.

But he didn't seem to hear her as he flicked his lighter and lit up.

Brooke watched him, studied his face, the firelight throwing shadow into the lines bunched up on his brow as he sat quietly smoking. He'd always been a pensive man, she thought. But tonight he seemed unusually preoccupied, and something told her that there was more to it than what had happened with Steiner. Even more than the fear of losing Le Val and everything he'd worked for. There was something else.

'What is it, Ben?'

He shrugged, took another drink.

'I know you,' she said. 'I can see something is troubling you.'

He said nothing.

'What happened in Switzerland?'

'You know what happened. I—'

'No,' she cut in gently. 'Not that. I'm asking you what *really* happened. You might have convinced Jeff with that story you told earlier on, but you didn't fool me. There's something else. Something you didn't want to tell.'

He didn't answer immediately. 'You're right,' he said finally.

'Then tell me.'

'It's hard to explain. I still don't really know what happened. I think I saw someone.'

'Someone?'

'Someone I used to know. Someone I wasn't expecting to ever see again. But I'm probably wrong. In fact, I've *got* to be wrong. It's impossible any other way.' He picked up his glass again and drank some more wine.

'Why? What's impossible? Stop drinking and talk to me.'

He shook his head.

'Who did you see?'

He was quiet for a long moment.

'Come on, Ben. Who was it? You know you can trust me.'

'It was a woman.'

139

'Oh.' She dropped her hands in her lap, fidgeting.

He glanced at her, seeing the look in her eyes. 'Not *that* kind of woman,' he said.

'What kinds are there?'

'Not an old flame. Nothing like that.'

'A former colleague?'

'Not that kind either.'

'An old friend?'

'Not exactly.'

'Then what?'

'Let's have another drink.'

'Let's not. Let's talk about this. Why don't you want to tell me the rest of it?'

'Because I can hardly believe it myself,' he said. 'Because I think it must mean I'm going crazy.'

Brooke was quiet, watching him. She reached out and touched his cheek, tenderly. 'You're not crazy,' she whispered. 'You're the least crazy person I've ever known.'

He grunted. 'People change. People lose it.'

'Not you.'

'What makes me any different?'

'You're a lot different, Ben Hope. So tell me.'

He leaned forward, elbows on knees, ruffling his hair with his fingers. 'I think I saw my sister,' he said quietly.

'Your sister?'

He nodded, slowly. 'My sister Ruth.'

She looked baffled. 'I didn't know you had a sister.'

'That's exactly it,' he said. His voice was just above a whisper, and she had to lean close to hear him. 'I didn't think I had, either. Not any more. Not for a long time.' Then he turned his head slowly and looked Brooke in the eye.

'Ruth's been gone for more than twenty years,' he said.

Chapter Twenty-Two

'I told you it was crazy,' he said when Brooke just stared at him. 'Someone lost and gone, someone who's just been a memory to me for most of my life, just turned up and is out there somewhere.'

'I don't understand any of this,' Brooke said, shaking her head.

'You've known me a long time,' he said. 'Remember when I quit the regiment?'

She nodded. 'It was such a surprise to me. I heard it through the grapevine that you'd just upped and left. Nobody could understand why. Then I didn't see you again for four years.'

'And you asked me then what had happened, and why I'd started up in kidnap and ransom work. Why I wanted to help look for people who'd been snatched. Especially kids.'

'I remember you didn't want to talk about it.'

'I couldn't talk about it. Not to anyone, not for a long time.'

'Are you going to talk to me about it now, Ben?'

He nodded. Stubbed out his cigarette, lit another and tossed more logs on the fire. And then, deep into the night, he told her the story.

* * *

It was one that he'd barely spoken of to anyone in twenty-three years, an episode in his life that only a handful of people knew about. And yet one that had marked him more deeply and shaped his world more decisively than any of the wars and adventures, loves and losses, ups and downs that he'd known.

He talked in a low voice, relating it to her almost matter-of-factly, though the pain stabbed him with every word.

He'd been sixteen years old when his whole life had changed. It had been a tradition in the Hope family to take turns choosing their annual holiday location. That year had been Ben's turn. He'd opened up an atlas, flipped a few pages and found himself looking at the great wide golden-coloured spaces that were North Africa. Thought about forts in the sand and heroic tales of Beau Geste and the Foreign Legion. Jabbed a finger down on the map and said 'Morocco'.

So Morocco it was. Springtime in Marrakesh had been hot and dusty and filled with amazing sights and sounds for the teenage Ben. Nine-year-old Ruth had loved it too. They'd always been close, but that spring they'd become inseparable companions. Ben had lost endless games of table tennis to her, taught her to dive in the hotel pool, sat up with her in the evenings reading *Lord of the Rings* out loud while their parents drank gin and tonic and played bridge with the other guests in the bar.

On the third day, Ben had spied Martina in the lobby. Just a year or so older than he was, she'd seemed infinitely more sophisticated and grown up, almost like some kind of movie star. It had been the first real infatuation of what had, up until then, been a pretty sheltered life. He'd never thought a girl like that would look at him twice, so when she'd coyly sidled up to him the next day and asked if he'd take her to visit one of the local souks, he'd hardly been able to believe it.

142

There was one problem. His parents had asked him to stay in the hotel with Ruth that afternoon while they went to a museum Ben's mother wanted to see without the encumbrance of kids. The solution had seemed simple: wait until they were gone, then meet up with Martina and bring Ruth along too. He'd felt a little guilty about disobeying his parents, but the lure of Martina had been too powerful a temptation.

It had been a heady couple of hours, basking in the glow of Martina's beauty and the way she'd wanted to hold his hand as they wandered round the crowded souk looking at all the stalls. There had been exotic crafts and jewellery, snake charmers and performers, amazing tapestries and spices, a whole other world. He'd bought a gift for Martina, and she'd hugged him. For a boy from his over-protective middle-class background, it was intoxicating.

That had been it. The moment that clinched everything that was to follow.

Because in that moment, when he'd taken his eyes off his little sister for maybe ten seconds, maybe even just five seconds, too long, he'd turned around and she was gone.

'And you never found her,' Brooke said softly now. There were tears in her eyes.

He shook his head. 'Everything possible was done, looking back. Embassy, police, the works. My parents even hired private detectives. It was two years before we finally admitted to ourselves that it was pointless carrying on with it.'

'White slavers?'

He shrugged. 'Probably. Nobody knows. But it had all the hallmarks, we soon found out. They whisk people away in seconds, and they can move them across enormous distances before anyone's the wiser. There's no telling where the victims can end up. They get sold into harems, or into prostitution.

A lot of them wind up as junkies. Most of them don't live very long.'

He let out a long sigh. It was still hard to think about, even harder to talk about.

Brooke was silent for a few moments. 'You told me once that your mother had killed herself.'

'Was I drunk?'

'A little.'

'It's true. She did.'

'Was it because of what happened to Ruth?'

'She never got over it. And she never forgave me. Neither of them did. By the time I was nineteen, they were both dead. Her from an overdose, him from what I think was a broken heart. I drifted for a while, then joined the army. The rest is history.'

He took a long slug of wine, then went on.

'The worst thing wasn't losing Ruth. It wasn't even knowing that I'd let it happen. It was not knowing *what* was happening. When I used to think about the things those men might be doing to her, I used to catch myself wishing that she could have been run over by a car or something. At least then it would have been over. Then I'd hate myself even more for thinking that way.' He paused. 'Years went by. And one day, I woke up and it hit me that my sister was dead. She just had to be.'

'And that made it somehow easier to bear, but at the same time you felt even more guilty that her death could be a relief to you.'

'There's no escape, is there?' he said, smiling weakly. 'You just live with it.'

Brooke looked down at her feet for a moment, gathering her thoughts. 'Ben, why do you think the woman you saw in Switzerland is Ruth?'

144

He turned to her. 'You think I'm imagining it?'

'Maybe.'

'That's what I thought, too. But I'm not.' He told her all what had happened in Switzerland.

'So what do you think?' he asked her when he'd finished.

'Run that last bit by me again. You chased after this person. You thought it was a guy at first, then realised he was a she. There was a struggle, and that's when you thought you recognised your sister.'

'That's pretty much it.'

'And you were so shocked that you just let her get away.' He nodded.

A crease appeared between Brooke's brows. 'What are the odds, Ben? That it's really her?'

'In principle, pretty small,' he admitted.

'And she was wearing a mask?'

'Standard military and security forces issue black three-hole ski mask. Same kind we use here.'

The line in her brow deepened. 'I don't get it. All this pain. Digging up all this past torment, inflicting this on yourself when you can't be sure. Because, you know, you really can't.'

'There's more to it.' He paused while he refilled their glasses. 'One day in autumn, when Ruth was about seven, she was helping my father rake up fallen leaves in the orchard and burn them in a garden incinerator. She was running around near the burner when she slipped and fell and touched her arm against the hot metal. The burn was pretty nasty, and the scar never went away. It was on the underside of her right forearm, about two inches long, crescent-shaped.' He smiled tenderly at the memory. 'It was actually quite pretty, smooth and white and perfectly formed. She even got to like it.'

'So this woman in Switzerland. This neo-Nazi terrorist or whatever the hell she is. You're going to tell me that she has the same scar?'

'Exactly the same.'

'And this is what you're basing it on? A scar that anyone could have?'

'Not everyone. I told you, it was very distinctive.'

'So distinctive, you remember it that clearly after more than twenty years?'

'It's her, Brooke. I know her. I felt her presence. I looked in her eyes. Ruth's not dead. She's out there somewhere, and I'm going to do what I should have done years ago. I'm going to find her.'

Chapter Twenty-Three

Ben awoke long before dawn, and Ruth was the first thing that came into his mind. He took a quick shower and pulled on jeans and a shirt, then went downstairs and walked straight over to his office. Grabbed a laptop, shoved it under his arm and took it back across the dark yard to the house. He made some coffee, then sat down at the kitchen table and ran an internet search on Hans Kammler.

Top of the results that flashed up on his screen was Kammler's online encyclopaedia page. It showed a black and white photo of a tall, slim, determined-looking man, caught mid-stride and glancing at the camera. He was wearing the insignia of an SS-Obergruppenführer, and his peaked cap bore the SS silver death's head icon that had become the twentieth century's most dreaded emblem of pure evil.

Ben sipped coffee as he read through the text. What Steiner had said about the man had been correct. Born in 1901 in Stettin, Germany, Kammler had trained as an engineer and gone on to enlist in the SS in 1932. Ten years later, now a general, he had been singled out as one of the Reich's most skilled technicians and personally appointed by Adolf Hitler to oversee the design and construction of facilities for the Nazi extermination camps, including the notorious gas chamber and crematorium at Auschwitz

– a task that he seemed to have attended to with single-minded fervour.

By 1944, Kammler's scientific expertise had taken him even higher within the Nazi hierarchy. He'd been tasked by SS boss Heinrich Himmler to head up the V-2 rocket programme that had rained devastation on London in the later stages of the war. At the same time, Kammler had been put in charge of something called the Special Projects Division, about which there seemed to be very little information available, but which Ben figured had been the German equivalent of the USA's Defense Advanced Research Projects Agency, DARPA.

The man's death was somewhat shrouded in mystery, too, with accounts ranging from suicide to execution by the Soviets alongside two hundred other SS soldiers in the final days of the war.

So much for the encyclopaedia entry. Ben clicked out of it and started exploring the other links that his search engine had thrown up. Somehow he didn't think the Hans Kammler on Facebook was the same guy he was after. And the scattering of other results didn't seem to offer up a great deal, either. Internet conspiracy theory nerds seemed to have run wild with speculation about Kammler's involvement with the Special Projects Division. Just about all of the remaining search results were links to misspelt and frequently semiliterate forum entries linking Kammler to everything from Nazi occult rituals to time machines to flying saucers.

Ben gulped back the rest of the coffee as he waded through the quagmire with building impatience and frustration. None of this could possibly have any bearing on why anyone would want to kidnap Maximilian Steiner. It was becoming clear that he was going to have to talk to someone – someone who not only knew more about Hans Kammler than the

148

internet could offer, but could also shed light on why Steiner's documents were so attractive to a gang of neo-Nazi kidnappers. He reckoned the world of Holocaust-denying fascists must be fairly small and close-knit. The problem was getting a foot in the door.

But he had an idea of who might be able to help.

He was just about to shut down the laptop when Brooke walked into the kitchen. 'Morning,' she said sleepily. She was still in her dressing gown, her hair tousled, eyes bleary.

Ben stood and pulled up a chair for her at the table. She slumped into it gratefully as he prepared a fresh pot of coffee and put it on the range.

'Christ,' she said, resting her face in her palms. 'Why did I drink so much last night?'

'My fault. Sorry.'

She looked up at him. 'Look at you. Fresh as a daisy. How do you do it?'

'Addled by a lifetime of self-abuse,' he said. 'So intoxicated, my body's given up caring.'

'Sure. Then you go out for a ten-mile run and you don't even get out of breath. Some alcoholic you are.'

For his SAS training Ben had once had to carry a thirteen-stone man with full kit and rifle up and down the side of a mountain. He wasn't sure if he could still do that. Maybe he should give it a try sometime, he thought.

Brooke's gaze flicked over to the computer. 'What were you looking up?'

'SS General Hans Kammler, inventor of the amazing Nazi time machine.'

'You're really going to do it, aren't you?'

'Look for my sister? Of course I am. I have to.'

The percolator was spitting and bubbling. He grabbed a mug, poured out Brooke's coffee, added a dash of cream the

149

way she liked it, and set it down in front of her. 'I know what you think about this,' he said as he sat down beside her. 'But finding people is something I do well.'

'If anyone can find her, you can.' She paused to sip some coffee. 'Oh, that's good. But the real question is, Ben, *what* are you going to find?'

Ben stared at his hands on the table.

Brooke went on, her voice soft and gentle. 'First, most likely, if you track down this woman, she isn't going to be your sister at all. She's going to turn out to be some crazy stranger who just happens to resemble the image you have of Ruth in your mind, the age she would have been now. Wishful thinking is a powerful force.'

'I wouldn't say it's wishful thinking to believe that my little sister came back from the dead as a Nazi.'

'That brings me on to the next bit. The worse bit. What if, by some bizarre chance, this person really is your sister? She won't be the little girl you remember. She'll have changed. Whether it's wearing a swastika badge or joining some kind of cult, you have to ask what makes an intelligent person gravitate to this type of extreme behaviour. You don't know what kind of mental or physical trauma she might have been through, what kind of people she's been associating with and what severe psychological disturbances she could be experiencing. She'll be someone you don't recognise. She might not even remember you.' Brooke paused. 'I'm sorry. I'm laying it on thick, and I don't want to hurt you. It's just that you need to understand, for your own sake as much as hers.'

'Everything you say makes perfect sense,' Ben said. 'But I won't change my mind. I'm going after her anyway.'

She nodded and took another sip of coffee. 'I knew that's what you were going to say. But promise me that if you find her, and she really is who you think she is, that you'll let me get involved. I mean, professionally. You're both going to need help to get through this.'

He nodded. 'It's a deal. And thanks. You're a real friend.'

'And you're a real worry.'

He looked at his watch. 'Time to make the first call of the day.'

'Who to?'

'There's a guy I know at Interpol. Luc Simon. He might be a place to start. I heard he's high up the food chain these days. He was a cop in Paris when he and I worked together.'

'Worked together?'

Ben shrugged. 'Blowing up buildings, taking down bad guys. It was never an official thing. We had a kind of understanding.'

'I won't even begin to ask,' Brooke said. 'I'm going for a long, hot shower.'

As she left the room, Ben walked over to the phone and dialled the number for the Interpol General Secretariat in Lyon. After giving his name and details to an endless series of receptionists and secretaries who seemed hellbent on preventing him from being put through to the person he wanted, he persisted and finally heard the familiar voice on the line.

'It's been a long time,' Simon said warmly. 'I didn't think I was going to hear from you again.'

'Neither did I, for a while there. You're a difficult man to get to talk to these days. Congratulations on your promotion, by the way. Commissioner. Pretty impressive.'

'I gather you've moved on yourself since we last talked. You're a respectable businessman now.'

'A regular tycoon. But I was calling about something else. I need your help.'

'Fire away. I'll see what I can do.'

'What do you know about neo-Nazis?'

Simon grunted. 'Plenty. It's a growing problem across Europe. You only have to look at the statistics for visitors to Hitler's birthplace to see the rise. We have extreme far-right groups sprouting up like toadstools all over the place – France, Holland, Austria, Italy, everywhere. Why do you ask?'

'What about Holocaust deniers?'

Simon thought for a moment. 'Well, a lot of our shaven-headed, armband-wearing friends make no effort to decry the Holocaust. In fact, some of them would be all too happy if it had been ten times worse. But then you have this diverse splinter group, associated with the neo-Nazi movement but in some ways quite distinct, who want to persuade the world that Hitler never really did these things and that the historical account has been fixed to vilify him.'

'And he was actually a great guy, he loved his mum, etc, etc.'

'You get the idea. Quite a strong little subculture going on there.'

'That's what I'm interested in. Anyone in particular stand out?'

'Before I say any more, Ben, I have to ask you why you want to know all this.'

'Personal interest,' Ben said.

'Nothing you'd like to share with me?'

'I'd rather keep it to myself, Luc.'

'Only I seem to remember the last time you and I were in contact, you left a bit of trouble in your wake. Like dead men and bullets all over Paris.'

'That was then, Luc. I've settled down now.'

'Maybe. But some people never change.'

'Trust me. I just want to talk to someone about a wartime document, written by someone called Kammler.'

'That's it? A document? You don't want to take the document from them, or anything like that?'

'No, I already know where it is. I just want to ask some questions. Nice and easy, nothing sinister.'

'So why not talk to whoever has it? Why go looking for someone else?'

'Long and boring story. Let's just say I'm not flavour of the month with the owner. Plus, I don't think he knows much. So, are you going to help me or not?'

Simon was quiet for a moment, and Ben could almost hear him thinking. 'There *are* a few prominent Holocaust deniers we keep an eye on,' Simon said. 'Now and then we pick one up for racial assault or firearms charges. It's not exactly top secret. These guys attract a lot of attention, if you know where to look.'

'So you wouldn't be risking anything by telling me a name or two.'

'I could tell you more than one or two,' Simon said. 'But here's the problem. I don't know exactly what you want from them, but I do know the way you work. I give you this information, you're going to start kicking down doors. They're not going to like that, and when they try to get in your way it's going to end with you wiping the floor with them. As a result of which, people like me will have to go in and clean up the mess. I'm not sure I like that idea.'

'You went out on a limb for me before, Luc.'

'And half of France got shot to pieces.'

'That won't happen this time.'

Simon paused again. 'Let's say I trusted you and gave you some names. It's not going to take you very far. These guys' thing is violence against the weak, stamping about chanting slogans, getting swastikas tattooed on their foreheads, breeding pit bulls and sawing off shotguns. Fine, it might satisfy you to kick some asses, but if it's historical information you're after, I have someone in mind who I think would be a lot more use to you.'

Ben smiled into the phone. The idea of meeting these characters with swastikas on their foreheads appealed to him. Just the kind he'd enjoy pressing information out of. People like that knew other people, giving him a whole network he could take down if necessary. He'd dealt with that type before. But first things first, and it sounded as if Simon had something interesting here.

'Go on.'

'There's a guy called Don Jarrett. A fellow countryman of yours. I think you'll be interested in him.'

'Who is he?'

'Let me start off with who he *was*. Back in the seventies and eighties, he was a very well-respected historian and author. Third Reich expert of the highest order, apparently. But then he started getting a little too pally with some of the old Nazi officers he hung about with for his research. He was seen at a lot of far-right rallies and his name went down on the list of people to watch. Then, a few years ago, he stepped up his profile by writing a book claiming that the Nazi Final Solution against the Jews was a fabrication, a con trick by governments. When he tried to back up the book sales with a European lecture tour, he was arrested in Germany, charged with illegally denying the Holocaust, and put in jail for three years. Only served half that, but while he was inside his wife left him, he lost his job and his home in England, and when he was released he went into exile. These days he keeps his head down and isn't a threat, though we still like to keep an eye on him. Bit of a loner, and a real cold fish. He might not be willing to talk to you. But if you could absolutely promise me that there'd be no trouble—'

'Where do I find this Jarrett?' Ben cut in.

'I'm waiting for that promise first. That you'll go easy, and be discreet, and all of those things that'll make me happy. Or else no dice.'

'Everybody's got me making promises today.'

'Still waiting.'

'All right, I promise,' Ben said.

'I hope I'm not making a big mistake here.'

'I won't lay a finger on him. Unless he makes the first move, in which case I swear to hide the body really, really well.'

'That's not funny.'

'Come on, Luc.'

'All right. Jarrett has an apartment in Bruges. He eats lunch at the same café in the middle of town, same time, every day. You'll find him there. Let me have your fax number. I need to go and talk to someone right now, but give me twenty minutes and I'll send over what you need.'

Chapter Twenty-Four

By the time Brooke came back downstairs fifteen minutes later, Ben had a map spread out across the table. On the chair was his old green army bag, packed, strapped and ready to go.

'You don't waste any time, Hope.'

'Just twenty-three years,' he said.

Brooke watched as he traced his route across the map. 'So where are you heading now?'

'Belgium.'

'What, right this minute?'

'I have another call to make, and I'm waiting for a fax to come through. Then I'm gone. I've got a lunch date in Bruges.'

'Looks like your Interpol guy came up trumps for you.' She looked at her watch. 'Better hurry, then.'

'I'll make it.' He folded up the map, grabbed the webbing shoulder strap of the bag and started heading for the door.

'Ben?' she said hesitantly.

He looked back at her. For a fleeting moment it struck him how good she looked standing there with her hair still damp from the shower. She had nice eyes. Something he didn't notice often enough.

'Maybe you'd like me to come along?'

'What about your lectures?'

'Jeff could stand in for me, couldn't he? Just this once?'

'I don't know if that would be a good idea, Brooke.'

She looked away, flushing. 'Shouldn't have asked. You're the boss.'

'It's not that,' he said. 'I'd be happy for Jeff to stand in for you, if you needed it. But this is something I have to do on my own.'

She nodded. 'I understand. When will you be back?'

'I don't know,' he said truthfully. 'Soon as I can.'

'I'm flying back to London the day after tomorrow. Call me there if I don't see you before, OK?'

Outside the sun was shining brightly and the air tasted fresh and sweet after last night's rainstorm. It felt like it was going to be a hot day. Ben looked around him as he walked across the yard, and on top of all the other things he was feeling, he felt a tingle of apprehension wash through him. He didn't want to lose this place.

He strode over to the office and walked in to see that Luc Simon's fax had come through already. He dumped his bag on the floor, tore the single sheet out of the machine and studied it. There were two police mugshots of Don Jarrett, a photocopy of a *Der Spiegel* newspaper cutting about his trial and imprisonment for Holocaust denial, and some information hastily jotted down in Luc's handwriting with the address and location of Jarrett's regular lunchtime hangout in Bruges.

Ben folded the paper into his pocket. Then he took a deep breath, picked up the office phone and dialled the number for the bank manager.

Five minutes later he had set up an appointment at the branch in Valognes. Dupont, the manager, was away fishing and couldn't see him for ten days. That suited Ben fine. He wasn't in too much of a hurry to find out whether or not he was about to lose his livelihood.

He wondered what Dupont's reaction was going to be when he told him how much money he needed to raise. As a going concern and with all the work he'd done on the place, Le Val had to be worth at least a million and a half. Business was better than he'd ever anticipated. The facility was bringing commerce to the area. Thanks to his clients and delegates, the local village brasserie had never had it so good. Ben was liked, and he was employing local people. Maybe the bank would look favourably on his needs.

Maybe. Or maybe not. But right now, he couldn't think about that.

As he was about to leave the office, the phone rang again. Ben knew the voice immediately. Shannon. Screaming at the top of his voice.

'Motherfucker, you're going to pay me that fucking money!'

'How's the back, Rupert?'

'I want the fucking money. I want it now.'

'You can't have it now.'

'I want it.'

'You'll get it when I have it. That's the best I can do.'

Shannon went on screaming down the phone about his lost contract, his ruined reputation, his damaged back, that bitch Brooke walking out on him, and Ben's personal responsibility for all the ills of the world. After about thirty seconds of furious invective, Ben had had enough and took the phone away from his ear. Even at arm's length, he could still hear the tinny little voice rasping from the receiver. He gently laid the phone handset down on the desk, turned and walked away. Shannon was still screaming at him as he shut the office door.

Something to worry about later.

From the office, Ben went over to the old converted Dutch barn at the side of the house where he kept the Mini, and tossed his bag onto the passenger seat. He'd always been a light traveller. He was carrying just a change of clothing, his well-worn whisky flask topped up with his favourite ten-year-old Laphroaig, two spare packs of untipped Gauloises and a few other travelling items.

In addition to which he'd packed something that Luc Simon wouldn't have been too happy about.

The pistol wasn't part of the official weapons inventory at Le Val, every item of which was registered and logged, serial numbers on file everywhere from NATO to the French Defence Ministry. It was a scuffed old plain steel Smith & Wesson automatic that had probably seen criminal use at some point in its life, the serial numbers filed off both frame and slide. The child kidnapper Ben had taken it from didn't need it any more, the same way he hadn't needed any food, water or air for the last six years. It had lain at the bottom of Ben's safe deposit box at the Banque Nationale in Paris for most of that time, and it wasn't until he'd cleared it out before moving to Le Val that he'd even remembered it was there.

He didn't expect any serious need for it in Bruges. But in his experience there was only one really effective way of liberating information from someone who didn't want to talk. There was no need to hurt them, or even to make specific threats. Just the sight of the weapon was usually enough, especially for a bookish type of guy like Don Jarrett.

Luc Simon would be pissed off. *Get in line*, Ben thought.

He fired up the Mini, drove out of the barn and across the yard. As he passed the house he glanced over and saw Brooke standing at the window watching him go. She gave a sad little wave.

On the track that led towards the road, he met Silvain Bourdon's minibus, waved at the driver and pulled to the side to let it by. Bourdon was the local guy whose taxi firm Ben used to shuttle delegates back and forth from the airport at Cherbourg. As the dusty minibus passed by, he could see the pasty faces of the eight insurance brokers who were here for Brooke's hostage psychology course.

Hating himself for leaving her and Jeff at a time like this, Ben drove on up to the road, passed through the gates and pointed the car east across France for the second time in three days.

Chapter Twenty-Five

Rory woke up in a soft bed. At first he thought he was at home, and it was all a bad dream. That he was going to sit up in bed and see all his things around him, his posters on the wall and his chess computer on the desk, his astro-binoculars on their tripod over the other side of the room, and then look out of the window and see the sun rising over the lake and hear the birds singing in the trees outside and the sound of his Aunt Sabrina's voice calling his name from downstairs.

But when he blinked away the bleariness and his vision came into focus, he saw where he really was and felt that cold, skin-shrivelling feeling down the back of his neck.

He was in a room he'd never seen before, and he had no idea how he'd got here. He only knew how very, very desperately he didn't want to be here. The stone walls had no windows, and the only light came from a dull naked bulb that hung from a wire above his head and was covered with spider's webs and the dried-out corpses of flies.

The other side of the iron bed frame, two men were standing watching him. One was tall with sandy hair, about the same age as his dad or maybe a little younger. The other was shorter, not much taller than Rory, with a ruddy complexion and thick dark hair.

Rory shrank away from them.

'You're awake,' the sandy-haired man said. He sounded English. 'You've been asleep for a long time.'

Rory could feel the bruise in the crook of his left elbow where the needle had gone in. He remembered now. The ship, the sea, the distant islands he'd seen from the deck when he'd managed to get away. The kidnappers who'd chased him. The way he'd managed to toss the stolen phone overboard before they'd caught him and dragged him roughly out from under the lifeboat and shaken him violently, asking him who he'd telephoned; how he'd struggled and kicked and screamed and spat in their faces as they'd held him tight and rolled up his sleeve and the horrible woman had jabbed the syringe into his arm. The last thing he could recall was being hauled back down to that stinking hold and being cuffed to the pipe again. Nothing after that.

He glared at the strangers at the foot of his bed and thought about his secret. He was smarter than they were. Only he knew that he'd talked to Sabrina. She and his dad would have called the cops. There had to be the biggest search of all time underway by now.

'You assholes had better let me go,' he said darkly.

The sandy-haired man grinned. 'Really?'

'Yes, really. Because my dad happens to be in the Special Forces, and if you don't let me go home right now, he's going to hunt you down and take you apart.'

'Your dad sounds like quite a fellow,' the sandy-haired man said. 'But the thing is, Rory, I know you're making that up. I've spoken to your dad. In fact, he and I are very well acquainted. And it might interest you to know that he's on his way here even as we speak. You'll be seeing him in no time.'

Rory frowned. 'Why?'

'Because he and I have some business to take care of. But that needn't concern you. All you have to do is sit quietly and wait.'

'I think you're lying.'

'You'll soon see, won't you?' the man replied. 'Anyway, now that you're awake, you might want to take a shower and change into the clothes we have ready for you. You must be hungry, too.'

'I don't want anything, jerkoff.'

The man smiled. 'Actually, the name's Pelham.'

'Fuck off,' Rory yelled at him.

'Now, Rory. I'm sure your father wouldn't like you to use language like that. We all have to try to get on, don't you think? Better for everyone that way.'

'Don't talk to me like I'm a kid,' Rory spat.

'You're a brave boy,' Pelham said. 'And I know you're also a clever boy who understands what's best for him. So why don't you settle down and behave, and the minute your father and I have finished our business together, it'll all be over.' Pelham smiled again. 'Now, I'm sort of in charge here, and I have a lot to do, so you won't be seeing too much of me.' He motioned to the man standing next to him, who hadn't spoken. 'This gentleman here is called Ivan, and he's going to be looking after you.'

'Hello, Rory,' Ivan said. His voice was gentle. Rory had heard accents like his in movies. He figured the guy was Polish or Russian or something. He glowered at him.

Pelham looked at his watch. 'It was good to talk to you, Rory. Ivan and I have to go now, but he'll be back in a minute to show you where the bathroom is and get you something to eat.' He turned to Ivan and they exchanged a few words in a language that Rory didn't understand. After that, they left the room and Rory heard the sound of a key in the lock. He stared at the door for as long as he could hold in his tears, then buried his face in the pillow.

No way was he going to let them hear him cry.

Chapter Twenty-Six

If Bruges was the best-preserved medieval city in Europe, the motorway that sliced through the countryside to its outskirts was one of the fastest and most modern. Ben reached the place with just about enough time to make his rendezvous, left the car in an out-of-town parking complex and boarded a bus heading for the historic centre.

Alone in the back row, he unfolded the fax sheet from his pocket and ran back through the details Luc Simon had sent him. The little family café-restaurant where Don Jarrett liked to have his lunch each day was right in the middle of the old town, off the largest of its squares. Afterwards, according to the Interpol agents who had been keeping tabs on him, it was the Holocaust denier's habit to take a daily stroll down by the picturesque canals.

Sweet, Ben thought.

He got off the bus on the edge of the old town and mingled with the many tourists in the squares and narrow cobbled streets. He bought a Belgian newspaper from a little newsagent stand, then checked his watch and went looking for the main square and the location of Jarrett's regular lunchtime haunt.

It didn't take long to find, and it was just as Luc Simon had said, next to the clock tower. On the adjacent side of the square was a bistro with an outdoor terrace. Ben took a parasol-shaded table between a romantic hand-holding young couple and an argumentative American family who looked like they were going for some kind of burgers-and-Coke speed record. He leaned back in the wicker seat and started flipping nonchalantly through his paper. Over the top of the pages he kept his eye on the restaurant entrance across the way.

Creatures of habit were easy to track. At 1.29 p.m. Ben saw a man cut across the square, head straight for the restaurant and go inside without glancing at the sign on the awning or checking out the menu beside the door. A regular customer for sure, but in his beige safari jacket and that conspicuous manner that the British always seemed to exude abroad, he wasn't ever going to pass for a local. There was a large book under his arm, which told Ben this was someone intending to sit alone for a while. He looked to be in his early sixties, with a curly ring of grey hair around a bald crown. A good deal heavier and paunchier than in the picture Luc Simon had faxed through from Lyon, but it was definitely Don Jarrett.

Now there was nothing to do except wait for the guy to have his lunch. A waiter came to Ben's table, and Ben ordered a beer and a plate of mussels with French fries. He paid in advance so that he could leave quickly if needed.

As he ate, he skipped idly through a few articles in the newspaper without taking in a single word, glancing frequently over at the restaurant window where he could just make out the top of Jarrett's head above the Kronenbourg logo painted on the glass. The Americans at the next table finally had their fill and went off to argue somewhere else.

At just after 2.15, Ben saw Jarrett walk out of the restaurant doorway with his book under his arm, take a right across the square and mingle into the crowds of tourists standing around and snapping pictures of the clock tower. Ben scattered a handful of euros on his table to tip the waiter and followed.

Away from the main square, the streets between the old buildings were winding and narrow. Ben hung back a hundred yards or so as Jarrett walked, keeping him in sight without being spotted. Up ahead, the sunlight sparkled between the trees and across the rippling waters of the canal. Jarrett took a left turn and trotted down some steps towards the towpath.

Ben followed. Jarrett walked on ahead, moving slowly, seeming to relish his surroundings. A couple of hundred yards further up the canal path, a pretty arched stone bridge spanned the water. Moored up to its side, bobbing gently on the current, was an empty tourist barge.

There was nobody about. It was quiet down here, just the gentle lap of the water against the stone walls and the warble of a blackbird perched overhead in a tree. Ben quickened his step. As he walked, he took the Smith & Wesson from his bag and slipped it discreetly into his jacket pocket.

Jarrett seemed to sense the presence behind him. He glanced over his shoulder, then half-turned, smiled and nodded with a polite 'Good afternoon' in English-accented French.

Ben didn't return the smile. 'Don Jarrett?'

Jarrett turned again and looked at him. The smile faded quickly, replaced by a wary glint in his eye.

'You are Don Jarrett, aren't you?' Ben said calmly.

'If you're a journalist, I won't talk to you. Not interested. So piss off.'

'I'm not a journalist,' Ben said. 'But I didn't come to Bruges for the sightseeing.'

As he said it, he drew the Smith & Wesson out of his pocket. Normally he would have carried it already cocked and locked, Condition One, the way he'd been trained. That way, you only had to flip off the safety and it was ready for action. Efficient, but not particularly theatrical.

Instead, he did it the showy way they did it in the movies, the way that gets you killed in real life, making a big deal out of reaching across with his left hand, racking back the slide and releasing it with that bright, splashy *shlak-clang* of metal on metal that he knew would strike fear into Don Jarrett's heart.

It did. And all the more so when Ben pointed the pistol at his head.

It wasn't even loaded. Something the guy didn't need to know.

Jarrett backed away fearfully. He raised his hands, palms out, eyes pleading. 'You've come to kill me, haven't you?'

'Expecting someone?'

Jarrett eyed him uncertainly, with the look of a man facing up to something he'd been resigned to for a long time. 'I've had threats.'

'Seem like a popular guy. But I'm not going to kill you. Unless you make me.'

Jarrett reddened. 'What do you want?'

'I asked them where I could find the biggest turd of a Holocaust denier going. They told me you were it. So here I am, and you and I are going to have a little chat.' Ben made a big show of uncocking the pistol, then put it back in his pocket.

Jarrett looked a little more relieved. The fear had drained away from his face to leave a flush of indignation in his cheeks. 'Who's *they*?' he demanded.

Ben shrugged. 'Them.'

170

Jarrett said, 'The same bastards who persecuted me, ruined my life and put me in jail.'

'I'd say you brought that on yourself, no?'

'I'm not a Holocaust denier.'

Ben smiled coldly. 'You're denying that, too?'

'They call me a Jew hater, a fascist, a terrorist. I'm none of those things, all right? I'm a revisionist historical scholar whose only crime was to ask questions about things that everyone else was afraid to. I've served my time. Now why don't you just bugger off and leave me alone?'

'Uh-huh. Now I have some questions to ask you.'

'What kind of questions?'

'Let's you and I go for a boat ride.'

Ben ushered the man down the path. He was pretty certain they weren't being followed by any of Luc Simon's people, but he didn't want eavesdroppers. The last thing he needed was to draw Interpol's attention to whatever it was that his sister had got herself involved in. That was something for him, and him alone, to deal with.

As they approached the bridge, a small thin man with a straggly moustache and a money pouch on a strap around his shoulder appeared at the side of the canal, hovered near the boat mooring and eyed them expectantly.

Ben pointed down at the barge. 'How much for the tour?' he asked, and the guy told him it was twelve euros each. The boat had a little wheelhouse at the front, and behind it was seating for about a dozen passengers. Ben reached for his wallet, counted out a hundred and eighty euros and handed it to the boatman. 'Just him and me. No other passengers. There's a little extra for you.'

The boatman shrugged and stuffed the cash in his pouch.

'I don't like going on the water,' Jarrett muttered. 'I can't swim.'

'Good.' Ben shoved him towards the edge and made him climb down the ladder to the barge. Ben went down after him and pushed him towards the stern, as far from the wheelhouse as they could get. The boatman climbed down, started up the gurgling engine and cast off.

The canals wound gently through the old medieval city, past ivied stone buildings and under trees that leaned far out across the water. Jarrett held on tightly to the chrome railing at the barge's stern, looking down at the wake that the barge's lazy propellers were churning up behind them. Ben stood next to him, watching him.

'I'm happy in this place,' Jarrett said quietly. 'I like the way people leave me alone. I can lose myself here and forget about all the shit that's out there, and all the things that were done to me.'

'I know exactly how you feel,' Ben said.

Jarrett looked at him in surprise.

'You feel betrayed. You showed the world what you thought was the honest truth, and you were stood on. You feel hard done by. And you know what? I don't give a shit about your burning martyr act. I despise you and I don't want to be here. But unfortunately, I need your help.'

Jarrett's face was twisted in hate. 'Like what?' he spat out.

'Like information.'

'On?'

'Your speciality,' Ben said.

'What's in it for me?'

'A lot, Jarrett. Believe me. Talk to me and good things will happen. Like not being found floating in the canal with a bullet in your brain. How's that for starters?'

Jarrett stared at him for a long time, then seemed to decide that Ben meant it. He let out a sigh, seeming to deflate a little so that his shoulders drooped. 'OK. I get the picture. What do you want to know?'

'I want to know why a bunch of neo-Nazi terrorists would be interested in Hans Kammler.'

Jarrett's eyebrows climbed up his high brow. 'Kammler? SS General Hans Kammler?'

'Is there another one I need to know about?'

Jarrett leaned on the rail and puffed out his cheeks. 'Might help if I knew what it was about Kammler they were after.'

'Right up your street,' Ben said. 'Some documents that could allegedly prove that the Nazi Holocaust didn't happen.'

Jarrett frowned. 'My street? Hold on. I've never said it didn't happen. Just that it was grossly exaggerated. That only just over a million died, not the six million that are claimed. And that it wasn't the big Jewish extermination it's cracked up to be. That was a Zionist fabrication cooked up by the British to help gain control over the Middle East by filling Palestine with poor, suffering Jewish refugees in 1947.'

'Save the lecture for someone who might actually swallow it,' Ben said. 'Just answer my question.'

Jarrett was silent for a few moments. The only sound was the singing of the birds, the soft burble of the boat and the distant throb of traffic. Finally he said, 'Well, I can see why a Holocaust revisionist might be interested in any documents written by Kammler, if they were to shed light on the Auschwitz business.' Jarrett nodded to himself. 'I can certainly see that.'

'What Auschwitz business do you mean?'

'I take it you're aware that Kammler was in charge of the SS Building Division that built the so-called death camp, and personally oversaw the design of the alleged gas chamber?'

'I'm aware of it,' Ben replied. 'I'm not so sure about the "so-called" and "alleged" part, though.'

173

Jarrett gave a grim smile. 'That's the whole crux of the debate. This is the very thing the bastards put me in jail for. You see, revisionists believe that the gas chamber you see today if you go on a guided tour of Auschwitz is really just a reconstructed air-raid shelter, dressed up to look like it was used for homicidal purposes, when in fact that's anything but the case. There's a whole load of stuff they don't want you to know.'

'They?'

'Yes, they,' Jarrett said hotly, and the thread veins in his cheeks burned red. 'Like the fact that the work camp inmates had their own theatre and swimming pool. The fact that there are virtually no traces of the lethal Zyklon B compound in the gas chamber walls, far less than in the delousing rooms where they used it solely for the inmates' hygiene. Even pro-Holocaust historians have admitted that ninety per cent of the stuff was used for routine health maintenance, as a pesticide. I mean, why go to the trouble of looking after your prisoners if you're just going to exterminate them anyway? Doesn't make sense. Then there's the little detail that the holes in the gas chamber ceiling, through which the Nazis were supposed to have poured the crystals to produce the cyanide gas, were demonstrably added after the war by the Soviets as a deliberate propaganda stunt.'

Ben listened carefully. This was exactly the kind of well-rehearsed poison he'd expected to hear from a man like Jarrett, and it just washed over him. What he found painful was the thought that his own sister, whose memory he'd clung to so dearly for all these years, could have ever bought into these terrible distortions.

He put that concern aside and focused on the matter at hand. 'So you're suggesting that these people want to get their hands on the Kammler documents because they believe they'll find evidence of what the gas chamber was really used for?'

'Showing that nobody was ever actually gassed there,' Jarrett finished with a smile. 'Exactly. But those are documents that I've never heard of before. I'd be kind of interested to see them myself. Where are they?'

'As if I'd ever tell you.'

'Shame. There are a lot of unanswered questions about Hans Kammler. Nobody even knows what happened to him, or why a guy so high up in the Nazi hierarchy, answerable only to Hitler himself by 1945, was never even mentioned at the Nuremburg Trials after the war. Deep conspiracy stuff. CIA plots and all that. Outside of my area.' Jarrett gave a dark chuckle. 'You'd have to talk to a guy called Lenny Salt for that kind of thing. Actually, he was interested in Kammler too, come to think of it. It was a long time ago. I'd forgotten until now.'

'Who is he?'

'Conspiracy freak. Some kind of scientist, I think, at Manchester University. Physics, it was. Strange-looking fellow. Came to one of my talks once.'

'One of your revisionist pals?'

Jarrett seemed about to object to Ben's tone, then bit his lip and shook his head. 'Hardly. He wasn't interested in my views at all. In fact, he was quite violently opposed to them. But I did get the impression that he seemed to know an awful lot about Kammler. More than I do, for that matter.' He paused, pursing his lips. 'And I'm sure he would be interested in these documents you mentioned, unless he already has them, that is.'

'He doesn't have them,' Ben said. 'I know that for a fact. How well do you know this Lenny Salt?'

Jarrett shrugged. 'About as well as you'd know anyone you

spent half an hour over a pint with. Like I said, we chatted about Kammler, then we argued, he called me a Nazi prick and left.'

'I think you have that effect on people, Jarrett. In fact, I'd say you got off lucky.'

The boat was approaching another bridge. There was a stone stairway leading up from water level to the street. 'This is where I get off,' Ben said. 'Enjoy the rest of your tour.'

'So you're done with me?' Jarrett said nervously. 'You're not going to shoot me now?'

'I don't think that would do much to change the world,' Ben said. 'You kill one rat, you have to kill them all. That's someone else's job. But I wouldn't sleep too easy if I were you.' He tapped the boatman on the shoulder and had him pull over to the side. Climbed the smooth stone steps and walked away.

As he was crossing the bridge he looked down to see Don Jarrett staring up at him from the back of the boat. Then it passed under the bridge and Ben didn't see him again.

Chapter Twenty-Seven

Adam O'Connor knew the exact number of paces up and down the length and width of his poky hotel room. He knew where every spider's web was in every corner, and he'd spent so long staring at the gaudy flower design on the faded wallpaper that he could have drawn it with his eyes shut.

After nearly two days of waiting, he was going stir crazy and beginning to feel as though he'd been trapped here all his life. His stomach was knotted with worry, so cramped it hurt to move. He'd barely touched the plates of stinking stew that room service had been bringing him. His door wasn't locked, and a few times he'd wrenched it open and peered out into the dim corridor. Nobody was even guarding him. Once or twice he'd wanted to run, and keep running until he got to a police station. But he knew that would be the worst thing he could do. They'd kill Rory.

If Rory was even still alive. At this moment, Adam had no way of knowing how – let alone where – his son was.

He checked his watch. The afternoon was ticking by. Then it would be evening. Another night of waiting. Why were they doing this to him?

Unable to prevent the image from looming up, he visualised Rory's face again. It was too much. Adam felt the salty tears well up and the next thing he knew he was sobbing uncontrollably, his shoulders heaving. Then his stomach heaved and flipped, and he dragged himself off the armchair and just made it to the bathroom. All that came up were a few strands of acid bile. He washed his face at the sink, splashed rust-coloured water over his cheeks and tried to calm himself.

People had always told him he looked younger than his age, but when he gazed in the stained mirror he saw a gaunt, unshaven, crazed-looking man a decade older staring back at him. His eyes were red, puffy and ringed with black, his cheeks looked hollow and the lines on his face were etched so deep they might have been carved with a knife.

That was when his resolve tightened even more and he knew his plan was the right one.

No other way.

What if you're wrong? What if you're misjudging the situation?

No other way, Adam. No choice. You were committed the moment you left home.

He stumbled back to the other room and slumped on the edge of the bed, feeling hollow and brittle. Time passed; he didn't know how much. He sobbed again for a while, then dried the tears with a handkerchief from his pocket and blew his nose, staring numbly into the middle distance.

Far away in the dark, misty world of his thoughts, he barely heard the footsteps outside. They walked up the creaking boards of the corridor and stopped at his door. There was a pause, then the door suddenly flew open and three people walked in.

Adam looked up and saw a woman standing there. She looked about thirty. Thin fair hair scraped back from her face, a square set to her jaw and a hard, impassive look in her eyes.

He hated her immediately.

To her left was a tall, lean man. The man to her right was half the height but twice the width, muscular, with arms that strained the seams of his jacket and a neck like a bull's. All three of them were watching him intently. The stocky guy had a black pistol in his hand. It was pointed at the floor but the way he was fingering it, he looked as though he wanted to use it soon.

Adam's thoughts focused through the fatigue. A woman and two men had taken Rory from *Teach na Loch*.

The woman spoke. 'You're Adam O'Connor?'

Adam couldn't place the accent. Something European, vaguely eastern. Maybe Czech.

'I'm O'Connor,' he said weakly. His own voice sounded strange to him, after not speaking to anybody for so long. 'Where's my son?'

'You'll see him soon enough,' she said. 'Keep your mouth shut and come with us. Try to talk to anyone, try to run, and he dies.' She held up a phone. 'I only have to press a button.'

They made him get his things together, then ushered him out of the room and down the dingy corridor, making him carry his holdall while the tall man held on to his briefcase. They passed rows of doors. No sound coming from behind any of them. No sign of life anywhere. Adam was glad to get away from this hateful place, and his heart soared at the idea that he was going to see Rory again. *He was alive.*

'Keep moving,' the stocky guy muttered, prodding him down the corridor. His accent sounded similar to the woman's.

'Who are you people?' Adam said.

The stocky guy cracked him on the back of the head with the pistol, hard enough to make him bend double and gasp with pain.

'I told you, keep your mouth shut,' the woman said without looking back at him. The tall man grabbed Adam's arm and forced him onwards. They went through a doorway marked 'PRIVAT', down a bare, narrow staircase that smelled of damp. The winding staircase led down to a rear exit that opened into an alleyway. Adam followed the woman out into the pale sunlight. The alley was edged with piles of old beer crates, cardboard boxes and bins that stank of rotting garbage.

A black unmarked van was waiting for them. The stocky guy wrenched open the back doors while the tall one took Adam's holdall from him and threw it in the front with the briefcase. A wave of the gun, and Adam clambered into the back. There were no windows, and it was empty apart from a mattress on the hard metal floor. The back doors slammed shut with a hollow clang, and he was in darkness.

More doors slammed, then the engine fired up and he was jerked almost off his feet as the van pulled away with a lurch.

The drive lasted a long time. Adam curled up on the mattress as the van chassis squeaked and rattled and the vibrations pulsed up through the floor. He could tell from the steady, dulling roar of the engine that they were on a fast road, maybe a motorway.

After what seemed like days, the engine note dropped to a rumble and the vibrations diminished as the van turned off onto a slower road and started swinging and swaying through bends. From the angle of the floor and the number of gear changes, he figured that they were climbing steeply up some kind of mountain road.

For a horrible moment, that made him think of Julia Goodman. Back in Dublin, what seemed like a lifetime ago, Lenny Salt had suggested that someone might have thrown her off a mountain. Adam hadn't believed him at the time,

180

but now everything was different. Anything seemed plausible. Was the same thing going to happen to him? Was his son already dead, and now he was going to die too?

But the van didn't stop, and nobody pulled open the doors to haul him out and pitch him over the edge of some terrible drop. The journey continued. It was colder now, as though they'd gained a great deal of altitude. Adam found a crumpled blanket on the mattress and pulled it over him. As he lay there huddled, the van left paved roads behind and was soon lurching and bouncing interminably over rough ground.

He lost all track of time. Reality began to merge with the nightmares in his head, and he drifted in a shadowy in-between state until the slamming of doors and the sound of voices outside startled him awake and he realised they'd come to a stop. More strange sounds, like the grinding of machinery and a juddering crash like a giant portcullis closing. Then the van lurched away again. Now the sound of its engine was echoey and hollow, as though they were driving through some kind of tunnel. It went on and on, and he sensed they were moving downhill in a slow spiral, as if driving into a huge subterranean car park.

Gripped by equal measures of curiosity and dread, Adam rolled off the mattress and clambered up on his feet again. Where were they taking him?

Then, suddenly, the van stopped again. He heard the front doors open and footsteps echoing as his three captors got out. The footsteps walked around the side of the van. The lock turned with a harsh grating noise, and suddenly Adam was dazzled and covering his eyes as the back of the van was flooded with white light.

Strong hands gripped him by the arms and he was hauled out. Half-blinded, he struggled to get his bearings. Concrete

181

under his feet. The air was stale and voices bounced off stone walls. It felt cold and dank, and something told him they were deep underground. There were several more people around him, talking rapidly in a language he was pretty sure wasn't German.

His eyes began to adjust to the light of the fierce spot-lamps, and now he could see they were in a large chamber. The walls were painted battleship-grey, streaked with damp and age. There were several more vehicles parked around, a couple of trucks and a Land Rover.

The woman, the tall, lean man and the stocky one with the pistol were in conversation with a group of four more men. They all had the same serious expression. Two were armed with small automatic weapons that hung from shoulder straps. Adam couldn't understand a word of what they were saying, but it seemed like a handover – and he was the goods.

The woman nodded, someone laughed and then one of the armed men grabbed him and led him brusquely across the chamber towards a steel door. He glanced over his shoulder and saw the woman and her two male companions walking away without a second glance at him.

Beyond the door, he found himself being marched down a stone corridor that seemed to have no end. The walls were the same pitted grey. They passed a stamped metal sign riveted to the stonework, its edges eaten away with rust. A stark red arrow pointed down the corridor by way of direc-tions, and underneath was faded black lettering in what looked to him like German. He couldn't understand 'BEFEHLSRAUM', but the word 'KOMMANDOSTAB' looked military.

'Where the fuck am I being taken?' he demanded.

No reply. His four captors marched him onwards down

the dank corridor. Here and there, puddles of stagnant condensation had collected on the floor, and dusty cobwebs hung from old pipework and the exposed wires that ran along the walls between lamps in wire cages. The switches and circuit breakers were ancient Bakelite affairs, as old as the peeling paint on the stone blocks.

The corridor curved around to the right. Some clanging iron steps, then a landing with more doors. Another sign, with more red arrows pointing in different directions. Whatever this place was, it was huge.

The men shoved Adam through one of the doors into what seemed like a storeroom. Judging by the layer of dust on the tables and shelves, the place hadn't been used in decades.

And when he looked around, he knew exactly how long. He stopped and gaped, blinking, disbelieving, at the age-worn banner that was hanging on the wall at the far end of the room. It was faded red, with a white circle in the centre about three feet in diameter.

Inside the circle was a Nazi swastika.

He whirled round to his captors, but they just shoved him roughly across the room and through another steel door, pushed him inside and shut him in.

He was in a cell. It was clean and warm, with a radiator, a metal-framed single bed, a sink, a toilet and a wardrobe. But it was a cell.

Adam O'Connor started beating on the cold steel door and screamed for his son.

Chapter Twenty-Eight

Ben was back at the Mini by three o'clock, and sitting at the wheel in the car park on the edge of Bruges, wondering what to do next. Europe was awash with sprouting neo-Nazi groups. Somewhere out there, one of them would lead him to this woman he believed was his sister. He could dedicate himself to tracking them down, infiltrating their meetings, shadowing them like a ghost, kicking down doors and breaking bones until he found the right shaven-headed, tattooed degenerate who could take him to her.

Luc Simon had been right. The way he was feeling right now, it would satisfy him to kick some arses.

But it could take months, years. It would dominate his life completely. Even if he was willing to risk incurring the wrath of Luc Simon and spending half his life dodging Interpol agents, time was a luxury he couldn't afford. He had Rupert Shannon's lawyer to worry about. The threat of losing Le Val hanging over him like the sword of Damocles. The stomach-churning prospect of having to go and beg for money from the bank, something he'd never had to do in his life before. And none of those things was about to go away.

But he couldn't just give this up and go home. The other alternative was to keep following the Kammler trail. If he could learn more about the kind of people who were interested in the SS general's work, find and talk to others who were chasing the same thing, he might find connections.

Ben thought about the man Don Jarrett had mentioned.

'All right, Lenny Salt,' he said out loud. 'Let's see if we can't dig you out. Maybe you can shine some light on this mess.'

He used his phone to do an online search on Manchester University. The Physics Department website was easy to find, but after trawling through the whole thing twice he could find no mention whatsoever of a Lenny Salt. He spent a few minutes checking through the other science departments as well, in case Jarrett had got it wrong. But no sign.

Then he tried typing 'Lenny Salt' into the search engine. He came up with about a million results, but none of them offered up anything promising.

He went back to the Physics Department site and figured out his next move. Late in June, the university would be deep into its holiday season. Few lecturers would be around, maybe just the odd one popping in and out of their offices, but there would be some kind of skeleton staff looking after reception. Ben scrolled down a list of lecturers and his eye landed on a guy called Tom Wilson. In his picture he looked about fortyish, heavyset and balding. He was smiling with his eyes like someone who'd have a sense of humour. Ben wondered whether he'd appreciate this joke.

He called reception. 'Physics Department,' said a woman's voice. She sounded young, and half-asleep with boredom. He could imagine her sitting there, manning an empty reception desk on a dull, hot afternoon, gazing out of the window at the sunshine and counting the minutes until she could get out of there.

For all he knew, she talked to Wilson every day of her

week and would see through the deception right away and slam down the phone. It was a one-shot deal, but it was the only shot he had.

He tried to sound breezy and laidback. 'Hi, this is Dr Wilson. Listen, sorry to bother you about this, but I'm trying to contact Lenny Salt and he's not answering his office line. Need to ask him something, but I've lost his damn mobile number. You wouldn't happen to have it there, would you?'

Silence down the phone.

When she spoke again, the bored slur in her voice was gone.

'Who did you say you were?'

'Dr Tom Wilson,' Ben said. He could feel this slipping away from him already.

Another heavy silence on the line.

'Tom Wilson, assistant head of department?' She said it suspiciously, but Ben could hear the smile curling on her lips.

'That's me.'

'Do you know your office number, Dr Wilson?'

Teasing now. Ben didn't reply.

'Lenny Salt doesn't work here any more,' she said. 'And he never had an office here. He was just the lab assistant. But you'd know that, wouldn't you, Dr Wilson?'

Shit.

'Student gags are usually reserved for Rag Week,' she said.

'You got me. But this isn't a student gag.'

'So you're not Tom Wilson, and you're not a student either.'

'Innocent on both counts.'

'I knew you weren't Wilson. Your voice is too nice. And the students are all callow youths.'

'I'll take that as a compliment,' Ben said.

'So who are you, caller?'

He shrugged. 'I'm Ben.' Sometimes frankness was the best way.

'That's a nice name. You're not trying to get me into trouble, are you, Ben?'

'I didn't get your name.'

'I didn't give it. It's Vicki. That's with an i.'

'I wouldn't dream of getting you into trouble, Vicki with an i.'

She gave a low laugh. 'Listen, Mr Nice-Voice-Ben. Even if I had a number to give you, I wouldn't be allowed. But I don't have a number, because Lenny Salt wouldn't ever give one out. He'd be too worried the CIA or someone would use it to track him down.'

'Got to watch those things,' Ben said. 'You never know with those guys.'

'And that's why if I were looking for that old fart, not that I would in a million billion years, I wouldn't even bother with the phone. I'd be looking up some weird shit online.'

'Some weird shit?'

'That's his website, someweirdshit-dot-com. But you didn't hear that from me.'

'I get the feeling Lenny wasn't your favourite person in the department.'

She snorted. 'He's a nut. And a creep. Thinks he's this big scientist. Not that I have any favourites in this place.'

'Any idea where he went after he left there?'

'I know he lives in a caravan or a camper, something like that. But he could be anywhere.'

'I really appreciate your help, Vicki. You're definitely the nicest and strangest Physics Department receptionist who's ever flirted with me on the phone.'

That low laugh again. 'I'll take *that* as a compliment. Buy me a drink sometime, if you want to thank me.'

'The very next time I'm in Manchester.'

'Look forward to it, Ben. You know where to find me.'

Then she hung up. Ben stared at the phone for a moment, smiling and shaking his head.

Leaning back in the car seat, he revisited the search engine and punched in the web address Vicki had given him. What he found there was no great surprise. The website was a paradise for conspiracy theorists. All the usual suspects were on display. The Diana murder. The real reason for the Iraq invasion. Bin Laden a US Intelligence agent. Area 51 and UFO cover-ups. The CIA observation posts on the far side of the moon.

Ben sifted through it all quickly, scrolling down the long list until he came to a header that read 'The Kammler Shadow Project: Fact or Fiction?'

Ben stared at it.

He clicked on it.

Page temporarily unavailable.

He sat thinking for a moment, then scrolled over to a tab that said 'Contact'. The page flashed up, and offered no number to call, no obvious email address like 'lenny@someweirdshit.com'. There was just an electronic form to fill in and submit.

Ben pondered the best way to draw the guy out. No point in coming straight out with 'I want to ask you questions' and then expect a call. He had to make Salt think he was offering something juicy. If Salt had been keen enough to travel to one of Don Jarrett's lectures, he might be interested enough to call back.

He wrote:

'Message for Lenny Salt. I have important information about Hans Kammler. If you want to know more, let's talk.'

He didn't sign with a name or offer a return email address, just typed in his mobile number and then sent the message.

He sat in the car a long time. He didn't know what he was waiting for, or whether Salt would be any use to him, or even where to go from here if it turned out to be a blind alley. Maybe back to Luc Simon for more names. Perhaps it was time to start kicking down doors after all.

Or maybe Brooke was right. Maybe he just should go home and try to focus his mind on the many troubles awaiting him there.

But he knew he'd come too far for that now. He couldn't walk away. He closed his eyes and tried to still his mind. So much to think about, and so little that made any sense.

It was about half an hour later, when the clock on the Mini dashboard was approaching quarter to four, that the phone buzzed in his lap and he realised he'd drifted off into an uncomfortable doze. His head jerked up at the sound and he was instantly alert.

'Who's this?' said a man's voice on the other end. The voice was filled with suspicion, deep and gravelly. Ben pictured a man in his sixties. The accent was east London.

'Is that Lenny Salt?'

'Who's this?' the voice said again.

'Just a friend, Lenny. Just want to talk.'

'You'll never track this number.'

'Like I said, I'm a friend.'

There was a long pause. Then: 'Info on Kammler, you say?'

'That's right.'

'I already have all the info I need on Kammler.'

'You just think you do,' Ben said. 'Wait until you hear what I have to tell you. Can we meet?'

Pushing for a meeting with a paranoid like Salt was a dangerous move, because it was all too easy to frighten him away – and once he was gone, he'd be gone for good. But Ben knew the only way to winkle him out of his shell and keep him there was to pin him down face to face. And if his instinct was right about Salt, all it would take was to arouse his curiosity enough.

It seemed to be working. The long silence on the phone tasted of wary interest, like a hungry cat struggling between suspicion and temptation over a morsel in a stranger's hand.

'We can meet,' Salt said. 'But strictly on my terms. You come to me.'

'No problem at all. Name the place.'

'Laugharne.'

Ben had to think where it was. 'Laugharne in Wales or Larne in Northern Ireland?'

'Wales.'

'That's where you live, on the Welsh coast?'

'I didn't say I lived there,' Salt said cagily. 'I said I'll *meet* you there. Tomorrow morning at eleven. Come alone. Wear a red scarf so I know you.'

A red scarf in the middle of summer, Ben thought. Great.

'OK, where exactly?'

'There's a castle on the bay. Take the path that runs along the side, towards the Dylan Thomas boathouse. Walk to the first bench and wait.'

'I'll be there.'

Chapter Twenty-Nine

By five o' clock Ben was sipping a scotch on the rocks in the departure lounge at Brussels airport, waiting for a UK-bound flight that would take him as close as possible to his destination. The Mini was in secure long-term parking, and the Smith & Wesson was scattered in pieces across the Belgian countryside.

Three hours after that, he was behind the wheel of a black rental Audi A5 Turbo Diesel speeding west up the M4 from Bristol airport over the Severn Bridge and into Wales. He hit Carmarthen, then more dual carriageway, then twisty rural roads led him through lush green countryside down towards the coast. By the time he got to Laugharne, the sun was setting. He checked into the first bed and breakfast he saw on the edge of town, spent an hour in a nearby pub over a couple of beers and a plate of ham sandwiches, then headed back to the B&B for an early night.

The next morning at five to eleven, he was pulling up at his rendezvous point. He slotted the Audi into the car park near the ruined medieval castle overlooking the bay, and got out. The sky was clear and the sun already hot. On the passenger seat was a red woolly scarf he'd bought at the airport in Brussels. He draped it reluctantly around his neck and made his way between the stalls selling local produce, clothing and bric-a-brac to tourists, then headed over a little hump-back bridge towards the walkway that skirted the base of the castle. A couple of passers-by shot strange looks at the man wearing the thick scarf on such a warm, sunny June day.

A sign saying 'Dylan Thomas Boathouse' pointed in the direction of a white stone cottage perched over the shore-line in the distance. Ben walked towards it. People were ambling up and down the pathway with dogs on leads, some tourists were taking photos of the castle towers, and a couple of artists sat in the grass at the foot of its craggy wall sketching the view across the bay.

Ben scanned the horizon. It was a peaceful place, the kind of place he'd have liked to hang around for a while. The tide was out, and the sand and shingle glittered in the sunlight. He spent a few minutes taking it all in, feeling the sun's warmth on his face, breathing in the rich tang of the sea and watching the gulls that circled and called to one another overhead. He wished he had the freedom to enjoy moments like this more often.

There were some wooden benches along the walkway. He went over to the first one as Lenny Salt had instructed, and checked the time. It was after eleven now.

Looking up and down the walkway, he watched the people going by. He saw portly middle-class tourists with cameras and walking sticks and plastic bags with gift-shop logos on them. He saw arty-looking literary types with open-toed sandals and scruffy hair, clutching volumes of poetry on their pilgrimage to the former home of the famous Welsh poet. He saw an old man bending down to pick up the dogshit that his overweight Labrador had deposited on the path, and dumping it in a bin.

But he didn't see anyone who answered to Don Jarrett's description of Lenny Salt.

Fifteen minutes later, he was beginning to wonder if he'd come all this way for nothing. Maybe it had been a mistake to trust that a paranoid conspiracy obsessive like Salt would turn up to meet him.

But Ben had a very well-developed sense of when he was being watched, honed over years of following people and being followed himself. And suddenly he was getting a feeling, like a tickle in his brain, that made him glance back towards the car park a hundred yards away.

He could see his big muscular Audi sitting there, sunlight reflecting off its windscreen. Three cars along was a vehicle that hadn't been there when he'd arrived. It was a red Vauxhall estate, a junkyard special with a lopsided number plate and a blue passenger door. Standing a few steps from the Vauxhall was a skinny, hunched, white-haired man wearing khaki shorts and a Hawaiian shirt. In his hand was a chunky black camera with a long lens, and he was staring in Ben's direction. Even at this distance he looked strangely out of place.

As Ben watched out of the corner of his eye, pretending to be following the line of a white cruiser that was tracking across the bay, he saw the distant figure raise the camera and he knew he was being photographed. Then the guy lowered the camera and went shuffling round the side of the red Vauxhall, looking jittery and furtive and shooting a final nervous glance Ben's way as he got in.

Ben saw a puff of blue smoke from the exhaust as the engine fired up, and heard it rev out as the guy hit the gas too hard in his hurry to get away. The Vauxhall reversed quickly out of its parking space, lurching on tired springs, headed out of the car park and turned right onto the main street through the village.

As it went, Ben saw the big tow-hitch sticking out from its rear, and he remembered what Vicki had told him about Salt living in a caravan.

Salt, you bastard.

Ben ran, dropping the stupid red scarf on the path as he sprinted back towards the car park. By the time he reached his car, the junkyard Vauxhall had disappeared out of sight down the road.

Chapter Thirty

As Adam sat slumped on the edge of the bunk in his neon-lit cell, only the hands on his watch gave him any clue that it was mid-morning by the time he heard the tinkle of keys at the door.

He turned slowly to face the two guards who walked in. One of them stayed by the door, pointing the muzzle of his stubby automatic weapon across the room at Adam's chest. The other one walked up to him, made a brusque gesture and whistled out of the corner of his mouth. The universal sign language for 'On your feet, asshole.'

Adam looked at him, then over at the one with the gun, who was clutching the weapon as though the prisoner might suddenly jump them and make a break for it. It seemed absurd.

'Who do you people think I am, James frigging Bond?'

If the two guards even understood him, there was no flicker of reaction on either of their faces. Their eyes were stony cold as they marched Adam out of the cell and through the storeroom. He glanced at the swastika banner on the wall. 'So let me guess. You're Nazis, right?'

No reply. He gave up talking to them as they walked him out across the landing outside, back down the metal stairway and down the twisting stone corridors. The place was a maze, and after a couple of turns he couldn't remember coming this way the previous day. A doorway led into a dim, dank room containing what looked like some kind of old service lift, a crude platform suspended by cables that vanished off into a dark shaft overhead. The guards walked Adam to the platform, then one of them stabbed an antiquated Bakelite button on a wall panel. A second later there was a grunt of machinery coming to life, and Adam felt the platform jolt under his feet. With a whirring and screeching of cables, the lift was cranked upwards through the hole in the ceiling and into the shaft. Up and up through the darkness for what seemed like forever. Then the machinery clanked to a halt and they stepped out. Another room, more doors, more incomprehensible signs. But the air seemed fresher here, and Adam thought he could detect the slightest hint of a breeze from somewhere.

One of the guards opened a door, and the other pressed his hand against Adam's back and shoved him through it.

He stumbled. 'Watch it, Hitler boy,' Adam muttered over his shoulder. The guard looked at him as though he could happily have shot him dead and left him where he dropped. He shoved Adam again, harder this time. Maybe provocation wasn't a wise option.

Then Adam stopped and looked around him at the place he'd just walked inside. His jaw dropped.

The cavernous space was built with the same stone blocks as the chamber he'd arrived in yesterday, but it was twenty times as large. The ceiling soared up like the roof of a cathedral, great archways overhead connected by a system of metal galleries and ladders. A huge, tattered swastika banner hung against the stonework. Sixty-five years ago, this place must have been swarming with German soldiers.

As a gust of wind ruffled his hair, Adam realised that the

giant hall was open to the elements and bright with the first natural light he'd seen since the alleyway in Graz. He turned to see where it was coming from.

And found himself staring out over a rocky valley that stretched as far as the eye could see. Eighty yards from where he stood, a vast stone arch opened up to the outside like the mouth of a cave. At first he thought the leafy green veil hanging over the entrance was vegetation, but then it hit him that it was military-style camouflage netting designed to conceal it from prying eyes.

Now he understood what the place was. He was standing inside a hollowed-out mountain. The sheer scale of it made him dizzy.

After a long career in science, Adam was no more a history expert than he was a linguist – but he'd learned enough about World War II from his background reading on Hans Kammler to know that the Nazis had built hundreds of hidden underground bunkers, experimental research stations and factories around occupied Europe, constructed by armies of forced labourers transported from Auschwitz and the other death camps. He'd read that some historians believed not all of those secret facilities had been found. It looked as if they'd been right.

Adam could barely imagine the construction project for a place like this. It would have been like a scene from ancient times, the building of the pyramids. Tens upon tens of thousands of workers labouring fifteen hours a day for months, even years. A huge mass of human ants driven back and forth by their masters, worked until they dropped dead with their shovel or pickaxe still in hand, while more doomed souls arrived under armed convoy from the camps each day to take their place. How many must have died here, nobody would ever know.

Between the mouth of the cave and where he stood was an aircraft, its fuselage and wings streaked red with corrosion. He stepped away from the guards and walked underneath one of the rusty wings. He'd seen this type of plane in documentaries. It was the infamous Luftwaffe Me 262 jet fighter, the revolutionary plane that could have won the war for Germany if its development hadn't come so late. But this one seemed to have some very strange engine modifications visible through its nose canopy – modifications whose function he could only guess at.

What had they been doing in here? Adam swallowed. He already knew the answer, but it was too incredible to contemplate.

The guards interrupted his thoughts, moving him on at gunpoint through more corridors. They stopped at a door and one of them knocked. A voice answered, and they went in.

Adam was surprised to find himself stepping inside a pleasant office. Classical music tinkled softly in the background. Behind a mahogany desk sat a sandy-haired man in a smart suede jacket. He stood as Adam was shown inside, and walked up to him with a smile. The guards left and shut the door.

Adam studied the man warily. He wasn't like the three hardcases who'd brought him from Graz, or the brutish guards. In his early forties or thereabouts, he was handsome in almost a dashing way, with a high forehead and twinkling grey eyes that hinted at high intelligence and a careful, logical mind.

'My name is Pelham,' the man said. The accent was English, educated, upper class. Adam's blood chilled as he recognised the voice. It was the one that had talked to him on the phone the day Rory was taken.

'It's a pleasure to meet you at last, Professor Connor,' Pelham went on. 'Or should I say, Professor *O*'Connor? You haven't been the easiest of men to find, changing your name like that.' He motioned to an open drinks cabinet behind the desk. 'Would you like a drink?'

Adam glared at him. 'I'd like to see my boy, you sonofabitch.'

Pelham shrugged, reached for a decanter and a glass and poured himself a measure. 'There's no reason why this should be an unpleasant experience for either of us,' he said. 'But suit yourself. Here, take a seat.'

Adam remained standing.

'My employer regrets that he can't be here personally to greet you. Unfortunately, his schedule just doesn't permit it.'

'Well, that's a shame. I'd have liked to meet this guy. Give him my regards. Who is he?'

Pelham smiled. 'Afraid I can't say.'

'No, I didn't suppose you could. Where's Rory?'

'Actually very close by. Closer than you might imagine. You'll be seeing him soon, I promise. And please rest assured that he's been very well looked after here.' Pelham smiled. 'Your son's a fine boy. You should be proud of him.'

Adam was palpitating with rage. The man's smooth charm just made him angrier.

Pelham smiled reasonably and sat at the desk. Setting down his glass, he laced his fingers together and leaned forward. 'Now, let's waste no more time. There's been enough delay already. It's thanks to our difficulty finding you that we first had to approach your colleagues, Drs Goodman and Miyazaki.' He frowned. 'Regrettably, they were of little assistance. We had to let them go.'

'Murdering bastard. They were my friends.'

'It's all down to you now, Adam. May I call you Adam?

201

I hope you understand the degree of trust we're placing in you, and that you'll co-operate with my employer's wishes. In a very real sense, what we're offering you here is the opportunity of a lifetime. A chance to achieve something quite extraordinary.'

Adam leaned across the desk, so that his face was just a few inches from Pelham's. 'What the fuck am I doing in this place?'

'Please don't play games with me, Adam,' Pelham said softly. 'You already know exactly what you're doing here. You're going to make the Kammler machine work for us.'

Chapter Thirty-One

Lenny Salt was pretty pleased with himself.

As he drove out of Laugharne as fast as the old Vauxhall would go, heading away from the coastline through the maze of winding lanes that criss-crossed the countryside like a spider's web, he had a big smile on his face. He reached out and patted the camera on the passenger seat. Nice work. He'd got some great snaps of the Red Scarf Man. That would teach Them to send some spook out to trick old Lenny Salt. Information on Kammler? Lenny smiled. *Yeah, right.* As if these people could tell him anything. Nobody knew more about Kammler than the Kammler Krew.

He thought about the man he'd photographed, magnified up close in the long lens. Probably mid to late thirties, in good shape. Almost certainly ex-military. Those guys all had that look about them. MI5 or CIA? he wondered. Then again, what did it matter which agency he was working for – it was all part of the same evil global fraternity.

Them. Lenny thought about Them a lot. The bastards were all in it together.

He'd seen this whole thing coming, for a long time. Had anyone listened to him? Had they fuck. And now look what had happened. Michio and Julia dead, and it was only a question of time before They got to Adam as well.

It's not paranoia when they're really out to get you, he thought. That was one of his favourite sayings, and it never failed to make him smile to himself, because he knew he was way too smart ever to let them catch him. He'd been too clever for Red Scarf Man today, same as he'd been too clever to let himself be duped by that girl last year, that German or whatever she was, the one calling herself Luna.

Luna – what kind of stupid made-up name was that?

Lenny grinned to himself at the memory of how he'd fooled her. Same system he'd used today. Agree to the meet, watch them from a vantage point, take the pictures and slip away. *Know your enemy*. That was another favourite saying of his, one he took seriously. This was war. It was a matter of survival.

As soon as he got back to the caravan he was going to download the pictures onto his laptop with the others: all the people who'd ever tried to follow him, lure him or pinch his ideas. He was still working on a lot of the names, and of course most of them were phoney anyway – that was the way They worked. But he had all the faces memorised, and he was always watching out for them, everywhere he went. More enemies would come for him in the future. He was certain of that – but he'd be ready for them.

They weren't going to get him. No chance. Not him, not wily old Lenny Salt. Always one step ahead, always on the move, untraceable, checking his emails from a different library or cyber-café every day, always paying cash and giving false names to the farmers whose bits of land he rented. Then, every couple of months, or whenever he felt the heat, he'd move on.

And now that Red Scarf Man was sniffing around, it was going to be time to pack up and relocate again. Away from west Wales, maybe up to Scotland this time. Or perhaps

Cornwall. Plenty of places to hide away there, and there was always a hippy retreat or new-age healing camp where you could buy a bit of hash.

After half an hour's drive Lenny was deep in the country-side. At the end of a long, twisty single-track lane he stopped at a farm gate, got out of the car and opened it, drove through and stopped again to shut it behind him. Cows looked up from their grazing and eyed the Vauxhall lazily as it bumped through the field. Across the other side, he reached the next gate and passed through into the wooded area where his camp was.

A few yards further up the track, half-hidden behind a sprawl of gorse and brambles, was the old Sprite caravan. He'd bought it cheap, in cash, from a secondhand dealer in the Peak District just before he'd left Manchester. As soon as he'd got it, he'd sprayed it with military surplus drab-olive paint to help it blend into the rural environments where he planned on spending the rest of his days. Home might be a box on wheels, but he liked to keep it nice and tidy.

Lenny got out of the car and walked over towards the caravan, avoiding the tripwire that was carefully stretched between two trees and attached to an alarm circuit. His hidden cameras watched him from the foliage.

Next to the caravan was his folding table, his deck chair and the barbecue that he grilled his food on. He fancied some sausages tonight. He climbed the aluminium steps to his front door, took the keys from his pocket and undid the two heavy steel padlocks to let himself in. It was hot and stuffy inside, and he pushed open the windows to let some air circulate.

Still grinning to himself at having fooled Them yet again, he stepped over to the fridge and pulled out a can of Old

Speckled Hen. Cracked the ring and raised the can in a toast to his cleverness.

'I'll have one of those too,' said a voice behind him.

The can dropped out of Lenny's fingers and hit the vinyl floor with a hiss of foam.

Lenny spun around.

The man from the castle walkway in Laugharne was standing in the doorway.

Chapter Thirty-Two

Adam gaped dumbly at Pelham, as if he'd been slapped.

'That's right,' Pelham said, clearly enjoying the look on his face. 'It's here. I wasn't joking when I said you were being given an incredible opportunity, Adam. You should be honoured. Welcome to the inner circle.'

'You found it.' Adam's voice was hushed with awe.

'It was found. Not by me. I'm just a man with a job to do, the same as you. Mine was to find someone who could make it work. We failed twice. Now you're here, we're not going to fail a third time.' He cocked his head. 'Are we, Adam?'

Adam was too stunned to formulate a reply.

'Good. Now, enough talk. I want to show you something that very few people have seen in more than half a century.'

Adam was still speechless as Pelham led him out of the office. The guards were standing outside the door, weapons dangling at their sides. They stood to attention as their boss strode out of the doorway and followed, pointing the guns at Adam's back. Pelham led the way back towards the hangar, past the corroded hulk of the Me 262 and over to a doorway on the far side of the huge space, where he stopped and gave a sharp command. One of the guards produced a large key and unlocked the door.

On the other side of it was a large circular chamber, fifty

yards across. Light streamed in from holes in the rough dome of a ceiling and Adam could make out the marks of picks and chisels in the craggy stone walls. He shivered as he thought of the doomed concentration camp slaves who had carved this space out of the solid rock of the mountain under the watchful eyes and cocked weapons of their Nazi masters. The smell of death was soaked deep into the walls of this place.

Running around the circumference of the chamber was a circular metal walkway, with a rail at chest height. Adam stepped to the rail and peered over the edge. His eyes widened. The centre of the chamber was an abyss, a round vertical shaft about fifteen metres across that plummeted straight down further than the eye could see. A rusted iron gangway led across from the edge of the chamber to a steel cage housing an open-sided industrial lift, the kind Adam had seen in pictures of old mines. Pelham walked briskly across the clanking gangway, opened a mesh door, and Adam followed him wordlessly into the lift. One of the guards accompanied them, and the other went over to a switch panel on the wall.

As the lift groaned downwards and the craggy shaft walls rolled by, Adam saw that the guard was looking down at his feet, fingering his weapon a little nervously. Nobody spoke. Down and down. Adam estimated they must be hundreds of metres inside the mountain. There was no ventilation down here, and the air was thick and foul.

The lift touched down and they stepped out into a circular gallery like the one above. A single arched passage led off it, lit down its length by age-yellowed lamps. Pelham led the way. The passage widened steadily, then came to a dead end.

Facing them, glowing dully in the lamplight, was a giant steel door. It filled the entire wall, tall and wide enough to drive a Panzer tank through. It looked to Adam like the entrance to the world's biggest bank vault. The rivets stamped into its edges were the size of baseballs, and six massive steel deadlocks cut deep into the rock. Painted onto the door's matt grey surface was a sign with a skull-and-crossbones image and the words 'VORSICHT: GEFAHRENZONE' in stark red letters.

The danger warning was loud and clear. Whoever had put that door in place must have known what terrible forces were to be contained behind it. Adam wondered if his captors had even the slightest idea of what they were dealing with.

Pelham gave a command to the guard. The man nodded, unslung his weapon and handed it to his boss. Stepped towards the huge door, dusted his hands and took a grip on the giant metal wheel, crusted with age, that was connected by a system of gears to the bars of the deadlocks. The guard braced his feet apart, paused a beat and then grunted with effort as he put his strength behind the lock. The wheel turned with a squeak, and the deadlocks began to draw back. Another turn, a few more inches.

Standing there with his mouth open and watching the locks slowly grind back across the door, Adam suddenly realised he hadn't breathed for about a minute. His heart was firing like a machine gun. Pelham watched his face, and a little smile curled at the edges of his mouth.

Adam gulped. He was about to witness something incredible, legendary. Something he'd spent years studying from afar, within the confines of his safe little world, relying solely on his own scientific knowledge and the sketchy evidence of a handful of witness accounts. The mythical Kammler machine. The lost Grail of super-esoteric science. Here he was about to lay eyes on it for the first time.

Now he knew that Michio and Julia had stood on this

spot, not so very long ago. Had they felt the way he was feeling now, quaking with terror and yet, somewhere deep inside, burning up with excitement?

The thought screamed at him from inside his head. *Can I make this thing work?*

The deadlocks had reached the end of their travel. The guard stepped away from the wheel, wiping the rust off his hands, then leaned his weight into the huge door and pushed hard. It began to open.

Adam felt Pelham's hand on his shoulder, and walked towards the dark doorway. The air wafting out of the shadows smelled dank, and Adam shivered with the cold that suddenly tingled up and down his body.

Then Pelham flashed a torch, found the handle of a switch and yanked it. Lights flickered into life and Adam's jaw dropped open.

He'd held an ingot of solid gold created inside a nuclear reactor. Watched the child-sized Honda ASIMO robot conduct a symphony orchestra. Stood inside a particle accelerator a mile underneath the ground as electrons slammed into one another at the speed of light. Witnessed the afterglow of a gamma ray burst when a giant star collapsed in on itself and a black hole was born. But he'd never seen anything like this before.

Under his feet, electric wires snaked like pythons towards the device in the middle of the vault. He followed them towards it.

Standing on a concrete plinth, the bell-shaped object was as tall as he was. He walked around its smooth sides, put out his hand and touched the cold steel casing.

Kammler's secret creation, shrouded in mystery for sixty-five years, the greatest enigma of the twentieth century. Maybe of all time. *Die Glocke*, the Germans had called it.

The Bell.

And here it was. Incredible.

The scientist in him was already hard at work, his eyes following the line of the joints in the strange metal casing until he'd located the bolted-on access panels in its underside. He had a pretty good idea of what was behind them.

Can you make it work? asked the voice in his head.

He knew the answer. *Maybe I can.*

But I'm not going to.

He turned. Pelham was standing a few feet away, watching his every move like a crouched leopard watching an antelope.

Wait for it, you bastard.

'I'm the last one who can help you,' he said.

'That's right, Adam. You are. That's why we've gone to such pains to make this as attractive to you as possible.'

'Meaning that if I refuse, you'll hurt my boy.'

'I hope that won't be necessary.'

'So I agree to help you, and then what? You'll just let us both walk away, go home? You take me for a complete idiot? You think I don't understand what's going to happen to Rory and me if I give you what you want? I don't know what kind of fool would agree to a deal like that.' Adam took a step closer to him. The guard was watching him with a frown, and the gun was pointing his way. But he didn't care. 'So I'm making you a new deal.'

'A new deal,' Pelham echoed blankly.

'That's right. You're going to start listening to *my* terms now. Here's how it's going to be. You think those papers I brought with me are my Kammler notes? Wrong. They might be useful if you're thinking of wiring up some smart house technology into this shithole. But the real stuff is right where I left it in my study back home, securely locked away in a password-controlled safe. And that's where it's going to stay until you let my son go.'

Pelham didn't reply.

'These are my terms. One, you let me take Rory safely home. Two, you let me see for myself exactly where this cosy little place of yours is. Three, you give me your guarantee that neither my son nor I will ever be harmed or threatened in any way again. Then, and only then, I'll agree to come back here and help you make that thing work.'

Pelham jutted out his chin and raised an eyebrow. Said nothing.

Adam pointed at the machine. 'Play fair with me and I'll give you what you want. But cross the line, and I'll make sure the authorities will be on this place like flies on Rottweiler shit. And I'll screw up that machine so bad, you'll have to sell it for recycling into Coke tins. Don't think I don't know how.'

'Have you finished?' Pelham asked quietly.

'That's all I have to say. Think about it.'

Chapter Thirty-Three

'Quiet little spot you've found for yourself here, Lenny,' Ben said.

Salt backed away. His eyes were wide and fixed on Ben as he reached his right hand back and fumbled for something on the Formica top behind him. Then his fingers closed on the wooden handle of the long barbecue fork and he snatched it up and pointed it like a weapon at Ben's stomach.

'Stay away from me or I'll skewer you.'

Ben looked at the fork. 'I think you'd better put that thing down before you go and hurt yourself.'

'Who sent you? Who are you working for?'

'Just myself. Sorry to disappoint.'

'What do you want?'

'To talk, Lenny. Nothing more.'

Salt clutched the fork tighter, standing there in a puddle of beer.

'You look like you've pissed yourself,' Ben said. 'Aren't you going to put that fork down?'

'You'll kill me.'

'Lenny, if I'd wanted to kill you, you wouldn't even have seen me.'

Salt blanched.

Ben reached slowly into his pocket, took out his wallet

and handed him a business card. 'This is who I am and what I do.' He nodded to the laptop on the bed. 'Check out the website. There's a picture of me.'

'I'm not connected here. No email, no internet.'

'Scared they might trace you?'

Salt nodded sheepishly.

'You need to do a better job. It wasn't hard to find you. And your snap-and-run routine needs work too.'

Salt was still frozen there, clutching the fork. The last of the beer had seeped out of the can and was trickling across the vinyl floor.

'For Christ's sake,' Ben said. 'I haven't got all day.' He stepped over, snatched the fork before Salt could react, and threw it out of the open caravan doorway. It whistled through the air and stuck juddering in a tree trunk.

Salt kept gaping speechlessly at Ben.

'Now clean that beer up, and let's go outside and talk.'

Salt hesitated, then tore off a length of kitchen roll from a dispenser next to the stove. He used the paper to mop up the puddle on the floor while Ben grabbed two more beer cans from the fridge and led the way outside. Salt joined him, watching him warily, and they sat opposite one another at the picnic table.

Ben snapped open his beer. 'I'm sorry if I scared you before, Lenny. I didn't want to.'

Salt grunted in reply, opened his own can with a spit of foam and took a long gulp, keeping his eyes on Ben. The business card was still clenched in his fist, and he scrutinised it carefully, first its printed front, then the blank back, staring at it as though it was the lost map to the secret US Government alien farm at Roswell.

'No invisible ink,' Ben said. 'No holographic cryptograms.'

Salt looked up. 'Tactical Training Unit? What does that mean?'

'It's my business. Just a training school.'

'Bullshit. It means you're military.'

'Was military,' Ben said. 'Not any more.'

'Sure. That's what you would say, isn't it?' Salt sneered. 'I don't talk to people like you.'

'I'm being completely honest with you. I've been out of the military for a long time now. I left there to do my own thing, and now I teach people how to do the same. I could give you the phone numbers of a dozen people who'd vouch for that.'

'Teach them to do what?' Salt asked suspiciously.

'To protect vulnerable people and stop bad things happening to them,' Ben said. 'And if something bad's already happened, to help them get out of it. To find people who've been kidnapped, or who've got into trouble.'

'So you're a detective?'

'Not exactly.'

'A cop?'

'Definitely not,' Ben said.

Salt narrowed his eyes. 'Are you looking for someone now?'

Ben nodded. 'Yes, I am. I'm looking for a young woman who might have got herself mixed up in something very dangerous. And I'm hoping you might be able to help me with information. I'll pay you for your time.' He dug some notes out of his wallet and held them up so that Salt could count them.

Salt's eyes flicked down to the money, then back up to meet Ben's. 'Cash up front.'

Ben tossed the money across the table. Salt palmed it and stuffed it in his pocket. He smiled. 'Now, what if I don't feel like talking?'

'Then I might feel like snapping your neck,' Ben said.

215

Salt swallowed. 'What information do you want?'

'I want to know about Kammler.'

Salt gave a dark little chuckle. 'Of course. Seems like everyone's getting interested in Kammler all of a sudden. There's a lot of weird shit going on, man.'

'Are you saying someone else has approached you?'

'Not for a while. I'm keeping my head down low.'

'What about before?'

Silence.

'The neck-snapping part still applies. I thought we had a deal.'

'There was the German.'

'What German?'

'This crazy German girl.'

'Go on.'

Salt shrugged. 'There isn't that much to say. It was about eight, nine months ago, just before I left Manchester. She emailed me, same as you did. Wanted to talk to me about Kammler. Said her name was Luna, and she was based somewhere in the Black Forest. Offburg, Hoffenburg, something like that.'

'Offenburg?' Ben knew of the place. It was close to Strasbourg, near the border between France and Germany.

Salt nodded. 'That's it. But I wouldn't take that too seriously, man. I knew right away she was phoney. Told me she sold ceramics.' He smiled knowingly. 'Like someone who sells ceramics would be genuinely interested in this stuff. I tell you, man, the covers they come up with are pretty fucking thin sometimes.'

Ben asked, 'Did she arrange a rendezvous with you?'

Salt nodded again. 'St Peter's Square in Manchester. She was very keen to meet. Flew over the same day. At least, that's what she said. The woman I saw might not have been the same one. Might have been one of her team, you know?'

'So you turned up for the RV.'

'Oh, I turned up, all right. Old Lenny always turns up.'

'But you didn't talk to her. You did what you did with me, took her picture from a distance and then buggered off. That's a very bad little habit, Lenny.'

Salt flushed angrily. 'Got to protect myself, haven't I? Can't be too careful.'

'Have you still got the picture?'

Salt hesitated a second, then shrugged and jerked his thumb back over his shoulder at the caravan.

'Let me see it.'

'What, now?'

'Right now, Lenny. It's important.'

Salt got up and went into the caravan. Ben heard him pottering about for a moment, then he re-emerged carrying a laptop and a battered screw-top tin labelled 'coffee'. He laid the computer on the picnic table, flipped it open and powered it up. While it was whirring into life he twisted the lid off the coffee tin. Ben caught the smell of ground beans. Salt shoved his hand into the brown powder, spilling a lot of it on the table, and came out with a small object wrapped in a miniature plastic Ziploc bag. He opened it, and Ben saw that the object was a computer USB flash drive.

Salt inserted it in one of the ports on the side of the laptop. 'You have to look away now,' he said, turning to Ben.

'Why?'

'Because I can't let you see me typing the password.'

Ben sighed and looked away. Salt rattled the keys, and then said, 'OK. You can look now.'

Ben turned back towards the computer as the contents of the flash drive came up onscreen. It contained a vertical list of JPG photo files, at least thirty of them.

'What is this?'

217

'Them,' Salt replied.

'Them?'

'My enemies.'

Ben scanned the list up and down. Salt had labelled each one with the date and place the picture had been taken.

'These are all people who've approached you?'

'Nah, nah. They wouldn't do that. It'd blow their cover. Most of these were just following me in the street.'

'So they could be anyone.'

Salt gave him a look. 'No way, man. I know when I'm being followed. So I take their picture, and then they don't come back, see, but they always send more. You've got to know your enemy.'

Ben didn't say anything.

Salt scrolled down the list of files, stopped and tapped a finger on the screen. 'This is her.' He clicked, and a photo of a woman flashed up.

Ben stared at it.

The photo was of a woman standing on a flight of steps leading up to what looked like a library. She was on her own, and even frozen on the screen she looked tense, as though waiting for someone but not quite sure what she was going to find when they turned up. It had been a dull, cloudy day in Manchester, and she was dressed for cool weather in a dark green fleece. She had the same slight build as the woman he'd chased in Switzerland, about five-eight, with shoulder-length blond hair blowing in the wind. There was just one problem.

Ben looked at Salt. 'She's got her back to the camera. You can't see her face.'

'Hold on. I got a better shot just after that.' More clicking, and Salt exchanged the picture for another. Same place, seconds later. Now the woman was turned towards the camera.

Ben's heart sank again. The definition on the face wasn't good. All he could see was a blur of features. She could have been anyone.

'Can you zoom in and sharpen it up?' Ben said.

Salt tapped a couple of keys and the image expanded. The woman's face disappeared offscreen, so that Ben got a close-up of the dark green fleece and the designer logo on its breast. Then Salt flicked another couple of keys and her face panned back into view. Salt used the cursor to draw a rectangle around her head, clicked down a sub-menu and the image suddenly sharpened into focus.

Ben was drawn into the screen, so that nothing existed outside of it.

It was her. It was Ruth. If there'd been any doubt in his mind until that moment, now it had been suddenly blown away into spinning fragments like flying debris in a bomb blast.

Chapter Thirty-Four

Adam's eyes fluttered open to a world of blurs and echoes.

What happened to me?

He blinked, struggling to focus on the kaleidoscope of images and jumbled pieces of memory that were swirling randomly through his brain. Faces hovered in front of him, distorted and elongated, like reflections in the back of a spoon. He knew the distant voices he could hear were talking to him, but he couldn't make out the words. Nausea washed over him, and his eyelids felt weighed down with lead. He sank his chin on his chest and groaned. Tried to move and found he couldn't. Looked down at his hands, saw his fingers groping like claws. His wrists tied down, his arms pinned. The sudden fear opened his eyes wider and forced his brain to sharpen.

He was sitting in a wheelchair in a small room with grey walls and a bare bulb for a light. He wasn't alone. One of the figures in the room with him, standing watching him with his head slightly cocked to one side, was Pelham. Behind him stood the two armed guards he'd seen before and another he didn't recognise.

Now he was beginning to recall what had happened. He remembered the Kammler machine in the vault deep below. He remembered what he'd said to Pelham. Then the sudden shock of the man tripping him to the ground, effortlessly, like he was nothing, and holding him down while the needle had lanced painfully into his flesh.

And now he was here. But where was here? He tried to speak, but something was clamped against his lips and it wasn't until then he realised he was gagged.

Pelham's voice, gentle and soft. 'Just a mild sedative, Adam. You've been out no more than a few minutes. You might get a bit of a headache, but nothing serious. Now, let's get started.'

A guard stepped forward and grabbed the handles of the wheelchair. Adam felt himself being swivelled round, and he suddenly saw himself dimly reflected in a big glass pane in front of him. He looked like a wild man, eyes staring, strapped to the chair by leather belts around his wrists and ankles and another one across his chest. The gag over his mouth was like a ping pong ball, pulled tight into his mouth by a buckle behind his neck.

The glass in front of him was a window, and he was looking through into another room.

'I'm sorry you decided to be difficult, Adam,' Pelham's voice said behind him. He could see the man's reflection standing behind the chair. 'I'm disappointed. I was hoping you and I could have a good relationship.'

Through the window, Adam saw the door open and some-body walked into the other room. He'd seen that face before. It was the woman who'd brought him from his hotel. She turned to the window with that impassive, steely gaze he remembered from Graz. Her eyes seemed to be searching, and he realised that she couldn't see him. The window was a two-way mirror.

The door in the other room swung open again and a man walked in backwards, pulling something into the room. Adam knew him too. He was the muscular, bull-necked man who had been with the woman in Graz, the one who had hit him in the back of the head in the hotel corridor. The thing he was pulling into the room was some kind of trolley. Adam's fuzzed-out brain took a second to register what it was.

When he did, horror shot up through him like lava in an erupting volcano.

The upper tier of the medical trolley was covered with shiny implements. Scalpels, drills, saws, needles. A large serrated knife. Beside it, a meat cleaver with a big square-nosed blade and a wooden handle.

The stocky man rolled the trolley across to the far wall and left the room. The woman took her time walking over to it. With her back to the two-way mirror she kneeled down beside it to pick something from the lower shelf, then stood up holding some kind of opaque plastic bundle. Adam watched as she unfurled it and realised it was an apron, the kind that slaughterers wore for butchering animals. She tied the apron strings neatly around her narrow waist, then reached into the front pocket, took out a pair of rubber gloves and pulled one on, then the other.

They're going to torture me, Adam was thinking. They're showing me the implements. He felt his bowels twitch.

But then the door of the room opened again, and the stocky man walked in backwards again clutching the handle of another wheeled trolley. This time it was heavier, and his tall companion from before was helping him with it.

But Adam wasn't watching them. When he saw what they were bringing in, he started screaming through the gag and thrashing against his bonds.

The trolley was a workbench on wheels. Lying on his back across its pitted wooden surface, chained to its four corners by his wrists and ankles, stripped to his underwear, was Rory.

All Adam could hear was the screaming and crying and pleading of his son as they wheeled him in.

'Let me go! Dad! Dad! I want my dad! Don't hurt me!' His back was arched as he struggled against the cuffs, the pale skin stretched over his ribs. He looked sickly and fragile and ill with terror.

Adam fought the leather straps holding him to the chair with every muscle in his body. He thought his heart was going to give out.

'I told you I was just someone with a job to do,' Pelham said quietly. 'And I always do my job. Even if it's not very pleasant. And this isn't going to be, Adam. I'm sorry.'

The two men wheeled the bench into the middle of the room, then stepped back to the side and let the woman take over. She glanced at the two-way mirror and nodded, and Adam saw a thin smile spread over her stony face. It was the first expression he'd seen on it. She seemed to be watching him, looking right at him as though she could sense his presence on the other side of the glass and knew what he was feeling.

'Her name is Irina Dragojević,' Pelham said behind him. 'The less you know about her background, the better. Of all the unsavoury things she does for a living, this is her favourite. She's an expert. That's why she was hired for this job, to do the things that the rest of us won't. She enjoys it, Adam. You can see it in her eyes.'

Adam was bellowing through the gag, twisting his head from side to side and trying to bite the material apart as he watched the woman walk slowly around the boy on the bench and go over to the instrument trolley. She ran her hand along the row of implements, like a chef selecting the best tool for the task in hand. A heavy hacker to chop through a tough joint, a long slim blade to fillet a fish. Her

224

fingers rested on the handle of a scalpel. She picked it up and examined the blade against the light, ran her gaze thoughtfully along the cutting edge. She shook her head, neatly replaced the scalpel and picked up the big meat cleaver. She weighed it in her hand and nodded to herself. Looked slowly back at the two-way mirror and one side of her mouth twisted into a smile of anticipation.

Next to her on the bench, Rory was struggling harder than ever, fingers clawing at the wooden bench, veins standing out horribly on his neck, screaming so hard Adam was terrified that his lungs would burst.

The woman's gaze swivelled down at the child. She stared for a moment, then drew back her free hand and slapped him across the face, twice, with cracks that echoed in the room.

'Quiet,' she said.

The harsh blows silenced Rory's screams. His chest heaved and he began to sob piteously.

Adam wasn't a violent man. He'd never enjoyed nor invited confrontation, never been in a fight, always dreaded trouble. Once, when he'd been a student in New York, a tough guy in a bar had spilled his drink to see if the shy boy would put up his fists. Adam had left the place as quickly as he could, and never returned.

But if he could have got free of the chair, he'd have been through that window like a missile and he would have sawn open that bitch's throat right there on the floor with a shard of broken glass and tasted the spray of her blood and spit in her face as she died.

'You still have time to reconsider,' Pelham said. 'I wouldn't like you to think I was being unreasonable.'

On the other side of the glass, the woman slid the blade of the cleaver along Rory's body, up his stomach to his chest, then over the trembling curve of his shoulder and down his arm. It stopped at his left wrist. Played on the skin, just hard enough to leave a white mark.

Then the woman took deep breath, looked as if she'd just seen God, and raised the cleaver eighteen inches in the air.

'*Noooo!*' Adam screamed through the gag.

The blade paused, catching the light. The woman glanced back at the mirror with raised eyebrows and a look that said 'Shall I go on?'

Rory wasn't struggling any more. His breath seemed to be coming in rapid gasps.

'Well, Adam?' said Pelham's voice in his ear as he bent close to him. 'Your choice. She'll start with the left wrist, then she'll do the left ankle and go on working her way round. She's waiting for me to tap on the glass. Once for no, twice for yes. What shall it be? Do you really want your son to be maimed for life?'

Adam felt fingers at the back of his neck, and the gag went slack. He shook it free and it dropped into his lap. He twisted his head round so that he could see Pelham in the corner of his eye.

'Make her stop,' he pleaded. His voice came out as a croak. 'Don't let her hurt my boy. Please. I'll do anything.'

'All this could have been avoided, Adam. You have to learn there are consequences to your actions.'

'Please,' Adam sobbed. His eyes were screwed up in agony. Mucus dripped in strands from his chin.

'You'll give me your word of honour? That you won't defy me again? Because next time I won't give you a second chance.'

Adam hung his head, breathing hard. Then nodded.

'I'd like us to be friends, Adam. I really would. And friends don't ever lie to each other. You're not lying to me, are you?'

226

'I swear to God. I swear. Don't hurt him.'

Pelham straightened, stepped over to the glass and tapped loudly, once. He held his hand there, and for a terrible instant Adam thought he was going to tap a second time. But then he took his hand away.

Behind the glass, the woman's eyes glinted with rage. She slammed the cleaver back down on the trolley, ripped off her gloves and apron and stormed out of the room. The stocky man and his tall companion moved in silence towards the bench and wheeled the trembling, whimpering boy back out through the door.

Adam was left staring at an empty room.

Pelham wheeled the chair round brusquely to face him. 'So let's start again, shall we?'

Adam nodded weakly.

Pelham undid the straps holding his wrists and ankles, then unbuckled the leather belt around his chest. Adam slumped in the chair. His hands were as pale as a corpse's, and the pain was excruciating as the blood started flowing back into them.

'You told me you left your notes in the safe in that smart house of yours in Ireland. Is that right?'

Adam let out a defeated sigh. 'In my study,' he whispered.

'Such a stupid thing to have done. Look at the time you've wasted, and the unnecessary stress you've inflicted on your son. No parent should ever allow their child to experience trauma like that. I only hope he can forgive you.' Pelham pulled up a stool, sat down and took out a little notebook and pencil. 'Right. Now that you've decided to see reason, you're going to tell me exactly where those notes are and how to get to them. Then I'll be sending Irina and her colleagues over immediately to fetch them, and I won't be expecting them to return empty handed. Understand?'

'I understand,' Adam murmured.

'Now, I know you're a very clever chap and you've got that whole house password-controlled. So I want you to give me all the necessary codes to get into and around it. Start talking.'

Adam told him everything. The passwords for the gate, the front door, the study, the safe, even the bedrooms.

Pelham looked pleased as he stood up and headed for the door. 'See how easy it can be?' He paused with his hand on the handle and waved the pad. 'I'm going to give this information to our friend Irina. Then we'll get you cleaned up and you can start familiarising yourself with that thing downstairs. Making that machine work is your life from this moment on, Adam. And your son's, too.'

When Pelham was gone, Adam sank his chin on his chest, put his hands over his face and sobbed. He didn't care about the guards in the room with him. Dignity no longer served any purpose.

Then he went rigid with fear as a thought struck him like a bullet to the head.

Sabrina. He'd forgotten all about her.

Oh, God. Sweet Jesus. Please don't let Sabrina still be there.

Chapter Thirty-Five

'Is she the one you're looking for?' Salt asked him.

'Yes,' Ben said quietly. 'It's her.'

'Any idea who she is?'

'Some idea.'

'You going to tell me? Could come in handy.'

'No, I'm not.' Ben had to speak carefully. He could hardly breathe.

'She's a spook, isn't she? One of Them. That's what They do, man, they hook them in. Brainwash them. Turn them into automatons to carry out their missions.' He pointed. 'I'm sure these are the bastards who killed Julia and Michio. It's all got to do with Kammler, see? The whole thing.'

Ben stared at him. 'Julia and Michio?'

Salt nodded through a swig of beer. 'Julia Goodman and Michio Miyazaki. They were part of the Krew,' he mumbled. 'Like me. We were all in it together.'

'I don't get it. What crew? You mean they were lab assistants like you at Manchester?'

Salt shook his head. 'No, man. Julia was my boss. She was head of department. Michio was a planetary scientist based in Tokyo. I'm talking about the Kammler Krew.'

This was getting more and more impenetrable. 'What happened to them?'

'Climbing accident. Heart attack. At least, that's what the official reports will tell you. But here's what really happened. I was in email contact with them all the time. Not every week, you know, but often enough. Then, bang, they're gone. Off the radar. Vanished. So I make a few enquiries, don't I? I'm told that Julia's taken a long holiday. OK, she was seriously into hiking and climbing, that kind of thing. But she never mentioned anything to me about a holiday. Next thing you know, she's fallen off a mountain in Spain. Dead, of course. Meanwhile, I hear from Michio's brother who tells me Michio was off on a research trip to America. Maybe that's true and maybe it isn't. But guess what? Wouldn't you know it, Michio gets stung by a scorpion, goes into shock, dies of heart failure. Both of them killed in a short space of time, and nothing to link them whatsoever except for one thing. Both members of the Kammler Krew. See? *Ha.*' Salt slapped the table.

Ben was feeling a growing surge of unease as he listened. It started in his guts and worked its way upwards until his throat felt clamped and his heart was thudding. If what Salt was saying was the truth, it meant that the stakes had just risen from attempted kidnap to actual abduction and murder.

And was Ruth part of it?

A dull roar filled his ears. His eyes lost focus.

Salt jabbed his finger again at the screen, making it wobble on its hinges. 'So who knows, man? What side is she on? The assassins', or someone else's? That's the world we live in, man. You can't trust anybody.' He paused, looking down at Ben's hand. 'Hey. You're bleeding on my table. I eat off this table.'

Ben followed his gaze and realised that he'd crushed his can in his fist without knowing it. The thin metal had sheared, leaving a sharp edge that had gashed his palm. A trickle of blood was dripping across his hand onto the wood. He wiped it away, struggling to clear his mind.

'I'm not getting this, Lenny. Why would these people, whoever they are, be going after scientists?'

Salt frowned at him, apparently taken aback, as though it was the stupidest question of all time.

'Maybe it's to do with tests of some kind?' Ben said, remembering what Don Jarrett had told him.

Salt's brow crunched up into a grimace. 'Tests?'

'Tests on the gas chamber. Poison residues in the ground, something like that? But why physicists? That would be something a chemist would do.'

Salt stared. 'You've got this totally wrong, man. This has nothing to do with gas chambers.'

'Holocaust deniers,' Ben said. 'It's about people who . . .' But he could see the deepening look of consternation on Salt's face, and his voice trailed off.

'No way, man.'

'But Kammler was the designer—'

'I know that,' Salt interrupted him. 'SS Building Division, and all that shit. But that's a whole separate thing. Forget about the Holocaust and all that. That's not why people are going after the Kammler stuff. This is about science.'

Ben stared at him. 'Science?'

'Weird, weird shit.' Salt shook his head. 'Like you wouldn't believe.'

'As in Nazi time machines and UFOs? You're right. I don't.'

'You've got to be open, man. There's stuff out there that would blow your mind. The Germans were developing all kinds of far-out technology in the war. Heard of the Foo Fighters? Those lights that the British bomber crews saw on night missions over Germany that would just, like, hover there and then go whizzing across the sky like nothing anyone had ever seen before or could explain? Who do you think made those? And where d'you think the Yanks stole it from

231

after the war? Philadelphia Experiment. Heard of that? US Navy special optical cloaking device, 1943? They made a whole ship disappear, man. Right into the ether, with all the crew on board. Then brought it back. Electromagnetic fields, anti-gravity. Weird science is all real, man. Everything you've ever heard of is real. But the fucking spooks use disinformation to cover it up, discredit a few scientists here and there so that nobody will take it seriously. Meanwhile the bastards know full well it's all true and they're hiding it from the world.'

Salt's voice started fading away into the background of Ben's thoughts, and after a while Ben could hardly hear him at all as he sat there ranting and gesticulating, his eyes wide with indignation, his wizened face cracked open in a snaggle-tooth snarl.

Ben closed his eyes and remembered that day in Switzerland. Replayed the events in the clearing, the kidnappers coming out of the trees in their black combat clothes and masks. The swastika badges on their jackets.

He remembered them clearly. He hadn't imagined it. And much as he despised the idea of his sister wearing that badge, until now he'd at least had some clear grasp of what was going on – or had thought he had. It had seemed to fit so perfectly with what Steiner had said. Yet what Salt was telling him blew the whole logic of the situation out of the window. Suddenly everything was changed, turned upside down.

Now his head was aching with concentration as he tried to make sense of it all. There was just one clear thread running through the mess. It was the clear, unalterable fact that, whatever the hell this was about, this woman calling herself Luna, but who was really his lost sister Ruth, had attempted to talk to Lenny Salt about Kammler. He didn't know why she had – that could come later. For now, all that mattered was the evidence he was looking at on the screen in front of him. She'd come a long way to talk to Salt, and that meant she was determined. Determined enough, perhaps, to want to talk to someone else when Salt failed to honour their rendezvous.

Ben thought about it for a moment, then looked up at Salt and asked, 'This group, this crew or whatever it was. Was it just you, Michio and Julia? Just the three of you?'

Salt shook his head. 'There were four of us, for a while at least. Until Adam dropped out.'

'Adam?'

'Adam Connor. O'Connor now. Changed his name. Irish roots, but he's American. He was Professor of Applied Physics at the University of New York.'

'You haven't mentioned anything happening to him. Does that mean he's still alive?'

'He was when I talked to him a few days ago,' Salt said.

'You told him your theory about Michio and Julia?'

Salt nodded. 'I warned him, and if he's got any sense he'll keep his head down, like me.'

'How did he react?'

'Oh, he probably thinks I'm paranoid. Mad old Lenny. Serve him right if they do get him.'

Ben paused, thinking hard. 'When did you take down the Kammler page on your website, Lenny?'

'When all this happened. To protect myself.'

'Before you took the page down, was Adam's name mentioned there?'

Salt looked puzzled. 'Yeah, it was, until he made me take it off. He didn't want to be associated with us any more. Thought it was bad for his reputation or something.'

'So Luna could have found him, the same way she found you.'

Shrug. 'I suppose.'

'Is Adam into conspiracies the way you are, Lenny?'

Salt flushed. 'No, he's got his head in the sand like everyone else.'

'So if she'd turned up, he wouldn't necessarily have tried to avoid her. But months later, nothing's happened to Adam. So she can't have been involved with whatever happened to your friends.'

'Maybe that's just what they want us to think,' Salt said. 'See how they fuck with our minds, man?'

Ben ignored him. He was thinking about this American guy. The man sounded like a sensible kind of person, as different from Lenny Salt as it was possible to be. Nothing made sense any more, and maybe it was an outside chance – but what if Adam had actually spoken to Ruth? He might know something. She might have given him a phone number, an email address. Even terrorists lived normal lives, lived in regular homes like everyone else. Or she might have given him a surname. Even a fake name could be a useful lead.

'You'd better give me O'Connor's number. I'd like to talk to him.'

'I can't give it to you. I don't have it.'

'Lenny—'

'Seriously, I don't have his number. I never did. I don't like to use phones, man. They're always listening.'

'I'm going to be pretty annoyed if I have to travel all the way to America just because you don't like to talk on the phone.'

'He's not in America any more.' Salt pointed west, through the trees. 'He's just across the water there.'

'Across the water?'

'Ireland. He moved there, out in the Wicklow Hills near

Dublin. Got a smart house business, lives out in the sticks by a lake.'

'Will he be at home?'

Salt shrugged. 'Don't see why not. He said something about expecting a visitor to stay when I saw him, so I don't think he's going anywhere.'

Ben looked at his watch. It was nearly quarter to two. He could drive from here to Pembroke Dock, catch the first ferry and cut across to Rosslare, then head north towards the Wicklow Hills. He should be there by nightfall.

Chapter Thirty-Six

Night was falling fast and early over *Teach na Loch* as the gathering storm rattled the glass in the windows. Sabrina looked out at the black clouds scudding across the sky and the ripples distorting the moon's glow on the surface of the lake. Then, as she watched, a cloud passed in front of the moon and the water went dark. The gently rolling hills were suddenly black, ominous silhouettes against the even blacker sky.

Not a prick of light anywhere to be seen, not a single person for miles. It made her feel very alone in the isolated house, and she found herself wishing she were back in noisy, cramped London.

The cream floor-length curtains suddenly swished shut without warning, making her jump before she realised that it was the house detecting the sudden change in the light and closing the curtains automatically. Three side lamps came on simultaneously a second later, the eco-bulbs glowing dull at first and then brightening.

'Would you like the fire on?' asked the soothing, electronic female voice from somewhere and nowhere.

'Go screw yourself,' Sabrina said to it. Every time she came here, Adam had installed some new piece of gadgetry, and

237

it always took her by surprise. Pretty soon there'd be a robot arm in the bathroom waiting to wipe your ass.

She walked over to the big, soft sofa, stretched herself out on it and went back to her thoughts.

Still no word from Adam all day. She'd been hoping he'd at least call her from Edinburgh to let her know when he was coming back. She'd tried calling him, but his phone was always off. And of course it was way too much to expect him to bother to answer the three messages she'd left him.

It was getting harder to know what to do. Why was Adam acting so oddly? Had he stashed Rory away at tennis camp so that he could go off with some woman he'd met? But that didn't make sense. If he'd met someone, why the furtiveness? It wasn't like he had anything to hide. Oh, wait, maybe she was married. That would explain a lot. He wouldn't want to let his little sis know about that kind of thing. Little sis who was pushing thirty but still had to be treated like a kid.

Or maybe Adam wasn't acting oddly at all, and he was right about Rory's practical joke, and there *was* a glitch with the email dates, and Rory had got himself another phone, and she was just winding herself up pointlessly with bull- shit delusions. That would make more sense, Sabrina thought – and it was almost certainly what the cops would have said about it all, if she'd been dumb enough to go to them. She'd been tempted a few times that day to call them. Glad she hadn't.

She jumped up from the sofa, a vision of a gin and tonic in a tall, frosted glass suddenly filling her mind. As she padded down the corridor in her bare feet, the house sensed the movement and turned lights on to guide her way. She walked into the kitchen and it was suddenly a blaze of white light.

'I *am* capable of flipping a switch, you know,' she muttered. 'Fucking smartass house.'

The house didn't respond. At least it didn't ask her, *Shall I put the kettle on?*

'Frank Sinatra,' she called out.

This time the house responded instantly with 'Come Fly With Me' from hidden speakers all around the room.

She mixed her drink, sliced a lemon, clinked ice in the glass and took a slurp. 'Cheers, Frank.' Then she added some more gin for good measure, left the kitchen and the lights escorted her back down the corridor.

What's the matter with you? she thought to herself. Why couldn't she just chill out and enjoy what was left of her vacation?

Well, maybe it's got something to do with being left all alone in a dark, creepy house that talks to you and makes things happen by themselves, with nobody around for a mile in every direction and a storm blowing outside.

As she thought this, a gust of wind hit the building and she was sure she felt it move.

'What is this place, Tornado Alley?' she muttered to herself. Wondering for a moment about what she would do if there was a power cut, she quickly reassured herself that her oh-so-scientifically-minded and supremely clever brother would have a genny down in the basement if it came to it.

She slumped back down on the sofa with her drink, grabbed the remote control, aimed it at the giant wall-mounted TV and pressed a button.

The TV stayed blank. Instead, a bright flame whooshed up to fill the electronically-controlled open fireplace below it.

Sabrina cursed. Why did all the goddamn remotes have to look exactly the same? She killed the fire with another touch of a button, chucked the remote down and picked up the right one to turn on the TV. Flipped through a bunch of channels and landed on a rom-com movie she'd seen years ago but liked enough to watch again.

She settled back against the cushions, getting in the mood and smiling to herself as Meg Ryan and Billy Crystal went through their bickering, fast-talking routine.

Suddenly, lights came on in the corridor. One after another, click, click, click. And stayed on.

She frowned. 'Adam, is that you?'

She half-expected him to walk into the room, brushing rain off his jacket and putting down his case, calling, 'I'm ho-ome.'

But there was no reply.

Sabrina muted the TV. 'Adam?' she called again. Still nothing. She got up from the sofa, stepped across the room and peered out into the corridor. The lights were already fading again.

'Is someone there?' There was a tremulous little edge to her voice that she wished hadn't come out. Her heart began to beat faster.

Outside, the thunder rumbled, and the rain lashed down harder on the windows and the skylights.

Sabrina was frozen to the spot, staring out into the dark corridor.

Something moved.

She tensed.

Cassini came slinking out of the darkness.

'Oh, Cass, you almost scared the shit out of me,' she sighed. 'Jesus.' She couldn't help but chuckle with relief as she scooped the cat off the floor and walked back to the sofa, holding him in her arms. 'Don't you ever think about doing that to me again, pal. OK?'

She went back to the sofa, took another gulp of gin and tonic and turned the movie sound back on. Cassini draped himself across her lap, so floppy he felt boneless, and she stroked him absently. She could feel the tiny vibration of his purring resonating through her, relaxing her.

'I would be proud to partake of your pecan pie,' said Billy Crystal in a funny voice up on the screen. Sabrina smiled.

And the cat's body suddenly tightened like a spring on her lap, and his needle-like claws dug through her jeans and stabbed into her skin. She let out a cry of pain. The cat was up on his paws, arched. Then he jumped off her and darted away.

Then Sabrina looked up and saw that the lights were back on in the corridor.

And that there was a man standing there.

Watching her.

Chapter Thirty-Seven

Sabrina shrieked and took off across the open-plan living room towards the stairs.

Too slow. The man was squat and heavy with muscle, but he was quick on his feet and in two powerful bounds he was on her. She went crashing into a side table, rolling and lashing out at him with her bare feet. A grunt as her heel connected with his eye socket; he let go of her and she scrambled to her feet and made the stairs. Her legs felt ready to buckle under her as she raced up the open treads. His footsteps pounded up behind her. Then she was on the landing and launched herself down the glass corridor.

The first door she came to was the master bedroom, and she grabbed the chrome handle with both hands and jerked it open. Staggered inside just as the man came sprinting down the corridor after her. He shoved his hand inside the door, and she slammed the edge of it hard on his fingers.

He let out a sharp cry. She yanked it open and slammed it again hard enough to sever those damn fingers – but he'd jerked his hand away and was roaring with pain outside the door as she braced her weight against it and remembered the password Adam had told her.

'Lock!' she shouted.

The house responded and the bedroom door instantly clunked as the mechanism engaged.

Sabrina stood there panting, her hands shaking, doubled over with the pain from the stitch in her side. She looked around her. She'd never been in Adam's bedroom before. There was a big leather bed, a bookcase filled with science and architecture books, a bureau and a sofa. Next to the sofa was her brother's prized candy-red Fender Stratocaster guitar, leaning up against an amplifier. Nothing she could use to defend herself. If this had been the States, there'd have been a pistol or a shotgun for home defence.

Calm. Calm. Pull yourself together. She'd read that in these situations, barring a loaded .357 Magnum in the bedside table drawer, the best thing to do was stay out of the way, let the thieves take whatever the hell they wanted and not confront them. She was safe in here. The locks were sturdy. Everything was fine. Stolen TVs and silver were easily replaced.

But how had he got past the security? This place was tighter than Fort Knox. Panic welled up like a tide. Her mobile was downstairs. She was stranded up here.

She glanced at the window. Rain was lashing on the outside of the glass. Maybe if she could get out onto the balcony and run round the outside of the house, she could scramble down the fire escape and get away.

At that moment she realised the sounds of pain had gone quiet outside the door. Suddenly she heard his voice again, just the other side of the thick wood. He didn't scream, 'I'm going to get you, bitch.' That would have been bad enough, but what she heard was even worse. He spoke one word, in a normal tone that scared her almost to death.

'Cassini.'

And the lock clunked open.

The lock clunked open and she stared at the handle in horror. Watched it turn, and before she could react or think to shout 'lock!' the door opened. And he was in.

She backed away across the bedroom, past the sofa towards the window. He padded in towards her. She could see the fire in his eyes and the bunched muscles under his rain-speckled shirt. The fingers of his right hand were bloody. His teeth were bared in a fierce grin as he stalked across the room.

Her hand brushed something hard. Adam's guitar, propped up next to the sofa. A big, heavy lump of solid wood, like a musical axe. She wrenched it up in both hands and swung it at his head.

The man stepped back out of the arc of the blow, and the momentum of the heavy guitar almost carried Sabrina off her feet. It smashed into the bookcase. Glass flew everywhere.

The man came at her. She recovered her balance and swung the guitar at him again with a grunt of effort, and this time it caught him hard on the shoulder. She was sure that she'd have shattered a normal man's collar bone, but with all the muscle on his upper body the blow just glanced off and he pawed the guitar out of her hands as he rushed her like an angry bull. He lashed out and backhanded her across the face, and she shrieked and went sprawling back across the bed. He grabbed her by the hair, hit her again.

Then he clambered on top of her, driving the air out of her with his weight, straddling her hips and pinning both her arms behind her head with one strong hand. She fought back, spat in his face, but he was heavy and powerful and there was little she could do to resist him. With his free hand he started ripping at her clothes, fumbling at the fastening of her jeans and yanking down the hem of her waistband. Started grabbing at his zipper.

245

No, no, no. Please. Not this.

He had her jeans down past her hips and she was screaming for him to stop when the bedroom door burst open and a woman and a tall man walked in. The woman was holding a stack of plastic CD cases.

Sabrina's attacker twisted round to look at the two of them, and muttered angrily in a language she didn't understand. The woman froze, taking in the scene, then stepped across to the bed. Her arm shot out and she grabbed a fistful of the stocky guy's hair. Jerked his head back harshly, making him cry out in pain, and dragged him off Sabrina.

Sabrina rolled off the edge of the bed, pulling up her jeans and trying to cover herself up. Her hands were shaking so violently that she could barely do up the button of her jeans. Across the bedroom, the woman still had the man's hair bunched up tight in her fist. His eyes were popping with pain. She wrenched his head back and forth a couple of times in disgust and then let him go.

Cowering by the side of the bed, Sabrina was on the point of thanking the woman for saving her from being raped. But then the woman turned to stare at her, and the cold look in her eyes made Sabrina recoil.

'Who are you?' Sabrina asked her.

The woman's stare bored into her. 'Shut up,' she said in English. Then she turned to the men and made a sharp gesture as she headed for the door. The tall man followed.

The stocky guy knew what to do. He scooped Sabrina up in his arms and dragged her out of the bedroom, ignoring her screams. She was powerless in his grip, and could feel the suppressed fury pulsing out of him. The woman led the way down the open-tread staircase, across the glass-roofed rear atrium and through the tall glass doors onto the rear terrace overlooking the lake. Rain was slashing down onto

246

the concrete, driven diagonally by the howling wind and hitting so hard it was bouncing. In the pale light Sabrina could see beyond the terrace and garden to the grassy slope down to the lakeside. The wind was churning up the water, and white-crested waves were rolling up the shore and breaking against the little wooden jetty where Adam kept his rowing boat.

Sabrina's bare feet hardly touched the ground as the powerful man hauled her out across the terrace. The woman turned to him, her blond hair plastered across her face by the wind, and issued stern, authoritative commands. He just nodded. Then the woman gestured to the tall man and led him away, up the flagstone path that skirted around the side of the house towards the front yard and out of sight.

The man dragged Sabrina closer to the lakeside. They were on the grass now, and she could hear his boots squelching on the sodden ground. Her hair was in her face and the rain stung her eyes and she could barely see. She writhed in his arms. It was like being clasped by a machine. His hand was pressed hard over her face, muffling her cries of protest. As he walked, half-dragging and half-carrying her, he stumbled on the rough ground and his fingers slipped an inch and she could open her mouth.

She bit hard, felt her teeth break skin and flesh.

He ripped his hand away and slapped her, then again. And again. She could feel his blood on her face. Heard the rasp of his voice close to her ear as he spoke to her in that strange language. Then he laughed.

She knew what the woman had told him to do. His job was to drown her in the lake.

She felt her heels drag on the stones as they neared the shoreline. His feet splashed into the water, and the icy shock took her breath away and made her heart stutter as he dumped her body into the waves. She screamed again, but it turned into a gurgle as he pressed a big flat palm against her face and drove her head down under the surface.

The water roared in her ears and filled her nose. Bubbles streamed out of her mouth. She flailed desperately with her hands, managed to fight free of his grip. Broke the surface and filled her lungs with air before he pushed her back down under the icy black water. She battled to hold her breath as her fingernails raked at his hands and wrists. But he was just too strong.

She knew she couldn't hold on much longer. In a few short seconds the water was going to come pouring into her lungs and he was going to hold her there until she drowned.

She was going to die. This was it.

Then suddenly she was gasping and wheezing and tasting air as her head burst free of the surface again. The man had let go of her. Through the coughing fit that racked her body she saw him go down on his knees, the water surging up to his neck and over his shoulders.

She blinked the water out of her eyes. A dark figure was standing behind the man, with an arm locked around his throat. A brutal twist, and Sabrina heard the crack over the roar of the wind as the stocky guy's neck snapped like a branch.

Then a hand was grasping her tightly by the arm and pulling her out of the lake.

Chapter Thirty-Eight

Ben hauled the coughing, spluttering woman up onto the shore. In his right hand was the automatic pistol he'd taken from her attacker's belt.

To come to an idyllic lakeside retreat to talk to a retired physics professor and find a gang of armed killers trying to murder a woman – Ben wasn't even trying to figure it out. The questions could come later, after he'd got himself and her out of this.

It had been on the approach to the house, the Audi's windscreen wipers batting away the thundering rain on full speed, that he'd spotted the beige Citroën Picasso parked at the gate. Innocuous enough, but a woman's scream of terror was a sound that could carry a long way, even through a stormy night. He'd killed his lights and engine and coasted the last few yards to the house, left the Audi hidden among the trees and come in over the wall. He could still hear the screaming as he'd sneaked through the grounds. Crouched behind a flowery shrub, he'd wiped the rain out of his eyes and watched the blond female and the tall man walk away around the side of the house and head back towards their car.

He'd been more interested in the woman. Everything about her cool, imperious bearing said that she was the leader. As she walked, she'd kept glancing at something in her hand.

Hard to tell from that distance, but Ben had thought it looked like she was holding a pile of CDs.

Then, as Ben had sat watching, his attention was quickly diverted to the second guy, the squat one with the muscles. It was becoming increasingly obvious that he didn't have good intentions towards the woman they'd dragged from the house.

In situations like that, it was hard to remain a passive observer.

Wishing there'd been time to conceal the attacker's body, Ben helped the frightened woman up the bank to the cover of the long grass, laid her down and crouched beside her in the shadows. Any minute now, the other two were going to be wondering what was keeping their friend so long, and they'd be back.

She shrank away from him, fear in her eyes. Water was dripping from her hair, and her clothing was soaked. Ben could feel his own wet shirt clinging to him, and the wind chilling his skin. He knew he had to get the woman inside the house quickly. Even in summer, hypothermia was a dangerous reality.

'I won't hurt you,' he said softly. 'What's your name?'

'Sabrina.' She wheezed, coughed up lake water. 'Who are you?'

'Sabrina, you're going to have to keep your head down. Don't do anything unless I say. Understand?'

The sound of car doors. Shouts carrying on the wind, right on cue.

'Slatan?' The woman's voice, harsh and edged with anger. The name and the accent sounded Bulgarian or Estonian to Ben.

He peered up over the long grass. The rain was moving on quickly. The wind tore a hole in the dark clouds and in the pale moonlight he saw the two figures approaching from the path along the side of the house, scanning right and left as they walked a few yards apart. Both had a grim, hard look and moved cautiously. Professional killers, Ben thought. And as they crossed the terrace to the edge of the grass, he saw the stubby black weapons they were holding in their arms that looked worryingly like Israeli Mini Uzi submachine guns. Sound suppressors, extended thirty-round magazines. The bright crimson dots of laser sight beams swept the lakeside. Whatever it was these people had come out here for, somebody wasn't taking any chances.

He quickly checked the pistol he'd taken from the dead man. Even in the dark, he could tell by touch what it was – a big-framed, old-fashioned Colt .45 automatic, maybe a Gold Cup or a Government model. It was a fancy piece, with an extended beavertail grip safety and a muzzle compensator to control recoil by diverting part of the gas blast from the barrel. But all the buttons and bells in the world couldn't disguise the fact that he had only eight rounds at best and barely visible iron sights that were next to useless for shooting in the dark, against state-of-the-art laser optics and the high-capacity fire-power of two machine guns. It didn't seem quite fair.

He shrugged to himself. One thing the SAS had taught him was that you did what you could with what you had. And he was lucky he had anything at all. He press-checked the breech. Glanced across at Sabrina and put a finger to his lips. Saw the whites of her eyes in the moonlight.

The woman and the tall man were about fifteen yards away when the woman suddenly stopped and pointed at the lake.

The floating dark shape in the water was exactly what Ben had been hoping they wouldn't spot. His stomach tightened like a fist as he watched and waited for their reaction.

The woman did pretty much what he expected. She was definitely the leader, and a decisive one. It took her less than two seconds to scan the long grass, jerk the cocking bolt on her Uzi with a ferocious snarl and let loose a ripping spray of gunfire that churned up the ground dangerously close to the grassy clump where Ben and Sabrina were hidden.

The ball was rolling. No choice. Ben could hardly make out his sights against the target but he fired back anyway. The flat punch of the .45 stabbed his ears and he felt the recoil kick back against his palm. Shooting almost blind, but he'd hit something, because the woman cried out and staggered back a step and fell, clutching her arm. The tall man instantly opened up with his Uzi, lighting up the night with his muzzle flash.

The sustained burst of fire drove Ben back down the slope, dragging Sabrina with him as clumps of earth and bits of grass showered down over them. Sabrina rolled in the dirt, wrapping her arms around her head for protection.

Ben scrambled back up the bank just in time to see the tall man helping the woman to her feet and the two of them retreating back towards the side of the house. He chased after them. Saw blood on the ground where the woman had fallen, and a trail of bright red spots along the path.

At that moment the moon was obscured by another black cloud and the grounds were plunged back into darkness. The man and woman were little more than shadows up ahead. Ben broke into a sprint. As he ran he pointed the Colt and let off three more blind shots that he instinctively knew all went wide of the mark. The flitting shadows darted around the side of the house and into the front yard. He heard running steps on the wet gravel. The sound of doors slamming and the Citroën's engine revving high, the rasp of spinning wheels.

Ben rounded the corner of the house and emerged into the yard just as the car was taking off at high speed. He fired at the taillights as they sped away from the gate and up the road, but they were already out of effective pistol range. He lowered the Colt and watched the headlamps carve through the bends, and then the Citroën was gone and the road was as black as the hills that merged into the night.

He turned away and started running back to Sabrina.

Chapter Thirty-Nine

The sky was clearing and the wind was dropping as Ben took Sabrina back to the house. He wasn't quite sure whether her passivity was a sign of trust for him or a symptom of shock, but her body was limp as he carried her in his arms, and her dripping hair nuzzled against his shoulder. She didn't seem able to speak, and the only sound she made was a weak sobbing as he carried her up the stairs to look for a bathroom. His first priority was to get her warm and dry. They could talk later.

He found the bathroom he was looking for on the first floor, and kicked open the door. Lights came on automatically as he carried her in, and he remembered what Lenny Salt had told him about Adam O'Connor's smart house technology business. He laid Sabrina gently down in a big cane chair in the corner, tore three fluffy cotton towels off a heated rail and wrapped them around her as he ran the bath to a temperature just warm enough to get her blood circulating again.

He kneeled down beside where she sat, checked her pulse and spoke softly to her. She murmured back. Her face was still pale, but colour was returning quickly. Once he was satisfied that she wasn't about to keel over, he left her alone to get out of her wet things and into the warm water, and went downstairs to check all the doors and windows. Everything had electronic locks that clunked like a car's central locking at the touch of a button. He checked each room in turn, the house sensing his movement and lighting the path ahead everywhere he went.

He could see no signs of a struggle anywhere, until he walked into the master bedroom back upstairs and found the rumpled bed, smashed bookcase and the electric guitar lying on the rug. Moving up to the second floor, the first door he tried led into what was obviously the bedroom of a young teenager. A single bed with an X-Men duvet set, a collection of electronic gadgets scattered across the floor, posters on the wall. He closed the door.

Across the broad, lushly carpeted landing from the boy's room was a darkened room with a half-open door. Ben went inside cautiously. Again the lights went on automatically for him as he entered, and he saw that he was in a large study.

Someone else had visited the room, and not long ago. Ben crouched down and felt the shoeprints on the carpet. They were still damp from the rain. Two sets of them, one larger and one smaller. The tall man and the woman had been here.

He stood up and looked around. The ultra-modern furnishings were sparse and tasteful. The walls were lined with framed black and white photos of space-age-looking houses in a variety of settings. Below a window overlooking the lake was a black leather swivel chair and a broad desk in ebony wood.

The damp shoeprints led past the desk to a wall safe in the corner. Ben went over to it and saw how the shoeprints were more concentrated here, overlapping as though the intruders had spent a few moments standing in this spot examining the contents of the safe. They hadn't bothered shutting the steel door after them, and it hung open. There was no keypad or dial visible anywhere, and he guessed that it was probably voice-activated using a password. No sign of forced entry. The intruders must have known the password.

Inside the safe were various folders and files marked with printed labels for things like tax and insurance, a couple of lockable steel cash boxes, a presentation case for an expensive Swiss watch, and two horizontal racks of CDs. Ben ran his eye along the double row of discs. None of them was music or DVDs. They were all computer files, and the professor appeared to keep his work life well organised because each little section was marked with labels obviously relating to his own smart house design concepts. CPU VOICE-ACTIVATION SYSTEM. IRIS SCAN RECOGNITION SYSTEM. EMERGENCY OVERRIDE SYSTEM. Ben ran his eye quickly along the line, then stopped.

There was an empty space in the rack where four CDs used to be. The label underneath the empty space was completely unlike the others. It said KAMMLER STUFF.

He gazed around the study for more clues. Nothing leaped out at him. He walked over to the desk. There were just a few items on its gleaming black surface. A chrome steel lamp, a closed MacBook and another framed photo, this time of a young boy of about thirteen smiling happily for the camera. Next to the computer was a phone handset off its charger with just one bar left on its battery life indicator, as though it had been left lying there for a few days by someone in a rush to get away. Near the phone was a ballpoint pen and a copy of the *Irish Times*, dated five days ago.

Noticing a scrawled note in ballpoint on the upper margin on the front page, Ben leaned down to read it. The scribble had been done in a hurry, but he could make out that it was a set of flight times from Dublin to Graz via Vienna, arriving 6.06 p.m. Austrian time.

He sensed a presence in the doorway and spun round quickly.

It was Sabrina. She was wrapped in a bathrobe with a towel round her hair and another one round her shoulders. Her eyes looked a lot brighter, and there was a flush of pink in her cheeks that hadn't been there before.

'I thought you'd gone.' She studied him curiously for a moment. 'You saved me,' she said softly. 'Thank you.'

'How do you feel?'

She gave a shaky chuckle. 'I'll live. Thanks to you. I don't even know your name.'

'It's Ben,' he said.

'Glad you showed up when you did, Ben.'

'You're probably wondering what I'm doing here.'

She tried to smile. 'Right now, everything is so screwed up, nothing seems that strange to me.'

'Is Adam your husband, Sabrina?'

She shook her head. 'He's my brother. Are you a friend of his?'

'I just want to ask him some questions. Where is he?'

'He's away on business.'

'In Austria?'

She frowned. 'Scotland. At least, that's what he said. But Rory's gone.'

Ben guessed that she was talking about the boy in the picture. 'What do you mean, he's gone?'

'He was kidnapped,' she blurted. 'I wasn't sure it was true, but now I know something's going on. I should have called the cops.' She looked at him as though a sudden thought had come to her. 'Are you—'

'No, I'm not the police. Nothing like that.'

258

'Then what are you? Just some guy who knows how to break necks and shoot guns?'

'I'll explain everything to you. But not here. We need to leave.'

She stared at him. 'Leave?'

'Your visitors seem to have found what they were looking for, but they might want to pay a return visit to tie up loose ends.'

Realisation crept into her eyes. 'You mean me?'

He didn't reply.

'Guess I don't have a lot of choice. Where are we going?'

'To the nearest pub.'

'Good. I need a drink.'

'Not to drink. To talk. Get some clothes on. My car's outside.'

Sabrina glanced up and down his body. 'You're soaked. You need to change. Try Adam's wardrobe.'

As she got dressed in the bathroom, he took her advice and found a change of clothes in the master bedroom. He gratefully stripped off his wet things, towelled himself down, and quickly pulled on the warm, dry clothes. The trousers were a thirty-six-inch waist, and he had to cinch the belt up tight to make them fit.

A couple of miles from the house was a small village with an inn. Ben parked up the Audi, left the Colt in his bag on the back seat and led Sabrina into the lounge bar. The fire was crackling in the chimney and the atmosphere was cheery with a lot of chatter and clinking of glasses. Irish folk music was playing for the benefit of the tourists, and shamrocks and Guinness logos lined the walls.

'Welcome home,' Ben said, looking around.

Sabrina shot him a curious glance.

'I used to live here in Ireland. Out west, Galway Bay.' He bought them each a double Bushmills and carried the drinks towards a little cubby-hole with a candlelit table for two.

Sabrina sat opposite him. Brushed the hair away from her face, sniffed and cupped her whiskey in trembling fingers.

'Let's talk,' he said.

Sabrina told him everything. About who she was, about her week's holiday in Ireland to be with her brother and nephew. About Adam's peculiar behaviour, the tennis camp and the Edinburgh conference and the strange phone call from Rory. 'The rest is pretty self-explanatory,' she finished. 'You saw what happened.' As she said it, her eyes clouded.

'I don't believe Adam's in Edinburgh,' Ben said. 'I'm pretty sure he took a plane to Austria. He'd been checking flight times before he left.'

'Why Austria?'

'Maybe to meet with the kidnappers and talk terms. Maybe that's where they're holding Rory. Maybe they've sent him on some kind of errand. Or else he's gone there looking for help, which could be a foolish move.'

Sabrina lowered her head against her hands. When she raised it and looked at him, her face was streaked with tears. 'Kidnappers. So you really think they've taken him?'

'I'm afraid that's what it looks like, Sabrina. I'm sorry.'

'But *why*? What do they want? Money, like a ransom? Adam isn't that rich. Richer than he was when he was an academic, but not what you'd call wealthy.'

'You don't have to be rich to be targeted by kidnappers,' Ben said. 'People will do anything to get their loved ones back.' He paused. 'But this isn't about money, I don't think.'

'Then what?'

'Information. I think they're using Adam for something, and Rory is their insurance policy.'

'My brother's a house designer. What information could he have that was so important?'

Ben asked, 'Did he ever mention the name Kammler to you?'

She looked blank, thought for a moment, then shook her head. 'Not that I can remember. Who's Kammler?'

'Your brother was involved in some kind of scientific research. He had some computer files on disc in his study safe. Those people took them. I think whatever is on those discs is what they were looking for.'

Sabrina was quiet for a moment, biting her lip in agitation. Then she reached for her bag and started rummaging in it.

'What are you doing?'

She found her phone. 'What I should have done days ago. I'm calling the cops. They'll know how to handle this.'

He shook his head and leaned across to grab her hand. 'That's not a good idea.'

'For Chrissakes, if he's in fucking Austria that's a lead, isn't it? Surely things can be done? Don't they have, like, Interpol and stuff for situations like this?'

'Look at me, Sabrina.'

She was quiet and looked at him.

'If you call the police, you're signing your nephew's death warrant.'

She went white. 'How can you know that?'

'Because Adam is under orders,' he said. 'That much is obvious. It's the reason he was acting strangely before he went away, the reason why he made up that cover story about the tennis camp and going to Edinburgh for business. The kidnappers will have made it clear to him that if he breathes a word of this to anyone, they'll harm Rory. The last thing anyone needs to do right now is start stirring things up.'

261

She didn't reply, looked down at the table.

'Now, imagine what you're going to put in motion if you involve the authorities in this. With all the best will in the world, it'll leak out. There's always someone willing to take a backhander in return for a juicy story. Television. Radio. Newspapers. A whole media circus, with the kidnappers watching every move. You might as well hold the gun to Rory's head yourself and pull the trigger.'

Alarm lit up her eyes. 'How come you know so much about all this stuff?'

'Because it was my job to deal with situations like this, and now I'm looking for someone who's been missing for a long time. I think that person is in deep trouble, and I have a strong feeling it's connected to the trouble your brother and nephew are in. Beyond that, right now I really can't say any more.'

She sighed. 'So what happens now?'

He leaned across the table and spoke gently. 'Sabrina, I do know one thing for sure. You weren't supposed to survive this evening. When those people go back to whoever sent them and report what happened, and that there's a witness—'

'They're going to come looking for me.' The words came out with a tremor, and she went a shade paler. Ben saw her pupils dilate with fear.

He nodded. 'It'll be easy for them to find out from Adam who you are and where you live. They only have to threaten Rory, and there isn't anything in the world he won't tell them. That's what kidnap is all about. Control.'

'It means I can't go home.'

'No. It could be dangerous.'

Her eyes brimmed with tears again. 'So where I am going to go? Stay with friends? What the hell do I tell them?'

'You tell them nothing. You can't be in contact with anyone you know. They can be traced, and you'd just be putting them in danger too.'

She looked helpless.

'Do you trust me?' he asked.

'I don't even know who you are. But you saved my life. What am I supposed to say?'

'London's a big place. You can easily lose yourself in it. I know someone there, a very close friend of mine whom I trust completely. I'll have to clear it with her, but I think she'd let you stay with her. You'd have to cancel everything, keep hidden, not even go out.'

Sabrina chewed her lip. 'For how long?'

'As long as it takes for me to sort things out.'

'Does that mean you'll find Adam and Rory?'

He took a deep breath. 'I'll find them.'

Chapter Forty

In the terrible place that Rory's world had become, all that separated night from day was whether he could see light under the cell door. When the light was on in the corridor outside, it meant it was day; and he lived in constant terror. When the corridor was in darkness, it meant his captors had gone to sleep. Like vampires, returning to their coffins, giving him a few safe hours to huddle in his bed and cry softly and try to be strong and brave and all the things he wanted to be. But more than anything, he wanted his dad to be here.

He had no idea what time it was or how long he'd been lying there under the sheets, burrowed in tight like a frightened animal. When he heard the cell door open and the footsteps walk across the stone floor towards the bed, every muscle in his body went rigid. A torch-beam scanned the room and he saw its circle of pale light land on the bed, shining through the sheets.

Whoever it was came closer, and he felt icy fingers of panic clench his heart as he thought of the hateful witch-woman who'd done those awful things to him just a few hours before. It was her. He could still feel the touch of the cold blade against his skin. Now she was back for more.

But when he felt someone sit on the edge of the mattress next to him and the warm, gentle hand on his shoulder, he knew it wasn't her. A joyful thought leapt through him at that moment. His dad was here, come to save him. He threw back the sheet and sat up in bed.

The face he saw, dimly illuminated in the torchlight, wasn't his father's. It was the short, ruddy-faced man who'd been bringing him his food.

Rory eyed him uncertainly. 'What do you want, Ivan?' he said with all the strength and confidence he could muster. There was still a shake in his voice, and he felt dizzy and sick.

Ivan put his finger to his lips. 'Shh. They do not know I am here,' he whispered in that thick accent of his. He flashed the light furtively back at the door, then let it shine back on his face. Rory could see the anger in his eyes.

'They should not have done that to you. I would not have allowed such a thing to happen. You must understand this, Rory.' Ivan reached into his pocket, brought something out and offered it to him.

Rory looked at it. It was a chocolate bar. He tore off the wrapper and ate greedily.

Ivan smiled as he watched him. 'Good,' he whispered. 'Eat. Get strong. You will need your energy.'

Rory chewed and swallowed until there was nothing left. Ivan gently took the wrapper from his fingers, stuffed it back in his pocket and handed him a tissue. 'Wipe your mouth with this. They must not know I brought you chocolate. They would kill me.'

Rory wiped the flecks of chocolate from the corners of his mouth and gave the tissue back to Ivan. 'Why?' he asked the man.

'Listen to me carefully. I am not one of them. I am here to spy on them.'

Rory's eyes widened and his heart began to thump. 'Are you a cop?'

266

'A special agent,' Ivan whispered. 'And I will get you out of here.'

'When?'

'Soon. Very soon, I promise you. But you must trust me. Will you trust me, Rory?'

Rory nodded quickly.

'Thank you. I know it is hard for you, and you are very scared. You are a good, brave boy.'

'Where's my dad? Is he here?'

'Shh. I think someone is coming.' Ivan turned off the torch, plunging the room into darkness. They both stared in the direction of the cell door. Any second now, Rory imagined the light was going to come on in the corridor and that woman was going to come marching in with the guards and find them together. They'd take Ivan away and kill him, and then he'd be alone again.

But nothing happened. The corridor remained dark and quiet.

Ivan let out a sigh of relief and turned the torch back on, shading its beam with his hand so that his face was half-lit and full of shadows. 'It is too dangerous for me to be here,' he whispered. 'I must go. I just wanted you to know that you have a friend in this place. I will not let them harm you. Everything will be fine. You have my word.'

'Ivan—'

'I will be back. Get some rest,' Ivan whispered. Then he slipped out of the door and Rory heard the soft click of the lock.

Chapter Forty-One

Ben called Brooke from Rosslare docks while he and Sabrina were waiting for the night ferry.

'Brooke? Sorry to be calling late. But I need a favour.'

'Fire away,' she said.

Without going into too much worrying detail, he outlined the situation. Brooke listened carefully, and when he'd finished she said, 'No problem. She'll be fine here. I'll make up the spare bedroom.'

He thanked her. 'I owe you one.'

The ferry crossing offered him a chance to grab some much-needed sleep. When they hit the Welsh coast dawn was breaking. Five hours of hard driving later, Ben was cutting through the south London traffic in driving rain and thinking of Jeff, probably well on his way to Nice by now for a week of sunshine, beer and pretty girls.

Brooke's place was in Richmond, a red-brick Victorian house split into flats. Ben had never been there before, and it wasn't until the door opened and he saw her standing there smiling at him that he was even sure he had the right place.

Her hair was loose over her shoulders, and she was wearing navy blue linen trousers and a light summer blouse the colour of her eyes. A string of jade beads hung around her neck.

She looked good. Really good. It wasn't until she said, 'Aren't you going to introduce us?' that Ben realised he'd been staring at her. He quickly introduced Sabrina, and Brooke said hello and led them both inside.

Stepping into Brooke's home felt a little strange to Ben, foreign yet oddly familiar, like a déjà-vu experience. Everything about the place – from the big comfy armchairs, to the cushions strewn everywhere, to the pine cones in the fireplace and the vases of fresh flowers and enormous pot plants that sat about on the polished wood floor – somehow spoke of her, *was* her. Django Reinhardt's 1930s gypsy jazz was playing in the background, and aromatic candles filled the apartment with the scent of vanilla and lotus.

'It's so kind of you to put me up,' Sabrina said.

'It'll be nice to have some company,' Brooke replied warmly. 'Now, I suppose you guys must want some breakfast.'

'Just some coffee,' Ben said. 'I'm not staying.'

'Would you mind if I freshened up first?' Sabrina asked.

'Sure. The bathroom's through there. Help yourself. There are towels in the airing cupboard.'

Sabrina left, and Ben stood about in the kitchen as Brooke made coffee. She served it in mugs and handed him one. His had a picture of the Pink Panther on it, and hers had Paddington Bear. She dribbled in a spoonful of honey, held the mug in both hands the way he liked, and sipped.

'Nice place,' he said, looking around him. The coffee was hot and strong. He took a big gulp and felt better. 'A bit more sophisto than Le Val.'

'I love Le Val,' she said. 'I'd swap it for this place any day.'

'I love it too,' he said quietly. Felt a twinge as he remembered the troubles there waiting for him.

'Won't you sit down? You look tired.'

'I'm fine.'

She looked at him with concern. 'What's happening, Ben? Last time I saw you, you were running off to Bruges. Where now?'

'Germany,' he said.

'Ruth?'

He nodded. 'It's her, Brooke. I saw a picture. No doubts.'

'I really hope you find her. Just remember what I said, about asking for help if you need it.'

'I haven't forgotten.'

'There's danger, isn't there?' she said, anxiously.

'A bit,' he admitted. He finished the last of the coffee, put down the empty Pink Panther mug and turned to go.

'You be careful, won't you?'

'Don't worry about me.'

'That's the stupidest thing you've ever said to me, Ben Hope. Of course I worry about you. You drive me completely nuts with worry sometimes.' Her cheeks had flushed red, and Ben was taken aback by the depth of emotion in her voice. She stepped quickly over towards him, put her arms around him and pressed her ear to his chest. Then looked up at him, and there was a tear rolling out of her eye and across the curve of her cheek. He reached up and gently dabbed it away with his fingers. Kissed her gently on the forehead. Then moved his mouth down and kissed her cheek, tasted the salty taste of the tear. Her skin felt soft against his lips.

She tensed and pulled away from him. 'Don't play with me,' she said quietly.

He frowned. 'I'm not.'

'I know you don't like me,' she said.

'What are you talking about? Of course I like you. I like you a lot.'

271

'But not the way I like you, Ben. Get it now?' The words seemed to come out against her will, as if they'd been kept submerged for a long time and she hadn't meant for them to come bubbling up.

He said nothing. Just looked at her, and could see the anguish in her face. It was a look he'd never seen before. It quickly turned to an angry blush, and she stepped away from him and went back to her coffee.

'Shit. I shouldn't have said that. Forget it, OK?'

Ben couldn't find the words for what he wanted to say. Before he had a chance to speak, Sabrina walked into the room, bringing a wafting scent of soap with her.

'I'd better be going,' he said. 'I'll be in touch.'

Chapter Forty-Two

Ben dropped the travel-stained Audi off at the rental place at Heathrow, boarded a flight for Brussels, and less than an hour later he was firing up his Mini for the drive to the Black Forest.

By late afternoon he was arriving in the town of Offenburg near the French–German border, a postcard-perfect little place surrounded by vineyards and filled with quaint old timber-frame houses and churches, outdoor markets and flower gardens. He checked into a small hotel, showered and then went down to the lobby to scour a regional business directory for local firms selling anything related with ceramics. There were a few arts and crafts shops around Offenburg, a gallery and a local pottery somewhere just outside the town that looked promising. By the time he'd worked up his list, the hotel bar was opening. He was first in. Downed a glass of Schnapps and then hit the road, deciding to start with the closest place and work his way outwards.

As detective work went, this was doing it the old-fashioned way, the hard way. In each of the ceramics and crafts shops he went to, showing the people there the picture taken by Lenny Salt that he'd transferred onto his phone, he got either a suspicious look followed by an offhand 'never seen her' or a completely blank stare. Then he tried the art gallery, but a guy in a suit who might have been a funeral director informed him that they dealt only with paintings.

The warmth of the day was cooling as the sun began its downward dip in the sky, and the wind was picking up. Ben's list was running a little short by now, but there was still the pottery shop on the edge of town. He found it easily enough, a kilometre or so into the peaceful countryside.

He'd been expecting something in keeping with the neat, prim little town nearby. This wasn't quite what he'd had in mind. The place was thirty yards back off the road at the end of a rutted driveway. As he stepped out of the car, some rangy chickens pecking in the dirt scattered and ran. A rusted sign for the pottery creaked to and fro in the breeze, and the stone buildings were just a year or two from dereliction, with the roof sagging dramatically in the middle. He walked around the building. The only sign of life about the place was the singing of the birds in the trees overhead. Weeds tufted up thickly through the cracked paving, and when he peered through the grimy window panes he saw nothing but uninhabited rooms littered with junk.

A little further up the road, Ben came across a farmhouse and knocked on the door. There was a furious barking of dogs inside, and then the sound of locks and bolts being opened before the door swung ajar and a little old man with a white beard squinted up at him and asked what he wanted. A Jack Russell terrier snarled at Ben from behind his legs.

'It closed down six, seven months ago,' the old man said when Ben asked him about the pottery place. 'Empty now.'

Ben showed him the picture. 'I wondered if you might have seen this woman there?'

The old man screwed up his face and peered at it, his nose almost touching the screen. 'She might have been one of them. Might not. Hard to say, I don't remember too good. There was a bunch of them in the place. Young people. They ran it together. Like hippies.'

'You mean like a co-operative?'

'Something like that,' the old man said with a shrug.

Ben asked if he knew who owned the building. The old man shrugged again, then shut the door and Ben heard the rattle of the locks and bolts.

He looked at his watch. It was getting too late in the day to make the kind of calls he needed to make to track the owners down. He dragged his heels back to the car and drove off.

So far, things weren't looking too promising. Maybe a forty per cent chance that this was even the right place. And a ninety per cent chance that its former occupants could be just about anywhere in Europe now.

Missing scientists. An SS general with a strange secret. A snatch attempt against a wealthy industrialist. And now some kind of bohemian commune that sold ceramics out of a semi-derelict farm shop in the Black Forest countryside.

He spent that night staring up at the ceiling of his hotel bedroom and counting the minutes until dawn. He drifted off sometime before first light, and woke to the rays of the sun creeping up the flower-patterned wallpaper by his bed. He threw off the covers, dressed quickly and grabbed a coffee in the breakfast room, waiting impatiently for the day to start. As soon as the hands on his watch hit 9 a.m., he started phoning round estate agents.

His enquiries drew blanks all the way. It seemed that whoever had let the co-operative make use of the building hadn't gone through an agent – or at least not one in the region. Maybe a more casual agreement, then, cash only. Maybe the place had been rent-free. It couldn't be worth much to live there.

But whatever the arrangement, someone had to be paying local taxes on the property. Which meant that somewhere there was a record on file that would lead him to the owner and then – with a bit of persuasion – to the people who'd last lived in it.

He checked a map of Offenburg and found that the Rathaus or town council office wasn't far from his hotel. The sun had disappeared behind iron-grey clouds and there was a chill in the air as he walked through the streets. The Rathaus was an imposing red and cream building on the corner of a street of neat old timber-framed houses. He pushed through the main entrance and walked across the reception foyer to the desk, where he spoke to an austere-looking woman with thin lips and dead eyes who seemed to enjoy informing him that unless he was a police officer or a licensed private investigator with proper ID to show her, there was no way she was going to disclose the identity or home address of the owner of the former pottery outside Offenburg. He stared hard at her for a long moment, until a flicker of nervousness appeared in those lifeless eyes. With that small victory won, he turned and pushed back out of the main entrance.

Out in the street, he looked up at the building. Below the arched clock tower was a balcony, and the stonework around the windows was ornately sculpted in classical German style. But he wasn't admiring the architecture. He was thinking about how easy it would be to get in there after dark, and find the records himself.

Easy enough. *Fuck it*. He hadn't come all this way to be put off by a sadistic petty bureaucrat. He walked away, already putting together his plan in his head. It wouldn't be the first government building he'd broken into.

But until dark, all he had on his hands was more time to kill. He couldn't bear the thought of sitting it out in the hotel, and he didn't feel like exploring the town much either. He walked back to where he'd parked the Mini, threw himself behind the wheel and punched the little car out through the traffic into the countryside. But if he'd thought that driving around aimlessly was going to help him get his mind off things, he knew right away that it was over-optimistic. As he drove, the road in front of him became the tunnel of his thoughts and he could feel despondency wrapping its arms around him. A weight of emotion settled heavy in his chest.

Had he lost Ruth forever? Was this just going to fizzle out?

Up ahead on the winding country road, he saw a line of horse riders, four of them, moving in single file, and he instinctively slowed the car and edged out to the left to pass them without scaring their mounts. He glanced at them as he purred by in second gear. The string was led by two women on big hunters, followed by a teenage boy on a grey and a little girl of about nine bringing up the rear. She sat astride her sturdily-built pony as if it was the most treasured thing to her in the world.

The leader gave Ben a nod and mouthed a thank you as the Mini passed by. He waved back glumly, put his foot on the pedal and accelerated gently away.

Then, fifty yards up the road, he stopped the car.

He looked back in the mirror. Watched the easy ambling gait of the big hunter up front, the sway of the rider's hips astride the saddle. Heard the clip-clop of horseshoes on tarmac.

The riders came closer, and he pretended to be searching for something in the glove box but was watching them all the way. As they trotted past the car, he stared again at the little girl.

Not at her. At what she was wearing. Zipped up tight to

her neck was a little green fleece jacket with an equestrian logo on it.

His fingers were trembling a little as he took out his phone and scrolled up the picture of Ruth standing there looking cold and windswept on the library steps in St Peter's Square in Manchester.

She was wearing the exact same type of fleece that the little girl was wearing. Same logo, same cut, same colour. He'd been too busy trying to make out her features to pay attention to the clothes. But now he realised that she was wearing exactly the kind of equestrian gear that the Ruth of his memories would have grown up wanting to wear.

With Ruth, it had been horses, horses, horses. What had started out as a fun activity for her at the age of four had quickly turned into a serious passion. By the age of seven, she'd been an accomplished junior rider with a whole wall of trophies and rosettes, and the dream she always talked about of becoming a champion show jumper had been looking more realistic with every new competition. The house had always been full of little riding boots and hats, bits of tack, horse pictures and books, hoof picks and all kinds of other equestrian paraphernalia. Those were the memories that made Ben smile.

Then his mind drifted to the ones that didn't. The memory of coming home from North Africa as a family of three and knowing that it was his fault. Of his mother, her face a mask of agony as she lay sobbing on Ruth's bed, clutching a little riding jacket as though Ruth was still inside it. Of the terrible months that had passed before his father had finally gathered up all the boots and riding hats, her tack and her saddle, and sealed them inside a packing case.

Ben returned to the present. Thought of the person Ruth was now. Whatever her life story had been, whatever the

278

reason why she'd never tried to find her lost family, was there a small part of her that was still the Ruth he'd known? A part of her that still loved horses, wanted to be around them?

Further up the road was a little white sign on a post. He couldn't make it out from that distance, but when the line of riders reached it they turned right up a track and out of sight.

He slipped the car into gear and followed. The sign at the side of the road bore a picture of a horse and the name of what appeared to be some kind of equestrian centre. Pulling up at the entrance to the track, he saw the riders pass through an open gate and up towards a large yard surrounded by stable-blocks. Behind the stables was an office with a car park, and he drove in and pulled up on the gravel next to a 4x4 hitched to a trailer.

Stepping out of the car, he looked around. He'd been in a hundred of these kinds of places with his sister. The smell of hay and straw, horse feed and manure filled his nostrils as he walked over towards the office. The two young women in boots and jodhpurs who were sitting at a desk over mugs of coffee and sharing a joke about something looked up at him as he stepped inside. One was about seventeen, stumpy with bad skin, and gazed at him through thick glasses. The other might have been a couple of years older, more self-assured, and gave him a smile. On her jacket was a name tag that said 'Hannah'. She had the broad shoulders and slender waist of a serious rider. An instructor, he thought.

He showed them the picture on his phone and asked if they knew the person in it. Blank looks, an exchange of rapid German, and they shook their heads.

'Can you tell me if there are any other stables or riding schools in this area?'

The stumpy one went on staring at him through her

glasses, but Hannah smiled again and said there were four. Politely ignoring the seductive looks she was giving him, he jotted down the details.

'Shame I can't drive you there myself,' she said. 'I'm working. But we're having a barbecue here tonight, if you fancy coming along.'

These German girls. He politely declined.

It took him two hours to drive around the countryside and find the first three places on his list. More horsey smells and sounds, more young women in riding gear. No sign of Ruth and nobody who seemed to know her. The peak of energy that had surged through him was beginning to wane again.

His spirits sank even more as he drove up to the last place on the list, eleven miles out of Offenburg, in the early afternoon. The establishment looked more like a country club than a riding school. The horses in the neatly-fenced paddocks were gleaming Arabs and thoroughbreds, and two little guys in uniforms jumped out to rake up the tyre tracks he'd left in the gravel.

He thought about driving off, then shrugged and slammed the door and wandered about the buildings. A talented young rider was cantering around the sand school with her feet out of the stirrups and her arms out like a plane. Grooms were leading nervy horses up and down the yard. Everything very slick, professional and expensive.

'Can I help you?' said a voice in German, cutting sharply across the stable-yard, not too friendly.

Ben turned to see a guy walking up to him who looked like a managerial type. Late forties, balding, gut and glasses and the angry red face of someone in a state of permanent belligerence.

'Maybe you can.' He showed the guy the picture on the phone. 'Do you know her?'

The manager stared at it for a second, frowned and then glanced up at Ben. 'Who are you?'

'I'm her brother,' Ben said. It sounded weird to hear himself say it.

'You're her brother?' the guy echoed doubtfully.

'You know her?'

'This is a members-only establishment,' the guy said. 'You are trespassing.' He snapped his fingers.

Ten yards away in an open stable, a very large groom in a blue overall was standing up to his knees in soiled straw and piling it into a barrow with a pitchfork. He was well over six and a half feet tall, and it seemed that whatever time he didn't spend mucking out horses, he spent pumping weights the size of truck tyres. At the sound of his manager's snapping fingers he instantly jumped to attention and strode over, trailing bits of straw and clutching the pitchfork like a gladiator's trident in his meaty fist. He stopped at his boss' shoulder and grinned down at Ben. His hair was cropped in a buzz-cut and his face looked like it had been beaten out of Kevlar, with eyes so far apart it was impossible to focus on both at once.

'You have thirty seconds to get the fuck out of here,' the manager said. 'Unless you want Johann to put his fork up your arse.'

Ben looked up at Johann and thought about how he'd go about breaking the guy in half. Violence was one option. Reasonable was another. He decided to go with reasonable.

'Johann, maybe you know her?' he said, and held up the phone for him to see.

Johann said nothing. The wide-set eyes darted at the picture, then back at Ben.

'Now get out,' the manager said with a smirk. 'Johann, make sure he leaves.'

281

Ben slipped the phone back in his pocket, turned and headed back towards the car park with Johann's muscular escort a pace behind him.

'You don't have to see me out,' he told the big guy. 'I'm not here to cause trouble. I was just looking for my sister, that's all.'

Johann's wide, flat face seemed to twitch, as though the effort of thinking was like turning over a big truck engine inside his head. Ben looked at him, and saw that behind the scowl were the eyes of a child.

When the giant spoke, the voice was deep and slow. 'Your sister?' he rumbled.

Ben had his hand on the Mini's door handle. He nodded. 'That's right, Johann. My little sister.'

'You look like her,' Johann said.

Chapter Forty-Three

Ben stood and stared at the big man.

'What did you just say?'

Johann blinked. The wide-set eyes darted sideways at the stable-block, as if he were scared of getting into trouble with his boss.

'It's OK, Johann. You can talk to me. You know her, don't you?'

Johann dipped his chin to his muscular chest and gave a slow, solemn nod. Ben believed him. The poor guy didn't have enough upstairs to tell a lie.

'I take care of Solo,' Johann said. 'She keeps him here.'

Ben had to hold the Mini door handle tight to stop himself from rocking on his feet. 'She comes here to ride?'

Johann gave another slow nod. 'Most afternoons. She is not here yet. Maybe she will come.'

'Does she drive here?'

Nod.

'What kind of car does she drive?'

'Big silver car. Like that one.' Johann raised one of his massive arms and pointed at a top-of-the-line Range Rover parked four cars down from the Mini.

'Listen to me carefully, Johann. It's my sister's birthday today, and I have a present for her. I want it to be a nice big

283

surprise. So when she arrives here, do not tell her that her brother was here. Do you understand?'

Nod.

'What is it you're not to say?'

'That you were here,' Johann repeated carefully. 'Her brother.'

Ben took out his wallet and shelled out a couple of twenty-euro notes. 'This is for you, Johann. You've helped me more than you know. You're a good guy.' He left the big man standing there looking at the money in his palm as he drove off.

Back on the main road, he found a layby within sight of the equestrian centre but shaded by enough overhanging foliage to mask his car. A perfect spot to sit and wait and watch the gates. He settled back in the driver's seat and lit the first cigarette.

Time passed. People came and went. The Jaguar X-type turned out of the gates and disappeared down the road. A while later, a black Subaru 4x4 towing a double trailer arrived. Some riders passed Ben's layby, returning from a hack, the horses sweated up. Ben sat and smoked, two cigarettes, then three, keeping low in the driver's seat.

He'd been sitting there for just under two hours and his watch was edging its way towards four thirty when he saw the silver Range Rover come up the road. Just one occupant. The car slowed for the gate and the indicator flashed, and as it turned in he got a brief but clear view of the driver. A woman, white polo shirt, short blond hair, wraparound shades.

Ben stubbed out his cigarette. His mouth was suddenly dry and his heart felt like he'd just done a three-hundred-metre sprint.

284

The Range Rover rolled up the drive towards the stable buildings, tyres rasping on the gravel, and pulled into the car park.

His first instinct was to drive in after her, go right up to her and talk to her. Tell her who he was. Just come right out with it. *'Ruth, it's me. Your brother Ben. Remember me? Where have you been the last twenty-three years?'*

But that was just his heart talking. The part of him that was still able to think rationally through the swell of emotions that was surging through him knew that the situation was a little more complicated than that.

He scanned the layout of the land. The equestrian centre consisted of the central buildings complex with the office, the stables and tack rooms and the main house, the paddocks and sand school, and a big prefabricated metal building that looked like it might be an indoor riding ménage. Maybe a dozen acres in all, but long and narrow. While the paddocks and riding areas were fenced with white wood, the outer boundary of the property was ringed with hedges. Most of the way round, what lay beyond the hedge was pine woodland. The trees extended all the way along the side of the road where he was parked, and there was just a single strand of barbed-wire fence between him and several hundred yards of thick, uninterrupted cover that would allow him to move unnoticed around the perimeter.

He got out of the car, shut the door quietly and crossed the road. There was nobody about. He peeled off his leather jacket and laid it over the barbed wire. Swung one leg over and then the other, slipped the jacket back on and made his way into the trees.

It didn't take him long to track around the edge of the equestrian centre. Staying well back in the sun-dappled shadow of the trees, he had a good view of the place. Good enough to see the angry manager strutting across the stable-yard, yelling at one of the staff. Good enough to notice the gentle giant Johann over at the dung-heap, discreetly tucked away behind the stable-blocks, emptying his wheelbarrow of soiled straw.

And good enough to spot the woman who was his little sister leading a shiny, well-groomed, expensive-looking chestnut gelding over towards the big metal building. She'd put on a riding hat and boots, and the horse was saddled and bridled. He watched her go in through the tall doorway. Waited a few seconds. Stepped out of the trees towards the hedge. Hesitated. Was this a mistake? Maybe, but he was way beyond recall now.

In three seconds he was over the hedge and running low across the stretch of clipped grass to the side of the indoor space. He skirted round its edge, pressed his back flat against the shiny corrugated wall and glanced around the corner to see if anyone had spotted him. Nobody had. In the distance, the manager was walking back towards the office, talking on a phone. The grooms and other staff carried on unsuspectingly with their business.

Ben slipped inside the building. The interior was like any other large industrial prefab construction, with H-section steel pillars and riveted joists holding up the high roof. The sand-filled arena at its centre was laid out with a course of jumps and brightly lit by neon strip-lights. Around the edges of the arena were rows of seats for spectators, all empty, the outer rows in shadow. He stayed back, near the wall.

And watched from the gloom as Ruth led her horse out across the sand. She seemed relaxed, and completely oblivious of his presence. The horse stood calmly as she tightened up his saddle girth, then she put her left foot in the left stirrup and nimbly mounted him. A gentle nudge of her

286

heels and he trotted off. She guided him briskly round the edge of the arena, picking up pace and warming the horse's muscles before putting him over the jumps. A grin spread across her face. She looked totally in her element.

More than ever, Ben wanted to step out of the shadows and go to her. But he held back, and the pain knotted up his stomach and his throat and tears prickled his eyes. She was so much the same Ruth he'd known back then, but also so different. He watched for twenty minutes as she expertly took the horse round the jumps, faster and faster and higher and higher. She cleared each pole faultlessly, just the way she'd always done as a little girl. Then she dismounted, gave the horse a warm hug and led him away.

By the time she was halfway back towards the stable-blocks, Ben was already over the hedge and working his way round through the trees to his car. Another half hour passed before he saw the silver Range Rover pull out onto the road and drive off. He followed it.

Now it was time to talk.

The Range Rover led him through the countryside. She drove at a steady fifty, slowing only to pass through a village, then over a narrow stone bridge across a stream. There was nothing about her driving that made him think she'd spotted the Mini following her. After eight kilometres he saw her indicator come on, and she turned into a rough lane. He hung back, and saw the Range Rover go bumping forty metres down the lane and then turn in through a gap in the wild, unkempt bushes.

He left the Mini in the shade of a tree, grabbed his bag from the passenger seat and started walking. By the gap where she'd disappeared was a lopsided sign in German that he translated to read 'ceramics workshop'. Peering around the corner, he saw the Range Rover parked in front of a long, low-slung whitewashed cottage. Someone had been practising their artwork on the side wall of the place – a spray-painted swirl of colours that he guessed was meant to look psychedelic. Dangling chimes tinkled in the soft breeze, and bees hummed among the flowerbeds. So far, so not the kind of place he'd have expected to find a cell of neo-Nazi terrorists.

Someone else was home. Next to the ticking Range Rover was a rusty VW Golf, and a battered Honda 750 motorcycle sat by an outhouse with a cat sleeping on its saddle.

Ben moved silently through the garden. The place had obviously been a smallholding once, but now most of the outbuildings were disused. A block-built garage that at one time would have housed a couple of tractors had been converted into a pottery workshop, with a potter's wheel and a long bench, both covered in clay dust. The flue pipe from the cold, ash-dusted kiln poked up through the tin roof. Swirly-coloured glazed plates and jugs and cups and vases crowded an industrial shelving unit against the wall. Ben didn't see any clay busts of Hitler up there.

He moved on. A nylon washing line hung between the corner of the house and a disused poultry shed, and a glance at the clothes on it told him that two women lived here, someone Ruth's build and someone a good bit heavier. Plus, judging by the different sizes of men's jeans hanging out to dry, at least two males.

He slipped back around the side of the poultry shed as the front door of the house suddenly opened.

Footsteps walking his way. Then a scrawny young guy in a sleeveless T-shirt, with long hair and a patchy beard, walked within a foot of him, stopped and turned and stared with saucer eyes. His mouth opened to yell in alarm.

Ben didn't let him make a sound. The guy was quick and

easy to subdue; four seconds later he was lying unconscious among the dried-out droppings on the henhouse floor. Ben crouched over him, studying him. No shaven head. No swastikas on the neck or arms. He opened up his bag, took out two plastic cable-ties and bound up the guy's wrists and ankles. Tore off a five-inch length of silver duct tape and stuck it tightly to his mouth.

Leaving the bag next to the unconscious body he stepped out of the poultry shed and slipped round to the rear of the house. Knocked on the door, three loud raps, then darted quickly back around the corner. After a few seconds' delay, the door opened and another man stepped out onto the cracked patio.

'Hello? Someone there?'

Ben peered out from around the corner. This guy looked a few years older than his bearded friend, maybe thirty-two. Good looking, short dark hair, a denim shirt splotched with dried clay. The potter. Ben found himself wondering if this was his sister's boyfriend. Better than the other one, at least, it occurred to him – and then he scolded himself for thinking such absurd thoughts at a time like this.

The guy was heading back inside when Ben came up behind him without a sound and took him down with a stranglehold that was just hard and long enough to make him pass out without doing any lasting damage. He glanced round, then dragged him to the poultry shed and dumped him there beside his buddy. Quickly trussed and gagged him, then got to his feet and closed the unconscious bodies inside. *Two down.*

At that moment, the front door flew open and a third person appeared in the doorway. Someone too quick and too sharp for Ben to duck for cover. But by that point, he didn't want to hide from her any more.

'Franz, where did you—' She stopped mid-sentence, and stared at him.

He stared back.

Face to face with his sister Ruth.

Chapter Forty-Four

Time seemed to pause as they stood there, frozen, eyes locked. They were just five yards away from each other, and it was the first really good view he'd had of her face. Her eyes were exactly the same blue he remembered from so long ago, but sharp now. The soft, round features of childhood were long gone, and had left behind them a certain hardness. The set of her jaw spoke of a strong will and a tough attitude. Another man would have found her attractive, her lean runner's build, the broad shoulders and trim waist. In all the pictures Ben had of her as a child, her hair was long and thick and lustrous. Cropped the way it was now, it gave her a severe look. But somewhere behind that dangerous, edgy exterior, she was still the Ruth he'd thought about every day for twenty-three years.

For a long second he looked into her eyes. Long enough to pray for a glimmer of recognition in there. He saw none. Then that suspended moment suddenly ended; time seemed to restart. She bolted back into the house.

Ben ran after her and managed to get his foot in the door before it slammed violently shut in his face. He crashed it open, pressed through the doorway, made a lunge for her arm. She darted out of his grasp, whirled around and with a scream she aimed a vicious kick at his groin. If he hadn't reacted in time and twisted out of the way, he'd have run straight into it and been crippled in agony.

Even in that moment, he couldn't help but admire her feistiness. Quick as a panther, she grabbed a wooden chair by the rungs of its backrest and jabbed the legs at his face. He ducked the blow, caught one of the spars. The cold part of his mind that had been forged through hard combat and even harder training told him he could ram the chair back at his opponent and smash their teeth in, end the fight there and then. He pushed that thought away, tore the chair out of her grip and dropped it.

She ran through another doorway and into a kitchen. On a wooden surface cluttered with saucepans and jars of utensils was a block of knives. In one fast movement she drew a long carving knife out of its slot and threw it at him. He twitched out of the way, felt the wind of the blade past his cheek, heard the hollow *thunk* and the judder of the blade as it embedded itself point-first in the doorframe a few inches to the right of his head.

Then she was escaping through the kitchen, bursting through a bead curtain and down a narrow corridor. He sprinted after her and saw her fly into a bedroom, slipping on bare varnished floorboards as she made for a single bed in the middle of the room. She somersaulted across it, dragging half the bedclothes with her as she rolled to the floor on the other side.

No way out of the room. She'd cut off her escape route.

But when she ripped open the bedside table drawer and came up from behind the bed with a pistol in both hands, he understood why she'd made for this bedroom. Fight before flight. Definitely his sister.

The numbing crack of the shot filled the small space. He threw himself down and hit the smooth floor, sliding feet first. Crashed into the bottom edge of the bed and flipped it violently up on its side, shattering the bedstead and jamming her between the mattress and the wall. She let out a muffled cry, and the pistol went tumbling out of her hand.

Ben was up on his feet before she could do anything, and tore the bed aside. She threw a punch at him, but she was disoriented by the impact and he easily slapped it aside.

It was time to finish this.

Every so often in his life, Ben had to do things he hated doing. This was one of the worst. With the heel of his right hand he delivered a short, hard, stunning blow to the side of the neck. She went limp and crumpled, knees buckling under her. He caught her before she could fall to the floor.

'I'm sorry, Ruth.' He laid her down on the broken bed, checked her pulse. When he was sure he hadn't done her any lasting harm, he picked up the fallen pistol, made it safe and stuffed it in his pocket. Then he grabbed her arms and flipped her body up over his shoulder.

He hadn't known exactly what his plan was as he followed her home, but now he realised there was only one option open to him if he wanted to get her somewhere quiet and have it out with her. He was going to have to smuggle her back over the border into France and west to Le Val. And he needed to move fast. He was pretty certain there were more than three of the gang living here. Sooner or later, someone was going to return home, and he didn't want to be there when they did. He might not be so lucky if four or five of them jumped him at once – especially if they were armed.

He carried his sister out to the poultry shed. Her two friends, the handsome one and the scrawny bearded one, were still out cold. He laid her very carefully down next to them and used more of the cable-ties to bind her wrists and ankles, taking care not to pull them so tight against her flesh. Then he taped her mouth and ran to fetch the car.

A body was a tight fit inside the boot of a Mini. Not the best car in the world for this purpose, he thought as he lowered her gently inside the cramped space, but he guessed that was something the designers hadn't felt the need to consider. He did his best to position her comfortably for when she woke up, then slammed the lid.

He stared pensively at the back of the car. Sighed, bit his lip, shook his head. No, that wasn't going to do at all. He had a long drive ahead, and it was a confined space in there with very little ventilation. He'd only just found her. The last thing he wanted was to suffocate her.

'Fuck it,' he said out loud. Opened up the boot, slipped the pistol out of his pocket. Thumbed off the safety, picked the best angle and emptied the rest of the magazine into the inside of the metal panel. The 9mm bullets punched neat round holes through the shiny green bodywork. Fourteen of them. When he closed the boot lid a second time, it looked like a colander – but at least she'd be able to breathe.

He walked back to the poultry shed, thinking about what he was going to do about the other two. If they'd been the kind of shaved-headed hard-nuts who normally went about wearing swastika badges, he might just have left them to rot where they lay. But these guys were different. Something else was going on.

He trotted over to the house, yanked the carving knife Ruth had thrown at him out of the doorframe, and snatched a black felt pen from the table where the phone was. He used the knife to cut the ties around the handsome one's wrists, then reached into his bag for another tie and attached the guy's left hand to the bearded one's ankle. He tossed the carving knife a few yards across the garden, so that they'd see it when they came to. The good-looking one would be able to use his free hand to cut himself and his friend loose, but not before they'd had to drag themselves several very difficult yards over the ground. That should delay things a bit.

One of the principal advantages of committing crimes against criminals was that they tended not to call the police to complain about it afterwards. But in Ben's experience you could never be too careful, and that was what the felt pen was for. He rolled the bearded guy over on his back and used it to write on his forehead.

ICH WEISS WER SIE SIND.

I know who you are, in big bold letters from temple to temple. The message ought to get them thinking. Ben smiled grimly at his handiwork, then got to his feet and ran back to the car, mapping out in his mind the best route into France without going through border checkpoints.

Chapter Forty-Five

On the way back to Le Val, Ben's phone rang. It was Brooke.

'Just wanted to check in and see how things were going.'

'Things are . . . interesting,' he said.

'Where are you?'

'On my way home. I should be there by midnight.'

'Did you find her?' Brooke asked after a pause.

'Yes. I did.'

'And it's definitely Ruth?'

'It's definitely Ruth.'

'I don't know what to say, Ben.'

'You don't have to say anything,' he replied.

'So what's happening? Where is she now?'

'Here with me.'

'She came with you?'

He hesitated. He'd already lied once to Brooke about his sister in the last few days, and he wasn't about to do it again.

'She's in the boot,' he said simply.

A moment's shocked silence on the line. 'What did you just say?'

'I said she's in the boot. But she'll be all right. She's tough.'

'Ben, do you realise what you're telling me? That the sister you lost because someone kidnapped her is now a prisoner in the back of your car because you went and kidnapped her back? This is insane. You can't go around snatching people.'

'I didn't kidnap her. I rescued her. That's what I do. I got her out of there, and now I'm taking her home and she and I are going to have it out.'

Another long silence on the other end. Then Brooke said firmly, 'Right, that's it. I'm coming over. I'll be there in the morning.'

'I can deal with it, Brooke. Stay put.'

'No, Ben. I seriously don't think you can. I think you need help. Maybe more than she does. Have you lost your mind?'

'What about Sabrina? You can't just leave her there on her own.'

'Sabrina will be fine. She can take care of herself.'

'I don't think—'

She cut across him. 'See you at Le Val.' Then, before he could protest, she ended the call.

He drove on into the night, thinking about his cargo in the back and how he was going to handle the situation when he got to the house. He had to admit he was flying blind now. No situation he'd ever found himself in before came remotely close to this.

Just before midnight, he arrived at the Le Val security gate and saw the figure of Raymond come out of the gate-house. He and his colleagues Claude and Jean-Yves were the three-man local security outfit Ben had hired to man the gates and patrol the perimeter. Ben rolled down the window and greeted him, trying to look as natural as possible without hanging around long enough for the guy to spot the bullet-riddled back end of the car or hear its occupant moving about inside. Raymond didn't notice anything.

Ben's heart thumped as he drove on through the gate.

This was it. He wasn't looking forward to the inevitable confrontation.

He parked the Mini inside the Dutch barn, and stepped outside to scan the buildings. What he was about to do didn't require an audience, not even a close and trusted friend like Jeff Dekker, and Ben was glad that this was happening while he was out of the picture. The whole place seemed deserted, apart from the four German Shepherds, led by Storm, who'd been sleeping in a nest of straw at the back of the barn and now came trotting over to the car to investigate. The dogs quickly picked up the scent of someone in the back.

'Leave,' he commanded them in a low voice, and they instantly backed off and retreated to a distance, watching intently with cocked heads and pricked ears as he opened the boot.

Ruth's eyes glittered in the moonlight, glaring up at him with rage and hate and fear like those of a cornered wildcat. She kicked and writhed as he bent down and lifted her out of the confined space, carried her over to the house and up the stairs to his private apartment. Once upstairs, he used her feet to shove the door shut, then laid her on the sofa and left her there struggling against her bonds while he went to attend to the windows. The whole house had sturdy wooden shutters that could be locked from the inside. Ben had fortified them with heavy-gauge steel wire, and only a really determined intruder with a sledgehammer would have got through them. He didn't think she could get out too easily, just in case she tried. He secured each window in turn, dropped the keys in his pocket, then fetched a bottle of mineral water from the cupboard and set it down on the low table by the sofa.

Then he kneeled down beside Ruth, gently peeled the tape away from her mouth and ignored the raging stream of abuse she fired at him as he snapped open his clasp knife and carefully sliced the plastic cable-ties around her wrists and ankles. She immediately tried to jump to her feet, and he shoved her back down. She sat glaring at him, rubbing her wrists.

He offered her the mineral water, and she grabbed it from him, took several long swallows and then dashed the bottle in his face. Her eyes blazed as she yelled at him in German. '*Du Scheisse, warum hast du mich hier gebracht?*'

Why have you brought me here?

He replied in English, and they were the strangest words he'd ever spoken in his life, a surreal moment that made the hairs on the back of his neck stand up. 'It's me. Ben. Your brother. I've brought you home.'

She stared at him for a long moment, her face wild and full of suspicion. 'You're not my brother,' she screamed at him. Just a trace of a German accent. 'What is this, some kind of twisted fucking joke?'

Ben's throat felt very tight. 'You're Ruth Hope. You couldn't possibly be anybody else.'

'You're a fucking liar,' she yelled. 'What have you done with Franz and Rudi?'

'Relax. Your little Nazi friends are fine. Probably licking their sores and pacing up and down wondering where you are.'

'Nazis,' she spat. 'We're not Nazis.'

'I think you'd better start talking to me, right now.'

'Fuck you. *He* sent you, didn't he?'

'He?'

'My fucking father. Where is he?' She looked about her, as if expecting someone to walk into the room and readying herself for the confrontation.

300

'I don't know who you're talking about,' he protested. 'What father?'

'I'm Luna Steiner,' she yelled. 'Do I need to spell it out for you, *arschloch*? My father is Maximilian Steiner. And last time I saw you, you were his bodyguard.'

Chapter Forty-Six

It was as though all the air had been sucked out of the room. Ben found it hard to speak.

'The Steiners don't have any children,' he said weakly.

Her face reddened. 'Who told you that?' she demanded. 'That lick-spittle Dorenkamp? Or my bastard pig of a father? Of course they'd say that, wouldn't they? I'm the dark little secret they want to keep quiet. Easier to pretend I don't exist.'

Ben reeled with confusion. 'Listen to me. You are my sister. When you were nine years old—'

But she didn't let him finish. Her arm flashed out. On the windowsill behind her was the old naval paraffin lamp he still used sometimes when the storms took out the power. She grabbed it and hurled it at him. It was a heavy lump of brass, and it could have put a dent in his skull if he hadn't ducked out of the way. It smashed into the chest of drawers behind him, splintering the wood.

'You let me out of here right now!' she shouted.

'Not until we talk and straighten this whole thing out. If you're Steiner's daughter, then why were you trying to kidnap him?'

'I need to go to the bathroom.'

'After. What about Adam O'Connor and his son?'

'I don't know what you're talking about. Let me go.'

303

'Why did you want the Kammler papers?'

She stared at him, her rage suddenly giving way to suspicion. 'What did that bastard tell you about Kammler?'

'Steiner? I think he told me a pack of lies.'

She snorted. 'Why am I not surprised?'

'And you're going to tell me the truth. I want to know what's going on.'

'Why the fuck should I tell you anything? Let me go to the bathroom, unless you want me to piss all over this pretty rug you have here.'

'All right. You go. But the door stays open.'

'So you can watch?'

'I don't want to watch my sister taking a piss.'

'I'm not your sister, buddy.'

He grabbed her arm as she strode towards the bathroom, and jerked her round to face him. She tried to get away, but he held her tight.

'That scar on your arm,' he said. 'You want me to tell you how you got it? You were seven years old. We were burning leaves. You, me and our father. Not Maximilian Steiner. *Our* father, I'm talking about, Alistair Hope. You tripped and fell against the incinerator. Do you remember?'

She said nothing. Her whole body was tense.

'Maybe you remember Polly? She was your horse. A Welsh mountain pony, twelve hands, grey. And then there was your fluffy toy dog. You called him Ringle-the-Wee and you wouldn't be parted from him. I still have him.' He pointed. 'I have a whole box of your things, there under my bed. Things I've kept all these years. Do you want to see them? Will that make you believe me?' He ripped his wallet out of his back pocket, opened it and took out a passport-sized picture. 'Look at this. It's you, about a week before you disappeared. I've carried it with me everywhere since.'

304

Ruth glanced at the picture, then stared at him defiantly. 'Stick it up your ass. Go tell it to your boss.'

Anger seized him then, and he shook her violently. 'Steiner didn't send me. He's not here. We're not in Switzerland, we're in France. Normandy, at my place. Steiner doesn't know you're here.'

'Let go of my arm. You're hurting me.'

He held her tighter. 'I came looking for you because I wanted to save you, Ruth.'

'Save me!'

'From yourself, you stupid little idiot. I don't know what crazy stuff you're into. I just know that it's going to end with you getting arrested or killed, all right? But if you want, if you really want, I only have to call Steiner and he'll send someone right over to pick you up. I'm sure he'd be very interested to meet the woman who's been trying to kidnap him. I might even take you there myself.'

Her eyes were full of alarm at his words. She twisted furiously against his grip. 'Let go of me!' she screamed at him.

He did, and she ran to the bathroom and slammed the door in his face, threw the bolt on the inside.

He thought about breaking the door down, then relented and stood there helpless with his head hanging. Maybe he needed to back off a little.

Perhaps Brooke was right – he couldn't handle this alone.

Feeling suddenly a hundred years old, as if every last drop of strength had been drained out of him, he left his quarters and locked the door. She couldn't escape from in there. Even if she broke through the shutters, it was a long drop to the concrete below, and there was no way she could climb down.

He trudged wearily down the stairs, snatched a bottle of whisky from the kitchen, carried it back through to the dark hall and sat with it on the bottom stair. He could hear the sounds coming from the landing above. It hadn't taken her long to figure out she was locked in. As he cracked open the whisky, she was already pounding furiously on the door, screaming to be let out.

Then, as he was into his second gulp, the smashing began.

He could only imagine what was happening up there. He sat there staring into the darkness and sipping the whisky, and after a while the sound of his possessions being hurled and broken into pieces just washed over him. He closed his eyes, felt his head nod. And gave in to it.

When he awoke, slumped uncomfortably on the stairs with just the half-empty bottle for company, the house was silent and sunlight was streaming through the hallway from the fan light above the door. He got to his feet, stretching and rubbing his back, and staggered through to the kitchen hoping that a strong coffee would drive away the sharp ache that had set up camp in his temple.

Someone else was awake, too. As he made his way down the hall the pounding and screaming started again upstairs. The sound of glass shattering. Another lamp, or maybe the mirror.

Let her get on with it. There couldn't be much left up there that wasn't already broken, anyway.

He was sitting at the kitchen table five minutes later, burning his tongue on scalding black coffee, when he heard the diesel chatter of a taxi pull up outside. The front door opening, familiar footsteps in the hall. He turned to see Brooke walk into the room.

'I told you you didn't have to come,' he said. 'But it's good to see you.'

'You look terrible. Where is she?'

He pointed upwards. 'Can't you hear?'

'What's she doing?'

'Smashing the place up. She's been doing it on and off since last night.'

'I need a coffee,' Brooke said, rubbing her eyes. 'I was up at five to catch the plane.'

Ben got up and poured her a cup. 'She says her name's Luna, and she's Steiner's daughter,' he told her.

'As in Maximilian Steiner, the guy she was trying to kidnap?'

He nodded. Another crash came from upstairs. More screaming.

'Why would she do that?' Brooke asked, puzzled.

'I don't know what's going on,' he said.

'I'm going up there to talk to her.'

'I'll come too.'

'No way, Ben. You're staying here. Don't interfere with this.'

'She's wild. She could hurt you.'

'I know what I'm doing.' Brooke gulped down her coffee and left. Ben heard her climbing the stairs. Her soft knock and her voice saying, 'Luna? Can I come in?' before unlocking the door. Then it clicked shut and he heard no more.

The two women were alone up there a long time. After ten minutes the smashing and yelling had become much less frequent, and after twenty it had stopped altogether. Ben knocked back cup after cup of coffee, pacing up and down in the kitchen and fighting the urge to go creeping up the stairs and listen at the door.

What the hell was happening? That was his sister up there – no doubt about that. And yet, she was – or said she was – Steiner's daughter. Steiner's adopted child? It was feasible, but the possibility was dizzying.

Questions poured through Ben's mind. Had Steiner known

of the connection all along, and somehow contrived to hire him for that reason? But that seemed impossible. Shannon would have had to be in on it too. Deliberately provoking Ben into hurting him, one unlikely event tripping the next like a line of dominoes. Absurd. So what was the answer?

Consumed with frustration and impatience, he just had to do something. He still had a card in his wallet with the main office number of the Steiner residence. He snatched up the phone and punched the keys, and asked for Heinrich Dorenkamp.

When the man came to the phone, Ben came right to the point. 'You told me the Steiners didn't have any children. Were you lying to me?'

A pause. 'I – ah . . .'

'Did the Steiners adopt a child? A girl of nine, more than twenty years ago? Yes or no, Heinrich? It's simple.'

'I'm afraid I cannot help with your enquiry,' Dorenkamp said in a stiff tone. 'I am very busy at the moment. Goodbye.' And hung up.

Ben was about to redial the number and get nasty when he heard the door open behind him and turned for the second time that morning to see Brooke walk in.

He glanced at his watch. She'd been up there for nearly two hours. She looked tired as she pulled up a chair and sat down.

He looked at her. 'Well?'

Brooke sighed. 'Well, we talked. She listened to what I had to say. And . . .'

'And?'

'And you were right all along, Ben. She's who you said, and she knows it. I think she knew it before I got here. Things you said to her last night, things that only her brother could have known.'

'So now I'm going to talk to her,' he said.

'There's something else, Ben. The situation's stranger than you think.'

'Meaning what?'

'She was convinced that her brother was dead.'

Chapter Forty-Seven

Ben pushed open the door to his quarters and kicked aside the debris that littered the floor. Everything that could be broken, overturned or torn down, had been. Brickwork showed through the plaster where a chair had slammed into the wall. The chair itself lay in splintered pieces on the carpet. The place looked as though a tank had driven through it.

'I'm sorry about the room,' said Ruth quietly from behind him. He turned and saw her sitting in the corner, hugging her knees. Her eyes were red and puffy, her face drawn.

'It's OK,' he said. 'I'd have done a lot worse. Not a stone left standing.'

'You and I,' she said. 'We're Hopes.'

'I'm glad you've come round to thinking so.'

She paused. 'I can't believe this is real. My brother's supposed to be dead.'

'It's been tried,' he said. 'But it hasn't happened yet.'

'I don't know anything about you.'

He nodded. 'We have a lot to talk about. And I think we'd better start at the beginning.'

'I could use some air,' she replied.

'You want to take a walk?'

*   *   *

The sun was shining brightly, just a whisper of a breeze stirring the treetops, as Ben took his sister into the forest that surrounded the Le Val facility. They barely spoke as they walked. He knew the paths through the woods better than anyone, better even than the wild boar and deer that had created many of them, and he led her deep into the woods towards the old ruined church. Storm trotted along behind Ben, keenly sniffing out the scents in the undergrowth.

They reached the ruin. Too much time had passed since his last visit to the place, and it was overgrown with wildflowers now that summer was approaching its height. Ben pulled back a hanging curtain of ivy and led Ruth through the crumbling archway. He sat down on a mossy stone, and she settled in the long grass at his feet as Storm went scouting around the walls.

He couldn't stop himself from staring at her. He was scared to blink in case she disappeared.

'It's weird, isn't it?' she said, half-smiling. 'Us being here like this.'

He nodded in agreement. 'Very weird. Can you talk about what happened to you?' he asked cautiously. After years of the worst speculation, it was a terrifying question to ask.

'I know what you're thinking,' she said. 'I've heard about what's done to the children the slavers take.'

'I've seen the things that are done to them.' He didn't even want to think about it.

'It didn't happen to me,' she said. 'Nobody raped me. Nobody drugged me. Really. I'm OK.'

He breathed out a long, long sigh. Like letting out twenty-three years' worth of pent-up pain. He said nothing for a few moments. Took a pack of Gauloises and his Zippo out of his pocket and offered her one.

'I don't smoke cigarettes,' she said.

'Don't tell me. You prefer the other stuff.'

She shrugged. 'It settles my nerves. I don't smoke it a lot though.'

Storm was scratching at the mossy earth at the foot of the wall, on the trail of a scent. Suddenly he stopped, stiffened, as if listening out for some imperceptible sound far beyond the range of human hearing. His shaggy hackles rose, and a long, low growl rumbled from his throat.

'Go and lie down,' Ben commanded softly. The dog glanced at him, then obeyed.

Ben lit a cigarette, clanged his lighter shut and dropped it back into the breast pocket of his denim shirt. 'Do you remember the day you disappeared?' he asked Ruth.

'It was a long time ago. It's like a dream.'

'Start at the beginning,' he said. 'Tell me everything.'

She leaned back against the rough stone wall. 'I remember being with them. The kidnappers. I remember being inside a car, or a truck. It's not so clear any more. They took me across the desert, and we met up with these other men. Like a rendezvous, in a tent pitched out there in the sand seas, the middle of nowhere. There was money on the table. I think they were meeting up to sell me on, you know? But then they started arguing. A fight broke out. One of them had a sword.' She chuckled. 'It was probably just a knife, but I remember thinking how huge it looked. He took it out, and another man shot him. They were so busy fighting, nobody saw me slip away. I ran and ran. I was scrambling up and down all these dunes that went on forever. I remember how hot the sand was. It burned my hands and feet. But I kept going, because I was so scared they were going to catch me. But then I remember hearing this strange noise behind me, like a roaring. I turned and saw what looked like a giant wave coming towards me.'

'A sandstorm,' Ben said.

She nodded. 'I just ran like hell. The roaring got louder and louder. Then I saw this old van, buried up to its wheels in the sand. God knows how long it had been left abandoned there, but it saved me. I managed to climb in the back before the storm hit. That's all I remember for a long time.'

Ruth paused. 'I woke up lying in a soft bed of blankets and skins. I was in a Bedouin tent. Faces looking down at me, of the people who'd found me after the storm. I was ill for weeks, from dehydration and shock. They tended me, nursed me and fed me, and then I just stayed with them.' She smiled wistfully. 'They were kind, wonderful people. They called me "Little Moon" in their language.'

'Because of the scar?'

She pulled back her sleeve and ran her finger along the white crescent shape on her skin. 'My little moon.'

'How long did you stay with them?'

'Three years, more or less. I don't really know. We moved around, setting up camp here and there. They sold camels, skins, beads. Never in one place for long.'

He shook his head in amazement. 'And all that time, we were searching frantically for you.'

'I often thought about you. All of you, but especially you, Ben. I cried myself to sleep every night for the first year. But, you know, time passes.'

'And children adapt,' he said.

'And so that's how it was for me. My new life, my new family. But I guess that they knew they couldn't keep me forever. A little white girl growing up among the desert people, someone would have noticed sooner or later. And someone did.'

'The Steiners,' he said.

'I remember when I first met them. We'd travelled near

an oasis to fill up with water. I was playing in the bushes with some of the other kids when this huge bus came along. The kids all ran over to it. I knew I wasn't supposed to, but I ran over as well. At first we all thought it was a tourist bus, but then when we got up close, we realised it was just these two people and their driver. All tourists seemed like rich folks to us, but this was just incredible. They were giving out toys and money to the kids, and we were all going wild. I was so excited, I didn't notice that my head garb had slipped down. That was when Silvia saw my hair, and my blue eyes. I remember her watching me, pointing me out to *him*.'

'Maximilian.'

She pulled a face. 'Prick. Then, anyway, next thing I knew, there was this whole discussion going on, and everyone was crying and saying I had to go. After that, everything changed for me. For the second time, I was taken from everything I'd known, my friends, my new family. Suddenly I'm on a plane to Europe, and then a helicopter and this amazing fairytale house, and I'm wearing these new clothes. It was winter there, and so cold. A whole different world. From a poor Bedouin urchin to this little twelve-year-old rich kid.'

'So then Steiner adopted you,' Ben said. 'And he named you Luna, taken from your Bedouin name. Except that he must have cut a few corners and greased a few palms to make the adoption possible.'

'Oh, he's very good at that.'

'So what should I call you? Are you Luna, or Ruth?'

'Everyone's always known me as Luna. I hardly remember what it's like to be Ruth any more.' She shrugged, smiled. 'But maybe I need to start learning to be her again. I'd like you to call me Ruth.'

At that moment, the dog got to his feet, his lip curling

back to show his fangs. Another long, low growl. He was intently focused on something behind the trees.

'Quiet,' Ben called over to him. Storm let out a little whimper and lay back down.

'What's bothering him?' she said, peering over towards the trees.

'There's probably a boar in there or something.' There were more important things on Ben's mind than whatever was preoccupying the dog. 'Why did you think I was dead?'

'I was brought up believing it. That's what Maximilian told me. He said there'd been this whole investigation. That he'd used every bit of his influence to find my family, and that what had come out was that my parents and my brother had been killed. I was only a kid. What was I supposed to think? At the time, I just accepted the reality I was presented with.'

Ben narrowed his eyes. 'Killed how?'

'An air crash, in India. A small tourist plane smashed into a mountain. He showed me the press cuttings. I saw it clearly. It was all there. Alistair Hope, his wife Kathleen and their son Benedict. He couldn't have got that wrong, could he?'

'No,' Ben said. 'I don't think there was any mistake.' Rage was building inside him. Steiner's wealth gave him the power to fake just about anything he wanted. But to deliberately fabricate a lie of this magnitude – why would he do such a thing?

'I don't understand,' she muttered. 'When I was seventeen I wanted to find out more about what had happened. Maybe I didn't totally trust Maximilian, I don't know. I hired a private investigator from Bern to trace information about you all. He came back to me with exactly the same stuff Maximilian had.'

Ben said nothing.

Realisation crossed her face like a passing shadow. 'The bastard got to him. Paid him off. Shit. I should have thought of it. More lies.' She shook her head.

'The question is why,' Ben said. 'Why has Steiner pretended all these years?'

'Are our parents still alive, Ben?' she asked suddenly, excitement flaring for a brief moment.

He sighed. 'No. He wasn't lying about that. They're dead. But it wasn't a plane crash.'

'What happened to them?'

It was hard to say it, but he told her the truth about their mother's suicide and their father's subsequent pining away. She paled as she listened, and buried her face in her hands.

'I hate him,' she said. 'I hate that evil bastard. I'll get him for what he's done to us all.'

'What about Silvia?' he asked. 'You think she was in on it too?'

Ruth shook her head vigorously. 'He lies to her about everything. Even after all these years, he's got her believing the sun shines out of his ass. She gave up everything for him, to live in that mausoleum. So, no, I don't think she's in on it. She's a good person, not like him. I was close to her once. I wish I still could be. My cousin Otto, too. I miss them.'

'What happened between you and Steiner?'

She shrugged. 'I grew up, and he couldn't deal with it. There was endless fighting. He wouldn't let me breathe. I couldn't do anything, couldn't have a horse, couldn't do this, couldn't do that. The more he tried to control me, the more I rebelled against him. Hanging out with people he disapproved of, smoking dope, getting involved in environmental causes, going on marches. He was probably afraid I'd cause a family scandal. In the end he gave me an ultimatum. Either toe the line or get out. I got out.'

'From teen rebellion to kidnapping,' Ben said. 'That was a big step up.'

'Yeah, well, you know why I took it. Because of the Kammler papers.'

'You're going to have to explain all this to me.'

Her lips curled into a dark, grim smile. 'OK, but I can do better than just explain. I can show you. Have you got a computer?'

'In the office.'

'Let's go. There are things you need to see. Then you'll understand.'

Chapter Forty-Eight

They left the ruined church and started making their way back along the leafy path through the woods. There was a closeness between them now that hadn't been there before, and it warmed him more than the June sun streaming through the trees.

'How much do you know about science?' she asked him as they walked slowly side by side.

'Just what I've picked up here and there,' he answered.

'You never studied it, then?'

'I studied theology, then war. Why?'

'I studied science,' she told him. 'Physics. University of Geneva was where I took my first degree. When I graduated I went to Bonn for my PhD.'

He stared at her in surprise. 'How does someone with a science doctorate end up selling pottery?'

'Because I happen to give a shit about scientific integrity. Science is meant to be the pure pursuit of knowledge for the good of the planet and its occupants, you know? But of course that's not the way it works. Like when a big telecommunications corporation uses bribes and threats to suppress studies that prove carcinogenic effects from mobile phone radiation. Or when astrophysics research projects get mysteriously shut down because someone inconveniently showed up major flaws in the Big Bang Theory. Little things like corruption and hypocrisy, I kind of have a problem with. I'd rather be helping Franz to sell his art than be part of that fucking machine. All it does is serve the establishment.'

'You're an idealist,' he said.

'Something wrong with that?'

'Not at all. I've had the same problem all my life.'

'Then you understand why I quit my career. But before that, it was my whole life. I was eighteen when I went away to Geneva. Maximilian hated me being away from home, but he was pleased I was following in his footsteps.'

'How so?'

'You didn't know? Before he made all his money, way back, he trained in chemistry and physics. Was pretty talented at it, too. That's what got him started in business – when he was a student he patented a heart drug that got taken up by a big pharmaceutical company and made him rich. Anyway,' she went on, 'off I went. I had everything money could buy. Maximilian bought me a luxury apartment in Geneva. I had a sports car, a fat allowance. Everything except freedom. He wouldn't let me have friends or go to parties with the other students. He always seemed to know what I was doing, like he was having me followed. Insisted I always came straight home for vacations and couldn't leave until term began again. That's why I was there, the summer after the end of my first year, when I overheard the phone call.'

'What phone call?'

'Between him and his brother Karl. Not long before poor old Karl died. Shame, I liked him. Maximilian had been collecting antiquities for years by then, and he was telling his brother about these documents he'd found by chance at some auction.'

'You mean the Kammler papers?'

She nodded. 'Of course, back then I'd never heard of Kammler. But he was telling Karl what an amazing discovery it was. Amazing and worrying, and how he'd been sitting up nights reading the stuff, becoming obsessed with it. I could hear Karl's voice on the speakerphone. He told Maximilian that if this stuff was even half true, he'd be out of business and that it was best to lock it away and not let anyone else see it. He was kind of joking, but I could tell that Maximilian was taking it really seriously. He was scared.'

'I don't understand. What was it about the Kammler documents that was spooking him so badly?'

They'd reached the office. Storm left them to go sniffing round the buildings, and Ben led Ruth inside.

'That's what I'm going to show you,' she replied. 'And it's going to blow your mind.'

'I've heard that before,' he said, thinking of Lenny Salt.

'Just wait and see.'

Ben fired up the laptop on his desk. As it whirred into action, he ran his eye over the pile of mail that was stacked up beside it. He was about to sweep the whole lot aside when he noticed the official Steiner logo on the envelope.

'That looks familiar,' Ruth said.

Ben tore it open, remembering the letter that Dorenkamp had mentioned. It was from Steiner's lawyer. An invoice for forty thousand euros in respect of damages incurred to property during Ben's brief period of employment. The letter finished tartly by warning that 'If the outstanding sum is not paid promptly within fourteen days, there will be further legal action and possible criminal charges.'

He tossed it down on the desk. Ruth read it and whistled. 'Even at my worst, I only managed to smash a few of his windows. What the hell did you do?'

'I had an argument with a smoke alarm. Now let's see what you have to show me.'

'Get ready,' she said. 'When you see this, everything you thought you knew about the modern world is going to change.' She sat in the swivel chair and he watched over her shoulder as her fingers rattled over the keys. She quickly entered a website URL and a box flashed up on the screen asking for a password. She rattled the keys again and hit ENTER, and the site opened up. Its design was basic, home-made, and Ben realised right away that its only function was as a repository for data files, secure storage for large amounts of information that could be accessed only by a chosen few.

'This is access only,' she said. 'Not open to the public. Rudi created it, and we uploaded all our research stuff onto it. I've never shown it to anyone on the outside.' She scrolled down an index of files, all with coded names that made no sense to Ben. 'You're a big boy,' she said, selecting one and clicking on it. 'I think you can handle it if I throw you right in at the deep end.'

As Ben watched, a video file loaded up onscreen and then began to play. The video seemed to have been filmed in some kind of warehouse. Bare brick walls, concrete floor.

'You're looking at a storage facility on the edge of Frankfurt,' Ruth explained. 'We hired it cheap, no questions.'

'Who's filming this?'

'I'm holding the camera. Franz was there too, operating the gear. A few other guys, too. All witnesses to what happened there.'

'Franz, the potter?'

'He wasn't always a potter. He was my colleague at Frankfurt University, where we were both teaching applied physics at the time this was filmed.'

As Ben watched, the camera panned slowly across a

massive bank of equipment that looked as if someone had salvaged it from a 1950s military base or the set of some antiquated science-fiction movie. Lights flashed, the display of an oscilloscope glowed green, the needles on gauges pulsed up and down. Banks of diodes and buttons and dials, wires trailing everywhere. The equipment was emitting an electrical hum. The camera panned across to reveal more of the warehouse, and more equipment wired together across twenty yards of the concrete floor.

'This was all stuff we bought as junk, borrowed or stole wherever we could and rigged up ourselves,' Ruth explained. 'There's a Van de Graaff generator, a bunch of tuning capacitors, and that thing there that looks like a giant dumbbell is a Tesla coil. Nothing fancy or expensive. That's the beauty of it.'

Ben didn't reply, watching without comprehension of what he was seeing. In an empty space a few metres from the machinery were two large items that could only be described as scrap metal. One was a huge rusting cast-iron hulk of an old mangle that looked as though it had been dragged out of a river and probably weighed over seventy kilos. Next to it was a truck axle and differential, complete with double wheels. Beside the axle lay a small dark object that Ben couldn't make out at first, then realised was a plain black baseball cap.

'What is this all about?' he asked.

'Just watch.'

Some voices could be heard offscreen from behind the camera. Then someone went 'Shh' and the room fell into a hush. The hum from the equipment grew louder. Lights began to flash faster. The readouts on the dials went wild.

'It's starting,' Ruth said. 'You're going to be amazed.'

Ben watched closely.

Nothing was happening.

'I don't see anything so spe—' he began.

And his voice trailed off in mid-word and his eyes opened wide as the baseball cap, the truck axle and the enormous mangle all suddenly sailed weightlessly up into the air.

Chapter Forty-Nine

The items hovered there, levitating without support. Ben stared hard at the screen, searching for tell-tale wires that might explain how this trickery was being done. But there were no wires, and what happened next made his jaw drop. While the baseball cap and the mangle floated in mid-air, the massive truck axle started to rotate slowly around on an invisible pivot. Then it suddenly took off, flashing across the warehouse faster than the eye could follow and smashing itself into the far wall with a loud crash and a cloud of masonry dust. A solid lump of metal, half a ton or more, zipping through the air like a lightweight arrow.

Propelled, apparently, by nothing.

At that point, the video clip came to an end, the image of the axle's impact freezing on the screen. 'We turned everything off then,' she said. 'Aborted the experiment. We couldn't control the movement or direction of the objects, and it was just too dangerous to continue. Then we packed up the gear and got the hell out of there before the warehouse owners discovered the damage to the wall.'

Ben tore his gaze away from the screen and turned to her. 'This isn't for real,' he said. 'It's got to be faked.'

'Come on. Open your eyes. To fake that on camera would cost millions. It would take the kind of CGI special effects

325

technology they use in the movies. Did that experiment look that well funded to you? No, Ben, this is real. And there's more.'

He looked at her, studied her face for traces of a lie and could see she was absolutely serious. 'OK. That was impressive. But what the hell was it?'

'It's not a magic trick,' she replied, allowing a smile. 'It's scientific reality. What I've just shown you was the most successful AG experiment Franz and I ever achieved.'

'AG?'

'Anti-gravity. The next one we did was a disaster. Nothing worked properly. Soon after that, the university cottoned on to what we were doing and found out that we'd borrowed some equipment from their labs without permission. We got sacked for conducting dangerous, unorthodox experiments – for which read experiments that the academic establishment and its corporate paymasters don't want the world to know about.'

Ben shook his head in confusion. 'Hold on. I thought that what you were going to show me had to do with the Kammler papers – stuff dating back to the 1940s.'

Ruth tapped the screen with her finger. 'That's exactly what this is, Ben. Harnessing hidden energies, tapping into the power of the ether. That's what Kammler's work is all about.'

'It sounds more like science fiction. Something from the future.'

'Wrong. Scientists have been talking about it for centuries. Benjamin Franklin said in 1780 that "We may learn to deprive large masses of their gravity, and give them absolute levity for the sake of easy transportation."'

'How did you get into this stuff?' he asked, still reeling from what he'd just seen and fighting to make sense of it.

'Remember I told you how I'd overheard Maximilian's phone call that time, when I was a student? Well, this is the stuff he was telling his brother about. As soon as my vacation was over and I went back to university, I started digging through every science text I could find that could explain what it was all about. Of course, the tutors did all they could to discourage me. It was years before I started seeing the deeper implications, and understanding that this radical, incredible thing was based on a complex phenomenon called Zero Point Energy.'

'I've never heard of it.'

'Not many people have. That's for two reasons. One, because the physics of it makes Einstein's relativity look like first-year maths. Secondly, because there are a lot of rich folks out there who stand to gain if this thing stays a secret. Zero Point Energy is, basically, free energy.'

He pointed at the screen. 'So you're saying Kammler's research was to make stuff float about?'

'There's much more to it than that,' she said. 'OK, I'll try to make it simple. As Einstein showed, we need to think of the universe and everything in it as an infinite soup of energy. Including you and me. We might think we're real and solid, but in reality we're just floating clouds of electrons. All that's stopping us from falling apart, or disappearing through the floor, is the interaction of electromagnetic forces. We're literally made up of and surrounded by gigantic, limitless amounts of energy.'

Ben frowned, absorbing the ideas.

'Now, when it comes to trying to exploit natural resources for human civilisation, our technology is limited to using the crudest methods imaginable. Fossil fuels are inefficient, wasteful and harmful to the planet. And they're running out fast. But imagine if we could tap into the natural energies

327

that surround us, literally pulling power out of the ether. We'd be rewriting the future of the planet. Each home with its own little Zero Point Energy reactor, providing unlimited power for heat and light. Free. Safe. Clean. No more toxic by-products to dispose of. No more gases pumping into the atmosphere, no more radioactive waste sitting at the bottom of the ocean. For the first time since the industrial revolution, humans would actually be living in harmony with the Earth instead of destroying it.'

'I get you, but I still don't see what this has to do with Kammler.'

'Kammler was the inventor of something called the Bell,' Ruth explained. 'A very special and completely unique device, commissioned by Hitler in 1943 or 1944 and built by Kammler's team of SS engineers and scientists. Not much is known about it, except that it was in development in a secret facility somewhere in Eastern Europe during the final years of World War Two. Whatever it was, it was so potent that it had to be kept locked inside a vault. Witness reports from the time claimed that it had strange powers, interfered with electrical equipment and emitted a weird blue light when it was turned on. Based on what we know about Kammler's research from leaked information at the time and vague references in some of his correspondence to fellow SS engineers, there's a very good chance that he was building some kind of Zero Point Energy reactor.'

'Reactor?'

'An instrument capable of extracting raw energy from the ether and converting it into usable power. Like electricity, but not artificially generated. Straight from nature. What we can create ourselves is a pale imitation.' She paused. 'But when Kammler disappeared in 1945, in the very last days of the war, so did all trace of his invention. Nobody knew where it was, whether it had even survived. US Intelligence spent years searching for it, but never found it. The same goes for his research papers, containing the secrets of his invention.'

'But you think Steiner found them?'

'That's right, Ben. I believe that's what he found by accident and has locked away – you can easily see why this stuff would be a threat to him. And from what he said that day on the phone to Karl, I think he knows not only the secrets of the Bell, but *where* it might be – its hidden resting place since 1945.'

'Let me get this right,' Ben said. 'You're saying that this Bell was a machine capable of drawing the energy out of thin air and converting it into usable power? Like a nuclear reactor, but without the need for fuel, and with no waste products?'

Ruth nodded. 'The future of our planet.'

'It's a little hard to imagine the Nazis as the inventors of a wonderful green technology that could save the Earth,' Ben said. 'Especially as they were in the middle of losing a war at the time. I'd have thought they had other things on their mind than green ideology.'

'There are other theoretical applications. Like the potential to create a super high-speed anti-gravity aircraft. There's some evidence that the Nazis might have been doing just that. And then there are other things, too.'

'Such as?'

'We're talking about energy, Ben. A limitless force of nature. If you control its release, harness it, you have a safe, clean reactor that can go on churning out endless amounts of power for all eternity. But if you speed up the process and let the energy come pulsing out much more strongly, you have something else altogether.'

Ben's stomach gave a lurch. 'A bomb.'

'Infinitely more powerful than the effect of merely split-ting the atom. While the Americans were developing the first nuclear weapons, they had no idea that their enemies were working on something that could potentially have made Oppenheimer's atom bombs look like kids' fireworks by comparison. It's safe to say that when Hitler gave Kammler's SS Special Projects Division carte blanche to develop this technology, it wasn't because he cared about the future of the environment. It would have given him the power to obliterate half of Europe. He could have won the war in a day.'

'So isn't it just as well that the Kammler research stays safe and secret?'

Ruth shook her head, resolute. 'No, Ben. The planet deserves it. Whatever dark side there may be to Zero Point Energy, it's no different from any other natural resource. Take electricity. You can use it to provide light and warmth and make people's lives better; or you can use it to fry a man in a chair. If we can just control that energy respon-sibly, we really do have the key to saving the planet.' Her eyes were bright with excitement as she talked. 'Think of it. The end of our dependence on fossil fuels. The total breakdown of the evil business empires based on raping the environment.' She smiled darkly. 'Including Steiner's. He has billions tied up in the aerospace and oil industries. Imagine the catastrophic losses he'd suffer if this technology broke through into the mainstream. Greedy capitalist bastards like him, plundering the planet's natural resources and holding them for ransom, would become as extinct as the dinosaurs.'

Ben now understood why Steiner had lied about the real nature of the documents in his safe, inventing the Holocaust denial angle to put any enquiring minds off the track.

'I think I get it,' he said. 'This is really just about you and him. You wanted your revenge on him, for what he represents to you.'

'No, Ben. I want what's best.'

'Really? That's why you and your radical friends decided to get tooled up with real guns and start playing at being kidnappers?'

'It was a long time before we even considered that kind of desperate measure,' she protested. 'Years of trying everything we could think of. Like the guy in Manchester I tried to talk to. I'd heard through the grapevine that he was this big Kammler expert. I flew all the way over there to see him, and—'

'And he never turned up to the meeting,' Ben finished for her. 'I know about Lenny Salt. If it's any consolation, I don't think he'd have been much help to you.'

'Then I tried to get in touch with this colleague of his called Julia something. Julia Goodman. But she never got back to me. Meanwhile, whenever we weren't trying to earn our living selling Franz's art or doing a bit of private science tuition here and there, we were scraping together money to hire equipment and premises to run more experiments. We kept hoping that we'd crack it. But there was something missing. We just couldn't quite get it to work consistently. One time in twenty, we'd get a positive result, and even then we couldn't work out why it was happening.' She sighed. 'In the end we sat down and realised we had no choice but to get hold of what Maximilian had in his safe. But it wasn't for lack of trying every other possible alternative. We didn't actually *want* to be criminals.'

'Couldn't you just have sneaked the keys out of his pocket like all rebellious kids do?'

'You don't understand. I haven't been back to that house for nearly eight years. I'm the estranged daughter, remember?

The crazy one who dropped out of society and went off on some crusade to save the Earth. Why do you think Dorenkamp told you there'd never been any Steiner children? I'm officially disowned, dead and forgotten. All I have is some money that's left from the Geneva apartment and the allowance they gave me.'

'You said you were close to Silvia and Otto, though. They might have helped you get inside the house.'

'Uh-uh. No way would I have done that to Silvia. She's a bad liar and Maximilian would have sussed her out right away. But I did try to work on Otto.' Ruth smiled. 'Poor, sweet Otto. It was about a year ago, I called him on his mobile, managed to persuade him to leave his golf clubs alone for a few hours. We met up for lunch in Bern, and I told him about these old papers of vague scientific interest that I wanted to look at. All he had to do was to go into Maximilian's study, open up the safe and photocopy them for me. But Otto's weak. He got cold feet, backed out. The big soft chicken's totally dominated by his uncle. So that didn't work either. Like I said, soon after that we realised we were all out of options. We thought, fuck it, go for it.'

'Dressing up like Nazis – I take it that was just a red herring for the police?'

She shrugged. 'We've all been active in green circles. Half our names are probably down on police files. They'd come knocking on our door pretty fast if a bunch of greenies started trying to take down the likes of the great Steiner. So we figured that with the Kammler SS connection, the best possible front would be to pass ourselves off as something the complete opposite of what we really were, some kind of neo-Nazi terror group. It wasn't hard to find the swastika badges. There were eleven of us involved, all committed. The first time, we almost got him. We were unlucky.'

'I heard what happened.'

'Then the second time, we had an even better plan. We spent ages working out every detail. But, as I recall, *someone* interfered.' She shot him a look.

'I'm glad I did, Ruth. You were risking your freedom, even your life, just because you believed that a bunch of documents written by some obscure Nazi loony almost seventy years ago was the key to saving the planet.'

'It's not a question of belief, Ben. These are facts.'

'I think you've been smoking too much of that weed of yours. You're stacking an awful lot of faith on this mumbo-jumbo.'

'That's neat, coming from someone who studied theology. You believe in a god that nobody can prove exists, that nobody's ever seen, and who never shows himself. I show *you* something real, and you choose to dismiss it without a second thought.'

'I don't know *what* I saw just now.'

She snorted, glaring at him, her temper rising fast. 'Yeah, it's easier just to close your eyes. Anyway, I don't care if you believe me or not. You wanted to know why we tried to kidnap Maximilian, and now you know. So maybe now you'll let me go back home.'

'To do what? To sell pottery? Or to pin your little Nazi badges back on and try to kidnap him again?'

'We're not going to stop trying. This is important.'

'I don't like what you're doing. What if someone had been hurt, or killed? You weren't shooting blanks that day.'

'It wasn't meant to go that far,' she said. 'I swear it.'

'You're throwing away your life.'

'I don't need your approval.'

'You might think you got away because you were clever, well trained and well rehearsed. The fact is, you were just lucky. If I'd been properly in charge of a close protection outfit that I'd had the opportunity to train and equip the way *I* wanted instead of just having to make do with amateurs, you and your friends would all be in prison now awaiting sentence. And if you keep trying, that's what you're going to come up against. You're going to get caught, Ruth. Ever been in a cell? I don't think you'd like it. If you thought Steiner was cramping your freedom, wait until you get a load of Interpol.'

She said nothing.

'And that's not all,' he went on. 'While you're running around playing your little games and dabbling in things that should be left well alone, people are being kidnapped and murdered for real. Julia Goodman, the woman you tried to contact?'

Ruth frowned.

'Dead,' Ben said. 'Along with another of her colleagues who was heavily into this Kammler stuff, someone by the name of Michio Miyazaki.'

She'd clearly heard the name, from the way she flinched.

'And have you heard of a man called Adam O'Connor? He's missing, and so is his young son. Whoever's out there doing this stuff is armed and means business, and it's clear that someone is paying them to take an interest in all this.'

'Someone like who? Maximilian?'

'I don't know,' he said. 'But I do know that anyone connected with this Kammler research is a potential target. Which includes you and your cronies, too. You're way out of your depth. You need to back right off.'

'Thank you for the lecture. But I'll take my chances. I can look after myself. I've done it for long enough. And I'd rather believe in something, and suffer the consequences, than not believe in anything at all.' She looked up at him hotly. 'So can I go now? Or am I your prisoner?'

'I ought to keep you locked up until you see sense.'

'Fuck you. You're just as bad as him.'

He could see the look in her eye. The argument was spiralling out of control, and the last thing he wanted to do was alienate the sister that he'd only just found again. He stepped towards her, put his hand on her arm. 'I'm sorry,' he said. 'You know I'd never stand in your way. If you want to go, go. Call Franz and tell him where you are. Or take the Mini. Here. It's yours.' He dangled the keys out in front of her.

She snatched the keys furiously out of his fingers, and he realised he'd already pushed her too far.

'Fine,' she snapped. 'I'm going to get some rest, and then I'll leave tonight.'

He pointed over to the trainee accommodation block. 'Pick any room you want. The sheets are all fresh.'

Without another word she turned away from him, wrenched open the office door and slammed it shut behind her. He watched her strut angrily across the yard, then powered down the laptop and left the office too.

There was no sign of Storm outside. Ben walked alone to the house, feeling frustrated. He was hoping to find Brooke sitting reading in the kitchen. She was becoming more and more part of the place. But there was no sign of her there, nor in the living room.

Then he heard the sound of someone moving around upstairs. Following the sound, he found the door to his quarters open. Brooke was crouched down on the rug, sweeping shards of glass into a dustpan. He saw that she'd been clearing up the debris. Broken chairs were piled in the corner, and the pictures that hadn't been destroyed were back on the walls. She'd gathered up the bits of broken glass from the smashed frames and propped them up neatly and safely out of the way against the wall near the sofa.

She hadn't seen him, and he watched her from the doorway. Kneeling there with her thick hair tied back loosely over her shoulders, she looked so serene and calm. He thought of the last time they'd been here together in this room, that evening spent sitting on the rug eating Marie-Claire's chocolate cake and drinking wine. It seemed so long ago now.

'Hi,' he said.

She looked up, and smiled back.

'Clearing this place up is my job,' he said. 'You shouldn't have.'

'Something to do while I stayed out of your way for a while.' She stood up, dusting off her hands. 'Anyway, it wasn't as bad as it looked. She didn't wreck quite everything.'

He walked into the room, closed the door behind him.

'You look shattered,' she said.

He sat on the sofa, and she walked over and sat next to him. He leaned back, closing his eyes, and for a few precious moments he was able to switch off and enjoy the soothing atmosphere of her presence. When he opened them, Brooke was watching him with a pained expression, like someone bursting to make a confession.

'Ben, I have something to say.'

He straightened up. 'What?' he asked, suddenly worried.

'I've been thinking – and maybe this isn't the right time to say it – but I'm not sure I should come here any more.'

He was silent as her words sank in.

'What I said to you in London. About the way I felt. The way I feel. I shouldn't have said that. But I can't pretend I didn't say it, any more than I can pretend it's not true.'

'I don't want you to stop coming here,' he murmured. He looked in her eyes. Very slowly, he reached out and stroked her soft cheek. Then, even more slowly, with his heart beginning to thud faster, knowing he was crossing a bridge he couldn't uncross, he leaned forward and kissed her.

This time, Brooke didn't pull away from his embrace. They moved closer together. The kisses started off gentle and soft. Then, as their breathing quickened, the kisses became deep and passionate. She reclined back on the sofa, clutching at his clothes, pulling him down on top of her.

And then the door burst open with a juddering crash and two men in black tactical gear carrying silenced Skorpion machine pistols stormed into the room.

Chapter Fifty

In the split second before anything else happened, Ben was already reacting. As he whipped round he locked on to the two pairs of eyes in the black tactical masks and he saw the intent in them. He'd seen that look plenty of times, the deliberately unthinking stony look, like the expression of a shark, that passes across a paid killer's eyes in the instant before he does his job. The clearing of the mind, removing all doubt, all hesitation, any last vestiges of humanity. No prisoners, no discussions. Gloved fingers were on triggers. Actions were cocked, safeties set to FIRE. The fat, stubby silencers were trained right on them.

The silence of the room gave way to a flurry of muted gunfire, like the ripping of corrugated cardboard, as both shooters opened up simultaneously. But by then, Ben had Brooke shielded with his own body and he was kicking out with his legs while hurling his weight against the backrest of the sofa. Bullets thunked into its wooden frame as it toppled over backwards. Their bodies sprawled on the floor as a swarm of splinters and ripped pieces of foam flew around them.

There weren't many good things about being on the wrong end of a Skorpion Vz61 submachine pistol in the hands of a man who knew how to use it. But even the most effective shooter couldn't do much about the combined effect of a rapid 850-round-a-minute rate of fire with the limited capacity of its standard ten-round box magazine. One quick dab of the trigger, a flurry of recoil against the shooter's palm, and the machine would have rattled itself empty. In a shade under three-quarters of a second, it was all over. That made the compact Skorpion an ideal assassination weapon. Walk into a restaurant with one under your jacket, go striding up to the target's table as he sits there innocently chewing on his *steak au poivre*, and before anyone knew what was happening the job was carried out and you were walking out of the place with a corpse in your wake. And a quick, clean assassination was exactly what these guys had had in mind for Ben and Brooke.

The problems arose when that opening gambit failed to claim its victim; and they intensified considerably when the intended victim was within arm's reach of an improvised weapon of their own and had the reflexes and the instincts to press their advantage while the assassins were too busy dropping their empty magazines and slamming in new ones to notice that the odds had shifted against them.

As Ben rolled across the carpet he found himself a foot away from the broken picture frames that Brooke had gathered up. His fingers closed on a big triangular shard of glass and he skimmed it like a Frisbee, across the top of the overturned sofa and straight at the shooter on the left, a fraction of a second before the guy was able to let off another burst of fire.

The glass whirled sideways through the air and caught him on the side of the neck, where the flesh was exposed between the collar of his combat vest and the ski mask. Its jagged edge ripped through the jugular vein like the blade of a meat slicer. The man's mouth opened into a screaming red hole in the mask and his left hand flew across his body to the gaping slash in his neck that was already spraying a livid jet of blood across the room. His knees crumpled under him and the muzzle of his Skorpion flailed out wide. As the shock almost instantly started shutting down his central nervous system, nerve endings overloaded with signals from the brain, his fingers twitched involuntarily.

And touched off the trigger of his weapon just as it was pointing at the other shooter's side. The weapon jerked under recoil, twisting upwards as though it had a life of its own. Ten rounds of 9mm raked the second shooter from thigh to chest, punching through every major organ on its way up. The man was dead before he hit the carpet.

The shooter with the slashed neck was the second to fall. He rolled and writhed and screamed as blood jetted under high pressure from his wound.

Even before he was down, Ben was up and over the upset sofa. He leapt across the room and landed in a crouch. Snatched up the fallen Skorpion that was still loaded and cocked. The guy he'd sliced was quickly bleeding to death. The rug was saturated with a spreading red stain, and squirts of blood were still pulsing weakly from the severed artery.

Ben could have made it easy for the guy, used the Skorpion to bring a quick end to the pain and terror of his last few moments of life. But having a loaded weapon in his hand was more important than showing mercy to his would-be killer.

Brooke was clambering out uncertainly from behind the fallen sofa. Ben ran to her. She was unhurt but visibly shaken as she gaped in horror at the bodies on the floor, the guns, the blood. He took her in his arms and held her tight for a second, both of them way beyond words.

Then he thought of Ruth and his guts turned to ice.

* * *

Just a minute before, Ruth had been sitting on the bed in her room, talking to Franz on the phone. She could tell from his voice that he'd been sick with worry.

'I'm sorry I didn't call you sooner.'

'Where the hell are you, Luna?'

'France. Don't worry, it's all fine.'

'You were kidnapped by this fucking maniac and now you tell me it's all fine? Have you any idea—'

'Look, things are complicated. It wasn't what it seemed like.'

'This guy trashed the house and tied me and Rudi up in the shed.'

She sighed, rubbing her hair. 'Yeah, I know, babe. I'm really sorry that happened. You OK?'

'No, I'm not OK. I've been going crazy. What are you doing in France?'

'Listen, I'm coming home and I'll explain everything to you. Just don't worry about me, OK? And don't worry about the guy either. Everything's cool. See you really soon.'

She'd put the phone down and gone back to fretting about the argument she'd had with her brother. Part of her wanted to go and find him, make up with him; another part was too proud to.

Other thoughts, too. *I am not Luna Steiner. I'm Ruth Hope.* It felt very strange, thinking that. Alien, yet somehow it made her glow inside.

The heavy thump from somewhere outside her door jolted her alert.

There it went again. Thump, *crash*. It was coming from inside the block.

She jumped off the bed and ran to the door. She was about to yank it open and step out when she heard the noise again. And then again, making her heart race with fear. Something was wrong here.

She turned the handle, slowly, cautiously, opened the door a crack and peered out.

Two guys in black were working their way systematically along the corridor that ran up the middle of the block, kicking down doors as they went and aiming small black automatic weapons into the empty rooms. In that moment, she understood intuitively that the adrenaline that was starting to speed through her body, making her hands shake and her knees go to jelly, was the instinctive fight-or-flight reaction of a prey animal in the presence of a predator. They were hunting for someone, and she knew that someone was her.

She'd opened the door just a millimetre too wide. One of the men turned and saw her. A yell as he alerted his buddy, and all at once they were dashing up the corridor towards her.

She burst out of the room and ran for her life. Right up ahead, beside the door marked 'TOILETTES', was the emergency fire exit. She grabbed the handle of the heavy door and ripped it open with a grunt. The two gunmen opened fire as they ran, two brief chattering bursts that strafed the wall and punched jagged, splintered holes through the wood of the exit door just inches from her body. She slammed the door shut and staggered out of the building. Found herself in a little walled yard on the other side with archways leading off it. She glanced around her, looking for a way to the main house. She had to find Ben. Where was he?

The emergency exit door opened and the two men in black came striding purposefully out, their weapons reloaded, glancing grimly around for her, motioning to one another. She darted through one of the archways, hoping they hadn't noticed her.

Then she skidded to a halt and let out a cry of fear as the man with the double-barrelled shotgun came out of nowhere and she was staring into the twin muzzles not three feet from her face.

Ben had emerged from the house and out into the hot sun just in time to see the second pair of black-clad intruders disappearing through the door into the trainee accommodation block.

He broke into a sprint. He had the Skorpion in his hand and the four spare magazines he'd lifted from the dead men in his pocket, but he still felt vulnerable as he ran across the cobbles, keeping low, skirting the edge of the buildings. No telling how many more intruders there were, and how they'd managed to get past Le Val's security guys. No time to stop to think about why they were here and what the hell was happening. And no time to get to the underground armoury room, just a few yards away under the innocuous-looking brick hut between the trainee block and the purpose-built gym. He had enough military hardware stored away inside the armoury's safes to hold off an entire regiment – but it might as well be a thousand miles away.

Brooke was right behind him, fierce and determined with the second Skorpion cupped in both hands. Ben had spent enough time on the range with her to know she could handle a gun and he trusted her to back him up.

He darted through the open doorway into the accommodation block, Brooke following. Saw the doors kicked open off the corridor, the bullet holes in the far wall and the emergency exit, and ran that way with his blood chilling in his veins as he thought of his sister. But every room in the building was empty. There was no sign of her, nor of the attackers. He ripped the exit door open so hard that he almost tore the handle off. Burst out into the little walled yard that separated the back of the trainees' block from Jeff's bungalow. The yard was empty too.

He froze as the two loud shotgun blasts boomed out from beyond the wall. At first he thought someone was shooting at him. Then he realised the shots had been for someone else. He raced towards the sound, his mind suddenly flooded with terrifying images. Convinced he was going to round the corner and find Ruth's body there. Torn up with buckshot. Vital organs shredded. Her blood spilling out across the ground. He almost cried out in horror. It was the kind of blind panic that he knew was liable to get him killed in battle, but at that moment he didn't even care.

He sprinted out of the walled yard, through one of its archways and round the corner through the back passage that ran around the wall of the bungalow. Up ahead was the little lean-to where Jeff kept his Land Rover. Ben whipped around the corner with the Skorpion thrust out in front of him and his finger tightening on the trigger.

Stopped dead in his tracks. Looked down and saw the bodies of the two men in black lying there a couple of yards apart. One sprawled on his back with a red hole a foot across where his heart and lungs used to be, shattered bits of rib poking through the carnage. The other propped up against the garage wall with his legs splayed out at impossible angles and his upper and lower halves only loosely connected by quivering intestines. A huge red flower of blood was painted up the wall behind him. At close range, there wasn't much that was more devastating than a shotgun.

'Ah, Jesus,' Brooke said, catching up and seeing the mess.

Ben looked up from the corpses to see Ruth standing there, looking small and frightened with her hands to her face. Shocked, but safe.

Beside her, cradling the shotgun, was Jeff Dekker. He nodded to Ben as he broke open the action to eject the smoking spent shells and quickly inserted the fresh pair that he was holding between the knuckles of his left hand.

'I should come home early from holiday more often,' he said laconically. 'There I was, sunshine and sand and beautiful girls everywhere, and all I could think about was this place. Couldn't rest for a second. If I'd known you were having a party I'd have come back even sooner.'

'Glad you showed up,' Ben said.

'Not sorry I kept this old twelve-bore in the toolshed, either. Thought it might come in handy for rats. I hate bloody rats.' Jeff used the shotgun barrels to point at the corpses. 'So what's the story on these guys?'

'Two more in the house,' Ben said. 'No idea who they are.'

'I don't suppose they'll tell us much now.'

Ben was walking over to Ruth when the bullet came out of nowhere and caught him in the chest. Somewhere through the bursting white flash of pain, he heard Brooke's distant scream. He staggered back two steps and keeled over in the dirt.

Chapter Fifty-One

Ben felt his body hit the ground, felt the breath burst out of his lungs with the impact. The pain in his chest was crippling. He fought for air, and sounds became a dull booming in his ears. As if from some remote place, he watched the others scatter in slow motion and dive for cover as gunfire blasted across from the Dutch barn next to the house. Bullets raked the ground near him, kicking up sprays of dust.

This is no time to die, he thought as he lay there. But for some reason that his mind couldn't grasp, he wasn't dead. He'd been down just a couple of seconds when he realised that his senses were already bouncing back, sharpening, focusing. He willed his body to move, and it did. Ignoring the pain that stabbed through his upper body, he rolled over and wedged himself in the gap between the bungalow and the lean-to.

A moment's silence as the shooters across the way reloaded, then another ripping rasp of silenced full-auto fire came from the barn and bullets sang off the wall right by his head.

He put his hand to where he'd been hit, felt the wetness seeping into his shirt. But it was cold, not warm, and when he looked at his hand there was no blood and the moisture on his fingers smelled like petrol.

He understood then what had happened. *Another life gone*, he thought grimly.

He risked a glance around the corner of the lean-to and saw a movement inside the shadows of the barn. Two men, same black tactical gear and ski masks. They were using the parked Mini Cooper as cover, scanning left and right across the yard with their weapons. Burst, reload, burst. It was a good vantage point, giving them an open view of the whole place. Jeff and the women were pinned down in the alley beside the bungalow a few yards away. Anywhere they tried to move, they'd be out in the open.

'Shotgun,' Ben called out to Jeff. An instant later, the weapon slid along the ground to within two feet of his reach. He stretched out a hand, then jerked it back as bullets ripped up the dirt. One of them whacked into the shotgun's stock, splinters flying.

He said a prayer and then threw himself out into the open. Hit the ground with his chest, and the pain seared through him again. His fingers closed on the shotgun and he snatched it up as he rolled out of the way of another spray of bullets that chewed up the spot where he'd been a millisecond earlier. He fired as he moved. Forty yards or so was a long shot for a double-barrelled shotgun, but he saw the window of the Mini vaporise into a cloud of glass fragments and one of the shooters spin away with a shout. Ben rolled again, let off the second barrel upside down on his back.

The Mini exploded violently with a deafening 'BLAM', its back end kicking upwards with the force as the steel shot pellets ripped into its fuel tank and sparks ignited the petrol. An orange fireball blasted out of the barn, bits of torn planking tumbled across the yard. The blast caught one of the shooters and just about tore him in half before he was lost in the thick black smoke that belched from the blazing car. The other was on fire as he came staggering out into the open. He dropped his weapon, went down on his knees and collapsed and started thrashing about desperately to put out the flames that were licking up his legs.

Ben scrambled to his feet and sprinted across the yard to the fallen man. Able to see him clearly for the first time, he noticed the secondary weapon the assassin was carrying strapped to his back – a high-performance crossbow with a mounted quiver full of murderous razor-tipped bolts.

Jeff got there a second later, and stared at Ben with an expression that said 'Why are you alive?' Ben reached into his breast pocket and showed him. The Zippo lighter was dented in the middle, squashed almost flat from the impact of the bullet. Jeff grinned.

Ben started stamping out the flames that were licking around the intruder's clothing.

'Let the bastard burn,' Jeff said.

'I want to talk to him.' Ben kicked a few more times, rolling the man over to quell the flames. He tore away the crossbow and looped its strap over his own shoulder, then pulled off the guy's smouldering combat vest and tossed it away. He started searching him roughly, not caring how much he hurt him in the process.

In a pouch on his belt he found a digital Nikon. He activated the camera and quickly found what he was looking for. An image came up on the screen. It was him and Ruth as they'd sat in the ruined church in the woods talking. He touched a button and saw another shot of the two of them walking back to the house. Now he understood what Storm had been growling for back there. The intruders had been casing the place before the attack, hiding in the woods.

He tossed the camera away and rifled again through the guy's belt pouch. The only other items in it were a phone and two photographs. One shot of himself, lifted from the Le Val website, and one of a slightly younger Ruth with a smile and long hair.

'So you came here to kill the two of us,' he said. The man's eyes looked up at him through the slots in the ski mask.

Brooke ran past them towards the barn, carrying a fire extinguisher to kill the blaze before it took over the whole building. She waded in through the smoke, dousing the flames with foam. The Mini stopped burning, thick foam dripping from blackened metal. Then, as Ben was about to start questioning the prisoner, she let out a cry of horror and threw down the extinguisher. She'd seen something in the barn. Ruth ran over and saw it too, putting her hands to her mouth.

'The dogs. They've shot the dogs.'

Ben ran over and felt sick at the sight. Four German Shepherds were piled in a lifeless heap in the corner of the barn, their bloodied bodies pierced through with crossbow bolts. Lying slumped over the top of the pile was Storm. Drops of blood plopped from the aluminium shaft that was protruding from his shoulder, splashing down into the red pool on the concrete floor.

Ben could hear Ruth sobbing behind him as he put his hand on the dog's body. Just the tiniest flicker of movement. He checked the animal's pulse. It was there, but it was weak. Storm's eyes half-opened and looked right into his, as if he were saying 'Don't worry about me.' He tried to raise his shaggy head, but the effort was too much. He licked Ben's hand, then his eyes closed and he fell unconscious.

'Will he make it?' Brooke asked.

'I don't know.' Ben turned and walked back towards the prisoner. Crouched down beside him and whipped off his mask. 'You speak English?' he asked him quietly.

The man nodded, squinting up with his teeth bared and his eyes glazed over with pain.

'Who sent you?' Ben asked. He spoke quietly, calmly. The rage was turning from hot red to a steady, controlled white.

No response.

'Ever been on a farm before?' Ben asked him.

Another nod, confused this time.

'Then maybe you've seen those machines they use to shred up sawn branches? Big whirring blades, chew through anything?'

The guy just stared. His eyes bulged. Sweat was pouring down his face.

'I have one of those machines,' Ben said to him. 'Right over there in the toolshed. If you don't tell me who sent you here I'm going to lower you slowly into it, feet first. You have three seconds to reply. One.'

'Fuck you,' the guy said through clenched, bloodied teeth.

'Two.'

The look of defiance melted a little, but not that much. 'I don't know!'

'You don't think I mean it, do you? Three.' Ben stood, grabbed the guy's ankle and jerked his body round brutally and started dragging him across the ground towards the toolshed. The guy kicked and struggled, yelling 'No! No!'

'Fire her up, Jeff,' Ben said. Jeff trotted ahead to the shed, yanked the tarp off the shredder, stooped down to prime the carburettor and then pulled the starter cord. The engine spluttered into life. As Ben was dragging the guy inside the toolshed, Jeff grabbed a coil of rope from a nail on the wall and flung one end over a beam. Ben took a fistful of the guy's hair, jerked him into sitting position on the concrete floor and looped the other end of the rope roughly around his chest. The machine whirred away next to them, blades gnashing like teeth, ready to devour anything that was thrown into its rusty maw and spew it out in little chunks from the outlet pipe underneath. Ben tugged the end of the rope and it went taut across the beam. Pulled a little harder, and the guy was lifted a few inches off the floor. Then a few more.

That must have been when he realised they were absolutely serious about feeding him to the shredder. 'OK! OK!' he shouted in panic.

Ben let go of the rope and let him slump back down. He unslung the crossbow. Bracing it between his chest and the floor, he yanked the bowstring all the way back with a click. Felt like a hundred and fifty pounds of pull. That probably gave the bow a velocity of over three hundred feet per second. He fitted one of the razor-tipped bolts and pointed the ungainly rifle-like weapon at the guy's face.

'Talk,' he said.

There was no hesitation now. The man spoke a single name. 'Steiner.'

Ben felt his mouth go dry.

His finger hovered over the crossbow trigger.

'Let me go now,' the man pleaded. 'I swear I'll never come back here again. I'll tell them you're dead. You and the girl, the way it was meant to be.'

'The girl in the photo. Steiner ordered her dead?'

The guy nodded. Ben looked in his eyes and believed him.

'Just let me go. I swear.'

'You shouldn't have hurt my dogs,' Ben said.

And fired the bow. The weapon recoiled in his arms as it launched the bolt with a *thwack*.

Chapter Fifty-Two

Rory looked up from the corner of his cell where he was sitting when he heard the tinkle of the key in the lock. When he saw it was Ivan, his fear ebbed away as quickly as it had mounted.

This time Ivan had one of the guards with him, one of the most surly and taciturn ones, but said something to him that made him stay out in the corridor while he came into the cell and half-closed the door behind him.

'I brought you something to read,' Ivan whispered with a nervous glance behind him to make sure the guard couldn't see. He reached into his jacket and brought out a tattered comic book.

Rory took it, grateful to have something to while away the hours with. He'd been here so long now, and the way day merged into night, he was losing all track of time and going slowly crazy. Ivan stood over him, smiling benevolently.

'Something else for you,' he murmured, handing the boy another chocolate bar.

Rory quickly hid the chocolate and the comic under his mattress, the way Ivan had told him to. Then he turned to the man, looking up at him with big, inquisitive eyes.

'Do you know where my dad is?' he asked him.

'I have not been able to find out much,' Ivan whispered.

'That man Pelham—'

'Shh.'

Rory spoke more quietly. 'That man Pelham said he was coming.'

Ivan lowered his voice a notch further. 'Pelham cannot be trusted,' he said. 'Don't believe him.'

'I don't understand,' Rory whimpered. There were times when he felt near the edge of hysteria, and that mood had welled up inside him more and more readily since the torture. It was as though some vital part of his inner core had been ripped out, leaving him as fragile as a sickly kitten.

'If Dad's not coming,' he sobbed, 'why am I here? What do they want with us anyway? When am I going home?' Tears streamed down his face.

Ivan laid a hand on his shoulder and looked earnestly into his eyes. 'Do not be so scared. I promised I would take care of you. And I will.'

Rory sniffed and smeared the tears away with his grimy sleeve. 'Are you in contact with the other special agents?'

Ivan looked back at the door, then nodded, smiled and put a finger to his lips. 'When it is time,' he whispered, barely audible, 'I will give the signal and they will come for us.'

'Can't it be now?'

'I still have work to do,' Ivan said. 'It's not over. But soon.' He cleared his throat, gesturing at the door. In his normal voice he said, 'You are to come with me. Time for your shower.'

Rory jumped up. The trips to the shower block were the only times he got out of the cell. In a world so limited and confined as his new environment, even something as simple as walking a few hundred yards through the dingy corridors to stand on cracked ancient tiles and get doused with lukewarm water from a rusty tank was something to look forward to.

Out in the corridor, the guard followed them. Ivan's hand was on Rory's shoulder all the way to the shower block, and the boy felt a little more protected with him there. As long as that terrible woman didn't come back to get him, he knew he could make it through this. He imagined how it would be when Ivan's special agent colleagues came storming through the place, taking out the guards one by one. How they'd drag the woman out from hiding, and put a gun to her head and blow her away. How Rory would watch, and smile to see it happen. After what she'd done to him, that would serve the witch right.

Running the scene through his mind as they walked, he looked round and up at Ivan with a conspiratorial smile. Ivan winked and gave his shoulder a reassuring squeeze.

They reached the shower block. Ivan opened the creaky door that led through to the washroom. A row of rusty metal shower heads fixed to the ceiling corresponded with a row of floor drains. It was a pretty Spartan arrangement. Ivan muttered something to the guard, who went off on some errand. Then he got the water running for Rory, turned it up as lukewarm as it would go, and left to give him some privacy.

Rory stripped off his clothes, bundled them on the side and stepped under the water. There was a rough piece of old soap lying on the floor, and he used it to lather himself up.

Ivan stood for a few moments around the corner, listening to the patter of the water on the tiles. Then he peeked furtively out into the corridor. He'd sent Miklós looking for Boris, and he knew that Boris was off duty and had gone off with some of the others to the nearest town, twenty kilometres away, to get his fill of beer and whores. Which meant the stupid Miklós would spend ages scouring the place, and he had time on his own.

Ivan slipped into a small room off the shower block that was used as an office. Inside the room was a desk, heaped with papers.

But he ignored it. Walked quietly over to the wall. Hanging from a hook was an age-faded framed print of Adolf Hitler, posing in uniform with the Nazi flag behind him and, below, the slogan 'EIN VOLK, EIN REICH, EIN FÜHRER' in gothic script.

He raised a trembling hand to the picture. Lifted the edge of the frame away from the wall.

A smile crept over his face and his heart began to beat faster.

He moved his eye to the peephole through to the shower block.

He watched as the naked boy soaped his smooth, young body. First the upper half. Then the lower half.

Ivan groaned softly to himself and started unzipping his trousers.

Meanwhile, down in the bowels of the mountain, inside the chamber behind the vault door, Adam felt the rising panic of desperation as he faced the task he'd been set.

'I don't think—' His words died in his mouth. He laid his hand on the cold metal shell of Kammler's machine.

Pelham was leaning against the wall a few feet away, watching him. They'd been there for hours.

'What don't you think?' he said calmly.

'I'm not so sure I can get this thing to work,' Adam groaned. 'I just don't get it. It's just . . . it's mind-boggling.'

Pelham pointed at the makeshift worktop that had been set up against the wall, and the laptop onto which they'd loaded the research files retrieved from *Teach na Loch*.

'You told me that once you had your notes, you'd be able to make it work. It's cost me a lot of trouble getting them for you.'

'I know what I said,' Adam said, fighting to keep his voice steady. 'But this goes way beyond anything I ever imagined. My notes are useless.'

'You're playing for high stakes, Adam. It would be wise not to forget that.'

'You think I've forgotten? I'm doing my best, goddamnit.' Adam glared at him, then looked back at the machine. It sat there silent, mysterious, unyielding, on its concrete plinth in the middle of the vault. The cold, smooth black metal shell gleamed dully in the lights. It seemed to him that the thing was taunting him, deliberately holding back the dark, terrible, wonderful secrets that were contained inside. Secrets that, he was beginning to fear, its inventor might have taken to his grave. The thought made him want to retch. He lashed out his foot at the bell-like casing.

Pelham peeled himself away from the wall and walked up to him with his hands in his trouser pockets. Adam could see the shoulder holster under his suede jacket, and the butt of the pistol he carried inside.

'Then your best will just have to be better,' he said.

Chapter Fifty-Three

Ben and Jeff leaped in the Land Rover and went skidding down the drive. They found Raymond and Claude unconscious, trussed up in the security hut near the main entrance to Le Val with tranquilliser darts in them. There was no sign of Jean-Yves, until they found the man bundled in the bushes two hundred yards away along the perimeter. All three men were unharmed apart from the effects of the powerful dope that the intruders had used to overpower them. Ben and Jeff loaded them into the Land Rover and carried them back to the house.

It took a few hours to clean up Le Val. Before anything else could be done, the bodies of the six intruders had to be disposed of. That was the easy part. In a sleepy rural area with a population of less than one person per acre of land, where the police very seldom needed to involve themselves in the locals' affairs, barring the occasional theft of a goat or a chicken, dead men could be made to disappear quickly, privately and permanently.

When that was done, it was time to start on the place itself. Jeff helped Ben to roll up the blood-soaked carpet and rug from the house, carry it downstairs and burn it. The bullet damage in the house and trainee block was going to have to wait.

The dogs were grimmer work. All but Storm were dead, and Ben buried them in the field behind the house while they waited anxiously for Drudi. The retired vet from Palermo was the kind of man who would ask no questions and keep his mouth shut. After he'd carefully removed the crossbow bolt from Storm, he gave his prognosis. No major organs had been affected. Storm had a long recovery ahead of him, but he was going to make it. Ben and Brooke carried the bandaged, heavily tranquillised German Shepherd into the kitchen and made him a bed out of blankets.

As they sat with him a while, Brooke unbuttoned Ben's shirt to take a look at his chest. There was an ugly purple rectangle on his pectoral muscle where the shape of the Zippo had been imprinted into the flesh by the bullet's impact. The bruise was going to be spectacular.

She held him tight, tearful and fragile now that the shock of that day's events was beginning to set in.

'I thought you were dead,' she whispered against his shoulder. He rocked her gently in his arms, kissed her hair. He didn't want to have to leave her, not now, not ever. But he knew he'd have to. He had unfinished business to take care of, and that meant a trip to Switzerland.

Ben and Ruth touched down at Bern airport first thing the next morning, and after a fast drive up through the mountains in a rental BMW they arrived at the gates of the Steiner residence. The uniformed security personnel on the gate recognised Ben, and there were some amazed glances at Ruth as they were quickly waved through into the estate.

'So, what's the plan?' she asked as they drove on down the private road and the château came into view through the trees.

'Straight in the front door,' he replied. 'Do what we have to do, then get out of here.'

'What are you going to do to him?'

'What he deserves.'

As Ben was pulling the BMW up in front of the main entrance, the familiar shape of Heinrich Dorenkamp came scuttling down the steps to meet them. The man had obviously just got the call from the security gate and he looked rattled.

Ben and Ruth climbed out of the car. Dorenkamp stopped in his tracks and stared at her. 'So it was true what they told me,' he said. 'It is you.'

'Long time no see, asshole.' Ruth shouldered past him, following Ben up the steps towards the house.

Dorenkamp ran after them. 'What are you doing here?' he asked nervously.

'Making a social call,' Ben said. 'Where is he?'

'You can't see him.'

'Don't get in the way, Heinrich, or I'm going to walk right over you. Where is he?'

'There is a meeting underway. He doesn't know you're here.'

'Good,' Ben said. 'That's the way I like it.' They'd reached the top of the steps. He shoved through the door and into the reception lobby, shoulder to shoulder with Ruth as they marched across the shiny floor and past the glittering warhorse. Dorenkamp stood helplessly in their wake.

'This place hasn't changed one bit,' Ruth said. 'Then again, some things never do. Where are we going?'

'Conference room. This way.' Ben pointed towards the main stairs.

A minute later they were on the second floor. Ben recognised the grand double doorway of the conference room. He went in without knocking.

Steiner was sitting at the top of the long table. Seated down its length to his left and right were a dozen men in grey suits and at varying stages of middle age, obesity and baldness, hunched over open files and whirring laptops that showed colourful flow charts and graphs and columns of figures. The man at Steiner's right elbow had been in the middle of saying something when Ben and Ruth walked into the room. He shut up. Thirteen pairs of eyes stared up in alarm. Steiner's face turned chalk-white, and his jaw dropped open.

'Meeting's over,' Ben said. He jerked his thumb back at the door. 'Everybody out.'

Silence up and down the table. Steiner's associates all turned to him. His pallor had turned to beetroot-red. He swallowed, hesitated, then gave a stiff nod. The twelve men instantly got up from their seats, hurriedly gathering up their papers and closing down their laptops, stuffing them into briefcases. They filed out timidly past Ben and Ruth, looking down at their feet, none of them daring to say a word.

As the last of Steiner's colleagues shuffled out, Dorenkamp appeared in the doorway. 'Sir, shall I call security?' he asked his boss.

'There'll be no need to do that,' Ben told him. 'But you can get Frau Steiner and Otto up here right now. Double quick.' He snapped his fingers.

'W-why?' Dorenkamp stammered.

'Because we're having a family reunion,' Ben said. 'And I want everyone to hear what the Great Man has to say for himself.'

Dorenkamp left, and they heard his jittery steps echo away down the hall as he went to attend to his duty.

Steiner was still staring wide-eyed at Ruth. The look of noble pride had completely melted away.

362

'You have a lot of explaining to do, Steiner,' Ben said.

'I know,' Steiner murmured with a weary nod.

'And then you're going to pay for what you've done.'

Steiner said nothing. Ruth was looking at him like he was something she'd scraped off her shoe.

After a few moments' silence, there were footsteps outside the door, and then it swung open and Silvia Steiner walked into the room. She looked just as well-groomed and elegant as Ben remembered, in a grey linen trouser suit and a gold necklace. She was followed by Otto, dressed as though Dorenkamp had fetched him straight from the golf course. Ben wouldn't have been surprised if he'd still been clutching his driver.

The PA was about to creep away when Ben called him back inside. 'I want you here too, Heinrich.' Dorenkamp hesitated, then walked in and shut the door behind him.

Otto slouched nervously to the back of the room and leaned against the wall next to the French windows. He smiled uncomfortably at Ruth and gave a little wave. 'Hi there, cousin.'

But Silvia was the one Ben was watching. She let out a gasp as she saw Ruth there. 'Luna!' They embraced tightly. Tears were in Ruth's eyes as she hugged her mother, and Ben could see the love that was there.

Silvia turned to her husband with a look of complete confusion. Steiner said nothing, just hung his head. Then Silvia turned to Ben with a frown of recognition. 'What is going on here?' she breathed.

'Let me introduce someone to you,' Ruth said to her. 'This is my brother Benedict. The one he—' she pointed at Steiner '—told me died in a plane crash. Does he look dead to you?'

Silvia gaped at Ben a moment longer, then turned aghast

to her husband. 'Is this right?' she said softly. 'Max, is this true? This man is her brother?'

'Yes, it's true,' Ruth said hotly. 'He lied to you, to me, to everyone.'

'Max, please say something,' Silvia muttered. She seemed unsteady on her feet for an instant, and had to lean against the table for support.

Maximilian Steiner said nothing for a long while. Then he heaved a sigh and pressed his hands flat on the table. 'What she says is true. I lied. I knew there was a brother still living. I paid to have the story of the plane crash fabricated.' He looked at Ruth. 'And years later, when you hired your own investigator, I protected my lie by buying him off too. I'm sure you have already worked that out for yourself.'

'But why, Max? Why?' Silvia burst out. 'Good God, does this mean her real parents are still alive too? That we took their child—'

'They're dead,' Ben said. 'You didn't take anyone's child.'

'But they didn't die the way I was brought up to believe,' Ruth said. 'All my life. Just lie after lie.'

Steiner held up his hands. 'Can I speak? Can I explain?' He paused, searching for the right words. 'Very well. I admit that I have been untruthful. But I did it only to protect you, Luna.'

'Forget Luna,' she said. 'My name's Ruth. Protect me? From what?'

'To protect you from the terrible knowledge that your real mother took her own life over the shock of your loss. And that your father's death was a direct result of it also. How could I burden a child with such guilt?'

Silvia was staring at him in utter horror, her fingertips white on the backrest of the conference chair she was leaning on.

'I lied to you too,' Steiner told his wife gravely. 'I thought I was doing it for the best. Perhaps I was wrong. I can see that now.'

'You deprived our child of her own brother,' Silvia said slowly. 'You say you wanted to spare her pain. But you brought her up believing this person she loved was dead. How could you have done such a terrible thing?'

'I knew who he was,' Steiner said, motioning at Ben. 'My sources told me that he had gone wild. Joined the army. A reckless and wayward young man, not yet twenty. I thought for a very long time about contacting him. But how could someone like that have taken on the responsibility of a child? He could have been killed in action, and then she would have suffered the pain of his dying anyway, but worse.'

'How very fucking noble of you,' Ruth said.

Tears had formed in Steiner's eyes. 'And we loved her,' he said to Silvia. 'I saw how happy you were, from the moment we found this beautiful little girl living in the desert and brought her into our lives. After what we had gone through, I couldn't bear that my dear wife could lose another child.'

Silvia Steiner slumped against the table with her head in her hands, weeping openly. Ruth ran over to her and held her. 'What's he talking about?' she asked. 'What child?'

Dorenkamp spoke for the first time. 'He is referring to little Gudrun,' he said solemnly. 'You never met her. She died, aged seven.'

'She fell off the pony I had bought her for her seventh birthday.' Steiner was staring down at the tabletop as he spoke, talking barely above a whisper and fighting to keep his voice steady. 'Her neck was broken. She was paralysed. The doctors believed they could save her. But shortly afterwards she slipped into a coma. Nine days later, she was dead.'

365

Ruth looked as though she'd been slapped. 'You knew about this all along?' she asked Dorenkamp.

Dorenkamp nodded.

'And you, Otto?'

Otto was still standing by the window, looking down at his feet. 'I'm sorry,' he mumbled. 'They told me never to tell you about it.'

Steiner looked at Ruth with red-rimmed eyes. 'Why do you suppose we never allowed you to have a pony, no matter how bitterly you wanted one? I was only trying to protect you. That is all I have ever done.'

'It's why you insisted on the Flash-Ball weapons,' Ben said. 'You knew that one of the gang trying to kidnap you was your adopted daughter.'

Steiner nodded sadly. 'I was terrified that she would be harmed if I sanctioned the use of lethal firearms. It's also why I tried my best to keep the police out of it. I hoped we could resolve the situation and come back together again as a family.'

Silvia looked up, wiping her tears away. She pointed at Ben. 'Max, when you hired this young man. You knew who he was?'

Steiner shook his head vehemently. 'I promise you, I was completely unaware of it. When the team leader, Captain Shannon, was injured, the name he gave me for his replacement was Benjamin Hope. I noticed the similarity with the name Benedict, but I put this down to mere coincidence. It was not such an uncommon name, after all. But then, one night after I had sacked the team, you, Silvia, made a remark to me that made me think again.'

'I remember,' Silvia sniffed. 'I had been trying to place his face. He looked so strangely familiar to me. We were getting ready for bed, when it suddenly occurred to me that the person he reminded me of was our own Luna.'

'So you did more poking around,' Ben said to Steiner. 'All you had to do was check out my website.'

'That is what I did, and I soon realised that Captain Shannon had misinformed me about your name. I thought back to what I had seen that day in the woods – the way you let the kidnapper escape so easily, as though you had suddenly been stunned by something you had seen. It seemed strange to me, and stranger still that this could have been the result of mere incompetence as I had initially assumed. Why would a man of such skill and training have done such a thing? Only when I discovered your real name did I realise the truth.'

'And you never thought to share this with me?' Silvia asked him.

'He wanted to tell you,' Dorenkamp replied. 'It was me who warned him against it.'

'We decided to wait and see what happened,' Steiner explained. 'I had a feeling that Luna's brother would go searching for her. That is his expertise. If anyone could find her, it would be him. I thought it would help to bring our family back together.'

Ruth's eyes were narrowed with fury. 'Don't listen to his bullshit, Mother. He wanted Ben to find me so that he could have us both killed. The easiest way to cover up all his lies and take me out of the picture at the same time. Nice and neat.'

Steiner's eyes opened wide as he listened to her words, and the colour drained from his face. 'No,' he quavered. 'You don't understand. I love you. I wanted you back. I . . . I swear I would never harm you. On my mother's grave . . .'

Silvia slapped him across the face. 'What did you do, Max?'

'Nothing!' Steiner protested. 'I don't know what she's talking about. I never—'

367

'Six professional assassins were sent to my home in France,' Ben said, looking hard at him. 'Their mission was to kill the two of us. They're not coming back. Before the last one died, he told me Steiner had sent him. And I know he was telling the truth. Men tend to do that, when they're about to have their legs chewed off.'

Steiner said nothing.

'Lie your way out of that one, Maximilian,' Ruth spat at him. 'You fucker.'

'It's the truth,' said a voice behind them.

They all turned.

Otto had stepped away from the window. 'It's true,' he repeated. 'Steiner did send them.' He pointed down the length of the conference table at his uncle. 'But I'm not talking about that sack of shit over there. It wasn't *that* Steiner. It was the Steiner that everyone forgets about. This one right here. Me.'

Then Otto dipped his hand into his jacket pocket and pulled out a .380 Beretta. Pointed it right at them and the strange little smile on his face spread out into a grin.

Chapter Fifty-Four

'Have you gone totally insane?' Ruth yelled.

Otto's grin broadened even more. 'Actually, I've got you to thank for this, *cousin*. Remember that time you came to me, wanting me to help you steal the old man's papers out of his safe? Well, that got me thinking. What was there about a bunch of antique documents that could be so valuable? Why was the old fucker keeping them a secret? So I had a little sneak peek and made a few photocopies. *Very* interesting. And I wasn't the only one who thought so, either.'

'You stupid bastard, Otto,' Ruth shouted. 'You have no idea what you're messing with.'

Otto's eyes bulged in sudden anger, the grin evaporating. 'Don't call me stupid,' he screamed. 'Everyone thinks I'm stupid. Otto the loser. Poor Otto, have to humour him.' He jabbed his chest with his left thumb, still holding the pistol steady in his right fist. 'But *I'm* the fucking smart one here. I know important people. People who respect me for just how fucking smart I am. So you call me stupid one more time and I'll kill you all right now.'

His rant had left him breathless. He wiped the spittle from his mouth with the back of his free hand, then went on.

'Yeah, that's right. I talked to people. Put the word out. And it wasn't long before I got a call. See, golf isn't just about hitting balls. It's about networking. Getting shit done. When you lot think "Oh, there's Otto out there playing his silly little game again", guess what? I'm organising. Planning.'

'Planning kidnap and murder,' Ben said quietly. The connections were flying together in his mind now. 'Using the Steiner resources and transport links to move people around the world.'

'I'm a businessman,' Otto smirked. 'So we did business. They wanted the documents, they got them faxed through pronto. They paid me a lot of money. Trusted me to run the show. So that's what I've been doing. Snatch a few fucking science geeks. So what? Who's going to miss them anyway?'

Ruth groaned. 'Jesus, Otto. Who *are* these people?'

'I don't think he even knows the answer to that,' Ben said. 'You think they'd trust him with that knowledge? They're just using him, setting him up to take the rap if anything goes wrong. As soon as they're done with him, they'll swat him like a bluebottle. But he can't see that. Can you, Otto?'

Otto shrugged. 'There you go again. Underestimating me. But that's OK, because you'll all be dead pretty soon anyway.'

'So where does a guy like you hire a mercenary team? What did you do, reply to an ad in the back of *Soldier of Fortune* magazine? Some rag-tag crew floating about Eastern Europe looking for easy work? You should have picked better.'

'Oh, you really think you know it all, don't you?'

'I know a lot,' Ben said. 'I know that these associates of yours are holding a young boy hostage to coerce his father into working for them. I know that whoever is payrolling this is after the weapons technology in those Kammler documents. I'm pretty sure you found the location of the Bell. And I also know that you can still make this all OK. Just put the gun down and tell me where your people are keeping Adam and Rory O'Connor.'

Otto sneered at him. 'Somewhere you'll never find them.'

'Do what he says, Otto,' Dorenkamp implored. 'It's the only way.'

'Yes, Otto,' Silvia said. 'Put the gun down.' She moved towards him tentatively.

Otto swung the pistol in her direction. His fingers were twitchy on its hard black rubber grip. 'Back, bitch.'

She stared at him, and at the weapon he was pointing at her. 'Am I dreaming this? You would pay to have your own cousin murdered?'

'Luna's not the only one in this family who listens in to other people's conversations,' Otto said. He wagged a finger at Dorenkamp, then at Steiner. 'I know you've been plotting to cut me out so I don't take over the business when you retire.' The finger pointed across at Ruth. 'And that you wanted to reconcile your differences with this little twit here, and make her your heir over me. Me! She's not even your flesh and blood. What, am I the one who fucking ran off, spat in your face, tried to *kidnap* you for Christ's sake? No. I was loyal to you. All these years, I've been taking your shit. Then what do I hear? I could hardly believe my fucking ears. That the long lost brother is back and he's going looking for his little sister. How sweet.' He grinned. 'And how convenient for me. All I had to do was wait and watch, and send in the Ninjas at the right moment. Problem solved.'

Ben took a step closer to him. Watching the muzzle of the .380. Assessing the distance and Otto's reaction time. If he could get a few steps closer, he might be able to get the pistol off him. 'Didn't quite work out that way, did it?' he said. 'Not for you, and not for your Ninjas either.' Another step.

But Otto wasn't that stupid. 'Back off, Major Hope.'

Ben stopped.

Otto looked pleased. 'Not so dangerous now, are you? Fine, so you managed to get out of it first time round. But a smart guy like me always has a Plan B. Why do you think I agreed to come up here today? Because I'm some little heel-hound at your beck and call that you can just order about? Think again. I came here to kill you all. And then I'm going to shoot myself.'

'Otto!' Silvia screamed.

'Don't worry, Aunt Silvia. I'll be fine. I'm just going to put one in my arm. Nothing too bad.'

'You wouldn't want to spoil your golf swing,' Ben said. He took another half-step forward.

'Everyone will think mad Major Hope came back for revenge,' Otto went on. 'He couldn't bear that he'd been sacked like that. You know what these Special Forces people are like. Maniacs. Psychopaths who live to kill. I heard the shots. Came running to see what was going on, and he shot me in the arm but I managed to get away to call the cops. Then he blew his own brains out before they could catch him.'

'Leaving you the only heir to the Steiner billions,' Ben said. 'You really are a clever guy, the way you've thought this out.'

'You'd better believe it,' Otto said.

'Really. I'm impressed.' *Keep him talking.* Two more steps, and he could chance it. He didn't care any more about taking a hit.

But the chance never came. Ruth had been standing there, to Ben's right and just behind, listening in dumb horror. She suddenly stepped forward and walked quickly towards Otto, holding out her hand. 'That's enough. Just stop, right now. Hear me? Give me the g—'

The deafening report of the .380 filled the room. Ruth

spun round from the impact of the bullet and fell to the floor.

Silvia let out a screech of horror. Dorenkamp stood frozen for a fraction of a second and then dived under the table for cover.

Otto backed away towards the window, his eyes bulging at what he'd done, clutching the gun with both hands.

Ben gaped down at his sister's prone body. Saw the quick spread of the blood through the material of her blouse.

But before he could react, he heard a roar of fury. Maximilian Steiner had said nothing for a long time and hadn't moved a muscle. Now he was on his feet. Kicking out his chair from behind him and charging around the side of the conference table at Otto.

Otto fired from the hip. Steiner staggered and kept on coming, and Otto fired again. Blood flew, but the billionaire's momentum couldn't be stopped by a small-calibre bullet. He slammed bodily into his nephew. The little black pistol spun out of Otto's grip and bounced across the floor as the two men crashed through the window with a splintering of glass and wood. Steiner drove Otto out onto the balcony. His fists were locked around his neck and he was shaking him violently, shoving him up against the white stone balustrade.

Ben fell to his knees beside Ruth. She wasn't moving. His hand was shaking uncontrollably as he felt for a pulse. *Don't-die-don't-die-don't-die.* When he felt it his heart did a backflip. Silvia threw herself down on the other side of her daughter's body and he had to push her out of the way as he feverishly checked to see where the bullet had hit. Ripped open the neck of her blouse and saw that the blood was welling up from a clean round hole in her shoulder. His fingers were slick with it as he felt for the damage. No bone fragments in the exit wound. The jacketed round had passed right through.

Silvia was wailing. Ben shook her with his bloody hands. 'Call an ambulance. Now.'

Then Ben was on his feet.

Just in time to see Steiner throw Otto right over the stone balustrade.

Ben reached the edge at the same moment that Otto's cartwheeling body hit the glass dome of the conservatory that was directly below the conference room window. He crashed right through it. Right down into the ornamental fountain below.

He never hit the water. His fall was abruptly halted by the bronze tines of Neptune's trident. Impaled like a trout on a harpoon. The spikes pierced through his belly and ribs and jutted out through his back. Otto screamed and thrashed for a few seconds, and then his body fell limp. The water of the fountain was turning rapidly pink as Ben looked away.

Maximilian Steiner lay collapsed on the balcony beside him and the blood began to spread across the stone floor.

Ben ran back inside for Ruth.

Chapter Fifty-Five

When the three ambulances shrieked out of the Steiner residence gates, Ben was riding with his sister, and he clutched her hand in his all the way to Bern. She drifted in and out of consciousness as the sedatives the paramedics had pumped into her took effect. Not long before they reached the hospital, her eyes fluttered open and she looked drowsily up at him from the stretcher.

'This was all my fault,' she murmured. 'It was me who told him about it. None of these things would have happened if—'

'Don't talk,' Ben said.

The ambulances screeched into the emergency room bays. Paramedics threw open the doors and Ruth was rushed out and wheeled hurriedly down white-lit corridors towards the operating theatre with her drip bag swaying on its stand. Ben walked with the gurney as far as the hospital staff would let him. Steiner was up ahead, the blood soaking fast through the sheets that covered his body, tubes in his mouth and nose. Two doctors burst out of a double doorway at the end of the corridor, one male, one female, already prepped for theatre.

'We'll take it from here,' the female doctor said, raising a hand to halt him. Ben stood back and watched as Steiner and Ruth were wheeled through the doors and out of sight.

Then all he could do was pace anxiously up and down in the waiting room as people came and went around him. Every second of waiting seemed like a week. After forty minutes, Silvia Steiner arrived. Her eyes were puffy and red as she joined Ben in the waiting area and perched herself on the edge of one of the chairs.

'Heinrich and I have just finished talking to the police,' she said. Her voice was husky from crying and weak with emotion, but as she went on there was a note of fierceness that Ben hadn't heard before. 'I told them that our nephew was insane with jealousy because he thought he was being denied his proper inheritance. He took a gun and tried to kill his cousin, and he would have killed us all if Max hadn't acted to defend us. Then there was a terrible accident and Otto fell off the balcony.' She reached for a handkerchief, dabbed her eyes and composed herself. 'That's what I told them. And I made sure that Heinrich said the same. That will be our story. The whole story,' she added.

Ben looked at her and admired her strength. Not just hers. 'Your husband's a hero,' he said. It sounded strange to hear the words coming from his own mouth. He squeezed her hand, and she squeezed back.

'Your name has been left out of it,' she told him. 'This is a family matter. Although I suppose you are family now, in a way.'

He thanked her. Just at that moment, the female doctor who'd talked to Ben earlier came striding up the corridor. The first piece of news was good. Ruth was fine. There had been no complications, no major damage. Her arm would be in a sling for a few weeks but would heal perfectly.

'My husband?'

'I'm sorry to say that Herr Steiner suffered a minor stroke

on the operating table,' the doctor replied gravely. 'We're doing everything we can. He's in intensive care right now.'

'When can I see him?'

'Not yet. But soon. Please try not to worry.' The doctor smiled and tried to look reassuring, then turned and hurried away.

Silvia Steiner fell back into her chair. Ben crouched beside her. 'He'll be OK,' he said. 'I'm sure of it.'

'Pray for him.'

'I will. And you look after yourself, Silvia.'

She looked at him tearfully. 'You're going?'

He nodded.

She gripped his arm. 'You go. Finish this.'

'I need to get into Maximilian's safe. Do you have the combination?'

She shook her head. 'But Heinrich does. You tell him that I said to provide you with anything you need. Anything. He won't give you any trouble.'

Before she'd even finished saying it, Ben was heading for the exit.

'You take care,' she called after him, but he wasn't listening.

The Steiner residence was a hive of police and forensic teams. The media were already at the gates, and pretty soon they'd be swarming all over Heinrich Dorenkamp for a statement about the tragedy that had seen Otto Steiner, heir to one of Europe's biggest fortunes, fall to a horrible death. The newspapers and TV would be full of it that night and probably for the next week, until a fresh disaster came along to turn everyone's heads the other way.

Silvia had been right. Dorenkamp didn't even try to resist Ben's request to see inside the safe. Five minutes after walking into the foyer, Ben was sitting alone at the billionaire's Louis

XIV desk, reading a sixty-page bound sheaf of waxy, yellowed papers that few eyes had seen since 1945. Each faded page was headed with a Nazi imperial eagle perched on a wreathed swastika, and the official seal of the SS.

Ruth wouldn't have been disappointed. The documents had it all. Detailed diagrams and cutaway drawings of the mysterious Bell, showing all its bizarre internal workings. Column after column of technical data whose meaning Ben couldn't even begin to decipher. Grainy photographs of what looked like some kind of enormous underground factory, a maze of tunnels and galleries, shafts and chambers, together with comprehensive plans of its layout. Everything he could have asked for was right here.

As well as some things that he didn't need to know, but found himself reading with a chill in his spine. Buried near the back, yellowed and faded with age, was a written military order dated 1944, and Ben's German was good enough to work out what it was. It was an order sanctioning the building of the secret facility under the supervision of the Kammlerstab, the general's own personal staff. This hadn't just been some disused munitions factory that Kammler had commandeered for his own use. The whole mammoth construction development had been undertaken for the single purpose of housing his special weapons project and keeping it a deadly secret from the outside world.

Two names were signed at the foot of the page. The upper scrawl belonged to Reichsführer Heinrich Himmler, Head of the SS.

Underneath it was an ugly, spiky flourish of a signature. The ultimate sanction. The mark of Adolf Hitler himself.

The next few pages were a detailed report on the construction of the secret facility, showing plans of the temporary railway that had carried trainload after trainload of forced labourers from the concentration camps to work on the project. Among the figures in the right margin were statistics of the number who had died, from exhaustion or disease, or from electrocution or drowning or tunnel cave-in, during the build. Tens of thousands of them, their unspeakable suffering reduced to an anonymous typed entry in a report, and all just so that Hans Kammler could keep his machine hidden from Allied Intelligence. The place had been a death camp in its own right.

Ben had read enough. He put the papers down on the desk. Reached for Steiner's phone and called Jeff at Le Val.

'What's happening?' Jeff asked.

'Plenty. I'll explain when I see you. Is Brooke still there?'

'She's back in London,' Jeff said. 'Left this morning.'

'Is she OK?'

'She's worried about you. Listen, someone called Sabrina phoned, asking about Adam and Rory.'

'That's what I'm phoning you for, Jeff. I need your help.'

'Thought you'd never ask,' Jeff said.

'I'm asking. Get over to the airport PDQ. I'm sending a private jet to collect you. You can't miss it. It's got the name Steiner written on the side in great big letters. I'll be waiting for you in Bern, and I'll brief you in the air.'

If Jeff was surprised, he didn't react. Or maybe nothing Ben did surprised him any more. 'Do I need to bring anything?'

'Just yourself,' Ben said. 'And as much tactical raid gear from the armoury room as you can stuff into two big holdalls.'

'Sounds like fun. Where are we going?'

Ben picked up the sheaf of documents, flipped a couple of pages and looked again at the faded map that had been drawn by SS General Hans Kammler sixty-five years earlier.

'We're going to Hungary,' he said. 'To a hidden Nazi base inside a mountain.'

Chapter Fifty-Six

The luxury interior of a private jet seemed like a strange place to unzip two big eighty-litre NATO-issue grey canvas holdalls containing a small armoury of light weapons and munitions, survival gear, woodland-camouflage combat clothing, gloves and boots. The equipment spilled out over the plush carpet and Ben ran through it all. Jeff had chosen well. He nodded.

'Perfect.'

By the time the jet had reached its ceiling altitude and was speeding eastwards towards Budapest, Ben was filling Jeff in on everything. Their destination was the largest mountain range in Europe: the Carpathians. *Kárpátok* in Hungarian, a rugged rocky arc that stretched for hundreds of miles beyond its borders through the Czech Republic, Slovakia, Poland, the Ukraine, Romania and Serbia. It was in the western Carpathians, buried in a desolate spot in the north-eastern corner of Hungary near the border with Slovakia, that General Kammler had built his secret facility sixty-five years ago. There it had remained, untouched, unexplored, virtually unknown. Now it was time to bust it wide open.

There was no telling what they were going to meet there. Otto Steiner might have hired a team of ten, or there could be a hundred armed mercenaries there holding the O'Connors. That was something to worry about when they got there.

It wasn't long after Ben had finished briefing Jeff that the fast jet touched down on a specially-reserved runway at Budapest Ferihegy International Airport. Steiner's influence had a lengthy reach, and Heinrich Dorenkamp wasn't slack in obeying the orders he'd been given. Ben and Jeff carried the two holdalls to a private room where a sober official handed over the keys to a Porsche Cayenne Turbo 4x4.

The high-speed non-stop bullet train from Budapest to the remote city of Miskolc took one hour and forty-five minutes. Ben meant to beat that time, and the big 4.8-litre car was the tool for the job. They carved eastwards across the country with their cargo on the seats behind them. Dusk was settling and the full moon was on the rise over the plains and forests as they bypassed Miskolc and began the winding journey upwards through the foothills of the towering mountains, stopping every so often to check the copy of Kammler's map. Upwards and upwards through dense woodland, the road carried them far away from any town or village until it had narrowed to a track. The Porsche was as good off-road as it was on tarmac, and they were jolted from side to side as Ben hammered it over the rutted ground, the powerful headlights picking out every rock and pothole.

Jeff pointed through the windscreen. 'There. The old railway.' Through the overgrown grass and brambles it was still possible to see where the earth had been banked to make way for the tracks ferrying the trainloads of death camp prisoners to their new home – for many of them, the journey to their grave. The rails themselves were long gone, hastily removed by the SS Building and Works Division in the closing months of the war before their presence could draw the eye of Allied aerial reconnaissance scouts. It had been many, many years since organised transport had come this way.

But someone else had been here, and recently. As the way became narrower and wilder through the tunnel of the trees, the Porsche's headlights threw pools of shadow into tyre tracks in the dirt. It looked as though a number of vehicles had used the route, four-wheel-drives and maybe a car with a wide wheelbase or some kind of van.

Ben eyed the map spread out on the dashboard. Kammler's drawings had been every bit as precise as could be expected from a man who was not only a trained engineer but a megalomaniac and a ruthless perfectionist. Everything was right. The co-ordinates were dead on. There was no question that the ominous black shape they could now see looming up ahead through the gaps in the trees, its rocky crags reflecting the light of the full moon, was Kammler's mountain. They were close.

Ben killed the lights, driving by moonlight. After another couple of minutes he swung a right off the track and bumped the car through the undergrowth until it was masked by foliage. He and Jeff got out, pulled out the holdalls. Waited for their vision to acclimatise to the dark, then started preparing for the task ahead. They didn't speak as they went through the old routine that had once been their whole way of life, pulling on the woodland camouflage clothing, lacing up their boots, re-checking and dividing up the weapons. The armament was simple but effective: two silenced Heckler & Koch MP5 machine carbines, two Browning pistols and two slim, double-edged, black-bladed killing knives in leg sheaths. In addition to that, Ben carried a cut-down Ithaca combat shotgun across his back while Jeff slung a stubby grenade launcher round his shoulder.

Aside from the weaponry and ammunition in their packs,

they each had a coil of slim, lightweight but very strong rope, which they slung diagonally around their bodies. Sub-vocal radio mikes and earpieces allowed them to communicate across a distance in the softest of whispers. The final piece of equipment for each of them was the ex-military Gen 3 zoomable night-vision goggles that attached to a head harness. Capable of operating in virtual zero-light conditions, the goggles turned the world a grainy, surreal sea-green.

The two men set off, moving like ghosts in single file. They made their way cautiously along the track, scanning far and wide ahead of them as they walked. The ground was rising steadily upwards, the wild forest slowly thinning out as they approached higher ground and the base of the mountain.

Ben couldn't stop thinking about what they were going to find there. Were Adam and Rory O'Connor still even alive? He battled his doubts away to the back of his mind and walked on. His goggles illuminated the way ahead in an eerie glow. He could sense Jeff's presence behind him, but the only sound he could hear was the beating of his own heart and the gentle sigh of the mountain breeze through the branches.

The crack of a twig and a rustle of foliage at two o'clock. Ben froze, raised his MP5.

The bear's eyes glowed like green torches in Ben's goggles as it stopped in the middle of the path and turned to look at them. Then it ambled on unhurriedly, its shaggy coat rippling as it walked. It slipped into the trees on the other side of the track and disappeared.

'Shit,' Jeff's whisper chuckled in Ben's ear.

They kept moving. The ground was sloping ever upwards and the gaps in the trees were getting wider. The mountain towered overhead.

Ben operated the zoom facility on his goggles, and the magnification of the grainy image in his eyepieces expanded from x1 to x10. He slowly, carefully scanned the terrain. Nature could do so much in sixty-five years to alter a landscape. The ravages of the weather, landslides, vegetation growth. It was hard to associate the crisp lines of Kammler's technical drawings with the rugged landscape in front of them.

But then he did a double-take, and held his breath as he zoomed in closer. *Yes, there it was.* Carefully blended with the tangle of overgrown bushes and brambles, visible only to someone who was looking for it, a thick sprawl of military camouflage netting veiled a rocky alcove right at the base of the mountain about sixty yards up ahead. He stared at it a moment longer, then zoomed the goggles back down to x1 magnification.

The question was, what was behind it? If it corresponded to the drawings, it was the twenty-foot-high steel doorway carved into the mountain by Hitler's slave army a lifetime earlier.

More tyre tracks were visible in the decayed leaf matter underfoot as they crept closer to the hidden entrance. Ben kneeled and put his hand to the ground. Fresh mud, the tread marks clearly imprinted. Someone had been here within the last twenty-four hours.

Jeff's voice rasped in Ben's earpiece. 'Whatever you do, don't move.' Ben froze, then turned his head very slowly to see Jeff pointing to a spot an inch from the toecap of his boot.

The tripwire was barely visible in the dirt, just a short section of it raised up enough to catch on an unsuspecting intruder's foot. It was almost certainly wired to a silent alarm somewhere inside the facility. Someone was definitely in there, and they didn't want to be found.

It took them almost half an hour to cover the last few yards, checking every inch of ground as they moved. Then, breathless with tension, they finally reached the camo netting. And carefully, very carefully, peeled back its edge.

Ben nodded in satisfaction. Sixty-five years' worth of brambles and moss and ivy had been recently clipped away to reveal the tall steel doors, exactly as in the drawings but now craggy and pitted with corrosion. He ran a gloved finger down their central edge and saw where some of the rust had flaked away from being opened. Moving his hand across to one of the massive hinges, he found it sticky with fresh grease.

But even if they'd been able to open them, going brazenly in through the front doors to face an unknown force of opposition wasn't an option Ben wanted to consider. When he'd studied Kammler's plans back in Switzerland, he'd spotted another way in that he liked a lot better. With just one reservation – one he didn't want to think about.

He stepped carefully away from the entrance. Now that he had his bearings, he had a pretty good idea of where to look. About two hundred feet up the mountainside and about three hundred feet to the left, the goggles on maximum zoom picked out what looked like the mouth of a rusted-out old oil drum protruding from the rocks, partially obscured by a shrub. He signalled to Jeff to follow him.

When they reached the oil drum, Ben saw he'd been right. It was the mouth of a chimney, six feet wide, and from Kammler's drawing he knew that its shaft drilled straight down about two hundred feet through solid rock to a chamber below. It had been hard to tell from the faded hand-written labels on the drawing what the purpose of the chamber was. He said nothing to Jeff as he unslung the rope coil from his shoulder and secured one end to a big rock. He tested the knot, then dropped the other end of the rope down the shaft. Jeff did the same as Ben climbed over the lip of the chimney and lowered himself down slowly fist under fist, clasping the rope between his boots to control his descent. He swayed from side to side as he went down, touching the metal sides of the vertical tunnel. Everything was a uniform green in his eyepieces, but he knew that if he flipped them up he'd be in total blackness. He glanced up, and saw Jeff's boots overhead as he slid down after him.

It was a long way down through the claustrophobic space, and after a couple of minutes Ben's arms were screaming. He worried about running out of rope and finding himself dangling helplessly over an unknown drop. But the rope kept coming, and after another thirty seconds he knew he was getting near the bottom from the indescribable stench that was rising up to meet him.

'Something stinks pretty bad down here,' Jeff's voice said in his ear.

It was a combination of every bad smell in the world. Burnt animal grease and decaying matter left to fester in water that was beyond stagnant. Putrefaction and filth of a kind that Ben didn't even want to imagine. Just as the smell was as bad as he thought it could get, it got worse. Moments later his feet splashed down into something that felt like mud. Cold liquid squelched thickly up around his legs and into his boots. He swallowed, fighting the bile that wanted to well up in his throat.

He let go of the rope and let his arms dangle by his sides to let the muscles recover. He was standing in what appeared to be a square stone-built chamber about thirty feet across. The squelchy soup was up to his knees. He looked down. It didn't seem like mud, but it was thick and cloying.

Then he looked up. And saw the rats. Hundreds of them, scuttling along the edge of the stonework above the surface.

Dropping down and swimming through the filth, their long tails wriggling behind them.

Jeff landed beside him, rubbing his hands. His face was contorted in disgust behind the goggles. 'What the fuck is this place?'

Ben didn't reply. He raised one foot with a sucking sound and started trying to wade towards the nearest wall. Embedded in the stone, steel rungs led up to the iron grate of a hatchway ten feet or so above their heads. He prayed it would be open.

Something hit him softly between the shoulders. He heard a high-pitched squeaking in his ear, and instinctively reached over his shoulder. His gloved fingers closed on something soft and furry. He flung the rat away, saw it twist in mid-air, its jaws snapping. It landed with a splash. Then another was scuttling up his leg, biting at his clothes. He lashed out and felt its back break.

They started wading quickly towards the edge, sloshing through the filth as fast as they dared without tripping and falling into it. Something nudged Ben's knee. At first he thought it was another rat, but then he looked down and realised.

There were *things* in the liquid. Things that had lain undisturbed for a long time had suddenly started floating to the surface as their feet churned up the sediment at the bottom.

The human skull bobbed away from him, staring sightlessly up at him in the green vision of his goggles. It was scorched and blackened and rat-gnawed, missing its jawbone. A bullet had shattered everything above the left eye socket. The teeth were torn out.

Then Ben felt something give way with a wet, brittle crunch under his boot. He stumbled. Another skull floated up, crushed and black and burnt. Then a section of rib cage, like the remains of an old boat. He kicked them away in disgust.

It was what he'd feared from studying the plans of the facility, and now he saw that his suspicions had been right. The chamber was the crematorium for the slave workers who had perished building Kammler's secret domain. The undiscovered mass grave of tens of thousands of nameless victims of the SS general's brutality. They were standing on human remains. Stacks of charred bone. The piled ash of burnt flesh and clothing, mixed with rainwater seepage over the years to create a sickening mulch.

They splashed through the horror. Ben's fingers closed on the bottom rung of the ladder and he hauled himself up the wall, closely followed by Jeff. There were gagging sounds in his earpiece as he reached the hatch, and he didn't know how much longer he could keep from vomiting himself. He muttered a prayer, pushed his fingers through the iron grating and gave it a hard shove.

It didn't move. It was either rusted shut, or it was locked from the inside. They were shut in here with the dead.

Chapter Fifty-Seven

Far away from where Ben and Jeff were trapped inside the crematorium chamber, separated by millions of tons of solid rock and a maze of tunnels and corridors, Adam O'Connor was on his hands and knees on the concrete floor of the vault, surrounded by dismantled electronic components, mechanical linkages, magnetic coils, bits of wire. A chaotic mess of spanners and screwdrivers and soldering irons and voltmeters lay scattered around him.

He hated the machine almost as much as he hated the woman who'd tortured his son. All his rage, all his frustration at the situation he'd been plunged into against his will, were obsessively focused on it. His shirt stuck to him with sweat. Days of beard growth covered his jaw, and his eyes were stinging from lack of sleep. His trousers were worn through from kneeling on the rough concrete, his hands were lacerated from all the rusted bolts he'd had to slacken in the confined space of the machine, his fingers covered in burns from soldering the thousands of corroded connections he'd found. Any one of them could have accounted for the fact that, so far, he just simply could not get the fucking thing to work. Every time he found a new problem his heart would soar, thinking *this is it*; only to sink again when he fixed it and put everything back together again, hit the big red activation knob . . . and the machine still just sat there.

Silent. Dead. Laughing at him. Just like it was now. Adam would have punched the loathsome thing, but his knuckles were too bruised and swollen from the hundreds of times he'd already done that.

He turned round and looked at Pelham. Every hour that Adam spent down here working on the Bell, Pelham was right there with him. Except that while Adam toiled and sweated and chewed his lip in terror of what was going to happen if he failed, Pelham had taken to lounging in a big armchair he'd had brought down for him, coolly reading newspapers and magazines while sipping on a long drink.

'This is hopeless,' Adam croaked. 'It'll never work.'

'You'll keep trying,' Pelham said without looking up. He flipped a page of the magazine he was reading. Took another sip of his drink.

'This thing is scrap metal. And even if it didn't have mice living in it, and every linkage wasn't seized solid, and every damn wire wasn't crusted up with corrosion, and the valves weren't rotted away to nothing, I still couldn't make it work.'

Pelham put down the magazine. 'We had an agreement, Adam. And frankly, your attitude is starting to wear out my patience.'

Adam dropped the spanner he was clutching and staggered to his feet, racked with cramp. He advanced on Pelham, enraged by the man's obtuseness. 'Listen to me. I'm not fixing a broken boiler here. This thing isn't like some household appliance that you just plug in. It's the most arcane piece of scientific hardware I've ever seen, and you're asking me to fix it with bits of crap from the local toolshop. I can't work in these conditions. I need a lab. I need more people. I need

392

proper equipment. Maybe if we could just break the whole thing down and analyse every component, we could—'

'This is it,' Pelham said, motioning at the room. 'This is as good as it gets. Live with it.'

'You don't understand how complex this thing is,' Adam shouted.

'You're supposed to be the expert,' Pelham said. 'That's why you're here.'

Adam could feel his face turning crimson as his shouts reverberated around the inside of the vault. 'And if I can't get it to work, then you know what? You know whose fucking fault that'll be? Not mine. Yours, asshole. *Your* fault, because if you fuckers hadn't killed my colleagues, if Michio and Julia were here with me now, the three of us might have figured it out. The way things are, you can do what you want, but you'll never see this thing working. Understand? It can't be done. So why don't you just pick up the phone and tell your employers, whoever the fuck they are, that it's over? That's it. And then you're just going to have to let me and my son go back to our lives.' By the end of the tirade his shouts had diminished to a sob. He couldn't talk any more.

There was silence in the vault. Adam steadied himself against the machine, panting.

Pelham spoke softly. 'You're tired, aren't you, Adam? Your nerves are ragged. You feel weak and confused and you don't know how you can go on.'

Adam's head sagged. He screwed his eyes shut and felt dizzy. He was one breath away from bursting into tears. 'Yes,' he whispered. 'If I could just sleep a while. Please. Then I'll keep trying. I promise. Forget what I said. I'm sorry. I'm just so tired.'

Pelham got up from his armchair, walked calmly over to Adam and put an arm benignly around his shoulders. 'Can

I tell you a story? I was a soldier once. Not your normal infantryman. We were something . . . special. Our selection training was very intense. You wouldn't believe the things we had to do. Just when we thought we'd been tested to the absolute limit, they moved it to the next level.' He smiled. 'You can't imagine what it feels like to be hunted like an animal, can you? Alone in the dark, running scared, no food except what you can catch with your bare hands, no shelter, no sleep for days on end. But that's what they did to us. They were teaching us to stretch the limits of what we thought possible, and those days taught me the most valuable lesson of my life. I learned that those extremes of fear, pain, fatigue were my friends, because they concentrated my mind. Made me find reserves of strength within myself that I'd never dreamed of. That's how I kept going. I made it through.'

Adam stared wordlessly at him.

'But not every man passed the test,' Pelham went on. 'Some were broken. They gave in. And you know what they said, those losers, as they were being carried off, crying like babies? "I'm tired."' He paused. 'What I'm saying is, I could let you go back to your cell right now, so that you could spend the next ten hours sleeping. But the truth is, Adam, I don't think it's going to help you to give in like that. Deep down, I think you have the strength to keep going. You just need help to find it within yourself.' He walked away from Adam and went over to the table beside his armchair. On it was a radio handset.

'What are you doing?' Adam said numbly.

Pelham picked up the radio. 'Irina, this is Pelham. Respond, over.'

A pause, then a fizz of static. Reception was poor inside the mountain. But then Adam heard the woman's voice reply and he felt his knees going weak.

'Fetch the boy,' Pelham told her. 'Bring him down to the vault. You know what I'm saying. Over and out.' He turned off the radio.

'No,' Adam said. 'No, no. You don't have to do this. I'll—'

Pelham pointed at the machine. 'You'll make it work, believe me,' he said. 'When she's cutting your son's face off, five minutes from now right here in this room while you watch, I guarantee that's going to concentrate the mind wonderfully. Let's see how tired you are then.'

Chapter Fifty-Eight

'Again. On three.'

Dangling side by side from the filthy rungs of the ladder, Ben and Jeff kicked against the iron grate of the crematorium hatchway one more time. The dull clang resonated through the chamber.

'I'm going to puke,' Jeff mumbled.

'Again,' Ben said. They'd been trying for what seemed like forever, and he could only hope that nobody had heard the noise. They swung their weight back from the hatch, then lashed out in unison.

This time, the clang of their boots on the iron grate was mixed with a screech as hinges rusted solid for over half a century gave way and the hatch moved. Not much, just an inch. But it moved, and Ben felt the relief scorch through his veins like whisky.

'We're nearly there. Once more.'

The final kick sent the hatch crashing open.

'You go first,' Ben said, and Jeff wasted no time in clambering past him and crawling out of the hole. Ben followed. After a few feet he was able to stand, and looked around him through his night-vision goggles.

They were in the rough-hewn stone anteroom from where the SS soldiers must have flung the bodies of the dead before sloshing gasoline over them and setting them alight. Maybe towards the very end, when the soldiers needed every drop of fuel to escape the approaching Soviet troops, they hadn't bothered burning their victims at all, but just shot those still alive in the back of the head and turfed the corpses into the hole to rot.

Ben thought about Don Jarrett, the Holocaust denier. Another trip to Bruges suddenly seemed like a very good idea.

If he ever got out of this.

Up three pitted stone steps and they were in a passageway. The air was dank and foul, but it felt like pure oxygen after the obscenity of the crematorium. The passage wound onwards. They unslung their weapons and flipped off their safeties as they came to an unmarked doorway. Ben counted *one – two – three*. A deep breath and they pushed through.

The light hit them. Across the corridor in which they found themselves, cobwebbed lamps strung together by loose wires threw a dim, yellowish glow that was unbearably bright with their goggles. They flipped them up, blinking to adjust their vision.

There was nobody about. They turned left and kept moving. They were on full battle-alert now, in that state of heightened awareness in which every muscle was tight, every nerve jangling and the mind racing with constant anticipation of what could be waiting around every corner. Life never felt more vivid than when death was just an instant away.

A door opened up ahead. Voices. Two men. Ben and Jeff pressed themselves flat into a shadowy alcove in the wall. Footsteps approached, and as the voices grew louder Ben could hear the two men were speaking Croat.

'I'm not gonna take much more shit from that bastard Pelham,' one of them was complaining bitterly *sotto voce*, as though he thought Pelham might be listening.

'Relax,' the other one said in a more laconic tone. 'Think of the money.'

'No fucking amount of money is worth being stuck in this hole. I hate this place.'

The men walked past where Ben and Jeff were hidden in the shadows, close enough to smell their body odour. The complaining one was stick-thin inside a rumpled leather jacket, with a facial twitch and long, greasy hair scraped back in a thin ponytail. The laconic-sounding one wore a khaki cold weather field shirt that looked like Russian military issue. His shaven head glistened in the lamplight.

Ben glanced at Jeff. He peeled himself silently off the wall as his fingers moved down to the hilt of the killing knife that was strapped to his thigh and drew it out of its sheath. Jeff was right at his side as they crept noiselessly but quickly up behind the men. The bald guy was Ben's. Ponytail belonged to Jeff.

Then they struck. Hard and fast. Ben clamped his hand over the bald guy's mouth and jerked his head back and stabbed the knife into his throat. In the movies, it zipped as easily through flesh as a hot knife through butter and left a clean, straight red line from ear to ear. In real life, to cut through the tough gristle and cartilage of a man's windpipe you had to saw brutally. Close your mind to what you were doing and keep sawing like crazy through the horrific mess until the blood was spraying out over your hand and the air was hissing out of the guy's lungs with that eerie gurgling sigh that you knew was going to haunt your dreams forever. Hold on tight until the victim's death struggles diminished and you could wipe the bloody knife clean on his clothes and move on and hope you never had to do anything like that again. Till the next time.

Ben and Jeff dragged the bodies into the shadows. They were in, and they were committed now. It was starting.

Chapter Fifty-Nine

Irina Dragojević stood back from the cell door as she watched her tall companion turn the key in the lock. Pelham hadn't said much on the radio, but he hadn't needed to. She had a very clear idea of what he wanted, because they'd already discussed the contingency plans. They were very persuasive, but the truth was she had no interest whatsoever in the outcome. The slim knife in the sheath on her belt was whetted and honed past razor-sharpness. When she thought about what she was going to do with it, and how nobody was going to stop her this time, her breath caught. The feeling was almost sexual. It dulled the throbbing ache in her arm where the bullet had creased it that day in Ireland. It made her feel whole and serene.

As she watched the cell door swing open, she heard that small, distant voice in her mind again.

Why do you do the things you do, Irina? Why?

There'd been a time, years ago, when she'd heard those voices often, and had been greatly troubled by them. But that had been before she'd come to see things clearly, to appreciate how beautifully simple it all was. The voice had no power any more. The power was all hers.

The tall man stepped inside the boy's cell. Irina went in behind him. She stopped. Narrowed her eyes as her colleague turned to stare at her in bewilderment.

The cell was empty. Rory O'Connor was gone.

Irina grabbed the radio.

Ivan's fingers were painfully tight around Rory's wrist as he led him quickly through the stone corridors. The man had barely said a word since he'd come bursting into his cell two minutes before, seemingly in a desperate hurry to get him out of there.

'Where are we going?' Rory asked.

'Somewhere safe,' Ivan told him. 'Things are beginning to happen.' He was frowning as he kept an ear open for fresh activity on the crackling radio handset in his jacket pocket. 'Come, we must go faster.'

'They've come for me? The other agents?'

Ivan nodded. Tugged on his wrist. 'Move faster.'

'Please, Ivan. Tell me what's happening.'

'Pelham sent Irina to fetch you, to hurt you again. I heard it on the radio. You are lucky. I was closer. I got there first.'

Rory shuddered and felt the colour drain from his face. He looked at Ivan and realised he'd never felt such a bond with anyone before. Except for one. 'Where's my dad?' he asked.

'Waiting for you on the outside,' Ivan said. 'Keep moving.'

Rory gulped air. He was going to get out of here. He was going to see his father. It would soon be over.

The radio fizzed into life. Through the spit and hiss of static, Rory listened to the exchange between the man called Pelham and the woman and his heart began to thump faster.

'I want him *found*!' Pelham yelled from the tinny speaker, and then the voices dissolved back into white noise.

'I won't let them find you,' Ivan reassured him. 'You are with me now. We are friends, no?'

'Yes, Ivan.'

They kept walking. Ivan was glancing furtively around him all the time, keeping an even tighter grip on Rory's wrist as he led the boy down passages he'd never seen before. 'Quickly,' Ivan kept saying. 'Quickly.' They came to a flight of steps leading downwards into murky shadows. Ivan turned on a flashlight and lit the way ahead. Down and down through a shaft that was carved out of the rock. It was echoey, and Rory could hear the steady plop of dripping water.

'Is this where we're meeting the other agents?' he asked breathlessly, and heard his voice reverberate off the walls.

Ivan didn't reply.

Then the staircase ended abruptly, terminating in an unfinished cul de sac. In the torchlight, Rory could see the pickaxe marks that scarred the rock face. The floor was littered with debris and old tools that had lain there so long, they'd rusted away to almost nothing. It was as though whoever had been digging the tunnel out of the solid rock had just stopped working one day, put down their tools and gone. He wondered what had happened. But more than that, he wondered why Ivan had brought him here. He turned and frowned up at his friend.

Ivan smiled in the beam of the flashlight. 'We are safe down here,' he said as he put a hand on the boy's shoulder. 'It is just you and me now.' Then he moved closer. His lips parted.

Rory stared for a second, and then he realised Ivan was trying to kiss him.

Chapter Sixty

Adam O'Connor was cackling like a lunatic as Pelham paced the vault with the radio in his fist.

'What do you mean, he's gone?' The man's composure had slipped away completely, and he was shouting in rage.

'He isn't here,' said the woman's voice through the spitting static.

'How could he have got out?'

'I don't know,' she replied.

Pelham yelled into the radio, 'I want him *found*!'

'Go for it, son,' Adam giggled to himself. 'We'll show these bastards.'

Pelham threw the radio down and stormed over to him. 'Oh, you think this is funny, do you, Adam?'

'The look on your face,' Adam laughed at him. 'You should see yourself right now. Your little world is just falling down around you. How're you going to explain this to your boss, asshole?'

'Laugh at this,' Pelham said. He reached his hand across his chest, pulled out the pistol that he wore under his jacket and cocked the action with a sound that rang around the stone walls. He aimed it in Adam's face. His jaw tightened.

'Shoot me then, jerkoff,' Adam taunted him. 'Let's see you make the machine work after I'm dead.'

The gun wavered.

'I'm all you've got,' Adam went on, waving his arms like a wild man. 'You're not going to shoot me.'

'Wrong,' Pelham said. He dropped his arm eighteen inches and squeezed the trigger. The pistol flashed and boomed in his hand.

Adam felt his leg get kicked out from under him and collapsed to the concrete floor, clutching his thigh. The blood began to pump out through his fingers. He pressed hard, desperately trying to stem the flow. He felt no pain, not yet. But he knew it would come. 'You shot me,' he mumbled in shock.

Pelham stood over him with the smoking pistol dangling loose at his side. 'I could have shattered the femur or split the artery and made you bleed to death,' he said calmly over Adam's screams. 'Next time I will. Get on your feet. Let's try this again.'

Rory twisted frantically away as Ivan's mouth sought his. He felt the material of his sweater rip in the man's fingers. Backed away against the wall, bewildered and hurt. He'd thought until this moment that Ivan was his friend. Suddenly he was alone again.

Ivan came at him, and Rory lashed blindly out with his foot. The kick caught Ivan squarely in the groin. Rory stood rooted in horror for a second as Ivan dropped the torch and fell to his knees with both hands clapped over his testicles and his eyes rolling back in agony. The boy grabbed up the fallen flashlight, turned and ran as hard as he could back up the winding staircase. He could hear Ivan's cries of pain and rage echoing up the carved-out shaft. Rory kept running like the wind. After what seemed like just a few seconds he could hear Ivan giving chase. He burst out of the mouth of the stairway and out into the lamplit corridor. He was lost now, his breath rasping in his ears, his heart in his mouth, no idea where to turn. The sole was flapping off his right trainer from where the kick to Ivan's groin had torn it half away from the shoe's upper. He pulled the shoe off and tossed it aside.

He could hear Ivan's running footsteps behind him, but a quick glance over his shoulder told him the man was out of sight down the twisty passages. Rory came to another junction in the corridor. Big signs on the wall that he couldn't understand. He turned right and kept going, hobbling on just one shoe for a few more yards until he knew he had to lose that one, too, or risk stumbling and twisting his ankle. He bent down and gripped the toe and heel of the shoe and yanked it off. The floor was cold and hard through his thin socks.

Rory stopped. Backed up a few steps to where he'd passed a round hole in the wall to his right. It was some kind of shaft, big enough for him to crawl into and hide. He shone the torch into the curving tunnel, put his hand to it and felt a breath of air caress his fingers. Maybe it led somewhere, and anywhere was better than here. He quickly climbed into it and started crawling as fast as he could down its length. Rusty metal under his hands and knees, not rock. It was a pipe of some kind, like an air vent, he thought.

And now he could really feel the breeze on his face. Cool, fresh, sweet air.

Air coming in from the outside.

Chapter Sixty-One

Ben worked the rusted iron bolt loose, creaked open the iron door and peered inside at the long, low, dark chamber. It was a primitive dormitory – row upon row of rudimentary bunks with open latrines just a few feet away. Skeletons littered the floor. Scores of them, gnawed apart by rats, covered in dust and cobwebs.

'Slave workers,' he said to Jeff. 'They must have starved to death down here when the Nazis abandoned the place.'

'Jesus Christ,' Jeff's voice said in Ben's earpiece.

They shut the door of the dormitory, and Ben grimly closed the bolt. He took the folded plan from his pocket, and studied it again. The gruesome discovery meant they were still in the lower levels, where the labourers had been housed. The next level up from there had been mainly for storage of equipment and provisions; then above that was the upper level with its complexes of operations rooms and offices, together with the barrack accommodation and shower blocks for the SS soldiers stationed at the facility. He and Jeff had agreed on the plane that it would be the most likely place to improvise a holding cell for a young hostage. As for Adam, it was Ben's guess that the kidnappers would have put him to work in the strange vault-like chamber which, as far as he could tell from the faded drawings, was the location of the mysterious Kammler invention. Deep inside the mountain, the chamber was only accessible from a lift shaft on the upper level.

'That's where we need to head for,' Ben said.

They moved stealthily onwards, using the map to find a crude service lift that rumbled up to the next level. They emerged cautiously into what looked like an underground car park, a broad arched concrete roadway leading off into the darkness. There was nobody about as they paused to get their bearings.

Jeff tapped the map with his gloved finger. 'Judging by the layout, I'd say we were just about here. So we need to follow this road. Looks to me like there's another service lift along there.'

Snick-snack. The sound of an automatic weapon's cocking bolt being worked, just a few feet behind them.

They turned. Bright torchlight blinded them. From behind it, the vague shapes of two men stepped out of the shadows.

A harsh voice said, 'Guns on floor.'

Very slowly and warily, Ben and Jeff put down their MP5s, then straightened up.

'Drop grenade launcher,' said the voice.

Jeff cursed under his breath as he unslung the weapon and tossed it down with a clatter.

'Also shotgun,' said the voice. Ben shrugged the cut-down Ithaca from his shoulder and dropped it on the pile.

'Remove head gear.'

Ben forced himself to peer through the blinding torch-beam as they dumped their precious night-vision goggles on the floor. The two guards were holding pistols. The one without a torch was clamping a walkie-talkie to his mouth. 'This is Dovzhenko,' he said into it. 'I have intruders on Level Two, Sector Twelve-B.'

'Hands on head,' the other one commanded, shining the light in Ben's eyes.

Ben laced his fingers together on top of his head, and Jeff did the same.

'Step away from weapons.'

Ben heard the triumphant smile in the guy's voice. He didn't have to glance sideways at Jeff to know that they were both waiting for the exact same thing.

Ben knew that there were only two types of mercenary soldier. There was the type who wore the army tattoos and told all the stories, but who'd never done half the things they boasted of and therefore didn't have the training to go with it. Then there was the type who maybe *had* done those things, maybe had seen a lot of action and been useful enough soldiers in their day – but they were all washed up now, worn out, cynical, living job to job, and too used to scrapping with tin-pot militia groups across weary, minefield-ridden Third World and Eastern European war zones to have any respect for the enemy. Either way, what the two types had in common was that they were sloppy soldiers and liable to make mistakes.

Ben also knew that tactics were a game. And in any game, winning was often just a question of riding it out until the opponent made that vital mistake. In armed confrontation, one of the rules was never to push your luck. Not even if all the odds seemed in your favour, not even if everything seemed to be going your way, not even if the other guy was completely at your mercy.

But to the sloppy soldier there was a huge kick, a supreme power-rush, to be gained from shoving the muzzle of a pistol right in the face of an unarmed enemy and yelling commands at them. And that sloppiness was exactly what Ben had been banking on. As though they just couldn't help themselves, the guards came right up close, pistols extended full-arm, the muzzles almost kissing his and Jeff's heads.

Much, much too close to get away from what happened next. The man called Dovzhenko let out a scream as Ben twisted his Glock out of his fist and felt the trapped trigger finger snap. As he was ramming the butt of the gun hard and fast into the man's teeth, Jeff had slapped the other pistol aside, wrestled it out of its owner's grip and clubbed him round the side of the head with it. It was all over in under two seconds.

But now things were about to get a little hotter. Ben pushed Dovzhenko down to the floor with his knee pressed into the back of his neck and the Glock to his temple.

'Where are the hostages?' he asked. It was a question he was only going to ask once.

The man never had the chance to respond. The arched roadway suddenly blazed bright with truck headlights and the growl of the diesel engine boomed through the echoey tunnel.

'Time to go,' Jeff said.

The big truck burst around the corner thirty yards away and came bearing down on them. There was no chance to pick up their discarded weapons as gunfire crackled out from the vehicle and strafed the concrete. Ben and Jeff sprinted away down the tunnel, returning fire from the pistols they'd taken from the guards.

No way they could outrun a truck.

As they ran, the headlights behind them cast long shadows on the curving tunnel wall up ahead and picked out a tall side doorway covered by a rusted steel shutter. There was a gap at the bottom, just big enough to squeeze through. Ben threw himself down and rolled under the bottom lip of the steel into darkness. Bullets hammered into the shutter as Jeff scrambled in behind him. The truck screeched to a halt outside, and they heard doors opening, voices shouting commands. Another burst of gunfire, and a line of dents punched into the shutter. Shadows appeared in the strip of light underneath. Ben fired at the gap, and they skipped away in retreat.

The two of them were safe in here – but they wouldn't be for long. Someone would be quick to figure out how to raise the shutter, or how to flush them out using gas or fire.

Stumbling around in the dark, Ben found an antiquated wall panel with a row of big switches, and threw them all. Dusty yellow lamps flickered into life, and he saw they were in an old vehicle workshop. Rusty fuel drums were stacked up against the wall next to a partially-dismantled BMW motorcycle and sidecar. In the middle of the concrete floor, a dusty tarpaulin was draped over a strangely-shaped object the size of a small van. Ben whipped the tarp away and clouds of dust billowed in the dim light.

'It's a Kettenkrad,' he said. He'd only ever seen pictures of the strange Wehrmacht all-terrain vehicle. It was a hybrid of a miniature tank and a military motorcycle. The six wheels per side were linked by caterpillar tracks, and the machine was steered by a bike front end with broad handlebars. He knew enough about them to know that they'd normally been used as tractors to haul trailers and light artillery. But someone had equipped this one with a pair of forward-facing German MG-34 belt-fed heavy machine guns, turning it into a formidable assault craft.

Outside in the tunnel, the truck gave a roar as it accelerated forward to ram the shutter. The metal buckled violently inwards, but held. The truck crunched into reverse and started backing away for another hit.

'They're going to get through pretty soon,' Jeff said, eyeing the buckled shutter.

413

'I know.' As he said it, Ben ran over to the stack of fuel drums. He grabbed one and shook it, heard the liquid swirling around inside. He carried it over to the Kettenkrad, quickly found the fuel tank hatch. The drum's nozzle cap was rusted solid. He stabbed a rough hole through it with his knife and started sloshing the fuel into the tank.

'You're crazy. That thing's been sitting dead for all these years.'

Ben didn't reply as he ran round to the Kettenkrad's driver's seat, searching for the dash-mounted ignition switch. He flipped it on and prodded the starter.

Nothing. The battery was dead. He swore.

The truck roared forward again and hit the steel shutter, harder this time. The crash shook the walls and echoed all through the tunnel. The shutter was grotesquely bulged and distorted, but it still held. The truck reversed. A couple more hits like that and it would be through, and Ben and Jeff would be cornered, outgunned and outnumbered inside the workshop as the guards came spilling in.

Ben ran round to the back of the Kettenkrad and found what he'd been hoping for. He snatched the crank handle from a clip on the bodywork, thrust it through an opening in the radiator grille in the rear, felt it engage on the crank-shaft. He said a prayer and turned the lever hard.

The engine coughed, then faltered and died.

The truck hit again, tearing the shutter from one of its roller mountings with a screech. The headlights streamed through the rips in the crumpled metal as it backed off for what Ben and Jeff both knew would be its final charge.

Ben tried the crank again. For a fraction of a second it seemed as though nothing was going to happen, but then he was suddenly engulfed in a cloud of smoke as the Kettenkrad spluttered into life. He leapt on board, twisted the motorcycle throttle and the engine gave a clattering roar.

Amazed, Jeff clambered up the side and dropped into the cramped space behind the twin machine guns. He swept away the thick layers of cobwebs, racked the cocking bolts.

'Ready?' Ben asked, blipping the throttle.

'What is it you always say?'

'Fuck it.'

'Then fuck it, I'm ready,' Jeff yelled over the roar of the engine.

At the same instant that the truck rammed the shutter, tore it clean off its mountings and came thundering inside the workshop, Ben was engaging the Kettenkrad's forward drive and lurching onwards with a clattering squeal of caterpillar tracks. He opened the throttle all the way. Twisted the handlebars and aimed the vehicle straight at the truck.

'Keep your head down,' Jeff yelled as they charged right into the blazing headlights. Ben hunched down behind the bars. But there was no way to be ready for the blast of two heavy-calibre machine guns just over and a foot either side of his head. The sound was devastating.

So was the impact on the truck. The flimsy bodywork was instantly shredded into ribbons and the windscreen exploded into glass dust as the truck swerved and went ploughing headlong into the fuel drums, rupturing them against the wall. The truck hit the far wall of the workshop at an angle with a massive crash and rolled onto its side, sending toolbenches and bits of machinery spinning through the air. Flames began to flicker inside the shattered cab.

The guards in the tunnel opened fire as Ben steered the Kettenkrad around the wreckage. Bullets pinged off the tractor's armour plating. Jeff swivelled the machine guns round in a sweeping arc just over Ben's head, cutting down three of the mercenaries in a bloody heap.

Now the Kettenkrad was roaring and clattering down the tunnel with the throttle wide open. The wind tore at Ben's hair as he twisted round in his seat to look at the carnage behind them. At that moment, the burning truck touched off the fuel drums inside the workshop. A huge rolling mushroom of fire swallowed everything within forty feet of the entrance. The mercenaries who had dived for cover as the Kettenkrad rumbled by were suddenly staggering about in flames.

The tunnel twisted hard left up ahead. Ben steered the handlebars into the turn, but he still had the throttle open all the way and the clumsy Kettenkrad went roaring into the bend too fast. He hit the brakes – and discovered with an icy lurch why the vehicle had been taken into the workshop all those years ago.

It didn't have any.

He tried closing the throttle to slow the thing down, but it was stuck open. Years of corrosion had affected the throttle cable, or the carburettor slide, or both. Unable to slow down, the vehicle slammed off the tunnel wall so hard that the handlebars were torn out of Ben's hands before he could whip in the clutch. They rounded the bend out of control at forty miles an hour with sparks screaming off the side of the bodywork.

What looked like a brick wall flashed up towards them. The Kettenkrad smashed into it with a heart-stopping crunch that sent Ben flying over the handlebars.

He was picking himself up painfully as Jeff clambered out of the trashed vehicle.

'Ever heard of using the brakes?'

Ben pointed. They'd crashed into the entrance to the service lift.

'Next level this way.'

Chapter Sixty-Two

Adam was bleeding all over the floor and fighting to keep from fainting with pain and nausea as Pelham stood over him with the pistol and forced him to reassemble the Kammler machine.

'There,' he gasped when the last bolt was tightened on the service hatch. 'It's done.'

'Make it work,' Pelham said through gritted teeth.

Adam thumped the red activation knob with the heel of his hand.

Nothing.

Of course, nothing.

The silent scream of frustration had to be vented. Not even caring about the gun in Pelham's hand, Adam snatched up a heavy lump-hammer and whacked the machine's casing with all the strength that was left in him. The clang filled the vault. He dropped the hammer on the floor. 'Look, just fucking kill me,' he panted.

And he and Pelham both stood back in amazement as the machine started to hum.

It was a low vibrating throb at first, rising steadily in pitch. The upper section of the bell started to rotate like the turbine of a jet engine. Faster and faster, and it suddenly seemed to

Adam as though the metal was beginning to glow with a strange blue-tinged light.

Both men were too astonished to speak. Then, as the rising hum became a tortured drone, something happened that nothing could have prepared Adam for.

The hammer moved – by itself. It was dragged across the floor, then suddenly sailed into the air and flew towards the machine. It slammed against the metal casing, ten times harder than Adam could have swung it, and stuck fast. Seconds later, the mess of spanners and screwdrivers and other tools that littered the floor, every metal object in the vault, went flying through the air, sucked towards the machine with incredible force. The pistol was torn out of Pelham's hand. He ran to the machine, tried to prise it off, but it was as though it had been welded to the casing.

Adam was sure he could feel strange effects inside his body. The electromagnetic field that the Bell was generating must be way off any Tesla scale, hundreds of times greater than an MRI scan. But something told him that the machine was only just beginning to power up. It was nowhere near its capacity yet. He stared at it. Everything that he and Michio and Julia had dreamed about was actually happening right there in front of him. The Kammler machine was drawing energy from the hidden dimensions within empty space, sucking it in like a giant lung taking in air, initiating the process of converting it into pure power. Terrifying, limitless amounts of power.

The drone was turning into a howl. Adam's vision was beginning to blur. Pelham staggered away from the machine, the incredulous look on his face lit blue by the intense glow coming off the casing.

Then the machine suddenly went quiet.

Oh, holy shit. Adam instinctively cringed down close to

418

the floor. Pelham opened his mouth to say something, but the words never came out.

The room seemed to explode as the magnetic field surrounding the machine suddenly reversed polarity. The metal objects stuck to the casing burst outwards in all directions like shrapnel from a bomb. Adam threw himself down flat as the steel toolbox went flying over his head like a missile and punched like a tank shell through the vault door. In the same instant, the lump-hammer spun violently through the air and took Pelham in the back of the head with such power that it went right through. Adam caught a nightmarish glimpse of the man's face disintegrating as he went down.

Now the whole vault seemed to shake. Rays of strange blue light shone through the dust that filled the air. The howl of the machine had resumed, building to a terrifying scream, and Adam could feel the force field vibrating his ribs. He could feel it in the very tissues of his organs. He scrambled to escape, crying out in pain from his injured leg. Pelham's pistol was lying in the dust. Adam had never so much as held a gun in his life, but he scooped it up and gripped it tight as he tumbled out through the ragged hole in the door.

He hobbled in flickering strobe-light down the passage leading to the circular gallery around the lift shaft. Jerked open the steel cage door, threw himself into the lift and slammed his fist against the Bakelite button, praying that the thing would work. Slowly, much too slowly, the lift began to grind upwards.

Nausea was pounding through his head, and it wasn't just from the gunshot wound. He was sure he could feel the solid rock around him vibrating.

He didn't know what was going to happen. All he knew was that the machine was out of control.

He had to find Rory. He had to find his boy.

Chapter Sixty-Three

Crawling on hands and knees, Rory had made his way deep into the air vent by the time he heard the movement in the shaft behind him and his heart froze.

He craned his head round in the confined space, and let out a cry of fear at what he saw. Ivan, crawling rapidly up behind him with his teeth bared in rage.

The shoes. Ivan had followed the trail of the fallen shoes.

The boy kept moving as fast as he could, but the man seemed possessed by some kind of demonic energy and he began to realise there was no way to outpace him.

'I'll get you,' Ivan's voice echoed up the metal shaft.

Rory kicked back at the hand that groped for his leg. His foot connected with something solid, but then strong fingers closed around his ankle. He felt himself being dragged back down the way he'd come. He clawed the rusty metal for a grip, but his fingertips just raked uselessly as he slid backwards.

Ivan was laughing now. 'Come here, little fish. Come to Ivan.' Rory thrashed out with both feet, but the man's grip was like iron.

It took several nightmarish minutes for Ivan to drag the boy all the way back out of the vent. Rory fought him every inch, until his breath was rasping and his fingertips were raw. Ivan pulled him clear of the mouth of the pipe and dumped him hard on the concrete floor. Slapped him across the face, twice. 'You will not run from me again.'

'You lied to me,' Rory screamed at him.

'That's right. I did.' Ivan hit him again, making him taste blood on his lips. Then the hands were running over his body, and he felt sick. He twisted away in desperation, managed to break free. Clawed up a handful of loose dust and grit and, as Ivan came close to try to kiss him again, he dashed it in his eyes. Ivan bellowed in pain and anger as Rory scrambled to his feet and ran like crazy through the twisting passages. He was working on pure survival instinct now, his mind as blank as a deer's running from a pack of wolves. Darting through an archway, he found himself staring up at a huge space carved out of the rock, with a gigantic lattice-work steel stairway that wound upwards through it to the next level.

Ivan was already gaining on him.

Rory grabbed the rusty handrail and started leaping up the steps. He could hear Ivan's racing footsteps hammering behind him. The boy's legs were like jelly, but he willed himself to keep going. He came to a landing where the stairway twisted ninety degrees, slipped on the metal floor and almost fell through the railings and out into the abyss. He managed to get back on his feet just as Ivan's hand came lashing out at him, wriggled away and ran madly on until he was nearly at the top. But the tumble had cost him precious seconds. Ivan's fingers closed on his belt and he cried out as he felt himself being pulled back. Ivan just absorbed the kicks. He pressed Rory down hard on the steps and started tearing at his clothes. His eyes were blazing and there was spit foaming in the corners of his mouth.

Rory was helpless to stop him.

Chapter Sixty-Four

Ben and Jeff moved quickly through the maze of corridors in the upper level, scanning left and right with their pistols. Ben checked the map again.

'We should find the access point for the main lift shaft down here somewhere. I don't think it's far away.'

'Something's wrong with this place,' Jeff muttered. 'I can feel it. It's weird.'

Ben had the same sensation. It was as though the air was crackling with energy, almost like static electricity, but somehow different. He'd never experienced anything like it before. He was convinced he could feel a thrumming vibration coming through the walls, growing steadily more intense with each passing minute.

'Listen.'

The sound of someone yelling, echoing up the corridor. The voice was high-pitched, but it wasn't a woman's. It was a boy's.

They ran towards the sound, and round the next bend they found themselves at the top of a tall iron stairway. A few steps down, a boy Ben instantly recognised as Rory O'Connor was lying on his back with a man on top of him. In the split second that he stood staring, Ben's first thought was that the man was trying to throttle him – until he realised what he was seeing.

The man was too intent on trying to tear the boy's clothes off to notice their presence. Ben stepped quickly over to him, grabbed a fistful of his hair and yanked him up and dashed his head against the steel railing. The man's hand flew to his belt and came out holding a pistol. Ben sent it spinning, headbutted him and threw him bodily down the stairway. The man went somersaulting down the metal steps, hit the landing. His fingers scrabbled for a hold on the rails as he slipped over the edge. His scream lasted about three seconds before he hit the stone floor down below, and then was silenced by a crunching impact that echoed through the cavern.

Ben and Jeff helped the pale, trembling boy to his feet and checked him over. 'Rory? We're getting you out of here.'

'Who are you?'

'I'm a friend of your Aunt Sabrina,' Ben said.

'I think my dad's here somewhere.'

'Well then, let's find him.'

In the time it had taken to save Rory from the attack, the thrumming in the air had intensified. It was getting more noticeable and uncomfortable every second. The kid looked scared. 'What's happening?'

'I don't know,' Ben said. 'But I don't like it.' He held on to Rory's arm as they moved quickly back along the corridors. By his reckoning, any time now they were going to reach the passage leading to the circular gallery where the access point was for the main lift shaft. If Adam O'Connor was down there working on the machine, they still had a chance of finding him. But Ben couldn't ignore the nasty feeling that they were running very short of time.

Jeff was rubbing his temple. 'Are you getting a headache? I don't know what's wrong with me, mate, but I'm feeling really weird.'

Ben was feeling it too. A strange kind of inner turmoil that was both mental and physical. It seemed to be coming from somewhere deep inside him, as though the cells of his body were being agitated, the way water molecules were vibrated by a microwave oven. The headache was steadily getting worse, rising at about the same rate as the strange sound that was now thrumming loudly through the facility, rising to a howl.

But that wasn't all he could hear as they drew nearer to the location of the main shaft. He strained to listen.

'I can hear someone calling your name,' he said to Rory.

Chapter Sixty-Five

As she and the tall man scoured the upper level for the missing boy, Irina knew something was badly wrong. She couldn't understand the strange sensations she was feeling, like ants crawling under her flesh and the worst headache she'd ever known building swiftly to an alarming crescendo inside her skull. She was sure it was something to do with the sound that was throbbing through the walls around them.

For several minutes now she'd been trying to raise Pelham on the radio and getting nothing but strange interference. The lights were acting strangely too, dimming and flickering as if all the electrical systems in the facility had gone haywire. Her instincts were telling her that this whole operation was quickly going into meltdown, and it was going to be time to evacuate.

They emerged into the wide open space that was the aircraft hangar, scanning left and right for any little hiding place the boy could have curled himself up into. Irina eyed the derelict Me 262, then clambered up onto one of the jet fighter's rusty wings and brusquely tore open the cockpit canopy. Empty. She swore loudly.

'He has to be around here somewhere,' the tall man said.

Irina jumped down from the plane wing, dusted the red powder off her hands, and strode onwards across the hangar.

Suddenly she stopped. Pointed. 'Look.'

A glistening blood trail traced a weaving line across the hangar floor. It led from the lift shaft gallery entrance. Her nostrils flared. She glanced at the tall man, and they began to follow the trail.

It led them away from the hangar and down the passages. Irina stopped to examine a bloody palm-print on the wall. Made by a man's hand, the blood still sticky and warm.

That was when they heard a ragged, hoarse voice calling out a single name over and over again. 'Rory! Rory!'

They found him just moments later, staggering along as if drunk, dragging his leg behind him and using the walls for support. It was the child's father. O'Connor.

The tall guy took out his pistol and aimed it down the corridor. O'Connor just stood there, swaying on his feet as though he was either resigned to a bullet in the head or he was just too crazed to understand what was happening.

Irina pushed the pistol aside. 'Let me.' Drawing the knife from her sheath, she began walking towards O'Connor.

The migraine in her temples was thumping violently, but she blinked the pain away. She had a job to finish. Pelham had told her that when this was all over, the child and his father had to be eliminated. And Irina Dragojević *always* honoured her contracts.

Her lips twisted into a thin smile as she approached him. He lowered his gaze down to the knife in her hand. She made no attempt to hide it. Better like this, when they knew it was coming.

'I know you,' he said. His voice was cracked with emotion and fatigue, barely audible over the growing sound that was shaking the ground under their feet.

She raised the knife. The flickering lamplight shimmered down the blade. She took another step closer to him.

'You're the bitch who hurt my child,' he said more loudly.

'That's right. And now this is for you,' she told him.

'And this is for you.' His bloody hand went to his pocket, and before she could react he'd drawn a gun. He pointed it at her and his face contorted as he squeezed the trigger.

Nothing happened. He tried again. Nothing.

Despite the pain exploding viciously through her skull, Irina began to laugh. Behind her, the tall man raised his gun and fired a single shot that blew O'Connor off his feet.

Adam felt the bullet tear through his shoulder and spin his body round. He hit the floor on his belly, gasping. The woman was howling with laughter as he scrabbled for his fallen pistol. His fingers closed numbly over its grip.

His vision faltered. *The lever.* The lever by his thumb. He pressed it, and it clicked upwards. He could sense her walking up to him, standing over him. The knife was coming. He was going to feel the cold steel any second now, carving into his flesh.

No. He mustn't give up.

For Rory.

He rolled over on his back and with all the strength he could muster he punched the gun out with both hands. Felt the smooth face of the trigger under his finger and squeezed it once, twice, three times, as fast as he could. The searing blast of the gun exploded in his ears.

The woman called Irina was standing right over him when he shot her. The first bullet took her under the chin and blew away half her face. The second blasted into her chest, and the third went through her hand.

The woman's tall companion let out a cry of rage as she went down. Adam fired at him, but even as the pistol went off in his hand, he knew the pain and dizziness had made him miss. Before he could get off another shot, the tall man had come running towards him and lashed out with his foot and kicked the gun out of his fingers. Adam tried to scramble away, but his strength was quickly failing him.

The tall man squatted down on his haunches in the blood and picked up the woman's knife. 'Now you're going to die bad,' he said.

Adam gasped as he saw the blade plunge towards him.

Then, in the next instant, he heard the shot and he was spluttering the tall man's blood out of his mouth.

Chapter Sixty-Six

Ben lowered the smoking pistol as the tall man crumpled to the floor with a bullet in his skull. Rory went running up the corridor, screaming for his father. Adam O'Connor's eyes opened wide in his bloodied face, and he let out a cry as his son flew into his arms. Rory hugged him, then saw the blood-soaked trouser leg and the pool of it on the floor under him, the ragged bullet wound in his shoulder.

'Oh, God, you're hurt!'

'I'm fine,' Adam sobbed. 'Now I'm just fine.' He held the boy tight in his arms, rocking him, tears cutting white lines through the blood on his face.

'I don't want to interrupt a happy family reunion,' Ben said as he and Jeff ran up to them. 'But we need to get out of here fast.' He had to raise his voice to be heard over the terrible noise. He and Jeff picked up the wounded man and supported him as they made their way through the passages. The noise kept building and building, driving them mad with its intensity.

'Need to find the main lift shaft,' Jeff shouted. 'Maybe it'll lead down to the exit we found.'

Ben shook his head. 'That only leads straight down to the vault,' he yelled back. 'We need to use the service lift we came up on.'

'Jesus. This whole place feels like it's going to blow apart.'

'The machine,' Adam muttered. 'It's out of control.' His head lolled sideways and his body went limp in Ben and Jeff's arms.

'Dad!' Rory screamed.

'He's just fainted, don't worry,' Ben reassured him. Adam's body was a dead weight as they carried him back the way they'd come. By the time they reached the service lift, the floor was trembling like an earthquake under their feet.

Just as Ben and Jeff were hauling the unconscious scientist on board the crude wooden platform, a massive shock seemed to ripple through the whole facility. It felt like an explosion, but with no blast – like a devastating pulse of pure energy capable of destroying everything around it. As the walls shook and the air seemed to thrum, the thick steel cables holding up the lift platform began to vibrate and buzz like plucked guitar strings. The platform began to judder.

Ben's eyes met Jeff's for a fraction of a second. They were both thinking the same thing. *Get off this thing now!*

They leapt off the platform, dragging Adam's slumped body with them as Rory watched in horror. At the same instant, the vibrating cables began to fray dramatically, and then parted with a lashing *crack*. The platform tumbled down the shaft, taking bits of masonry with it. Jeff lost his balance and almost went down with them, but Ben grabbed his webbing belt and hauled him away from the crumbling edge.

'There's no other way out of here,' Jeff yelled, pointing down the empty shaft. 'We're trapped.'

Ben's mind raced, fighting the rising tide of dizziness that was beginning to overcome him. He felt a tug on his sleeve and turned to see Rory standing there gesticulating back down the corridor. 'I know a way,' the boy shouted.

'What way?'

'Trust me. I found it.'

There was no choice but to follow the kid. Ben and Jeff manhandled the unconscious scientist as his son led them at a run back towards the stairway where they'd found him.

The moment they started down the metal steps, Ben knew they weren't going to get out in time. The stairway was rocking and swaying dangerously as they clattered down it. Struts and rails were cracking and breaking off, falling down around them. A guillotine blade of sheet metal crashed down, narrowly missing them and tearing away a section of framework. The whole construction lurched sideways and began to topple slowly over.

Seconds after the four of them had reached the bottom, the stairway fell apart. Debris rained down, burying Ivan's body where it lay on the cavern floor. They ran. Adam was beginning to come round as Ben and Jeff hauled him along.

'This way!' Rory was yelling. 'Here! This is it!'

Ben looked where the boy was frantically pointing. 'Where does it lead?'

'Some kind of air vent. Like a big pipe. It goes all the way through to the outside.'

Ben looked hard into Rory's eyes, blinking to focus his vision. 'You're sure? You've been in?'

'Some of the way in.'

Ben took a deep breath. It seemed insane, but it was their only option. The facility was rumbling like the world's biggest volcano about to erupt. 'Can you crawl?' he asked Adam.

'Just leave me here,' Adam slurred. 'Get my son out.'

Ben ripped his tactical webbing belt out of his trouser loops. 'You're going up that vent if I have to drag you. Hold this and don't let go.'

Then it was the frantic scramble up the tunnel. Rory led the way, followed by Jeff. Ben half-dragged Adam behind him on the end of the belt, praying it wouldn't snap. After half a minute of crawling, he could taste the cool air from outside and there was a definite glow of moonlight up ahead. But would they ever reach the end? The metal walls were heating up fast, burning their hands and knees. The nausea was crippling.

At that moment, the world seemed to come apart. The explosion was like nothing Ben had experienced before. A horrible sensation of weightlessness as they seemed to be falling, falling, followed by a barrage of enormous impacts. The steel pipe was as fragile and vulnerable as a twig tossed around in a hurricane. Ben heard Rory's scream of terror as it rolled over and over, battering them around inside. The pipe groaned as unimaginable outside pressures tried to stamp it flat. An ear-splitting shriek of rending steel, a cascade of dust and stones showering over them.

And then, nothing. As suddenly as the insane forces of destruction had reached their climax, it was over. There was silence, just the sound of grit and pebbles slithering down the inside of the pipe, and the soft groans of the others.

Ben raised his face out of his arms and blinked. The awful sensation was gone, the headache and nausea quickly clearing. Raising himself on his hands and knees, he realised he could stand. The pipe had ruptured above them, creating a jagged opening through which he could see moonlight and twinkling stars. He slowly, painfully got to his feet. A couple of metres away, Jeff was doing the same, looking stunned, his hair white with dust.

Rory stirred, let out a whimper and went scrambling over to his father. Adam O'Connor groaned in pain and joy as he sat up and hugged him.

The moon shone down on a transformed landscape. Kammler's mountain was gone. It had collapsed in on itself, the facility swallowed up, vaporised. All that was left was a giant crater of rubble and debris and twisted metal, like the scene of an air disaster without the plane.

Ben knew he'd never be able to describe what they'd just witnessed. The power of Kammler's machine was too incredible to contemplate. Now it was buried forever in its rocky grave – the Nazi weapon that might have saved the Earth or destroyed it was going to remain a secret for the rest of time.

Nobody spoke for a long while, just breathing the air, listening to the silence and savouring what it felt like to be alive. Ben stepped over to where father and son were holding each other tight. He put his hand on the boy's shoulder. 'You saved us, Rory.'

Adam O'Connor gripped Ben's hand in his bloodstained fist. '*You* saved us.'

Ben just smiled.

'Who the hell are you, anyway?'

'Nobody much,' Ben replied. He looked towards the sweeping forest, and pointed across the tree line to where they'd left the Porsche Cayenne, a few hours and a lifetime ago. 'There's a car down there. Let's get you to hospital, and then home.'

Chapter Sixty-Seven

While Adam was getting patched up in Budapest the next day, Sabrina flew out from London on a Steiner aircraft. Meanwhile, Ben was on the phone to Switzerland. Heinrich Dorenkamp told him the news. Ruth was on her feet and had already discharged herself from hospital after arguing with the doctors. As for Maximilian Steiner himself, he had come out of intensive care, weak and grieving for his nephew, but stable and headed for a full recovery.

Ben didn't bother watching the news, because he knew nothing would ever come to light about the incident in the wilds of Hungary. What had happened there was buried and gone, just as surely as the legacy of SS-Obergruppenführer Hans Kammler. Nobody would ever know the whole truth about who had been behind it. With Otto Steiner dead and his operation in ruins, the faceless, nameless figures who'd financed the project would now slip back into the shadows and wait for their next opportunity. That was just the way things worked. Always had, always would.

Ben hung around for a while in the hospital while Adam and Rory were reunited with Sabrina. He smiled to himself at the emotional scenes. Things hadn't worked out too badly in the end.

He walked away without anyone noticing. Jeff was sitting

in the Porsche outside. Ben climbed in next to him, and they headed for the airport.

It was the next afternoon, when Ben was sitting with Storm in the kitchen at Le Val, feeding him pieces of sirloin steak and watching him grow stronger by the hour, that he heard a car outside, and a minute later the door opened.

He turned, half expecting to see Jeff.

It was Ruth. Other than the sling around her arm, she looked fine.

'Is he all right?' she asked, looking with concern at the bandaged dog.

'People who've been shot don't just travel about the place,' he scolded her.

'Would you take that kind of advice from anyone?'

'No,' he admitted.

She swiped a glass off the side, pulled up a chair at the table and poured herself some of the wine he was drinking. 'How are you, bro?'

'I heard about Maximilian. I'm glad he's going to pull through.'

She shrugged. 'Me too. I feel pretty bad about what's happened.'

'Some of the things you did were wrong,' he said. 'But you did them for the right reasons, and that's what's important.'

'You're too nice to me. Fact is, I have some changes to make to my life. A lot of amends to make, and it starts here. Did Heinrich tell you that Maximilian is thinking of retiring?'

Ben shook his head. 'Meaning what?'

'Well, Silvia's not interested in running a business. So, with Otto gone, that just leaves me.'

'Sounds like something new for you,' Ben said.

'Franz will help me. We're going to build the greenest

multinational corporation you've ever seen. Use its power and money to do something for the world.'

'Something that doesn't involve Zero Point Energy?'

'Maybe that's still a little ahead of its time. We'll find other ways to make a difference.'

'Something tells me you'll do pretty well.'

She smiled. 'Now, enough about me. Did you call Brooke?'

'We've left messages for each other.'

'You're nervous about talking to her.'

'Things were left a little up in the air,' he said.

'She and I have been talking a lot on the phone. She told me a few things. Like the fact that your business is in deep shit because of that guy Rupert Shannon.'

With all that had been going on, Ben had almost managed to forget the Shannon situation. The prospect of losing Le Val returned like a toothache. 'Back down to earth with a thump,' he said.

'Is it true?'

'It's true. But I'll sort it out somehow. I'll be talking to Dupont at the bank soon. Whatever happens, we'll survive.'

'Well, maybe you won't need to,' she said enigmatically as she reached into her bag and took out an envelope.

Ben slipped out a single folded sheet from inside. It was a letter from the new CEO of Steiner Enterprises, Ruth Steiner-Hope. He smiled at that.

'Read it,' she said.

The letter was brief and straightforward, an offer to re-instate the original contract with Rupert Shannon and his team. Ben read it twice, then looked up at her with a frown. 'But you don't need them any more. Especially as they weren't much use in the first place.'

She chuckled. 'Shannon will be so keen to grab the dough, he won't read the small print of the new contract that'll be attached when this is posted in the morning. It basically states that they're being hired for general duties. No specific mention of bodyguarding. Which means we're going to put them to work mucking out the new stable complex I'm building, mowing the golf course and sifting out the swimming pools. If they refuse, it's their choice. Either way, you're off the hook.'

Ben folded the letter back into the envelope and handed it to her. 'Thank you, Little Moon.'

'There's a condition. Something I want you to do.'

'Name it.'

'I want you on a flight to London. You've got to go and see Brooke.'

Two hours later, cutting northwards over the Channel on board his sister's personal jet, he dialled Brooke's number.

'It's me,' he said.

'At last. Where have you been?'

'I'll tell you about all about it when I see you.'

She was quiet for a second. 'I don't know when that will be, Ben.'

'It'll be within the hour,' he said.

She said nothing, but he could hear the smile in her silence.

'You and I started something,' he said.

'Yes, we did,' she replied after a beat.

'How would you feel about picking up where we left off?'

'You and me?'

'You and me.'

There was a pause. 'See you in an hour,' she said.

Read on for an exclusive extract from the first book in the thrilling new VAMPIRE FEDERATION series coming from Scott in summer 2010.

SINCE THE DAWN of civilisation, vampires preyed on human beings, drank their blood and regarded them contemptuously as an inferior species, a mere disposable resource. For aeons, the vampires ruled.

But things have changed. With the birth of the modern age and the explosion in human communications and surveillance technologies, many vampires realized that they could no longer carry on the old ways. Something needed to be done, if the ancient culture was to survive.

In the last quarter of the twentieth century, the powerful World Vampire Federation was founded to control and oversee the activities of the vampire community. No longer would vampires prey unrestricted on human beings and turn them into creatures like themselves. New biotechnologies enabled the Undead to walk in daylight, living among us, in our cities, our streets. Strict laws were imposed to control vampire activity and allow their community to carry on. Quietly. Unnoticed. Undisturbed.

These laws were enforced by the Federation's Vampire Intelligence Agency, or VIA, with a licence granted by the Ruling Council to hunt and destroy transgressors.

But not all the vampires were willing to obey . . .

Prologue

The Scottish Highlands
November 1992

Outside the cottage, the storm had reached its peak. Rain was lashing out of the starless sky, the wind was screaming, the branches of the forest whipped and scraped violently at the windows.

The lights had gone, and the old place was filled with shadows from flickering candles. The twelve-year-old boy had been cowering at the top of the creaky stairs, listening to the argument between his parents and his grandfather and wishing they'd stop. Wanting to run downstairs and yell at them to quit fighting. Especially as he knew they were fighting about him . . .

. . . When the thing had come. A creature that looked like a man – but could not had been a man.

The boy had seen it all. Watched in speechless horror, peering through the banister rails, as the intruder crashed in the door and strode through the hallway. The argument had stopped suddenly. His parents and his grandfather were staring at the thing. Then the sound of his mother's scream had torn through the roar of the storm.

The creature never even slowed down. It caught his father

and his mother by the arms. Whipped them off their feet as though they were nothing. Like dead leaves. It dashed their heads together with a sound that the boy would never forget. Candles hissed, snuffed out by the blood spray.

Then the thing had dropped the bodies and stepped over them where they lay. Smiling now. Taking its time. And approached his grandfather.

The old man backed away, quaking in fear. Spoke words that the boy could not understand.

It laughed. Then it bit. Its teeth closed on the old man's throat and the boy could hear the terrible gurgle as it gorged on his blood.

It was just like the stories. The stories his parents hadn't wanted his grandfather to tell him. The boy shrank away and closed his eyes and wept silently and trembled and prayed.

And then it was over. When he opened his eyes, the intruder had gone. He ran down the stairs. Gaped at the twisted bodies of his mother and father, then heard the groan from across the room.

The old man was lying on his back, his arms outflung. The boy ran to him, knelt over him. Saw the wound in his grandfather's neck. There was no blood. All gone.

Claimed by the creature.

'I'm dying,' his grandfather gasped.

'No!' the boy shouted.

'I'll turn.' The old man's face was deathly pale and he gripped the boy's arms so tightly it hurt. 'You know what to do.'

'No—'

'It has to be done,' the old man whispered. He pointed weakly at the sabre that hung over the fireplace. 'Do it. Do it now, before it's too late.'

The boy was convulsed with tears as he staggered over to

the fireplace. His fingers closed on the scabbard of the sabre, and he unhooked the weapon from its mounting. The blade gave a soft zing as he drew it out.

'Hurry,' his grandfather croaked.

The boy pushed the sword back into the scabbard. 'I can't,' he sobbed. 'Please, granddad. I don't want to.'

His grandfather looked up at him. 'You must, Joel. And when it's done, you have to remember the things I told you.' His life energy was fading fast, and he was struggling to talk. 'You have to find it. Find the cross. It's the only thing they truly fear.'

The Cross of Ardaich. The boy remembered. Tears flooded down his face. He closed his eyes.

Then opened them. And saw that his grandfather was dead.

The storm was still raging outside. The boy stood over his grandfather's body and wept.

And then his grandfather's eyes snapped open and looked deep into his. He sat upright. Slowly, his lips rolled back and he snarled.

For a second the boy stood as if mesmerised. Then he started back in alarm as his grandfather began to climb to his feet. Except it wasn't his grandfather any more. The boy knew what he'd become.

Candlelight flashed on the blade as he drew the sabre. He raised it high and sliced with all his strength – the way the old man had taught him. Felt the horrible impact all the way to the hilt as it chopped through his grandfather's neck and took the head clean off.

When it was done, the boy staggered out into the storm. He began to walk through the hammering rain. He walked for miles, numb with shock.

And when the villagers found him the next morning, he couldn't even speak.

1

Eighteen years later
October 27

Pockets of thick autumnal mist drifted over the waters of the Thames as the big cargo ship cut upriver from the estuary, heading for the wharfs of the Port of London. Smaller vessels seemed to shy out of its way. With its lights poking beams through the gloom, the ship carved its way westwards into the heart of the city.

On the approach to the docks, the beat of a helicopter thudded through the chill evening air.

Eight sailors of mixed Romanian and Czech origin were assembled around the helipad on the forward deck, craning their necks up at the sky at the approaching aircraft. At their feet lay a pair of steel-reinforced crates, seven feet long, that had been wheeled up from the hold. Most of the crew preferred to keep their distance from them. The strong downdraught from the chopper's rotors tore at the men's clothing and hair as its pilot brought it down to land on the pad.

'Okay, boys, let's get these bastard things off our ship,' the senior crewman yelled over the noise as the chopper's cargo hatch slid open.

'I'd love to know what the hell's in there,' said one of the Romanians.

'I don't fucking want to know,' someone else replied. 'All I can say is I'm glad to be shot of them.'

There wasn't a man aboard ship who hadn't felt the sense of unease that had been hanging like a pall over the vessel since they'd left the Romanian port of Constantza. It hadn't been a happy voyage. Five of the hands were sick below decks, suffering from some kind of fever that the ship's medic couldn't figure out. The radio kept talking about the major flu pandemic that had much of Europe in its grip. Maybe that was it. But some of the guys were sceptical. Flu didn't make you wake up in the middle of the night screaming in terror.

The crewmen heaved each crate aboard the chopper and then stepped back in the wind blast as the cargo was strapped into place. The hatch slammed shut, the rotors accelerated to a deafening roar, and the chopper took off.

A few of the ship's crew stood on deck and watched the aircraft's twinkling lights disappear into the mist that over-hung the city skyline. One of them quickly made the sign of the cross over his chest, and muttered a prayer under his breath. He was a devout Catholic, and his faith was normally the butt of many jokes on board.

Today, though, nobody laughed.

Crowmoor Hall
Near Henley-on-Thames, Oxfordshire

Forty miles away, the gnarly figure of Seymour Finch stepped out of the grand entrance of the manor house. He raised his bald head, peered up at the sky. The stars were out, seeming dead and flat through ragged holes in the mist that curled around the mansion's gables and clung to the lawns.

Finch couldn't stop grinning to himself, even though his hands were quaking in fear as he nervously, impatiently awaited the arrival of the helicopter. He glanced at his watch.

Soon. Soon.

Eventually he heard the distant beat of approaching rotor blades. He rubbed his hands together. Took out a small radio handset and spoke into it.

'He's coming. He's here.'

2

The Carpathian Mountains, Romania
October 31

It was getting dark as Alex Bishop emerged from the path through the woods. Across the clearing, she could see the old tumbledown house. She just hoped that her informant had been right. Lives were on the line.

She quickly checked the equipment she was carrying on her belt, unsnapped the retaining strap on the holster. The steps on the porch were rotten and she overstepped them, treading carefully. She went to the front door, all peeled paint. It swung open with a creak and she could smell the stench of rot and fungus.

Inside, the house was all in shadow. She stepped in, peering into the darkness. The door creaked shut behind her.

Her sharp ears caught something. Was that a thump from somewhere below her feet? She stiffened. Something was moving around down there. She followed the sound through the front hall towards a doorway. A rat, startled by her approach, darted into the deepening shadows.

A muffled yell from behind the door. Then another. Shrill, scared, all hell breaking loose.

Someone had got here before her. She kicked the door open with a brittle cracking and splintering, and found herself at the top of a flight of stone steps leading down to the cellar. She wasn't alone.

Alex took in the situation. Three young guys in their twenties. One of them lay writhing in a spreading, dark pool of blood. Two still on their feet, one clutching a wooden cross, the other holding a mallet in one hand and a stake in the other. Both howling in panic, wild, demented, as the cellar's other occupant rose up from their friend's body and took a step towards them. His mouth opened to show the extended fangs.

Vampire.

The guy holding the cross rushed forward with a yell and held it in the vampire's face. It was a brave thing to do, textbook horror movie heroics, but foolish. If he'd been expecting the vampire to cover its face and hiss and shrink away, he was in for a shock.

The vampire didn't blink an eye at the cross. Alex knew he wouldn't. Instead, he reached out and jerked his attacker brutally off his feet. Pulled him in and bit deep into his shoulder. The young guy fell twitching to the ground, blood jetting from his ripped throat.

There was nowhere for the third guy to run as the vampire turned his attentions to him and backed him towards the corner of the cellar. The young man had dropped his mallet and stake, and cowered pleading against the rough wall.

The vampire stepped closer to him. Then stopped and turned as Alex walked calmly down the cellar steps. He stared at her, and his bloodstained mouth fell open. Recognition in his eyes.

'Surprise,' she said. Reached down and drew the Desert Eagle from its holster.

The vampire snarled. 'Federation scum. Your time is over.'

'Not before yours,' she said.

And fired. The explosion was deafening in the room. Even in Alex's strong grip, the large-calibre pistol recoiled hard.

The vampire screamed. Not because of the bullet that had ripped a fist-sized hole in his chest, but because of the instant devastating effect of the Nosferol on his system – the lethal poison developed by the Fed chemists and issued under strict control to VIA field agents like Alex Bishop.

The vampire collapsed to the cellar floor, writhing in agony, staring at his hands as the blood vessels bulged out of the skin. His face swelled grotesquely, eyes popping out of their sockets. Then blood burst out of his mouth, and his hideously distended veins exploded in a spatter of red that coated the floor and the stone wall behind him. Alex turned away from the spray. The vampire went on twitching for a second, his body peeled apart, turned almost inside out, blood still spurting from everywhere; then he lay still.

Alex holstered the gun and walked over to the young guy in the corner, grabbed his arm and hauled him to his feet.

He gaped at her. 'How did you—'

She could see that he had wet himself with fear. These amateurs had no idea what they were into.

'It takes a vampire to destroy a vampire properly,' she said as she unzipped the pouch on her belt. Before he could react, she'd taken out the syringe of Vambloc and jabbed it into the vein under his ear. He let out a wheezing gasp and then lost consciousness. By the time he woke up, his short-term memory of what had just happened would be completely erased.

Alex replaced the Vambloc syringe and took out the one that was loaded with Nosferol. Leaving the young guy where he lay, she stepped over to his two dead friends and injected each of them with 10ml of the clear liquid. Standard procedure, to ensure they stayed dead. She carefully capped the needle with a cork and put the syringe back into its pouch.

Two minutes later she was heading back out into the evening with the unconscious body over her shoulder. As she strode out of the house she tossed a miniature incendiary device into the doorway. She was halfway to the trees before the whole place went up in a roar of flame, bathing the murky woods in an orange glow.

Hiding the traces of another day's work.

'Rest in peace,' she muttered. She took out her phone, keyed in Rumble's number at the London HQ.

'Harry. You were right. It's happening.'